Matthew Reilly is the Australian-born author of five adult bestsellers: *Contest*, *Ice Station*, *Temple*, *Area 7* and *Scarecrow*. He wrote his first two novels while studying law at the University of New South Wales and now writes full-time, producing novels and screenplays and creating television series. He lives in Sydney.

Books for older readers by Matthew Reilly

Ice Station
Temple
Contest
Area 7
Scarecrow

MATTHEW REILLY

HOVER CAR RACER

MACMILLAN CHILDREN'S BOOKS

First published 2004 by Pan Macmillan Australia Pty Ltd

First published in Great Britain 2004 by Macmillan
This edition published 2005 by Macmillan Children's Books
a division of Macmillan Publishers Ltd
20 New Wharf Road, London N1 9RR
Basingstoke and Oxford
www.panmacmillan.com

Associated companies throughout the world

ISBN 0 330 44016 0

1 3 5 7 9 8 6 4 2

A CIP catalogue record for this book is available from
the British Library.

Printed and bound in Great Britain by Mackays of Chatham plc, Kent

For Matt Martin

ACKNOWLEDGEMENTS

Hi there, Readers!

As you will quickly notice, there is one thing entirely new about *Hover Car Racer*: the race maps and the artwork. While I've always had maps and diagrams in my books, with *Hover Car Racer* I knew I'd need something more than I'd ever seen in a novel before. Fortunately for me, this gave me the opportunity to work with one of Australia's finest graphic designers, a young man from Brisbane named Roy Govier, from Xiphos.

While Roy had previously designed the missile on the cover of *Scarecrow*, this was a *much* bigger task. For six months, he took my (let's face it, pretty pathetic) sketches and turned them into awesome 3-dimensional race maps and flying hover cars. I thank him for his huge efforts.

Beyond that, as always, there are many others to thank: the wonderful team at Pan Macmillan, led by my incredible publisher, Cate Paterson (who has pretty well become the godmother of mass-market fiction in this country). Jane Novak: my fantastic publicist. Sarina Rowell: my hardworking editor. Behind the scenes, I am also indebted to Ross Gibb, Paul Kenny, Jeannine Fowler and James Fraser for their guidance and experience. And, of course, my sincere thanks once again to all the sales reps at Pan Macmillan who visit bookstores every day to sell in my books. Publishing is a team game, and they are a sensational team.

And, lastly, the greatest thanks of all must go to my wife, Natalie. I remember when she came home from work one day and found me, an allegedly grown man, surrounded by an absolute mess—model parts, glue, paint all over my hands—and I held up the very first model of the

Argonaut and said: 'Look what I made! A hover car!' Or the other time when she came home from work and found half of the living room submerged beneath a giant seven-foot-tall styrofoam model of a Mayan pyramid. In both cases, she just smiled at me and said, 'That's *great!*' Every writer should have this kind of encouragement. No, seriously, this is why I have said before: to anyone who knows a writer, never underestimate the power of your encouragement. Thanks, Nat!

Now, enough with all that. It's time to race!

MR
Sydney, Australia
September 2004

PART I

JASON AND THE ARGONAUT

Imagine twenty fighter jets racing around a twisting turning aerial track, ducking and weaving and overtaking at insanely high speeds and you've just imagined a hover car race.

Rand Thomasson
3-time Hover Car Racing Champion

A FEW YEARS FROM NOW . . .

INDO-PACIFIC REGIONAL
CHAMPIONSHIPS:
GULF OF CARPENTARIA
AUSTRALIA (GATE RACE)

Gates

Gulf of Carpentaria

Hells
Creek

Sydney

AUSTRALIA

100 Point
Zone

90 Point
Zone

GRANDSTANDS

SANDBARS

60 Point
Zone

50 Point
Zone

80 Point
Zone

40 Point
Zone

30 Point
Zone

SWAMP

70 Point
Zone

20 Point
Zone

10 Point
Zone

START/FINISH
and PIT AREA

The race was barely nine minutes old when Jason Chaser lost his steering rudder.

At 690 kilometres an hour.

The worst thing was, it wasn't even his fault. Some crazy kid from North Korea driving a home-made hunk-of-junk swamp-runner had lost control of his car while trying to pull an impossible 9-G turn and had crashed spectacularly into the crocodile-infested marshes right in front of Jason, sending sizzling pieces of his car flying in every direction—three of which punched *right through* Jason's tailfin like a volley of red-hot mini-meteorites, rendering his steering vanes useless.

Jason jammed back on his collective, and somehow managed to right the *Argonaut* with only his pedal-thrusters just as—*shoom!-shoom!-shoom!*—three of the other top contenders whizzed by, rocketing off into the distance, kicking up geyser sprays in their wakes.

The *Argonaut* slowed to a complete stop, hovering three feet above one of the thousands of water-alleys in the vast swamp at the edge of the Gulf of Carpentaria.

The Bug's voice came in through Jason's earpiece. The Bug was Jason's navigator, co-driver and little brother. He sat in the back of the *Argonaut*'s cockpit, slightly above and behind Jason.

Jason bit his lip as the Bug spoke.

Then he shook his head determinedly. 'No way, Bug. I didn't come here to bow out in the first ten minutes. We're not out of this yet. You just plot our course, I'll do the rest.'

And with that he gunned the thrusters, flinging the *Argonaut* back into the race.

When they had arrived in Pit Lane earlier that morning, Jason and the Bug had sensed an unusual level of excitement in the air.

It was a good crowd—80,000 bustling spectators taking their places in the giant hover-grandstands overlooking the Gulf.

Of course, this was nothing like the crowds they got at the pro events. There, anything less than a million spectators was seen as a poor showing.

Part of the excitement stemmed from the fact that this year there were five drivers, including Jason, who were in contention to take out the regional championships and thus garner a precious invitation to the International Race School, gateway to the professional circuit.

But it was in Pit Lane itself that the excitement was at its highest.

Everyone was whispering and pointing at the two distinguished-looking gentlemen being shown around the VIP tent by Randolph Hardy, the portly President of the Indo-Pacific Regional Directorate of the IHCRA, the International Hover Car Racing Association.

Whispered voices:

'Gosh, it's LeClerq! The Dean of the Race School . . .'

'. . . other one looks like Scott Syracuse, the guy who

was in that accident in New York a couple of years ago and almost died . . .'

'Someone was saying they're here to scout for *extra* candidates for the Race School . . .'

'No way . . .'

Jason eyed the two visitors strolling through the VIP tent with Randolph Hardy.

The older man was indeed Jean-Pierre LeClerq, Principal of the International Race School, the most prestigious racing school in the world.

Located in Tasmania—an enormous island at the bottom of Australia that was wholly owned by the Race School—it was more a *qualifying* school than a strictly teaching institution. While lessons were certainly taught there, it was your ranking in the School Championship Ladder that really mattered. It was that ranking that got you a contract with a pro racing team after your year at 'the School'. Not surprisingly, the Race School had produced nearly half of the drivers currently on the Pro Circuit.

LeClerq was a regal-looking fellow, with a perfectly-groomed mane of white hair and an imperious bearing. His suit looked expensive. Jason figured it probably cost more than his entire car did.

The man beside LeClerq was far younger, in his early 30s. He was sort of handsome, with intense features and impenetrable black eyes. He also walked with a cane and looked like he'd rather be at the dentist having root canal therapy than be here at the Indo-Pacific Regional Championships.

Jason recognised him instantly. He had the man's collector-card in his bedroom back home.

He was Scott J. Syracuse, otherwise known as 'The

Scythe', one of the best racers ever to have helmed a hover car . . . until he busted the neurotransmitters in his brain in a horrific crash at the New York Masters three years ago. These days, modern medicine could fix just about any broken bone in your body, even a busted spine, but the one thing man hadn't figured out was how to fix the human brain. If you busted your brain, your racing career was over, as the Scythe had found out.

Just then Syracuse turned and his ice-cool eyes locked on Jason.

Jason froze, caught staring.

A full second too late, he looked away.

Truth be told, he actually felt embarrassed under Syracuse's glare. All the other drivers here wore co-ordinated outfits that matched the colour schemes of their cars. Some even had the new Shoei helmets. Others still had full pit crews wearing their team's colours. Jason and the Bug, on the other hand, wore denim overalls and their dusty farm-boots. They raced in old motorcycle helmets.

Jason scowled. He could hide his eyes, but he couldn't hide his clothes.

He also couldn't hide his hover car from Syracuse's level gaze. But that was another story.

The *Argonaut*.

Car No.55.

It was Jason's pride and joy, and he spent every spare minute he had working on it. It was an old Ferrari Pro F1 conversion that he'd found in a junkyard four years ago—one of those early hover cars converted from old Formula One cars.

It had the bullet-shaped body of an old F1 car, complete with nosewing, hunchbacked fuselage and wide tail rudder, but with the added features of a navigator's seat tucked immediately behind the driver's cockpit and a pair of swept-back wings stretching out from its flanks.

Most incongruously for an old F1 car, however, it had no wheels. Hover technology—the six shiny silver discs on its underbelly called *magneto drives*—had made wheels unnecessary.

While he liked to think otherwise, Jason knew it wasn't a real Ferrari Pro F1. Only the chassis. The rest of it was a hodge-podge of machinery and spare parts that Jason had scrounged from farm vehicles and the local wrecker's yard. Even its six race-quality magneto drives—a mix of GM, Boeing and BMW mags—were second-hand.

Despite its eclectic innards, the *Argonaut*'s exterior was beautiful—it was painted blue-white-and-silver in a way that accentuated the car's fighter-jet-like shape.

Jason himself was 14 years old, blond-haired, blue-eyed and determined. At school, he was good at math, geography and game theory. He wore his sandy-blond hair in a messy 'mohican' style reminiscent of the retired English footballer, David Beckham.

At 14, he was also rather young to be at the Regional Championships. Most of the other drivers at this level of racing were seventeen or eighteen. But Jason had finished in the Top 3 in his district trials just like the rest of them, which meant he had as much right to be here as they did.

With him as his navigator was the Bug—his brother, and at 12, even younger. With his tiny body and his big thick-lensed glasses, the Bug confounded a lot of people. He didn't talk much. In fact, the only people he would speak to were Jason and their mother, and even then only in a whisper. Some of the doctors said that the Bug was borderline autistic—it explained his excessive shyness and social awkwardness while also explaining his mathematical genius.

The Bug could tell you what 653 × 354 was . . . in two seconds.

Which made him the perfect navigator in a hover car race.

The Carpentaria Race was a 'gate race'.

The most famous gate race in the world was the London Underground Run—a fiendishly complex race through the tunnels of the London Underground system—and the Carpentaria Race was based on the same principle.

Instead of doing laps around a track, a gate race had no actual track at all. Rather, it took place over a wide area of open terrain 600 km wide by 600 km long. In today's case, that terrain was the vast swampland on the edge of Australia's Gulf of Carpentaria: a marshy landscape that featured a labyrinthine network of narrow waterways cutting through the swamp's eight-foot-high reed-fields and the high coastal sandbars of the Gulf itself.

Positioned at various points around this maze of natural canals were approximately 250 bridge-like arches through which the racers drove their hover cars. As your car whizzed through a gate-arch, an electronic tag attached to your nosewing recorded the pass.

Passing through a gate gave you points. Gates further away from the Start-Finish Line were worth more; those that were closer, less. The furthest gate from the Start-Finish Line, for example, was worth 100 points. The nearest, 10 points.

The trick was: there was a strict time limit.

You had three hours to race through as many gates as you could, *and then get back to the Start-Finish Line.*

This final element was crucial.

Every *second* that you were late coming back cost you *one point*. So coming home just a minute over the three-hour mark would cost you a massive 60 points.

The driver with the most points won.

Which made it a tactical race in which navigators played a key role.

No driver, no matter how skilled or fast, could get through all the gates in the allotted time—which meant *choosing* which gates to go for within that time limit. And since computer navigation programs were strictly forbidden at all levels of hover car racing, having a good navigator was crucial.

Add to that pit stops—magneto drives overheated, coolant tanks needed to be refilled, compressed-air thrusters had to be replaced—and all the many vagaries of racing, and you had a serious strategy contest on your hands.

The *Argonaut* screamed across the marshland, rushing through a narrow alleyway flanked by walls of eight-foot-high reeds, kicking up a whitewash of skanky swampwater behind it.

610 km/h . . . 620 . . . 630 . . .

With his steering fins flapping uselessly inside his broken rear spoiler, Jason steered with his two rear thrusters instead—alternating left and right, incredibly using his pedals to control the speeding bullet that was his hover car.

The Bug had plotted their course well. Every trip to the pits allowed Jason to see the big electronic leaderboard mounted above the main grandstand, with its up-to-the-second tally of all the racers' accumulated scores so far:

	DRIVER	NO.	CAR	POINTS
1.	BECKER, B	09	*Devil's Chariot*	1,110
2.	RICHARDS, J	24	*Stormbreaker*	1,090
3.	TADZIC, E	19	*San Antonio*	1,010
4.	YU, E	888	*Lantern-IV*	1,000
5.	CHASER, J	55	*Argonaut*	990

The accident had hurt them.

Lost them a lot of time. And no matter how hard Jason tried—and he tried as hard as he could—steering with his feet just wasn't as good as steering with his hands.

And with each trip to the pits, he could see the *Argonaut* falling further and further behind the leaders, dropping down the leaderboard.

What made it a hundred times worse was the identity of the driver who was leading: Barnaby Becker, a senior from Jason's school back home in Halls Creek.

Becker was 18, red-haired, freckled, cocky and rich. His father, Barnaby Becker Sr, was a businessman who owned half of Halls Creek.

Mr Becker had bought his son one of the best production hover cars money could buy—a beautiful Lockheed-Martin ProRacer-5. He had also once employed Jason's dad, a fact which Barnaby—a nasty kid if ever there was one—never failed to remind Jason of.

Nevertheless, Jason flew on, right to the end, zinging through as many arches as the broken but valiant *Argonaut* could manage, following the Bug's revised course.

It didn't matter.

As the giant clock above the Start-Finish Line ticked over from 2:59:59 to 3:00:00, and the last hover cars shot across the Line to the cheers of the 80,000-strong crowd, the *Argonaut,* piloted by Chaser J, was at the bottom of the leaderboard.

Jason pulled his beloved car to a halt in his pit bay and dropped his head.

In the most important race of his life—in front of 80,000 people; in front of the most distinguished pair of spectators he would ever race in front of—Jason Chaser had come stone-cold last.

The world was changed forever with the invention of the hover car.

Indeed, over the course of human history, few inventions could claim such an instantaneous and immediate global impact.

Gutenberg's printing press, Nobel's dynamite, the Wright brothers' flying machine—sure they were all impressive, but their impact on the world paled in comparison to the global *revolution* that was brought about by Wilfred P. Wilmington's hover car.

Much of the fuss had to do with the 80-year-old Wilmington's extraordinary decision to make his amazing new piece of technology freely available to anyone who wanted to exploit it.

He didn't patent it. He didn't sell it to a major corporation. Not even a special delegation led by the President of the United States himself could convince him to keep the technology solely for the benefit of the US.

No. Wilfred P. Wilmington, the eccentric backyard inventor who claimed that he had more than enough money to live out his twilight years in relative comfort, did the most extraordinary and unpredictable thing of all: he gave his technology to the world for free.

The response was immediate.

Since hover technology required no gasoline to fuel it, the oil-producing countries of the Middle East crumbled.

Oil became meaningless, and the United States—the world's largest consumer of oil—cancelled all its Mid-East contracts. The fortunes of the Saudis and the Sultan of Brunei went up in smoke in the blink of an eye.

Car companies embraced the new technology and—aided by their already-existent factories and mass-production assembly lines—they pumped out hover cars by the million. The first Model-T/H (for 'Hover') Ford rolled off the Ford Motor Company's production line barely one year after Wilmington's incredible announcement. BMW, Renault and Porsche followed soon after.

They were quickly joined, however, by an unlikely set of competitors: aeroplane-makers. Lockheed-Martin, Airbus and Boeing all began to produce family-sized hover vehicles too.

Overland travel became faster—New York to L.A. now took 90 minutes by car. Seaborne cargo freighters crossed the world's oceans in hours not days.

The world became smaller.

Professor Wilmington had originally named his discovery an 'electromagnetically elevated omni-directional vehicle', but the world gave it a simpler name: the hover car.

The technology underpinning the hover car was disarmingly simple and wonderfully universal.

Every moment of every day, upwardly-moving magnetic waves radiate outwards from the Earth's core. What Wilmington did was create a device—the 'magneto drive'—that *repelled* this upwardly-moving magnetic force. And while scientists marvelled at Wilmington's clever fusion of ferromagnetic materials and high-end superconductors, the general public revelled in the result.

For the result was perpetual hover.

So long as the world kept turning, hover cars could retain their lift. And so the public's greatest fear about hover technology—cars dropping out of the sky—had been assuaged.

Hover technology spread.

Passenger cars and hover buses filled cities. Cargo freighters zoomed across the seas. Children's hover scooters became all the rage. And of course the world's military forces found their own uses for the new technology.

But the advent of any new type of travel technology—boats, cars, planes—always brings forth a certain kind of individual and the hover car would be no exception to this rule.

Soon after the spectacular arrival of this new form of human movement came the arrival of a new kind of person: part race-car driver, part fighter pilot, all superstar.

The hover car racer.

The official presentation of prizes was enough to make Jason puke.

High on the podium, Barnaby Becker stood smugly between Regional Director Hardy and the Principal of the International Race School, Jean-Pierre LeClerq.

Smiling for the cameras, LeClerq handed Barnaby the winner's trophy, a gigantic bottle of Moët champagne, and a cheque for a thousand dollars.

Jason did notice, however, that Principal LeClerq's offsider, the ex-racer Scott Syracuse, was not on the stage. In fact, Syracuse was nowhere to be seen.

LeClerq shook Barnaby's hand, then he took the mike.

'Ladies and gentlemen,' he said. 'This being the end of the regional season, I have another presentation to make. With his victory today, young Master Becker has topped the local competition ladder, and as such, has won for himself another prize: he has won an invitation to study at the International Race School. Master Becker, it would be our honour to have you as a student next year.'

With that, LeClerq handed Barnaby the famous gold-edged envelope that every young racer dreamed of receiving.

The crowd roared their approval.

Barnaby took the envelope, thanked LeClerq, and then he punched the air with his fist and popped the cork on his champagne bottle and the festivities began.

Watching from Pit Lane, Jason just stared at the scene with his mouth agape, devastated.

Beside him, the Bug shook his head. He whispered something in Jason's ear.

Jason snuffed a laugh. 'Thanks, man. Unfortunately, you're not the Principal of the Race School.'

Then he spun on his heel and went back to their pit bay to load up the *Argonaut*.

The Bug scurried after him.

When they got back to their bay, they were surprised to find that someone was already there.

Scott Syracuse was standing in the doorway to their pit bay. He was leaning inside it, peering up at the *Argonaut*'s damaged tail section.

'Er . . . hi there. Can I help you?' Jason said.

Syracuse turned, leaning on his cane. He levelled his cool gaze at Jason. 'Master Chaser, isn't it?'

'Yes.'

'An appropriate name for you based on today's effort, don't you think? Scott Syracuse. I'm here with Professor LeClerq. I teach with him at the Race School.'

'I know who you are, sir. I have your bubble gum card.' Jason felt stupid as soon as he said it.

Syracuse nodded at the *Argonaut*. 'Your steering rudder's broken.'

'Yeah. I got hit by some debris from that crazy kid who tried to pull a 9-G banking turn.'

'When did that happen?'

'About nine minutes in.'

Syracuse stopped, turned abruptly.

'Nine minutes in? So how did you steer after that? Thrusters?'

'Yep.'

'Let me get this straight. You lost your steering nine minutes into the race. But you continued on anyway, steering with your *pedals* instead of your steering wheel.'

'That's right, sir.'

Syracuse nodded slowly. 'I wondered . . .'

Then he looked directly at Jason. 'I've got another question for you. You started the race differently to everyone else—you headed out for the gates on the western side of the course while most of the others went north-east. Then you got hit and changed your race-plan.'

Syracuse pulled a map of the course from his back pocket. On it were little markers depicting all of the 250 gates on the course.

'Can you tell me what your original plan was?'

Jason swapped a glance with the Bug. 'What do you say, Bug?'

The Bug nodded—eyeing Syracuse warily.

Jason said, 'My little brother here does our navigating. He's the guy who plotted our course today. We call him the Bug.'

Syracuse offered the map for the Bug to take.

The Bug stepped behind Jason.

Jason took the map instead. 'He's a little shy with people he doesn't know.'

Jason handed the map to his brother, who then quickly—and expertly—drew their race-plan on it. He handed the map back to Jason who passed it on to Syracuse.

Syracuse stared at the map for a long moment. Then he did a strange thing. He pulled out *another* map of the course, and compared the two. Jason saw that this other map also had markings on it, showing someone else's race-plan.

At last, Syracuse looked up, and gazed closely at Jason and the Bug, as if he were assessing them very, very carefully.

He held up their race-plan.

'May I keep this?'

'Sure,' Jason shrugged.

Scott Syracuse pursed his lips. 'Jason Chaser, hover car racer. It's got a nice ring to it. Farewell to you both.'

Jason and the Bug arrived back home in Halls Creek around seven that evening, with the *Argonaut* strapped to a trailer behind their dusty old Toyota hover-wagon.

Halls Creek was a little desert town in the far northern reaches of Western Australia. The exact middle of nowhere, Jason liked to say.

The lights were on in the farmhouse when they arrived, and dinner was on the table when they walked in.

'Oh, my boys! My boys!' Martha Chaser cried, running to the door to greet them. 'Jason! We saw it all on the television: that silly boy who crashed right in front of you! Are you both all right?'

She swept the Bug up into her arms, engulfing him in her wide apron-covered frame. 'You didn't hurt my little Doodlebug, did you?'

The Bug almost disappeared in her embrace. He seemed very content in her arms.

'He's okay,' Jason said, taking a seat at the table. 'Only thing he suffered was the humiliation of coming dead last in front of Jean-Pierre LeClerq.'

'Who?'

'Never mind, Mum.'

Just then, their father, Henry Chaser, came into the

kitchen, his overalls caked with dust from a day's work on the station.

'Well, hey there! The racers return! Good racing today, sons. Tough call with that kid who banged up your tail.'

'Damn idiot mangled our steering,' Jason groaned as he wolfed down some mashed potato. 'Wrong place, wrong time, I guess.'

'Oh, no,' Henry said, smiling. 'No, no, no, no. *You* lost your steering, Jason. You *put yourself* in the wrong place at the wrong time.'

'Now, Henry, leave them be . . .' Martha rolled her eyes. Her husband was a hover car racing enthusiast. He watched it on the television all the time, loved to analyse it—the classic couch coach. It was he who had introduced the boys to mini-cart racing in the back paddock at the ages of five and three.

Jason took the bait. 'No way, Dad! I didn't put myself in the wrong place. It was just plain bad luck . . .'

'No it wasn't,' Henry said. 'It was *racing*. I think this was a good lesson for you both. Racing not only involves beating the other top contenders—it also involves *avoiding* those who *aren't* as talented as you are.

'Sometimes racing isn't fair, Jason. Sometimes you can do everything right in a race and *still* not win. Hell, I remember once in the Sydney Classic, the leader was ahead by two whole laps and then he got sideswiped by a tail-ender coming out of the pits. Just like that, he was out of the race—'

The doorbell rang.

Henry Chaser got up, didn't stop talking. '. . . Guy was way out in front and he just got *nailed* by this stupid rookie. God, what was his name? Hell of a driver, he was. Young fella. Got wiped out a couple of years ago. Ah, that's it, it was . . .'

He opened the door. And remembered. He turned back inside. '. . . Syracuse! That's who it was. Scott Syracuse.'

He turned to face their visitor.

Scott Syracuse stood in the doorway. Tall and formal.

Henry Chaser almost swallowed his own tongue.

'Oh. My. Goodness,' Henry stammered. 'You're . . . you're . . .'

'Good evening, sir. My name's Scott Syracuse. I met your sons at the race today.'

'Ah . . . ye—yes,' Henry Chaser said.

Jason stood up. 'Mr Syracuse? What are you doing here?'

Syracuse remained in the doorway. 'I came to ask you a question, young Master Chaser. Oh, and your brother, too.'

'Yeah . . .'

'I was rather taken with the way you drove today, Master Chaser. With your feet and with your heart. I believe that with the proper training, your skills could be sculpted into something very special. I also ran your little brother's race-plan through a professional course-plotting program on a computer. His race-plan was 97% efficient. Almost the optimal plan for that course. But you guys didn't receive the gate layout until two minutes before race-time. Your little brother formulated that race-plan in the space of two minutes *in his head*. That's impressive.

'In short, I think you two make quite a team. Nobody else caught my eye today, but you two did. And now that I work at the Race School in Tasmania . . .'

Jason felt his heart beating faster. 'Yes . . .'

'Master Chaser,' Syracuse said. 'Would you and your brother like to come and study at the International Race School under my supervision?'

Jason's eyes went wide.

He spun to face his mother. Her eyes were tearing up.

He looked at his dad. His mouth had fallen open.

He turned to the Bug. The Bug's face was a mask. He slowly kicked back his chair and came over to Jason, stood on his tiptoes and whispered something in Jason's ear.

Jason smiled.

'What did he say?' Syracuse asked.

Jason said, 'He says your race computer must be broken. His race-plan was perfect. Then he said, "When do we leave?"'

PART II

RACE SCHOOL

THE INTERNATIONAL RACE SCHOOL
HOBART, TASMANIA

Dangling off the bottom of Australia is a large island shaped like an upside-down triangle.

Once known by the far more intimidating name of Van Diemen's Land, it is now simply called Tasmania.

It is a rugged land, tough and forbidding. It features jagged coastal cliffs, ancient rainforests and a winding network of long open highways. Dotted around its many peninsulas are the grim sandstone remains of British prisons built in the 19th century—Port Arthur, Sarah Island. Names you didn't want to hear if you were a 19th-century criminal.

Once Tasmania was the end of the world. Now, it was just a pleasant two-hour hover-liner cruise from Sydney.

Jason Chaser stood on the deck of the liner as it sailed up the Derwent River, and beheld modern Hobart.

With its elegant mix of the very old and the very new, Hobart had become one of the world's hippest cities. Two-hundred-year-old sandstone warehouses blended beautifully with modern silver-and-glass skyscrapers and swooping titanium bridges over the river.

Through a quirk of fate, the entire island was owned by the International Race School, making it the single largest privately owned plot of land in the world.

Back in the early 2000s, the Australian state of Tasmania had been in decline, its population both ageing and dwindling. When the population fell below 50,000 people, the Australian Government took the extraordinary step of privatising the entire island. Tasmania was bought by an oil-and-gas company that never saw hover technology coming. In the liquidator's sale of the dead company's assets, the island-state was bought by Phillip T. Youngman, the leader of a strange group of people who planned to create a school for the nascent sport of hover car racing.

The rest, as they say, was history.

As desert boys, Jason and the Bug had never seen anything like the east coast of Australia.

Their cruise liner had swept past Sydney on its way to Tasmania. Just off Sydney, stretching down the Pacific coastline, they'd seen the famous Eight Dams—a simply amazing feat of mass-scale construction. A few years ago, engineers had literally held back the Pacific Ocean while they built eight massive hydro-electric dams a few miles out from the coast.

The eight waterfalls that now streamed majestically down the faces of the dams provided an endless supply of clean power with an added bonus: the waterfalls were the second most-visited tourist attraction in the world behind the Pyramids, and a spectacular backdrop to the annual hover car race held in Sydney—the Sydney Classic—one of the four Grand Slam races.

The cruise liner pulled into the dock at Hobart.

Jason and the Bug grabbed their bags and made for the gangway bridge—

—where they were cut off by two surly youths.

'Well, if it isn't little Jason Chaser again,' Barnaby Becker sneered, blocking their way. At 18, Becker was a full head and shoulders taller than Jason. He was also now the Indo-Pacific Regional Champion, a title that garnered some respect in racing circles.

Barnaby nodded to his navigator: Guido Moralez, also 18, with shifty eyes and a slick sleazy manner.

'I dunno, Guido,' Barnaby said. 'Tell me how a little runt who comes stone *motherless* last in the regionals gets to come to Race School.'

'Couldn't tell ya, Barn,' Guido said smoothly, eyeing Jason and the Bug sideways. 'But I hope they're up for it. You never know what sort of accidents can happen in a place like this.'

This exchange pretty much summed up their trip.

After their unexpected invitation to come to Race School, Jason and the Bug hadn't seen Scott Syracuse. He was taking a private hover plane to Tasmania, and had said he would meet the boys there. Unfortunately, this meant Jason and the Bug—already outsiders on account of their ages—had had to endure the taunts of Becker and Guido all the way to Tasmania.

Barnaby, knowing that Jason and the Bug lived with adoptive parents back at Halls Creek, took particular joy in including the word 'motherless' in most of his snide remarks.

The Bug whispered something in Jason's ear.

'What! What did you say?' Barnaby demanded. 'What's with all this whispering, you little moron? Why don't you talk like a man?'

The Bug just stared up at him blankly.

'I asked you a question, punk—' Barnaby made to grab

the Bug by his shirt, but Jason slapped the bigger boy's hand away.

Barnaby froze.

Jason didn't back down, returned his gaze.

'Ooh, I smell *tension*.' Guido Moralez rubbed his hands together.

'Don't you touch him,' Jason said. 'He talks. He just doesn't talk to people like you.'

Barnaby lifted his hand away, smiled. 'So what did he say, then?'

Jason said, 'He said: "We ain't motherless."'

The Race School was situated directly opposite the dock, on the other side of the wide Derwent River, inside a shimmering glass-and-steel building that looked like a giant sail.

Jason and the other new racers were led into the School's cavernous entry foyer. Famous hover cars hung from the ceiling: Wilmington's original prototype, the H-1, took pride of place in the centre, where it was flanked by Ferragamo's Masters-winning Boeing Hyper-Drive and an arched gate from the London Underground Run.

'This way,' their guide said, leading them into a high-tech theatre that looked like Mission Control at NASA. An enormous display screen up front faced fifteen rows of amphitheatre-like seating. Each seat was fitted with a computer screen. A gallery at the very back of the theatre was provided for the media and at the moment it was full to bursting.

'Welcome to the Race Briefing Room,' the guide said. 'My name is Stanislaus Calder and I am the Race Director here at the School. Trust me, all of you drivers will come to know this room very well. Please take a seat. Professor LeClerq and the teaching staff will be joining us shortly.'

Jason looked around the room, checking out the other racers.

There were about twenty-five drivers in total, most of them older boys of seventeen or eighteen. Nearly all of them sat with two companions: their navigators and Mech Chiefs. Jason and the Bug didn't have a Mech Chief, having always done their own pit work. Syracuse had said they would be matched up with someone upon the start of classes.

Jason saw Barnaby Becker and Guido sitting up the back with some other older boys. A few girls were scattered about the room, most of them wearing the black coveralls of Mech Chiefs, but the assembled crowd was largely male.

One girl, however, caught Jason's eye. She was very pretty, with an elfish face, bright green eyes and strawberry-blonde hair. She looked about seventeen, and sat all on her own, way over at the right-hand end of the front row.

It took Jason a moment to realise that not a few of the reporters in the media gallery were gazing directly at her, pointing, trying to get photos of her. Jason didn't know why.

'Close your mouth and stop drooling,' a husky female voice said from somewhere nearby.

Jason turned to find the girl seated immediately behind him also staring at the pretty girl in the front row. 'Ariel Piper is way outta your league, little man.'

'I wasn't looking at her like *that*,' Jason protested.

'Sure you weren't.' The girl behind him was about sixteen, with a round face, bright flame-orange hair (with matching flame-orange horn-rimmed glasses) and a wide rosy-cheeked grin. 'I'm Sally McDuff, Mech Chief and all-round great gal from Glasgow, Scotland.'

'Jason Chaser, and this here's the Bug, he's my little brother and my navigator.'

Sally McDuff assessed the Bug for a long moment. 'The

Bug, huh? Well aren't you just the *cutest* thing. How old are you, little one?'

The Bug went pink with embarrassment.

'He's twelve,' Jason said.

'Twelve . . .' Sally McDuff mused. 'Must be some kind of mathematical wiz if someone invited him here. Nice to meet you, Jason Chaser and his navigator, the Bug. I imagine we'll be running into each other again over the course of this year. Hope you get a good mentor.'

'What do you mean?'

'Gosh, you are a newbie. Getting through Race School ain't just about being a great racer. Having a top teacher makes a huge difference. Apparently the best is Zoroastro. The Maestro. His students have taken out the School Championship three out of the last four years. Word is, Charlie Riefenstal is light on homework and heavy on track-time, so a lot of drivers want to get him.'

'What do you know about Scott Syracuse?' Jason asked.

'Syracuse. Yeah. Teaching full-time this year. I heard he did some fill-in teaching last year when the full-timers went on vacation.'

'And . . .'

'Apparently, his students were relieved when their regular mentors got back. They say Syracuse works you long and hard. Lotta theory. Lotta pit practice—over and over until you get it right. And a lot of homework.'

'Oh,' Jason said.

'Why do you ask?'

'No reason.'

At that moment, the rear doors to the theatre rumbled open and everyone fell silent. Jean-Pierre LeClerq entered the Briefing Room, followed by about a dozen teachers and lecturers, all dressed in flight uniforms. Last in the long line of Race School staff, Jason saw Scott Syracuse, limping along with the aid of his cane.

Principal LeClerq took his place behind the lectern on the stage.

'Ladies and gentlemen, sponsors, assembled members of the media and most importantly . . . *racers*. Welcome to the International Race School. The year has barely begun and yet the world of hover car racing has already seen some great upheavals'—Jason could have sworn LeClerq glanced over at Ariel Piper when he said that—'but here at the Race School we have adapted accordingly and while the debate has been *vigorous,* we welcome change.'

The media photographers clicked away on their digital cameras. Their photos would be on news sites around the world in seconds.

LeClerq continued: 'To the new intake of candidates, I say this: welcome. Welcome to the hardest, most demanding year of your lives. Make no mistake, this school is a crucible, a cauldron, a daily trial-by-fire that will push your skills, your minds—your very characters—to their limits.

'Race School is not for the faint-hearted or the weak-kneed. You will experience the elation of victory . . . and the deflation of loss. You will all partake in the School Championship, while those of you who actually win a race will have the extra privilege of participating in the mid-season Sponsors' Race.

'Some of you will emerge from this crucible forged and strengthened, and hence worthy of the title "racer" . . . and from that, worthy of a contract with a professional team. Others among you will not—you will be broken. But take heart, it is no disgrace to withdraw from Race School. Just being invited to come here in the first place means that you are something special.

'Speaking of something special,' LeClerq grinned, 'I am pleased to announce that we have a surprise for you all today. To give this year's Commencement Address we have a very special guest, an alumnus of this school and, let's be frank, a rather famous individual. Ladies and gentlemen, to give the Commencement Address, I present to you the best student I ever taught . . . Alessandro Romba, the current World Champion!'

The auditorium came alive.

Heads turned in delighted shock. Murmurs raced across the room. Jason almost fell out of his seat.

At the lectern, Jean-Pierre LeClerq gave a satisfied smirk—he had sprung his surprise perfectly.

Alessandro Romba was quite simply the most famous man in the world.

La Bomba Romba.

The reigning world champion on the Pro Circuit, he was the lead driver for the Lockheed-Martin Factory Team. He was also Italian, drop-dead handsome, and perhaps the most daring man to ever helm a hover car: his nickname 'La Bomba'—the Bomb—was very well-earned.

He endorsed aftershave lotions, Lockheed-Martin hover cars, and Adidas sportswear. Not a week went by when his face did not appear on the cover of some major magazine or newspaper.

When Alessandro Romba strode out onto the stage from the wings, the entire audience fell into a respectful hush. Not a few women in the crowd primped their hair.

He embraced LeClerq like a son hugging his father, and then he stood behind the lectern and smiled that million-dollar grin.

The media cameras clicked like machine guns.

★ ★ ★

Thirty minutes later, La Bomba Romba concluded his speech to roars of approval and a standing ovation.

Jean-Pierre LeClerq retook the lectern.

'Thank you, Alessandro, thank you. It will come as no surprise to any of you that in his year at Race School, Alessandro romped away with the School Championship by a record twenty points. I understand that he will be staying for lunch and is happy to sign autographs too.

'But to some administrative matters: I will now call out each candidate's name and assign them to their mentors. Your mentor will be your teacher here at Race School—as well as your guidance counsellor, your confidant and your surrogate parent. Each mentor will be responsible for three driving teams.

'So. Starting alphabetically. Team Becker, driver Barnaby, you will be under the tutelage of Master Zoroastro. Team Caseman, driver Timothy, Master Raul. Team Chaser, driver Jason, you will be assigned to Master Syracuse: Mech Chief to be assigned. Freeman, driver Wesley . . .'

Jason turned to the Bug. 'Well, little brother. It's time to start Race School.'

THE INTERNATIONAL RACE SCHOOL
PIT LANE

Pit Lane pulsed with the noises and smells of racing.

The whirring *hum* of magneto drives. The whine of hover cars screaming down the straight. The acrid smell of spent drives and the sweet mint-like odour of green coolant liquid.

After the formalities of the Opening Ceremony were over, it was straight to the racetrack for the new candidates. Their bags were all taken to their dorms, where they would meet them later. Their cars had been unloaded from the liner during the ceremony, and were waiting for them in the pits.

Naturally, Jason and the Bug got lost on the way to Pit Lane.

Race School was a pretty big place, with no fewer than six practice courses and thirteen competition courses, all fanning out from a central pit area on the banks of the Derwent called Race HQ. Finally, they found Pit Lane, with the *Argonaut* sitting inside a bay emblazoned '55'.

Scott Syracuse was already there, waiting for them.

'Master Chaser. Master Bug,' he said. 'So nice of you to join us.'

Standing with Syracuse were seven other students—two drivers with their navigators and Mech Chiefs . . . plus one extra student.

The seventh person was someone Jason recognised.

Sally McDuff.

'Oh, no way . . .' Sally said, seeing Jason and the Bug approaching.

Syracuse said, 'You've met already?'

'Yeah, at the Opening Ceremony,' Sally said.

Syracuse said, 'Well, then, for what it's worth: Jason Chaser, meet Sally McDuff, your Mech Chief. Ms McDuff hails from the wilds of Scotland but don't hold that against her. She's a gifted pit technician. For their part, Ms McDuff, aside from being inexcusably late, the Chaser brothers are quite a driving team.'

Jason nodded to Sally.

Syracuse indicated the other two drivers—both were big eighteen-year-olds, one Asian, the other African-American. 'This is Horatio Wong and Isaiah Washington. They will also be studying under my tutelage this year.'

Both Wong and Washington towered over Jason and the Bug. They eyed them as if they were insects.

'Now,' Syracuse said. 'Today is Monday. On Wednesday, you will contest the first race of the year. Like all races here at Race School, points will be awarded for the first ten cars on a sliding scale from 10 for the winner down to 1 for tenth place—points that will be tallied for the School Championship.

'During your time here at Race School you will partake in every variety of hover car race: gate races, lap races, sprints, knockout pursuits and enduros. Wednesday's race is the traditional Race School opener: a SuperSprint 30-2-1: Last Man Drop-Off. Thirty laps, but every two laps, the last-placed car is removed from the field. It's fast, furious, and unforgiving to racers who fall behind. There are no spectacular comebacks in a Last Man Drop-Off.'

Syracuse eyed them all closely, his gaze electric.

'Now, I know a lot of other teachers allow their charges to prepare in relative peace for this first race, using it as a kind of test-the-water, shake-off-the-rust, get-a-feel-for-the-place race. I do not view Race 1 in this way. I view it as a race. A race to be run and hopefully won.

'Nor do I believe in wasting valuable teaching time. Therefore, I will give you all two hours to prep and examine your cars, to make sure they arrived safely, and for those who haven't met to get to know each other.

'We will commence formal lessons in two hours, at 1600 hours, starting with Electromagnetic Physics in Room 17. I have arranged for Professor Kingston, the head of the physics department, to give you all a special private lesson.

'This will be followed by two hours of Pit Practice commencing at 1730 hours. Dinner begins at 1900, but you can always eat later. As for tomorrow morning's Race Tactics class, I expect that all of you will have read pages 1–35 of Taylor's *The Racing Mind* plus *The Rules of Hover Car Racing*, all of which you will find on your dorm computers. There *will* be a quiz. Any questions?'

The nine students just stared at him in shock.

'No?' Syracuse said. 'Good. See you in two hours then, in Room 17 for some physics.'

Sally McDuff walked in a slow circle around the *Argonaut*, frowning.

She eyed its hunch-backed fuselage, touched its coolant receptacles. 'Hmph.' Then she dropped to the ground and slid herself under the car, lying on a hover-plank.

Jason and the Bug just watched.

'Hmmm . . .' Sally's voice came from under the car.

She re-emerged. Stood up, put her fist to her chin, thinking hard, gazing critically at the glistening blue-white-and-silver hover car.

'It's crap,' she said, pronouncing the last word in the Scottish manner: *craaap*. 'An absolute honest-to-goodness cobbled-together piece of crap. Little Bug, I can't believe a smart guy like you would fly around in this thing. Him,' she jerked her chin at Jason, 'I could believe, but not you.'

The Bug smiled. He liked Sally McDuff.

But she wasn't finished.

'Hell, there must be nine different cars making up this thing. I mean, I can see why she flies fast, but she must be hellishly unstable: you've got the standard six magneto drives along the underbelly of the car, but it's a mix-and-match of three different brands. Luckily, you won't have to worry about that here: the Race School provides us with magneto drives.

'Your Momo directional prism is top quality, but like all the good stuff, Momo prisms wear easily and this one's only got a few races left in it. And what *the hell* did you do to your thrusters, man! Looks like you've been dancing on your pedals! They'll have to be completely stripped, greased and rebuilt. And you've eaten up your coolant hoses to within an inch of their lives.'

'We had a problem with the steering in our last race back home,' Jason said quickly, defensively. 'As for the rest, geez, I did build her myself—'

Sally held up her hand. 'Easy, tiger. Easy. I wasn't finished. After all that, she's a tough little nut, this *Argonaut*. Looks like you've put her through absolute hell and she's still begging for more. I like tough cars, cars with guts, character, *haggis*. And this car has haggis. Hell, I even like the paint job. And don't you worry, young Chaser. There isn't an engine alive that Sally Anne McDuff can't tune to peak performance.'

For the next two hours, Jason and Sally talked (with the Bug speaking through Jason), about their cars and past races, their homes and their dreams involving the racing world.

Sally wanted to be Mech Chief in a pro team. She was the youngest of nine children and all of the others were boys: all grease monkeys and car freaks. She had spent her early years watching them tinker with their hot rods—but it was only when she got her own car at age 14 that she revealed the extent of her knowledge: her own tinkering produced a veritable hover *rocket*. Her father, a stout old Scot named Jock McDuff, was so proud.

Jason told her about himself: living in Halls Creek in far north-western Australia with his adoptive parents. Martha and Henry Chaser couldn't have children, so for many years they had raised orphans. So far, over the course of 40 years, they had raised 14 parentless kids.

They had found Jason at the local orphanage as a four-year-old. Seated next to him in the playroom had been the Bug, a tiny troublesome boy of two who, they were told, only became quiet when he was with Jason.

When Martha and Henry decided to adopt Jason, they faced an unexpected problem: the four-year-old Jason wouldn't leave the Bug behind. Simply wouldn't leave without him. The dean of the orphanage also begged them to take the Bug, too, since there would be no end to the howling if Jason were taken away without him.

And so Martha and Henry Chaser had simply shrugged and decided to adopt the two of them.

★ ★ ★

Four o'clock came round and they went to their first formal class with Scott Syracuse. It was a killer physics lesson on the workings of magneto drives and the principles behind Wilfred Wilmington's invention and by the end of it, Jason was mentally exhausted.

Which made the ensuing two hours of pit practice absolute torture: over and over again, he would swing the *Argonaut* into their pit bay, bringing it to a halt underneath an enormous spider-like mechanism called a pit machine.

The pit machine had eight arms, all of which performed different tasks at the same time: magneto drive replacement, coolant refill, compressed-air replenishment, fin realignment—its operation supervised by Sally, the Mech Chief.

'Clean pit stops are the lifeblood of hover car racing!' Syracuse yelled above the din of his three teams. 'Races are won and lost in the pits! Every variety of race contains pit stops—some, like the Italian Run, even require the *pit crew* to travel overland to meet their car at multiple pit areas!

'Pit stops provide races with that crucial element of strategy! *When* should you pit? Should you pit one more time when the finish line is only three laps away? Can you make it round the final lap on only one magneto drive?'

Syracuse smiled. 'But before you can formulate pit stop strategies, you have to master the pit stop itself!'

At that moment, as Jason swept into his pit bay underneath the giant claws of his pit machine, he realised—too late—that he'd overshot the pit bay by about twelve inches.

'Chaser! Hold it there!' Syracuse yelled. 'Everyone! Freeze! Please observe. Ms McDuff, initiate the pit machine.'

Sally hit the switch.

The pit machine's eight-pronged claws descended around the *Argonaut*—and abruptly stopped, realigned themselves, moved forward a foot, then went about their repair work.

The delay was about five seconds.

'Not good enough, Mr Chaser!' Syracuse said. 'Your pit machine will be loyal to you. But are you being loyal to it by performing a sloppy pit entry? Your competitor just blasted out of the pits four seconds ahead of you and won the race. Imprecision is punished severely in racing. If you are imprecise, *you will lose*. I don't know about you, but I do not race to lose.'

Another time, while his pit machine replaced his six undercar magneto drives, Jason—in his eagerness to get away quickly—let the *Argonaut* creep forward over the white line painted on the ground, marking the forward edge of his pit bay area.

There came a shrill electronic scream.

The pit machine immediately withdrew into the ceiling, refusing to work on the car.

'Mr Chaser!' Syracuse called. 'Pit Bay Violation! You just earned yourself a 15-second penalty for illegally creeping out of your pit bay during a stop. Fifteen seconds in a hover car race is an eternity. Again, you lose.'

'But—' Jason started.

Syracuse stopped him with an icy glare. 'Don't resist your mistakes, Mr Chaser. Learn from them. To err is human, to make the same mistake twice . . . is stupid.'

And with that, mercifully, the pit practice ended.

It was 7:45 p.m.

It was late. Jason and the Bug and Sally were exhausted. And they still had reading to do for tomorrow.

'Thank you, people,' Syracuse said. 'I'll see you tomorrow morning.'

And he left.

'Could've said, "Nice work today, kids,"' Jason said.

Sally clapped him on the shoulder. 'Nice work today, kid.'

'Thanks.'

Jason walked to the dining hall, alone. The Bug and Sally had both gone off to their rooms to rest—Jason was going to bring them some food later.

Ahead of him walked Horatio Wong and Isaiah Washington, Scott Syracuse's other two charges. Neither Wong nor Washington even attempted to include Jason in their conversation.

Wong was complaining.

'What is his *problem*? I mean, why should *I* have to attend a damn *physics* class? So long as my Mech Chief knows what's happening inside my car, I just want to be left alone to drive it.'

'Totally,' Washington agreed. 'Hey, he pinned me for a pit bay violation. God, everybody does it. When was the last time you saw any racer pinned in a pro race for a pit bay violation? Never! Scott Syracuse wasn't that great a racer when he was driving on the tour anyway. What makes him think he's such a great teacher now?'

Wong lowered his voice, did a Scott Syracuse impression: *'To err is human, to make the same mistake twice is stupid.'*

The two of them laughed.

'Talk about bad luck,' Washington said. 'Why'd we have to get the teacher from hell?'

They came to the dining hall.

All of the other students at the Race School were already well into their dinners, having started at seven. Wong and

Washington quickly grabbed a couple of trays and joined a table of boys their age, taking the last available seats.

Jason scanned the room for a place to sit.

Many of the racing teams were eating with their teachers, laughing, smiling, getting to know each other. Syracuse hadn't even offered to dine with his students.

At one table, Jason saw Barnaby Becker and his crew, eating with their teacher, a skeleton-thin man with a beak-like nose.

Jason recognised the teacher instantly: he was Zoroastro, the celebrated former world-champion racer from Russia. One of the very first hover car racers, Zoroastro was still regarded by many as perhaps the most technically *precise* driver ever to grace the Pro Circuit: he was almost mechanical in his exactness, never missing a turn, just wearing his opponents down until they cracked under the pressure.

Now, as a coach, he was so good—and so vain—that he only deigned to teach two driving teams, not three, as all the other teachers did. And the Race School indulged him.

Which brought Jason's gaze to the other young driver seated with Barnaby and Zoroastro.

He was a strikingly handsome boy of about eighteen. He sat high and proud, and he scanned the dining room as if he owned it. He was dressed completely in black—black racing suit, black boots, black cap—perhaps to match his jet-black hair and deep dark eyes.

His absolute coolness rattled Jason.

Alone among the racers in the room, his sheer confidence was unsettling. It was said that the very best hover car racers behaved as if they owned the world: you needed a kind of narcissistic super-confidence and self-belief to propel yourself successfully around a track at close to the speed of sound.

Jason made a mental note to keep an eye on this boy in black.

He resumed his search for a place to sit.

A quick survey revealed that there was only one option, and it was a strange one.

Over in the corner of the dining hall, seated at a table all by herself, sat Ariel Piper, the pretty girl he had seen at the Opening Ceremony.

Jason grabbed a tray of food and went over to her table.

As he arrived there, he realised that Ariel Piper was even more beautiful up close. He hoped she didn't see his face flush slightly.

'Hi,' he said, 'is it okay if I sit here?'

Ariel Piper looked up at him suddenly, as if roused from a daydream, as if she were surprised to hear a human voice so close to her.

'Sure,' she said sarcastically, 'so long as you're not afraid to catch cooties.'

'Come on. I can't catch cooties just from sitting near you,' Jason said with absolute honesty. 'You only catch cooties from *kissing* a girl—' He cut himself off, blushed bright pink, before adding quickly: 'Not that I came over here hoping to kiss you, miss.'

Ariel Piper snuffed a laugh at that, and examined Jason more closely. At seventeen, she was lean and graceful, and way too old for a fourteen-year-old like him. Never had Jason wished more that he was three years older.

Then she said, 'You don't know anything about me, do you?'

Jason shrugged. 'Nope. Just that you're a student here at the Race School, like the rest of us. I'm Jason Chaser, from Halls Creek, W.A.'

'Ariel Piper. Mobile, Alabama.'

'Why did you say that about catching cooties? Are you sick or something? Is that why you're sitting over here all by yourself?'

Ariel gazed at Jason, a curious smile forming on her pretty face.

'You race with girls back in Halls Creek, Jason?'

'Sure. All the time. Some of the girl racers back home are the most vicious and dirty—I mean, competitive—racers in the district.'

'Okay, then. Have you ever seen a girl racer on the Pro Circuit?'

That stopped Jason.

'No . . .' he said slowly. 'No, I haven't.'

Ariel said, 'That's because, until now, the Race Schools haven't admitted girls, and since the Race Schools are the prime entry route to the Pro Circuit, there are no female pro racers. Mankind is funny. We've had all this progress, all these advancements in technology, equality and equal opportunity, but some prejudices die hard. People still see men and women differently in the world of sport.'

'But entry into the School is pretty well set,' Jason said. 'You either get invited or you get an automatic exemption by winning certain regional championships.'

'That's exactly right,' Ariel said. 'And I won the South-East-American Regional Championships. After I did, I applied for entry into the International Race School. But the School didn't admit me. They didn't let me in because I was a girl.'

'But that's just stupid,' Jason said. 'If you can race a hover car, it shouldn't matter whether you're a boy or a girl.'

Ariel said, 'Fortunately for me, Jason, the Australian High Court agreed with you. And they *forced* the School to accept me. It took a hell of a fight, but I got in.'

And suddenly the penny dropped, and Jason understood the presence of all the photographers and journalists at the Opening Ceremony, all focused on Ariel Piper.

He also now understood why she was sitting over here in the corner, all alone, ostracised. And he'd thought that *he* was an outsider because of his age.

'And so now I'm here,' Ariel said, 'and I'm wondering if it was all worth it. In just one day, my mentor has treated me twice as hard as his male racers. Girl Mech Chiefs will at least talk to me, but they won't risk eating with me. And forget about the male racers. Then there are all the sideways looks in the corridors and the pit area, the media attention, hell, even the Principal doesn't want me here . . .'

She looked away and Jason saw that her eyes were beginning to fill with tears.

'*Hey,*' he said firmly. He tried to think of what his mum would say in this situation, and he got it: 'No. Don't cry. Don't let them *see you cry*. Then they've won.'

That scored.

Ariel raised her head, sniffed once, sucked back the tears.

Jason said, 'Ariel, I don't know you that well, but I know this. You're here. Now. At Race School. And the only thing that matters at Race School is this: racing. If you can hold your own on the racecourse, people'll come round.'

She turned to face him. 'You know, you're pretty smart for a fourteen-year-old.'

'I can be a little slow on the uptake,' he said, 'but just like on the track, I catch up. If it helps, and if you want me to, I'll be your friend while you're here, Ariel.'

'I'd like that, Jason. Thanks.'

And with that, they started eating together.

THE INTERNATIONAL
RACE SCHOOL:
TASMANIA, AUSTRALIA
RACE 1: SUPERSPRINT 30-2-1

===== Course

TASMANIA

Hobart
Port Arthur

HOBART

RACE SCHOOL, TASMANIA
RACE 1, COURSE 1

Race day.

The roar of hover cars filled the air.

Blurring bullets with racers and navigators inside them whipped past Pit Lane. Large floating grandstands filled with cheering spectators enjoyed the carnival atmosphere of the opening race of the Race School season.

Race 1 had been simply electrifying from the start.

A crash on the first corner had seen two cars tumble into the banks of the Derwent River at 500 km/h. They'd touched as they'd turned, then flipped and rolled and bounced with frightening speed, shedding pieces of their fuselages as they skimmed the river's surface, before they came to twin thumping halts, their racers (and navigators) safe in their reinforced cockpits and their cars now only good for a trip to the Maintenance and Rebuilding Shed.

Jason had never seen anything like it.

The *pace* of the race was far faster than anything he'd ever been involved in. The intensity was furious. It was the difference between amateur stuff and pro racing.

The race was indeed a 'SuperSprint 30-2-1: Last Man Drop-Off': 30 laps, and every 2 laps, the last-placed car was removed from the field.

Since there were 20 starters (a few racers had pulled out

due to technical problems with their cars), that meant that the last two laps would be fought between 6 cars.

The course was tight—winding its way westward through the rainforests of lower Tasmania before returning to Hobart via the treacherous southern coastline of the island.

Such a tight course was brutal on magneto drives, which meant that pit stops would be required every seven or eight laps—creating a (very deliberate) dilemma near the end: did you pit near Lap 30 or did you try to get to the Finish Line on ever-diminishing magneto drives? Of course, if you were in the pits when everyone else crossed the Start-Finish Line to complete a lap, leaving you the last-placed car, you would be eliminated.

The first two cars eliminated were, naturally, the two who had crashed so spectacularly on the first turn—which meant that the remaining eighteen cars could drive in safety for the next six laps: the third elimination would not occur until the end of Lap 6.

Winding, bending, chasing, racing.

Jason saw the world rush by in a blur: the lush green leaves of the rainforests became streaking green paint-strokes. The sharply twisting road near Russell Falls—one of the great sights of Tasmania—became just another over-taking point, a spot where you could take someone under brakes.

Sweeping around the coastal cliffs and down the ocean straight.

730 km/h.

S-bending through a series of silver steel archways that jutted out from the wave-battered southern coastline.

550 km/h.

Then braking hard to a bare 210 km/h to take the final turn: a wicked left-hand hairpin around Tasman Island, a tall pillar-like rock formation not far from the ruins of the 19th-century prison at Port Arthur.

Then, finally, heading back up to the Derwent River—the home straight—hitting top speed: 770 km/h.

RACETIME: 15:00 MINS
LAP: 5

The *Argonaut* screamed down the straight, swept round the deadly Turn One, and shot into the rainforest.

It was Lap 5, and out of 18 cars, Jason was coming 10th and feeling pretty good.

Which was precisely when his left-rear magneto drive inexplicably went dead.

Immediately, his car lost some 'traction', became harder to handle. Race-spec hover cars customarily have six disc-shaped magneto drives on their undersides. Losing one is bearable, losing two is like driving a wheeled car on a wet road. Losing four is like driving on an ice-skating rink.

Jason's drive console lit up like a Christmas tree.

Sally's voice exploded through his earpiece: '*Jason! You just lost your Number 6 drive!*'

'I know! What happened?'

'*I don't know!*' Sally's voice said. '*According to my telemetry screens, it just packed up and died, lost all power!*'

'Bug!' Jason said quickly. 'What do you think? Bring her in?'

The Bug's voice came in through his earpiece.

Jason nodded: 'Damn right it'll be close. You sure we can make it?'

The Bug mumbled something.

'Good point,' Jason said. 'Sally: The Bug's right. We're 10th, a lap-and-a-half away from the next elimination. Everyone else is probably planning on pitting after Lap 8. If we pit now, we'll go straight to last, but if we can pull a good stop, we'll have a whole lap to catch up. And we'll be on a fresh set of mags. It's our best option.'

'*Then come on in, my boys!*' Sally roared. '*This is what it's all about! I'll be waiting!*'

The *Argonaut* took the final Port Arthur hairpin perfectly, and as the leaders shot off down the Derwent on Lap 6, Jason pulled his car into Pit Lane.

He hit his mark perfectly.

The clock started ticking.

00:00

00:01

The pit machine—now christened by Sally as the 'Tarantula'—descended on the *Argonaut*, six of its arms removing the car's six underside magneto drives, while its other two arms respectively replenished Jason's coolant tank and recharged his compressed-air thrusters.

00:04

00:05

Jason was tapping his foot impatiently. Every second spent in here was a second lost.

Shoom!-shoom!-shoom!

The hover cars that had previously been behind him now whizzed past the pits.

'Come *on!* Come *on!*' he whispered.

00:08

00:09

A ten-second pit stop would be great.

Shoom!

Suddenly the last-placed car shot past the pits. They were now officially last.

The Tarantula was almost done. Only the coolant hose was still connected to the *Argonaut*. Jason, keen to rejoin the race, leaned forward on his accelerator, creeping forward—

'*Pit Bay Violation! Car 55!*' a shrill amplified voice boomed out from some track-side speakers. '*Fifteen second penalty!*'

'What!' Jason yelled.

And then he saw the Pit Bay Supervisor—the teachers took it in turns to be Supervisor and today it was Professor Zoroastro, Barnaby's mentor and also the mentor of the mysterious boy in black. Right now, he was pointing at the *Argonaut*'s front wings.

They were exactly two inches over the pit bay line.

'Oh, no way!' Jason shouted.

A red boom gate whizzed down in front of the *Argonaut*, preventing it from leaving the pits. A digital timer on the horizontal boom counted down from 00:15.

Now every second seemed an eternity to Jason.

00:10
00:09
00:08

Jason looked over at Sally. Behind her stood Scott Syracuse—his arms firmly folded.

00:02
00:01
00:00

The boom gate lifted and the *Argonaut* shot off the mark, blasting back out onto the course.

★ ★ ★

The six brand-new magneto drives under him gave Jason a new lease of life.

The *Argonaut* flew like a bullet, gripping the tight turns of the rainforest section as if it were travelling on rails.

With its new mags, it had a grip advantage over the other cars, whose own magneto drives were now nearly six laps old.

Sally's voice: '*You're twenty seconds behind the second-last-placed car, Car 70, and gaining. Nineteen... now eighteen seconds behind...*'

The Bug spoke.

'I know,' Jason replied. 'I know.'

They were gaining roughly one second for every two kilometres. But there were only 40 kilometres left to run on this lap.

At this rate—provided Jason raced an almost perfect lap—they'd only catch Car 70 right at the Start-Finish Line.

Whipping past Russell Falls.

Ten seconds behind.

Out round the cliffs, onto the ocean straight—just in time to see Car 70 whip around a faraway bluff.

Six seconds.

Weaving through the S-bends of the coastal arches— and suddenly, the tailfin of Car 70 was close.

Four seconds behind.

And then Jason saw the Port Arthur hairpin up ahead, saw the building-sized rock pillar that was Tasman Island.

That was the passing point.

And he had new mags and the other guy didn't.

Car 70 hit the hairpin.

The *Argonaut* took it wider, cutting inside 70's line.

And the two cars rounded the curve together, flying dangerously close to the jagged rocky pillar—

—and the *Argonaut* emerged with its winged nose level with Car 70's bulbous snout!

The crowds on the grandstands leapt to their feet.

The local TV commentators went bananas at the audacity of the move.

Car 70 and the *Argonaut* raced down the Derwent side-by-side, neck-and-neck until—*sh-shoom!*—they crossed the Start-Finish Line together.

RACETIME: 18:02 MINS
LAP: 7

The official loudspeakers blared:

'*End of Lap 6, eliminated car is Car 70. Racer Walken.*'

The crowd cheered.

Jason floored it—while Car 70 slowed, its driver punching his steering wheel before pulling off into the Exit Lane at the end of the straight.

The *Argonaut* was still in the race.

RACETIME: 01:15 HOURS
LAP: 25

Almost an hour later, Jason was still in it.

Coming 6th.

The end of Lap 25 saw the final eight cars enter the pits more or less together.

Jason stopped the *Argonaut* on a dime.

The Tarantula descended, did its stuff.

Entering the pits just in front of Jason had been the boy in black.

His car was a super-sleek Lockheed-Martin ProRacer-5, painted entirely in black and simply numbered 1. It was rather presumptuous to number your car '1', since in the pro world, that number was allotted to the champion of the previous year. But at Race School, a racer's number was his or her personal choice.

The Black Boy's pit machine worked with extraordinary precision—attaching new mags, filling his car's coolant tanks, pumping in compressed air.

And then suddenly the boy in black was gone, booming out of the pits a full three seconds ahead of Jason.

It must have been a 7-second pit stop.

How did he do that! Jason thought. *Damn, he's good.*

The Tarantula finished and Jason jammed down on the collective, rejoining the race.

RACETIME: 01:21 HOURS
LAP: 27

Three laps to go. Seven cars left on the track.

The next elimination was the result of a huge crash out on the coastline: the car coming 2nd had lost two mags while wending his way through the S-bends of steel arches—his mags had not been attached properly during his last pit stop and had fallen off.

The result was a 500 km/h frontal crash into one of the solid-steel arches. A shocking explosion followed, but the racer and his navigator had survived by ejecting a nanosecond beforehand.

Which meant that when the field next crossed the Start-Finish line, that driver was eliminated—the fourteenth and last elimination of the race.

So now everyone had pitted three times—as such all were travelling on mags of the same age.

Six cars left. Two laps.

It was now a dash for the Finish Line.

MATTHEW REILLY

Superfast and supertense. One mistake and you were out. Pressure-driving time.

Place check:

Jason was in 5th place.

The boy in black, in his sleek black Lockheed-Martin, Car No.1, was coming first.

Jason could see Barnaby Becker—in his own maroon-coloured Lockheed—up in 2nd place.

In 3rd, hammering at Barnaby's tail, was a French youth in a Renault X-700. The French driver was throwing everything at Barnaby, but Barnaby was foiling his every attempt to get past.

In 4th place was a red-and-white Boeing Evercharge-III. This was Ariel Piper's car, No.16: the *Pied Piper*.

Good on you, Ariel, Jason thought. *Hang in there.*

Then came Jason, followed by Isaiah Washington, in last place.

The six cars took the bend at the end of the straight and entered the rainforest for the last time.

Past the falls and out to the ocean straight.

Nothing in it.

Then they entered the S-bends of the coastal arches and suddenly, without warning, the *Argonaut* shuddered violently and its tail flailed out wildly behind it like a stunt car in an old movie skidding on a dirt tack and Sally McDuff's voice was blaring in Jason's ear.

'*Jason! My telemetry just went berserk! Both of your rear magneto drives just lost all power!*'

Jason grappled with his steering wheel. 'I kinda noticed that, Sally!'

Steel archways whistled past him, inches away, just as Washington's car zoomed by, leaving the *Argonaut* in last place.

'Damn it!' Jason yelled. 'We're screwed! Damn it, we got so far . . .'

They were indeed screwed. With only four mags, Jason couldn't maintain the high levels of speed and control necessary to keep up with the others.

The *Argonaut* fell back. But Jason kept on driving. He was determined to finish the race—and get the 5 points for coming 6th—even if it meant limping over the line a long way behind the leaders.

He burst out from the S-bends to see the wide-open bay leading to the Port Arthur hairpin.

He saw the all-black Car No.1 bank into the final turn with clinical precision, disappearing behind the huge rocky pillar, closely followed by Barnaby—still holding off the French racer in the Renault—and then Ariel Piper swooping in close behind them.

And then it happened.

Ariel's car didn't take the left-hand hairpin.

Instead, it just kept on going straight ahead, shooting out and away to the *right*, heading for the open ocean.

Jason's eyes almost popped out of his head.

'What the—?' he said.

Washington's car took the final turn—pleased now to be moving up into 4th—and headed for home.

But Jason just kept watching Ariel's hover car.

It was now shuddering violently and listing away to the right—the absolutely wrong direction—shooting off into the distance in a superwide right-hand arc.

'Something's wrong,' Jason said. 'If she missed the turn, she would have pulled up by now . . .'

Then came the realisation.

'She's lost control of the car.'

And as he said those words, Jason saw the final hairpin

approaching, and suddenly he had a choice: he could finish the race—and get the 6 championship points for coming 5th—or he could help Ariel.

The Bug pointed out that the School would send out recovery vehicles to get Ariel.

'No,' Jason said. 'Look at her. She's too far gone. They won't get to her in time. We're the only ones who can help her.'

And with that, he made his decision.

Instead of taking the final left-hand hairpin turn himself, Jason banked the *Argonaut* right, booming off after Ariel's out-of-control hover car.

The commentators had never seen anything like it.

That the *Pied Piper* had missed the final turn under intense pressure was nothing new. But that the *Argonaut* had shoomed off into the distance after it was!

Two orange-painted truck-sized recovery vehicles were dispatched from Race HQ—standard practice for a race mishap. They couldn't know that this was no ordinary mishap.

The *Argonaut* zoomed low over the ocean, came alongside the tail of the red-and-white *Pied Piper*, both cars turning in a wide right-bending arc.

'Sally! Get me Ariel's radio frequency!' Jason yelled into his radiomike.

Sally did so, and as the *Argonaut* pulled alongside Ariel's shuddering car, Jason saw Ariel grappling with her steering wheel.

'Ariel! What's wrong?'

'*I've lost power in all my right-side magneto drives, Jason! They all switched off at exactly the same time, just as I was about to take that last hairpin!*'

'What kind of control have you got?' Jason asked.

'*Nothing! It's like everything just cut out at once! Thruster controls are gone! Electronics are unresponsive— I can't even shut down—and my other mags are losing magnetism fast.*'

This was bad. Ariel's left-hand magneto drives were bearing the weight of her whole car, and were thus losing their power twice as fast as they should have been. They were also driving the car in a wide circle, banking right.

What made it worse was the sight looming up ahead.

The southern coastal cliffs of the Port Arthur Peninsula rose up out of the ocean like a gigantic wall. High ocean waves crashed at their feet. Ariel's wide right-bending arc had brought her round a full 270 degrees: she was now rocketing northward, about to crash into the coastal cliffs.

'Ariel! You have to eject!' Jason yelled.

'*No!*' Ariel shouted back.

'No? Are you crazy! Why not?'

'*Jason, if I eject, the* Piper *will smash into those cliffs, and I won't have a car anymore. And without a car, I'll be out of Race School!*'

'And if you die, you'll also be out of Race School!'

'*I am not going to eject!*'

The cliffs were approaching.

Fast. Wide. Immovable.

There couldn't be more than ten seconds to impact.

Jason thought quickly.

'All right . . .' he said.

He gunned his engine and swung the *Argonaut* in underneath Ariel's speeding red-and-white car.

The cliffs rushed toward them.

Nine seconds . . . eight . . . seven . . .

The body of the *Pied Piper* cast a dark shadow over

Jason and the Bug, blocking out the sun. Jason saw the underbelly of the *Piper* less than a foot above his open cockpit.

Six . . . five . . . four . . .

The cliffs were very close now.

Then Jason pulled back on his stick, causing the *Argonaut* to gradually rise . . .

Clunk! The arched hunchback of the *Argonaut* clanged against the underside of the *Pied Piper*. Its wide flat tailfin also touched the bottom of Ariel's speeding car, providing a kind of three-point stability.

Three seconds . . .

And Jason gunned his thrusters, taking the weight of two hover cars with the engine of one.

The two cars rose together—slowly, painfully—one balancing on top of the other.

Rising . . . rising . . .

Two seconds . . .

Further . . .

One second . . .

The cliffs were right on top of them now, rushing forward. The *Pied Piper* was going to clear the clifftop, but the *Argonaut*, it seemed, was not.

Too late.

Impact.

The radio aerial on the underside of the *Argonaut* was ripped clean off by the clifftop as Jason rushed over the cliff at astronomical speed.

But they'd made it, clearing the clifftop by inches, pushing Ariel's car over it.

The danger averted, the Race School recovery vehicles swept into position on either side of Ariel's car, capturing her inside a fat beam of electromagnetic energy that extended out between them. The *Pied Piper*'s stability returned immediately and the two recovery vehicles guided it back to Race HQ.

For his part Jason pulled the *Argonaut* away from the recovery vehicles and returned to Pit Lane.

As they entered the pits, the Bug said something to Jason.

'Shut up, you cheeky monkey,' Jason replied.

The *Argonaut* cruised to a smooth touchdown in its pit bay, where it was met by Sally McDuff, Scott Syracuse and a crowd of buzzing onlookers.

Sally was smiling broadly.

Syracuse was frowning darkly.

Among the crowd were a phalanx of photographers and local journalists.

'You are one crazy little fella!' Sally roared, yanking Jason bodily from his cockpit and giving him a friendly thump on the helmet. 'But mark my words, young man, don't you ever put my little Bug in danger like that again!'

Jason smiled, turned to face Syracuse.

'Congratulations, Mr Chaser,' Syracuse said. 'You just made a name for yourself. You also failed to finish the race, which means you lost the 6 championship points that would have gone with 5th place. We'll discuss this later.' And with that Syracuse turned and left.

Cameras flashed. The journalists shouldered each other out of the way, shouting their questions, asking Jason what had compelled him to risk his life to save Ariel.

But after the initial frenzy, there came a shout: Ariel Piper had just arrived back in the pits. The media pack dashed off and Jason was left in his pit bay with the Bug and some peace and quiet.

He sat down, caught his breath. The Bug plonked down beside him.

After a few minutes, Sally came over. 'I just checked your rear magneto drives on my personal electrometer. Guess what? Those mags were only ten per cent charged when they were attached to the *Argonaut*.'

'What?' Jason said. 'Only ten per cent? Where did you get them?'

'Same place as everyone else,' Sally shook her head. 'The School's Parts and Equipment Department. It's where all the cars at the School get their equipment. But wait, there's more.'

'Yes . . .'

'You remember that other magneto drive that crapped out on you early in the race and forced you into the pits around Lap 5? Well, I checked it too. It was also under-charged. Same level. Ten per cent.'

'So what do you think it means?' Jason asked.

'It means,' Sally said, 'that either we got *galactically* unlucky getting three bogus magneto drives in our allotment . . .'

'Or . . .'

'Or someone set us up,' Sally said.

The words hung in the air.

'Someone arranged for us to collect three bogus mags from the Parts Department. Think about it. I picked up eighteen magneto drives for this race, three sets of six. We were going to have to use all of them at some point today. So we were destined to wipe out or at least have an unscheduled pit stop at some stage. Jason,' she frowned, 'I think someone sabotaged our car today.'

A few moments later, Ariel Piper came by their pit bay. The media tornado had got what it needed from her—some sound-bites to match their footage—and had gone on its way.

'There he is, my knight in shining armour,' she said.

'Hi,' Jason said. He introduced Sally and the Bug.

'Thanks for what you did out there,' Ariel said. 'And for understanding why I couldn't eject.'

'Forget about it,' Jason said. 'You woulda done the same for me.'

Ariel shook her head. 'I don't know about that, Jason,' she said. 'For some of us, heroics aren't the natural first instinct. But thanks again.'

She stood up to go.

'Oh, and one more thing,' she said. 'My Mech Chief, Bonnie, did some quick diagnostics on my car when I got back. Some of my magneto drives had apparently been doctored before the race, drained of ninety per cent of their power. And my onboard electronics had also been infected with a time-bomb computer virus that was programmed to go off late in the race—which was why I lost all control on the last turn.'

'No way . . .' Jason said. 'We got bogus drives, too. But not the other stuff.'

Ariel locked eyes with him. 'Someone didn't want me to finish this race today. And if it hadn't been for you, it would have been worse—a lot worse. I'm scared, Jason. I think someone wants me out of Race School permanently.'

PART III

ENEMIES WITHIN

PART III

There was no rest for Jason and his team after the high drama of Race 1.

The races continued—at the rate of two per week, usually held on Tuesday and Thursday, with classes in between.

One thing quickly became clear: the boy in black, the winner of Race 1, was a seriously good racer.

He also won Race 2.

And Race 3.

Jason managed to come fifth in Race 2, but 'DNF'd' Race 3—Did Not Finish—on account of another mysterious mechanical problem, this time a bottle of thinned coolant.

The boy in the all-black Car No.1 won by a mile on each occasion—and each time he was shadowed by his stablemate, Barnaby Becker. As a result, both of them flew to the top of the Championship Ladder, at 30 and 27 points respectively.

Their mentor Zoroastro strutted around the Race School like a coach with the two top-placed racers in his stable—while behind closed doors other racers complained that Zoroastro's drivers were unfairly driving *as a team*, with Barnaby flying obstruction for the supercool boy in black.

It took only a few questions for Jason to find out who this mysterious and talented boy in black was.

His name was Xavier Xonora, and it turned out that he was Zoroastro's nephew. Now, not only was he blessed with dashing good looks, great driving skills, an incredible racing pedigree and a top-of-the-line Lockheed-Martin car, Xavier Xonora also had one other thing going for him.

He was a *prince*.

A solid-gold bona-fide prince. His parents were the king and queen of the Principality of Monesi, a small sovereign European state not far from Monaco.

Whenever he walked by, the Mech girls at the Race School tittered and whispered. Every society mother in Hobart begged him to attend their dinner parties, hoping the young prince might take a liking to their dreamy-eyed daughters.

Jason and the Bug would bump into him occasionally in the pits. One time Jason smiled and said, 'Hey, Xavier.'

The Prince froze in mid-stride. Turned.

'If you insist on speaking to me, you will address me as *Prince* Xavier or Your Royal Highness,' he said, before moving on, nose held high.

'O-*kay*,' Jason said after him. 'Like that's gonna happen.'

Life at Race School was just non-stop.

Classes, races, homework and sleep.

For Jason, grappling with the sheer pace of Race School life was difficult.

While he loved the chance to race nearly every other day, no sooner were you finished with one race than you were back in the classroom analysing it. And then it was straight into the simulator, the race lab, or the pits to prac-tise, practise, practise.

Worse still, for Jason and the Bug a special arrangement had to be made for them to do regular schoolwork in between their racing classes.

It amounted to more information than Jason had ever

absorbed in his whole life and at times it was a struggle. While he was certainly smart, he had never been comfortable with the timetabled nature of school life. It was all he could do to keep up.

Scattered in among his racing classes were regular sessions in the School's giant centrifuge—a huge mechanical arm (with a race-car cockpit attached to its outer extremity) that swung in fast sweeping circles. Like the old Dynamic Flight Simulator at NASA, this centrifuge was designed to test each racer's G-force tolerances.

Jason invariably blacked out around 8-Gs, which was the average. Some other racers and navigators could get up to 8.5 or 8.7 before losing consciousness. It was perhaps surprising then when it was discovered that the student who could withstand the most G-forces was . . .

. . . the Bug.

The little guy could withstand an astonishing 9.3-Gs on the centrifuge—and still perform certain physical and mental tasks. And while many of the other students gagged or vomited when they were on the centrifuge, the Bug spent the whole time squealing with delight, like a kid on a roller-coaster.

Jason and the Bug were living in their own dorm room in the east wing of the Race School.

It was a high-tech white-walled three-level apartment—with recessed bunk beds, auto-fold-down sofas, and even a sliding pole to allow quick access between the multiple levels. In effect it was a kid-sized apartment, and as such the best cubbyhouse in the world. It even had spectacular views over Storm Bay.

Jason loved it, loved the independence of it.

But the Bug was different.

For all his astounding mathematical abilities (and his incredible results on the centrifuge), he was still essentially just a quiet little 12-year-old from a dusty desert town who missed his mum and his dad.

So late at night Jason would sit with him as they wrote long emails home, and when they got a reply several minutes later, the Bug would leap up with delight.

Then they'd sleep and suddenly the alarm clock would be ringing and it would be time for the next race.

And what a variety of races they were.

Gate races, enduros, sprints and last-man drop-offs, on an equally varied array of courses.

After 15 races, however, the points ladder didn't look good for Jason and the *Argonaut* team. It looked like this:

INTERNATIONAL RACE SCHOOL CHAMPIONSHIP LADDER AFTER 15 RACES			
DRIVER	**NO.**	**CAR**	**POINTS**
1. XONORA, X	1	*Speed Razor*	118
2. BECKER, B	09	*Devil's Chariot*	105
3. KRISHNA, V	31	*Calcutta-IV*	102
4. WONG, H	888	*Little Tokyo*	100
5. WASHINGTON, I	42	*Black Bullet*	99

Prince Xavier had won an astonishing five of the fifteen races, garnering 10 points for each win. He'd also had strong finishes in the other races, giving him a whopping 118 points out of a possible 150.

Of the twenty-five racers in total, languishing down near the bottom of the ladder was:

20. CHASER, J	55	*Argonaut*	79

After their zero-point efforts for not finishing Races 1 and 3, Jason and the Bug had started the season at the bottom of the competition ladder.

They'd had a couple of podium finishes since—mainly in gate races and the superlong enduros (long-distance races that lasted up to eight hours)—and the points they got for those lifted them slightly up the ladder.

But then around Race 9 they were suddenly beset by technical problems again.

After the 'depleted magneto drives incident' of Race 1, Sally McDuff had started electro-checking their drives before each race. In Races 9 and 12, she found that they had *again* received depleted mags from the Parts and Equipment Department.

But other technical problems also surfaced.

More thinned coolant in Race 13. A mystery computer virus that occasionally caused the Tarantula to malfunction. It was as if in every race they were fighting against an army of invisible gremlins constantly getting into their systems. If they finished at all, it was only after a huge effort.

So one day, Sally went off to the Parts and Equipment Department to investigate the faulty parts, only to return an hour later, fuming.

'Stupid greasy punk. The desk guy just waved me away,' she growled. 'Said, "Sorry, honey, but it wasn't us. You mustn't have taken good enough care of the ones you were given." Honey? *Honey!* So I told him we got six dodgy mags in one race and he just shrugged and stared at me. It was like talking to an Easter Island statue.'

Their mentor, Scott Syracuse, offered little sympathy.

It didn't help that their stablemates under Syracuse—Wong and Washington—were in the top five on the ladder and performing well in the same races, and experiencing no technical problems at all.

It made Jason appear simply unlucky, or worse, just not good enough.

The beautiful Ariel Piper was having similar problems—with magneto drives and faulty parts. After her near-catastrophic experience in Race 1 caused by a virus in her pit computer, she had installed a new firewall which seemed to have stemmed that problem. She was currently in 12th place—solid but unspectacular for the first girl to attend the Race School.

In any case, a key feature of the School's racing season was fast approaching and it was particularly troubling Jason.

The mid-season Sponsors' Event—a feature race held in front of the School's sponsors, benefactors and famous ex-students—would be held after Race 25, and it was only open to those students who had *won* a race during the season.

The Sponsors' Event was a huge opportunity to perform in front of some of the major players in the pro racing world. The thing was: Jason hadn't yet won a race, and with 15 races already down, he was fast running out of races to win.

Either way, it was time to address his team's problems. It was time to go to the source of all the depleted drives, thinned coolants and faulty parts.

The Race School's Parts and Equipment Department.

The International Race School's Parts and Equipment Department was housed inside a gigantic warehouse behind Pit Lane near the banks of the Derwent River.

It was a colossal structure, so big in fact that the School had built a glorious silver grandstand on top of it, giving a superb view of the main finishing straight.

On a rare spare afternoon, Jason, the Bug and Sally McDuff came to the student entrance, opened it—just as a stocky bull-necked youth with a bristly shaved head emerged from the Department.

Sally watched him go with interest.

'Do you know who that was?' she said.

Jason squinted after the bull-necked youth. 'No. Who?'

'His name is Oliver Koch. He is Xavier Xonora's Mech Chief.'

'Is that so?'

They entered the Parts Department, came to the service desk that separated visitors from the cavernous interior of the warehouse. The gritty odours of grease, rubber and coolant pervaded the air.

They were met by a weasel-faced young man named Wernold Smythe. Smythe lazily wiped his grease-covered hands on a rag. He was about 26, laid-back, and creepy.

'Can I help you?' he asked, wedging the rag into one of the low-slung hip pockets on his overalls.

'Yes. I'm Jason Chaser. Team *Argonaut*. We've been

having some problems with equipment coming out of the Department. Mags which aren't fully powered up, thinned coolant.'

'You didn't get faulty mags from here,' Smythe said quickly. 'Doesn't happen.'

'But we did. Our mags were only 10 per cent charged.'

Smythe leaned forward. 'No, *you didn't*. Every mag that goes out of here is electro-checked on the way out.' Smythe jerked his chin at Sally McDuff. 'Maybe your Mech Chief screwed up: left 'em too close to a power-drain source, like a portable pit machine generator or a microwave transmitter.'

Sally growled. 'I'd *never* leave a magneto drive next to a microwave transmi—'

'It's happened before,' Smythe shrugged. 'As for coolant. We hand it out in the original manufacturer's bottles, with the seals intact. I got some complaints from a couple of other racers—kid from India and that Piper chick. Y'all probably just got a bad batch. In any case, I'll note your complaint.'

Just then, the Bug tugged on Jason's sleeve, whispered something in his ear.

Jason nodded—then he glanced at the greasy rag protruding from Smythe's hip pocket.

He said to Smythe: 'Would you mind if before our next race my Mech Chief observes you electro-checking our mags before she takes them away from here?'

Smythe's face turned to ice. 'I don't think I like your tone. Are you suggesting something?'

'Like what?'

'Are you suggesting that I'd deliberately allow depleted mags to be given out to certain racers?'

'Let's just say I'm tired of being "unlucky". I just want to ensure that I don't suffer another bout of unluckiness tomorrow.'

Smythe said coldly: 'I answer to my boss, Department Chief Ralph A. Abbott. He answers to Jean-Pierre LeClerq. How about this: you get me a note from Abbott or LeClerq and I'll let your Mech Chief observe tomorrow's electro-check. Until I see that note, why don't you just *get lost* and leave me to do my job.'

His snake-like stare became a fake smile. 'Now, unless there's anything else I can do for you, I have to go.'

Jason and the others left the Equipment Department.

As they walked, the Bug whispered in Jason's ear.

'Yeah, I saw it,' Jason said.

'Saw what?' Sally asked. 'What did the little guy say to you in there?'

'It's not what he said, it's what he saw. The Bug saw something in Smythe's pocket,' Jason said. 'When we came in, Smythe stuffed his rag into his pocket. But he didn't stuff it in far enough. The Bug saw a wad of hundred-dollar bills sticking out from under it. I can't imagine a grease-monkey like Werny Smythe goes to work with that kind of cash on his person.'

'Which means . . . ?' Sally said.

'Which means he got that money recently. Today. And who was in the Department just ahead of us?'

'Oliver Koch . . .' Sally said.

'That's right. Xavier Xonora's Mech Chief,' Jason said.

The Bug whispered something.

'No,' Jason replied. 'I don't think we can dob them in yet. Just seeing some money in his pocket isn't enough evidence to prove our case. But I think we're gonna have to keep an eye on Smythe and Prince Xavier's team.'

The next day, Jason found himself rocketing north along the eastern coastline of Tasmania in the *Argonaut*, powering through driving rain.

Ducking, weaving, blasting, charging.

He swooped left, banking into a high-speed turn that took him across the mid-section of Tasmania.

There was good news and bad news.

The good news: he was coming 3rd in this race, behind Horatio Wong and Isaiah Washington.

The bad news: there were only three cars in the race.

It was a three-man practice race between Jason and the other two students of Scott Syracuse: Wong and Washington.

It was the day before Race 16 and while most of the other teachers had given their students a rest-and-preparation day before the race, Syracuse had organised for his charges to have a private race of their own on Course 9, a track which circled the lower half of Tasmania.

Despite the atrocious weather, the *Argonaut* was absolutely flying.

It shoomed out over the Serpentine Dam, bending south toward Wreck Bay.

The only problem was, it was almost a quarter of a lap behind the other two racers—thanks to an unexpected malfunction of the Tarantula during its first pit stop. The big pit machine had simply shut down halfway through the stop, meaning that Jason and the Bug had just had to sit helplessly in their cockpit while Sally McDuff frantically rebooted the robot.

The damage was a full quarter lap.

And this was only a 10-lap race.

Being a longer, more open circuit, pit stops were assumed to be necessary every four laps. Or not.

So at the end of Lap 8, Jason had to make the call.

To pit or not to pit?

To not pit—while the other two cars did—would allow him to catch up and even overshoot them. It was a daring move, and something Wong and Washington certainly wouldn't expect.

It was also not altogether unprecedented: some of the greatest come-from-behind wins on the Pro Circuit had come from drivers who had audaciously skipped their last pit stop.

But the trade-off was lower-powered magneto drives. Could Jason complete the last two laps on ever-diminishing drives? If he drove perfectly—absolutely perfectly—maybe he could.

'Let's do it,' he said to the Bug when he turned onto the home straight and saw both Wong and Washington predictably enter the pits.

So Jason gunned it—

—and shot past the entry to Pit Lane.

Wong and Washington both snapped round at the sound of the *Argonaut* booming away up the straight.

Jason drove hard.

He had two laps to complete and every second he made while the other racers were stopped in the pits was a second he had up his sleeve.

Up the coast he went, then banking left, cutting across the island.

The others finished their pit stops, blasted back out onto the course—in hot pursuit.

Jason urged the *Argonaut* on.

The other two cars closed the gap. But this course wasn't as tight as some of the other tracks and hence wasn't as brutal on magneto drives. Wong and Washington weren't catching up all that quickly.

The Bug told him their magneto drives were down to 15%.

'We can make it,' Jason replied.

The *Argonaut* hit the western coast, shot down the shoreline. Zoomed round the southern tip of the island, then pointed north and once again saw the home straight.

Shoom! It whipped across the Start-Finish Line.

'One lap to go,' Jason said.

'*Come on, Jason . . .*' Sally McDuff's voice said in his earpiece.

Wong and Washington's cars blasted across the Start-Finish Line, gaining on Jason like a couple of hungry sharks.

The gap was ten seconds and closing.

Cutting left across the island.

Nine seconds.

The *Argonaut* was becoming very slippery.

Its mags were running at 10%, the Bug reported.

'*Jason, conserve your mags! Use your thrusters more!*' Sally said over the radio.

'We're okay!' Jason said. 'We've just gotta hold out for half a lap!'

Across the top of the dam. Nose into the rain.

8%

He took the left-hander onto the southern coast more gently, losing more time.

4%

Wong and Washington were close behind him now—
2%

The final stretch was a long 'sweeper' round the southern coastal cliffs of Tasmania and not too tough on mags.
Jason managed to stay out in front.

Then he hit the final left-hander and . . .

. . . slowed.

0.4% . . . 0.2% . . . 0.0%

'No!' he yelled.

He received no response when he pushed forward on his
collective.

Wong and Washington whooshed by the *Argonaut*,
rocketing away up the home straight, disappearing into the
distance, becoming specks.

Wong would cross the line first, winning by 0.3 of a
second.

Jason punched his steering wheel. 'Damn it!'

He engaged his emergency power reserves to guide the
Argonaut up the straight and limp over the Start-Finish
Line, pounded by the pouring rain.

Upon returning to the pits, wet and soaking, he found
Wong's team dancing in jubilation. Washington's team was
also happy to have finished so strongly.

And Scott Syracuse was just standing there, shaking his
head.

'Mr Chaser. Mr Chaser. A bold move. But also a *very* stupid one. In over two thousand official hover car races at this
school, only ten have ever been won by racers who skipped
their last pit stop. That's a success rate of 0.005%. It might
look audacious when you see Alessandro Romba do it on
television but statistically, skipping your last stop is a foolish
tactic. Please don't do it again whilst you are under my tutelage, lest someone think I actually encourage such folly.

'Mr Wong, good racing. Exceptional pit work on the part of your Mech Chief. Mr Washington, your cornering needs work, but you finished well. And Mr Chaser: you have a lot to do. Work on your tactics and get your Mech Chief to check your pit machine more closely before each race.'

Syracuse turned to leave. 'That will be all for today, people. I'll see you tomorrow for Race 16. As usual, be in the pits two hours before racetime. Good night.'

And he left.

The next few races passed without any major incidents—no faulty parts or depleted magneto drives.

Just good hard racing.

The *Argonaut* had some promising finishes. A third, then a fifth, which lifted it up the rankings to 15th.

Ariel Piper caused a minor sensation when she stole victory from Barnaby Becker on the final turn of Race 18. But after that, she was bogged down with technical problems again and in the next three races, she DNF'd twice and fell down the ladder to 14th.

Ariel didn't mind: her win in Race 18 had guaranteed her a start in the much-anticipated Sponsors' Event.

Jason, however, was still winless.

He had come close in Race 22—a gate race around the craters of the old mining town of Queenstown, coming second to Xavier Xonora. Again, it had been pouring with unseasonal rain that day—so heavily in fact that several of the gate-arches collapsed in mudslides and the race was nearly cancelled.

In the race, however, the Bug had excelled himself, coming up with a very clever race-plan that none of the other navigators—not even Xonora's—had even considered.

Jason executed the plan well, but Prince Xavier was an incredible racer—and absolutely awesome in the rain—and his navigator's race-plan, while more conventional than the Bug's, was just as effective with Xavier at the wheel, and the Black Prince held on to win the race by a bare point.

Jason kicked himself. Their plan had been superb. Sally's pit work had been great. It was *his* driving that had let them down. He had been the weakest link.

And now they only had three races to get a win.

Another strange thing happened that day.

As Jason stood on the winner's podium with the Bug and Sally, he noticed Barnaby Becker—who had come 9th—gazing up at him from the crowd, with his and Xavier's mentor, Zoroastro, beside him.

Jason noticed Zoroastro point up at the Bug and whisper something to Barnaby.

Barnaby nodded. Only Jason saw the gesture, from way up on the podium. What it meant, at first he didn't know.

That evening he found out.

As he and the Bug were returning to their dorm from dinner later that night, they found that the lights to their stairwell were not working.

The entire area was dark and silent. Foreboding.

They climbed the stairs, but had only got halfway up when four shadowy figures—two above them, two below—appeared from the shadows.

Trapping them on the stairs.

The two boys above them were Prince Xavier and Barnaby Becker. The two boys below: the stocky Oliver Koch and Barnaby's navigator, the sly Guido Moralez.

Moralez emerged from the darkness.

'Well, well, well, if it isn't the kindergarten class. Good race today, kiddies. Not good enough, but still a sterling effort.'

'Thanks . . .' Jason tried to go up the stairs, but Barnaby and Xavier blocked him.

Moralez climbed the stairs, eyeing the Bug. 'You little fellas like those gate races, don't you. Like the strategy of them. Like the idea of setting your own course.'

'What do you want with us?' Jason said.

'Chaser, Chaser,' Moralez said. 'That's your problem, you know, it's always about *you*. But this isn't about you. No. This is about *him*: your little navigator here. I just want to talk with him. Congratulate him on plotting such a great course today. Give him a little prize.'

Moralez cracked his knuckles, stood over the Bug. Then he formed a fist, held it in front of the Bug's bespectacled face. 'Here's your prize, you little four-eyed freak.'

Moralez made to punch the Bug in the face, but Jason rushed forward at the last moment and pushed the Bug out of the way—and in doing so, received the full force of the blow instead.

Jason hit the wall. Hard. Blood spilled from his nose.

'Hoo-ah! Ouch!' Moralez sneered. He moved again towards the Bug, who backed up against the wall, cowering, defenceless, utterly terrified—

'No!' Jason called, standing up on wobbling legs and again moving in front of the Bug. 'You don't *touch* him.'

The Bug hated to be touched, absolutely *hated* it. Hell, he only let two people in the whole world even hug him: Jason and his mother. He didn't even let his father cuddle him. A full-blown punch from Guido Moralez would probably send him into a catatonic state.

Jason had to do whatever he could to prevent this creep from touching the Bug . . . even if that meant acting as an alternative punching bag.

'You wanna pick on someone,' he said to Moralez, 'pick on me . . . *loser*.'

The bait worked.

'Loser? *Loser!*' Moralez sneered. 'You little punk . . .'

Whack! He punched Jason in the gut, the blow sudden and strong. Jason buckled over—winded—but remained standing.

He swallowed.

Raised his head.

Looked Moralez right in the eye. Baited him again.

'You . . . hit . . . *like a girl*,' he said grimly.

Two more lightning-quick blows from Moralez dropped Jason to his knees.

Moralez moved in.

'Enough!' Prince Xavier's voice echoed from the top of the darkened stairwell.

Moralez rubbed his knuckles as he stepped away from Jason. 'You forgot what I told you when we arrived here: you never know what kinds of accidents can happen in a place like this. See ya round, Chaser.'

Jason just stared up at the silhouette that was Xavier Xonora. 'Next time, Xonora,' he said, 'take us on where it counts. On the track.'

The shadow made no reply.

Then as quickly as they had appeared, the bigger boys left, melting away into the darkness, and Jason and the Bug were alone in the stairwell.

The Bug rushed to Jason's side, tears in his eyes, put his arms around his brother.

Jason sat up, touched his nose. 'Ow.'

The Bug whispered something.

Jason looked at him. 'That's okay, little brother. Anytime.'

The next morning, in the Race Briefing Room, there came a big surprise.

Accompanying Race Director Calder onto the stage was none other than the Principal of the Race School, Jean-Pierre LeClerq. He took the lectern.

'Racers,' he began. 'I have an announcement to make. Some excellent news has come through. I have just received word from the Professional Racers Association regarding Race School participants in the annual New York Challenger Race.'

A buzz filled the room.

The New York Challenger Race was part of the week-long New York Racing Festival, the high-point of the hover car racing year, held in October. The climax of the Festival was the New York Masters Series: four different kinds of race, held one race per day—a supersprint, a gate race, a multi-car pursuit race and, last of all, a long-distance quest race. A veritable feast of racing, the New York Masters title was the most prestigious hover car racing title in the world and the last of the four Grand Slams.

The New York Challenger Race, however, was traditionally held two days *before* the Masters series. It was an intricate lap race through a street circuit that traversed the avenues and parks of New York City.

Entry was by invitation only and the race normally featured up-and-coming racers from the satellite leagues.

Schools like the International Race School were often given a couple of invitations to disperse as they pleased. Participating in the New York Challenger Race was not just an honour—it was also an incredible opportunity for an unknown racer, since it was a chance to race in front of the pro-racing teams who would be assembled in New York for the Masters.

'I am pleased to announce,' LeClerq said, 'that the Racers Association has allocated the International Race School *four* places in this year's New York Challenger Race!

'In keeping with the School's long-standing tradition in matters such as this, the four invitations to the Challenger Race will be allocated to those racers occupying the top four positions on the Race School Championship Ladder at the end of the school competition in September.'

The buzzing in the room intensified as racers and their teams quickly conferred, calculating their chances of coming in the Top 4.

It was now late May. There was still a long way to go in the School Championships.

Jason, the Bug and Sally formed a huddle. Jason's face was a little cut and bruised.

Sally whispered: 'The Top 4? Geez, can we make it?'

'There's a lot of racing left in this season,' Jason said. 'Just about everyone can still make it. Either way, it certainly gives us something huge to race for.'

At that moment Principal LeClerq cleared his throat, getting everyone's attention again.

'I also have another announcement to make,' he said, 'this one concerning the annual Sponsors' Event to be held here at the Race School this coming weekend. Two things. First, the format of the Sponsors' Event.'

The format of the Sponsors' Event changed every year: some years it was a gate race, others an enduro, sometimes it was even a series of races.

'This year's Sponsors' Event,' LeClerq said, 'will take the form of a tournament: a day-long series of knockout one-on-one pursuit races.'

Once again, the room rippled with excitement. Such a format was similar to a professional tennis tournament: as you beat one opponent, you went through to the next round, until by the end of the day, only two racers were left to fight out the final. Every race was do-or-die, which made for very exciting racing.

But then LeClerq went on. 'My second announcement about the Sponsor's Event is more administrative. As I am sure you are all aware, the Event has long been scheduled to take place this coming weekend, in front of all of the School's sponsors and benefactors.

'Owing to the inclement weather of late and its effects on our courses across the island—mudslides, high seas along the coasts—it has been decided that Races 23 and 24, set for today and Tuesday, will be cancelled. Weather permitting, Race 25 will go ahead as planned on Thursday.'

The announcement made Jason gag. '*What!*' he whispered in disbelief.

But everyone else in the room, it seemed, had been dazzled by the New York Challenger announcement and appeared unfazed by this.

'No *way*,' Sally McDuff said. 'They just canned two races . . .'

'And we haven't qualified for the Sponsors' Event yet,' Jason said.

They looked at each other, not even needing to say it.

If they were going to race in the all-important Sponsors' Event at the weekend, they had to win Race 25 on Thursday.

Second wouldn't cut it anymore.

Now they had to *win*.

The next few days went by very quickly.

Luckily, the weather brightened, and while Races 23 and 24 were still cancelled, Race 25 was cleared to go ahead as scheduled on Thursday.

Scott Syracuse continued with lessons, even going so far as to schedule new classes on the days that had previously been set aside for Races 23 and 24. Most of the other teams had been given those days to rest or work on their cars at their leisure.

It was odd then that on the Tuesday—the original day for Race 24—*both* Horatio Wong and Isaiah Washington fell mysteriously ill, and so missed Syracuse's new classes. Tired as they were, Jason, the Bug and Sally still went.

That same day, the format for Race 25 was revealed.

Put simply, Race 25—the halfway race in the School season—was a doozy.

It was an enduro, an eight-hour marathon on the School's second-longest course, a multi-faceted track that snaked its way around the island of Tasmania, hugging the coastline, occasionally jutting inland. Since each lap would take an astonishing 24 minutes, the race was only 20 laps long. But this course came with two very special features.

The first feature was a worthy imitation of the signature feature of the Italian Run: *a short cut*.

The famous short cut in the Italian Run sliced through the heel of the 'boot' that is Italy. As such, the term for

successfully exploiting such a short cut is: 'cutting the heel'.

The Race School's short cut sliced across the main isthmus of the Port Arthur peninsula at the town of Dunalley, offering the game racer a 30-second jump on the rest of the pack—*if* he or she could figure out the correct route through a short underground maze.

And the second feature: ***demagnetising ripple strips*** on all the hairpin turns and S-bend sections of the course.

Colloquially known as 'demon lights', demagnetising ripple strips are a standard feature on the pro tour and particularly nasty. They flank the curves on a hover car course and look rather like wide runway lights that float in the air.

Put simply, they are a method of enforcing disciplined driving. If you stray off the aerial track and fly *even for a moment* over some demag lights, your magneto drives lose magnetic power at an exponential rate. Thus your car loses traction and control. Dealing with demag lights is simple: don't run over them.

Since Wong and Washington weren't around, Jason, the Bug and Sally took the opportunity to talk to Syracuse about tactics for Thursday's all-important race.

'What about the short cut?' Jason asked. 'Should we try to cut the heel?'

'No,' Syracuse said quickly. 'The short cut is fool's gold. It looks like a good option, but in truth it's not an option at all.'

'What if we're behind and it's the only chance we have?'

'I still wouldn't go near it,' Syracuse said. 'It's a trap for the unwise, for those who *like* short cuts. Indeed, it's designed to appeal to their greed. I would only use it if I knew the correct way through it beforehand.'

'But we *can't* know that,' Sally said. 'The peninsula mine

tunnels are strictly out of bounds. We're not allowed to check them out beforehand.'

Scott Syracuse cocked his head sideways. 'No, Ms McDuff. That's not entirely true. There *are* legitimate ways of mastering such mazes, if you have the patience . . .'

He left the sentence unfinished, looked directly at them. 'Unless you know the secret of the maze, I would suggest you not use the short cut in Thursday's race.'

With that they finished early, around 2:30 p.m.

Jason and the Bug returned to their dorm—weary, beat.

Truth be told, at that moment, Jason was feeling as low as he had ever felt at Race School. He felt overtired from too many classes, underappreciated by his teacher, out of his depth with his fellow racers, and out of races to win.

Which was probably why he was caught off-guard when he and the Bug arrived back at their apartment to find a pair of visitors waiting outside their dorm room, large shadows at the end of the hall.

At first Jason froze, fearing another confrontation with Xavier and Barnaby, but then he heard one of the shadows speak:

'*Where's* my little Doodlebug!' a booming woman's voice echoed down the corridor.

He smiled broadly.

There, standing outside his and the Bug's dorm room, were their parents.

The Chaser family went out for the afternoon.

They drove out to the ruins of the mighty 18th-century convict prison at the tip of the Port Arthur peninsula, where Martha Chaser unrolled a picnic rug and spread out an array of sandwiches and soft drinks.

And Jason and the Bug spent a wonderful afternoon sitting in the sunshine talking with their parents.

The Bug sat nestled alongside Martha Chaser, looking very content, while Jason told their parents about everything that had happened to them at the International Race School since he and the Bug had last emailed.

He told them about their continuing technical problems, about recent races, about the Black Prince and Barnaby's backroom thuggery (which Martha didn't like at all and wanted to inform the authorities about, but to Jason's relief Henry Chaser stopped her by saying, 'No, dear, this is a battle for the boys to fight'), and about Scott Syracuse's relentless class schedule that didn't seem to be replicated by any of the other teachers at the School.

He also told them about Race 25, the race that he and the Bug had to win if they were to get a start in Saturday's all-important tournament.

'First of all, son,' Henry Chaser said gently, 'let me just say this about your teacher, Mr Syracuse. Never *ever* worry about having the "hard" teacher. Trust me, the hard teachers are always the best teachers.'

'Why?'

'Because the hard teachers *want you to learn*. This Syracuse guy isn't here to be your best friend, Jason. He isn't here to have a fun old time. He's here to *teach*. And it sounds to me like he's teaching as hard as he damn well can. What about you: are you *learning* as hard as you can?'

Jason frowned at that. 'But he never says "well done" or "good job".'

'Ah-ha. So that's it,' Henry Chaser said. 'You want to get some positive feedback out of him. Want to know how to get that?'

'Yes.'

Henry Chaser smiled enigmatically. 'Jason. When you start learning as hard as you can, I guarantee he'll start treating you differently.'

Jason sighed, bowed his head.

His father clapped him on the shoulder. 'It's okay, son. You're only 14. You've got to learn these things sometime. Now. To more important matters. Tell me again about this race on Thursday that you have to win at any cost.'

Unfortunately the afternoon had to end, and as dusk descended, the Chasers packed up their stuff and started the drive back to the Race School.

On the way back, with the Bug fast asleep beside him, Jason gazed idly out the window of their car, watching the landscape whistle by.

As such, he wasn't really paying attention when Henry pulled over abruptly—to help a biker on the side of the road.

Jason watched as his father, illuminated by the headlights of their car, walked over to the young man crouched beside his bike.

Jason couldn't see the biker's face, but he noticed that the man's hover motorcycle—a nice Kawasaki XT-700 trail rider—was completely covered in a strange grey powder.

'Need a hand, partner?' Henry Chaser said into the darkness. 'Or a ride?'

The biker waved him off. His riding leathers were also, Jason noticed, totally covered in the grey powder.

'Nah. Just fixed it,' the biker called. 'Got some dust in the mag switches.'

Sure enough, he had fixed the problem. The young man's bike hummed to life and he straddled the hovercycle, reaching for his helmet.

And in that instant, Jason saw the young man's face.

Then the hover bike raced off into the night, and Henry Chaser returned to the car, shrugging.

Jason, however, sat frozen in his seat.

He had recognised the biker.

It was Wernold Smythe, the clerk from the Race School's Parts and Equipment Department.

'Sounds like it'll be a tough race,' Henry Chaser said as he dropped Jason and the Bug off at the Race School. Henry and Martha were going to stay at a caravan park in Hobart for a few days and watch Thursday's big race.

Henry said, 'Eight hours means a lot of pit stops—your Mech Chief is in for a long day. And stay away from those demon lights. Run over some of those and your race is over. And watch out for other drivers ramming you onto them. Oh, and Jason . . .'

'Yes, Dad?'

'Always remember the Bradbury Principle.'

'Yes, Dad,' Jason sighed. His father *always* said that. It was Henry Chaser's contribution to sport: the Bradbury Principle. Jason ignored it and got serious: 'What do you think about cutting the heel?'

'Wouldn't touch it,' Henry said. 'The pros rarely cut the heel in the Italian Run and for good reason. It's a Venus flytrap: looks pretty and alluring from the outside, but it'll just eat you up. It'll put you either further behind or out of the running completely.'

'That's just what Mr Syracuse said,' Jason said.

'Scott Syracuse said the same thing?' Henry said. 'Oh! Of course—' he cut himself off, chuckled.

'What?' Jason asked.

Henry Chaser smiled. 'Scott Syracuse once tried to cut the heel in the Italian Run. It was the last time he raced the Italian Run; a few races later, he had that huge crash in New York that ended his career.

'That time in Italy, Syracuse was way back in the pack because of a collision he'd had with another car, so he decided to try and cut the heel. Now, if you cut the heel in Italy, you can gain up to *four whole minutes* on the rest of the field. It woulda put him back in contention.'

'And what happened?' Jason asked.

'Two *hours* later, the race was over and he still hadn't come out,' Henry said. 'He didn't emerge until *four hours* after the race, and even then, he came out the way he went in. Didn't even find the way through. By the time he reached the Finish Line in Venice, they were dismantling the grand-stands! No wonder he advises against cutting the heel.'

'Yeah,' Jason said, frowning. 'No wonder.'

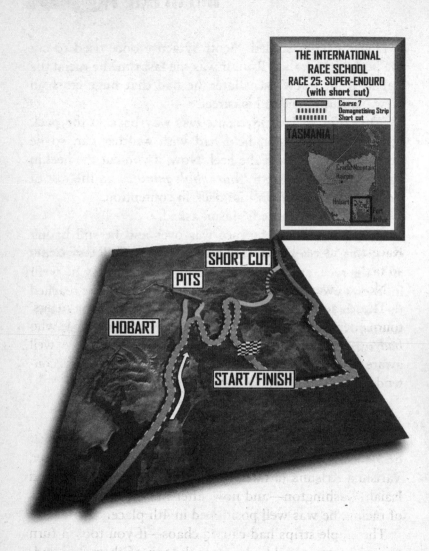

THE INTERNATIONAL
RACE SCHOOL
RACE 25: SUPER-ENDURO
(with short cut)

Course 7
Demagnetising Strip
Short cut

TASMANIA

Cradle Mountain
Region

Hobart

Port
Arthur

SHORT CUT

PITS

HOBART

START/FINISH

Race 25 was easily the most hard-fought race of the season so far.

No-one was giving an inch.

Those racers who hadn't yet qualified for the Sponsors' tournament were going all-out for the win. While those who *had* qualified were racing just as fiercely—they were well aware that if a pre-qualified racer won, it meant one less contender to deal with on Saturday.

The intensity of the racing was simply furious.

And at Lap 11, Jason was still in it.

After narrowly avoiding a wild three-car crash on Lap 2, he had stayed in touch with the early leaders—Xavier, Varishna Krishna (a talented young racer from India) and Isaiah Washington—and now, after more than four hours of racing, he was well positioned in 4th place.

The ripple strips had caused chaos—if you took a turn too wide, you would edge over the top of them and suddenly your magneto drive levels would drain before your eyes.

The big crash on Lap 2 had been the direct result of the ripple strips, and it had taken out some of the contenders in this race.

It was Barnaby Becker's fault.

He had slid out over the ripple strips flanking the tight hairpin near the pits. He had stayed over the demag strips for almost five seconds, enough to deprive *all six* of his magneto drives of nearly all of their power. Out of control, he had slid back across the track, collecting two other racers—among them Ariel Piper—on the way through, ending all of their races.

Ariel wasn't pleased.

For his part, Jason felt he was handling the strips pretty well—not perfectly, but well. On any given lap, he might edge over a couple of them and lose a little bit of power. But judging by the similarity of their pit-stop schedules, it didn't seem as if any of the other contenders were doing any better.

Significantly, no racer had attempted to use the short cut.

The leaders completed Lap 11, and flocked into the pits—Jason among them.

He swung into his bay and the Tarantula descended on the *Argonaut* from above, its arms bristling with magneto drives and coolant hoses.

Jason gulped down some energy drink, breathed hard. Their pit stops had been good in this race. Their mag drives and computer systems seemed okay—

And suddenly the Tarantula froze in mid-action.

'No!' Jason yelled.

Sally McDuff dived for the Tarantula's console, started tapping keys. 'The system's crashed again! Damn!' she yelled. 'I have to reboot!'

She typed fast on the computer.

Jason snapped round—

—to see Krishna, then Washington and then Xavier zoom out of the pits, one after the other, rejoining the race.

'Sally! Come on!'

'Almost there . . . !' she called back. 'Almost there!'

'Damn it!'

The seconds ticked by—every one of them sinking the nails deeper into Jason's coffin.

10 seconds . . .

15 . . .

20 . . .

'Got it!' Sally called.

The Tarantula completed its work, then swooped up into the ceiling and Sally yelled 'Go! Go! Go!' and Jason floored it and the *Argonaut* shoomed back out onto the course—

—to be met by a surprising sight.

Just outside Pit Lane, Jason saw Car No.1—Prince Xavier's black Lockheed, the *Speed Razor*—splayed sideways in the centre of the track, stopped. Xavier was waving his fists at an orange hover car crashed into the treeline nearby.

Jason deduced what had happened immediately.

As Xavier had been exiting the pits, the hapless driver of the orange car—a perennial tailender named Brent Hurst—had been zooming by, completely unaware of Xavier emerging from Pit Lane. A near miss had ensued, with the *Speed Razor* fishtailing to a halt, while Hurst had missed the next turn, hit the ripple strips and gone careering off into the treeline.

By the time Jason had emerged from the pits shortly

after, Xavier was powering up and so the two of them rejoined the race together, 20 seconds behind the leaders, with the *Speed Razor* just in front of the *Argonaut*.

Over the next three laps, try as he might, Jason couldn't narrow the gap on the leaders.

There was another pit stop, but since everyone was pitting more or less as well as each other, the lead time between the two leaders—Krishna and Washington—and the rest of the pack, led by Xavier and Jason, remained at about 20 seconds.

It was with the completion of Lap 14 that Jason realised. *He was running out of laps.*

There were only six laps to go, with most racers planning for two more stops, and he wasn't gaining at all.

This was terrible. With an enormous 20-second gap to reel in, he just couldn't win—and he *had* to win this race! Unless . . .

'Sally! Bug!' he yelled into his radiomike. 'Quick poll! Next lap, do we try the short cut?'

'*Jason, I don't know . . .*' Sally said. '*If you screw it up in there, we'll lose for sure.*'

'We're already going to lose!' Jason said. 'Unless we get some galactic good luck. Bug?'

The Bug whispered his reply.

'That bad, huh?' Jason said. 'Are there any stats you *don't* know, little brother?'

The Bug's analysis didn't give him confidence. Only one hover car racer had ever actually won a pro race by successfully utilising a short cut maze—out of 165 short-cut-equipped races. Not good odds.

'We're screwed,' Jason said aloud.

The laps ticked over: 15, 16 . . .

The lead gap remained 20 seconds.

Hell, Jason thought, he couldn't even get past the Black Prince.

Lap 16 saw more pit stops.

Krishna and Washington were leaving the pits just as Xavier and Jason swept into them.

As the Tarantula went to work, Jason looked over at Xavier's busy pit bay.

In the midst of all the activity around the *Speed Razor*, Jason saw Xavier chatting animatedly with his Mech Chief, Oliver Koch. And beyond it all, Jason saw someone else standing at the back of their bay, a young man who wasn't wearing the charcoal-black uniform of the *Speed Razor*'s team—

Jason froze.

The young man standing in the very back of Xavier's pit bay was Wernold Smythe.

'Hey, Sally,' Jason said. 'How long has Werny Smythe been in Xavier's pit bay?'

'He arrived a few laps ago. Started talking to Koch about something.'

Jason looked back at *Speed Razor*'s pit bay: saw Xavier and Koch talking. Koch was making sharp hand gestures, as if he were giving Xavier detailed directions.

Then Jason checked out Wernold Smythe again. He remembered seeing Smythe two nights ago, by the side of the road, covered in grey powder, with his hover bike similarly covered.

And suddenly it hit Jason.

'Bug! The short cut at Dunalley. It's an abandoned mine, right?'

The Bug said that it was.

'What kind of mine?'

The Bug said that it had been a coalmine.

'A coalmine . . .' Jason said. 'Limestone powder . . .'

'Jason? What are you thinking?' Sally asked.

Jason said, 'Coalmines use limestone powder to guard against flammable gases oozing out from the walls. It's a grey powder that miners spray all over the walls of a mine. Covers everything. I read about it in a thriller novel once.'

'So?'

'So, I happened to see Werny on Tuesday night, out on the road to Port Arthur, completely covered in grey powder . . .'

And with those words the picture became clear in Jason's mind.

'That's what Koch and Xavier were paying Werny for!' he exclaimed. 'They weren't paying Werny to give us faulty parts. Koch and Xavier were paying Werny to go out and map the short cut for them, to find a way through it! Holy cow, guys, we just got galactically lucky.'

Voom!

The *Speed Razor* blasted out of the pits—just as the Tarantula lifted up and away from the *Argonaut*.

His face set, Jason jammed his thrusters forward and took off after Xavier as though his life depended on it.

Prince Xavier's *Speed Razor* blasted out of the pits pursued by the *Argonaut*.

The pits were situated right on the mouth of the Derwent River, in the middle of the course's most fiendish section of hairpin turns, each of which was skirted by demagnetising ripple strips.

Xavier ripped around the first turn, a sharp left-hander, banking steeply, closely followed by Jason in the *Argonaut*.

The next turn was a tight right-hander—and the point at which racers could take the option of cutting the heel of the Port Arthur peninsula at the Dunalley isthmus.

Right on cue, Prince Xavier took the alternative route and charged *left*, leaving the course proper, going for the short cut.

The crowds in the mobile hoverstands gasped.

That the leaders had already taken the longer and safer route made the move daring in itself. But that it was Prince Xavier Xonora—dashing and handsome and the championship leader—who had decided to go for it thrilled them even more.

But then something even more astonishing happened.

The *Argonaut* took off after the *Speed Razor*, zooming toward the short cut behind it.

The two cars rushed toward the Dunalley isthmus. As he flew, Jason could see the wide blue ocean beyond the narrow strip of land.

But in the foreground, built into the front edge of the isthmus like a cannon emplacement—as if guarding the way—yawned the squat concrete entry tunnel to the short-cut mine.

The *Speed Razor* didn't hesitate. It disappeared into the mine at 300 km/h.

Jason swallowed. He had to stay close to Xavier—since Xavier knew the way through.

The black entry tunnel to the mine rushed toward him like the open mouth of a hungry giant. Jason drew in a sharp breath.

'Hang on, Bug. Here we go!'

And with that the *Argonaut* shot underground, disappearing into the blackness of the mine.

Rocketing through darkness.

The close square walls of the abandoned mine whipped past Jason at astonishing speed, the whole underground world illuminated only by the sabre-like beams of his headlights. Each tunnel was about the width and height of an old railway tunnel.

Up ahead, he saw the glowing red tail-lights of the *Speed Razor* descending into the bowels of the Earth, following the steep entry tunnel straight down. Then without warning, the red lights cut left, having arrived at the bottom of the entry tunnel.

Jason shot off after them. He had to keep those tail-lights in view—

The Bug said something.

'I know! I know!' Jason yelled back. 'I'm trying to stay with him!'

The *Speed Razor* swept momentarily out of sight, and Jason followed it, only to find himself staring at a fork of two tunnels . . . and no tail-lights in sight.

A bolt of ice shot up Jason's spine.

No . . .

Then he saw the tail-lights way up the right-hand fork and relief swept through him and he took off after them.

The mine flattened out and the *Speed Razor* swept through it at rocket speed, taking turns easily, a sharp left here, a sweeping right there, with the *Argonaut* close behind it.

And then Jason noticed that the tunnels had started to slant upward. They were approaching the surface. Trailing close behind the *Speed Razor*, he rounded a final bend before—

—blinding sunlight assaulted his eyes.

They were out!

They'd got through the short-cut maze.

The eastern coastline of Tasmania stretched gloriously away to the left, with Prince Xavier's *Speed Razor* rocketing away along it.

The *Argonaut* blasted out of a trapezoidal pipe halfway up the coastal cliffs and banked sharply to avoid the specially-placed set of demagnetising strips at the junction of the short cut and the regular course, just as—*shoom! shoom!*—two cars boomed past him on either side.

Varishna Krishna and Isaiah Washington!

The former race leaders!

And suddenly Jason's eyes widened.

Thanks to the Black Prince, the *Argonaut* was back in the race.

The next lap-and-a-half saw some of the fiercest racing of Jason's life.

Through the S-bends up at the top-right corner of Tasmania, winding between Cape Barren Island and Flinders Island—trying to avoid the demag strips while also trying to overtake his foes.

And then Varishna Krishna tried to slip past Xavier at

the hairpin next to Pit Lane, but Xavier cruelly blocked him, forcing the Indian out over the ripple strips.

Krishna reeled, skidding wide, and as he did so, Washington managed to slip past him into 2nd place. Jason tried to snatch the opportunity as well, but Krishna regained control of his car at exactly the wrong time, and not only did he shut Jason out, he also made him slow down a fraction.

Jason swore.

And so, by Lap 18, with only two laps to go, he was still in 4th, in what was now essentially a four-horse race, behind three of the best drivers in the School: Xavier, Washington and Krishna.

With the race almost eight hours old now, everyone was running on depleted mags, depleted nerves and depleted energy levels. The sheer intensity of their battle had meant that all of the top four racers had at some point touched the ripple strips in the last few laps, thus further losing traction.

Which meant, with two laps to go and their magneto drives starting to feel slippery, they'd each need to make one last pit stop.

Halfway round Lap 18, Sally McDuff's voice came through Jason's earpiece.

'Jason! The other crews are preparing for their final pit stop. You wanna come in with them now or wait till the next lap?'

Jason pursed his lips, assessed the situation.

His magneto drive levels were at 39% of full strength. Two laps on this course would consume about 30%: 15% per lap. The remaining 9% allowed him maybe three bumps on the ripple strips.

You have to win. Second place isn't an option today.
The Bug seemed to read his mind, and said so.
'Thirty-nine per cent. We can make it . . .' Jason said.
The Bug was doubtful.
Sally, listening in on the radio, said: *'Jason, no. Not again. Don't even think it.'*
'They won't be expecting it,' Jason said.
'Jason, it didn't work in that training race with Wong and Washington. And you remember Syracuse's stats. Skipping the last pit stop has a success rate of 0.005 per cent.'
At that moment, the Bug reminded Jason of another piece of Scott Syracuse's wisdom: *To err is human, to make the same mistake twice is stupid.*
Jason's eyes narrowed.
'We're gonna do it.'
And so, as the three lead cars decelerated into the pits for their final pit stops, to the absolute amazement of the crowds, the *Argonaut* swept past the pit entry and zoomed off down the track, trying to put as much distance between it and its rivals before they came out of the pits, hungry to chase him down.

Jason hit the short-cut tunnel on the fly and, guided by the Bug's photographic memory of their previous trip through the labyrinth, took the same route they'd taken before.
They emerged from the other side, banking a little too wildly, and Jason touched the demag strips on the outside of the track and his magneto drive levels dropped 3%.
'The others are out of the pits now, Jason!' Sally's voice warned in his ear. *'They're hunting you down!'*
The *Argonaut* swept round the course.

Jason concentrated intensely.

His magneto counter ticked steadily downwards.

The other three cars gained on him, rocketing round the course on fresh mags. But Washington and Krishna didn't have the nerve to follow Xavier through the short-cut tunnel and they fell behind, taking the long way round, and in doing so, effectively put themselves out of the running.

The Black Prince, however, took the tunnel fearlessly, and as such, he kept gaining on the *Argonaut*.

Then, on the other side of the course, Jason hit the demag strips bounding the Cradle Mountain hairpin, just a glancing blow, but enough to send his mag meter whizzing down another 3%.

The *Speed Razor* kept coming. On the long straights, Jason could see it looming in the distance in his mirrors.

Mag levels: 18%.

The *Argonaut* came to the sharp hairpins near the pits. Despite the fact that he took them extra carefully, to Jason's horror, he clipped the ripple strip on the super-sharp right-hand hairpin just before the Start-Finish Line and suddenly his mag levels were at a bare 15%.

Jason knew what that meant.

With only one lap to go, on ever-declining mags, and with a ruthless competitor looming up behind him on a fresh set of magneto drives, he had to do a perfect lap.

The *Argonaut* cut left, banking toward the short-cut isthmus, commencing the final lap.

The crowds in the stands were on the edge of their seats. Among them, Henry Chaser sat with his hand held to his mouth. Martha Chaser seemed quite content beside him, head bowed, doing some knitting.

The *Argonaut* raced into the short-cut tunnel for the last time.

The *Speed Razor* also banked left, heading for the isthmus, starting the final lap.

The *Argonaut* zoomed up the coast.

The *Speed Razor* entered the short-cut mine.

The *Argonaut* zig-zagged between the upper islands.

The *Speed Razor* roared up the coast.

At Cradle Mountain, Jason slowed dramatically to take the turn that had cost him some magnetism on the previous lap. The *Argonaut* was sliding all over the place now, handling like someone trying to walk on an ice skating rink, going at a torturously slow 450 km/h.

The *Speed Razor* was doing 600 km/h and accelerating.

Halfway round and Jason's mag levels were down to 7.5%. Just enough to get home—if he didn't touch any ripple strips.

Down the wild western coast of Tasmania—with the *Speed Razor* now looming large in his mirrors.

Xavier's car moved surely and securely, always gaining. The *Argonaut* slipped and slid, limping home.

Everyone could see where this was heading.

At their current speeds, the *Speed Razor* was going to catch the *Argonaut* right at the death.

Mag levels: 3%

Jason floored it down the last long sweeper, bracing himself for the series of dreadfully tight hairpins guarding the Finish Line—hairpins that he was going to have to negotiate perfectly. One touch on the ripple strips now would end his race.

Mag levels: 2%

'Come on . . .' he willed himself. 'Come *on* . . .'

Prince Xavier's black Lockheed now filled his mirrors.

The *Argonaut* took the left-hander into Storm Bay at a pathetic 325 km/h. Glowing red demag lights whizzed by it on either side.

The *Speed Razor* took the same turn a split-second later, doing 450.

The *Argonaut* shot past the pits, slowed to a crawl to take the first right-hand hairpin.

The *Speed Razor* launched itself into the same turn.

The two cars were almost level.

Mag levels: 1%

Jason swung left, into the second-last turn of the race—a left-hand hairpin—just as the *Speed Razor* came alongside his tail.

Then it was into the last corner of the race, a tight right-hand hairpin, and here Xavier made his move, tried to overtake Jason *on the outside!*

The two cars roared round the final turn *side-by-side*.

Henry Chaser leapt to his feet.

Sally McDuff prayed before her monitor.

The crowds in the stands rose as one.

And the two hover cars—the blue-white-and-silver Car 55 and the all-black Car 1—whipped out of the last turn and rocketed down the home straight and in a blur of speed, crossed the Line together.

LAP: 20 [OF 20]

To the naked eye, it appeared as if the two cars crossed the Finish Line together, but the official laser digital photo of the finish of Race 25 would later show that after eight hours of racing, after twenty hard-fought laps, Car No.1, the *Speed Razor*, driven by Xonora X, travelling at 365 kilometres an hour and accelerating, had crossed the line 4.2 cm behind Car No.55, the *Argonaut*, piloted by Chaser J, and travelling at 320 kilometres an hour.

After a perfect lap from its daring young driver, by the paintwork on its nosewing, the *Argonaut* had qualified for the Sponsors' tournament.

PART IV

THE TOURNAMENT

CHOOKA'S CHARCOAL CHICKEN RESTAURANT
HOBART, TASMANIA

The Bug squealed with delight as he popped the top off his well-shaken can of Coke and sprayed it into the air like a triumphant pro racer on the winner's podium uncorking a bottle of Moët champagne.

Beside him, Jason and Henry Chaser cheered; threw their fists into the air.

It was Thursday night and the Chaser family was celebrating Team *Argonaut*'s win in Race 25, and its subsequent qualification for the Sponsors' Tournament on the coming Saturday.

Family tradition dictated that it was 'winner's choice'— the family member (or members) being celebrated got to choose the restaurant and the Bug had quickly chosen his favourite restaurant in all the world: the chicken burger chain, Chooka's Charcoal Chicken.

Which was why the entire family—plus Sally McDuff, who was by now an honorary Chaser anyway—now sat around a plain formica table surrounded by the remains of chicken burger wrappers, onion rings, French fries, and Coke cans. Everyone was laughing and smiling and recounting their favourite moments of the nail-biting race.

Well, not quite.

At one stage in the dinner, Jason noticed that his mother

wasn't joining in the festivities but was, rather, staring off into space, seemingly lost in thought.

'Are you all right, Mum?' he asked.

She turned abruptly, as if roused from a dream, quickly regathered her smile. 'I'm fine, dear. Just thrilled for you boys.'

The world had been spinning for Jason since his down-to-the-wire, skip-the-last-pit-stop win over Prince Xavier earlier that day. His memories of the afternoon were a blur of images:

He remembered returning to the pits after the race, being lifted out of the *Argonaut* by a jubilant Sally, high-fiving the Bug, standing on the podium in his battered boots and denim overalls, and watching on the big screen as the 10 points Team *Argonaut* received for winning elevated the *Argonaut* to 12th on the Championship Ladder.

He also recalled Scott Syracuse coming over to him after the victor's presentation, and looking at him closely.

'You skipped your last pit stop again, Mr Chaser.'

'Yes, sir. I did.'

'You weren't worried about making the same mistake twice?'

'No, sir. I knew I could make it this time.'

'So you decided not to take my counsel?'

'No, sir. I just decided to follow something else you told me about mistakes, way back when we were doing pit practice and I kept creeping out of my pit bay.'

Syracuse frowned. 'What was my advice then?'

'You said I shouldn't resist my mistakes. That I should learn from them. So I decided to learn from my last mistake—the other time I skipped my last pit stop, I shouldn't have. This time, it was okay.'

'By exactly 4.2 centimetres . . .' Syracuse observed.

Jason smiled. 'My dad once told me you can win by an inch or a mile, sir. Either way, it's still a win.'

And with that, for the first time Jason could remember, Scott Syracuse smiled.

He nodded graciously. 'Well done today, Mr Chaser. I can't possibly imagine what awaits us when you race in Saturday's tournament.'

He began to walk away.

'Mr Syracuse!' Jason called after him. 'My family's in town and we're going out to celebrate tonight.' He paused. 'Wanna come?'

Syracuse hesitated for a moment, as if this were the most unexpected question in the world for him.

'Sure,' he said at last. 'That'd be . . . very nice. What time?'

Jason told him.

Syracuse said, 'Well, I have some work to do, some lessons to prepare, so I might be a little late. But I'll be there.'

And sure enough, Syracuse arrived at the restaurant exactly 45 minutes late, just as a classic Chooka's ice cream cake with the *Argonaut*'s number 55 on it was delivered to their table.

As Syracuse joined them, Jason wondered if he ate takeaway chicken burgers very often. As it turned out, Syracuse handled his greasy burger with ease.

It took all of four seconds for Henry Chaser, official armchair racing expert, to start asking Syracuse all about his professional career.

'You know,' Henry said, 'we were talking about that time you tried to cut the heel in Italy once. That time you got caught in there for—what was it—four hours?'

'Four and a half,' Syracuse corrected.

'What happened?'

Jason also waited for the answer.

When he spoke, Syracuse seemed to choose his words carefully: 'Let's just say, I didn't expect my career to end in New York later that year.'

And with that he looked to Jason, as if expecting him to deduce what such a cryptic answer meant.

Jason thought about it.

'You didn't expect to crash out later that year in New York,' he repeated aloud. 'Which means you expected to race in Italy again, in future years . . .'

'Correct.'

Then it hit Jason.

'No *way* . . .'

Syracuse nodded slowly. 'You've got it.'

'You were doing *research*,' Jason said. 'You were *reconnoitring* the Italian short cut for the next year.'

Syracuse nodded, impressed. 'Well done, Mr Chaser. To this day, you're the first person to have figured that out.'

Jason couldn't believe it. It was so deviously clever. He said: 'Everyone thought your taking the short cut was a desperate attempt to catch the leaders, but it wasn't. You had no intention of catching the leaders at all, or even winning the race. You spent four hours searching the maze, working out its secrets *so you could use them in future years*.'

'Four and a half hours, thank you very much,' Syracuse said. 'And then Alessandro Romba wiped me out in New York later that season and I never got to use that knowledge. Tough break. But I thought your use of the short cut in today's race—following that Xavier fellow in—was just as clever. I hope you were taking notes as you went through. Because that knowledge will be with you whenever that short cut is used from now on—well, at least until the School reconfigures it.'

Jason beamed at Syracuse's praise, and glanced over at

his father, recalling his words from two days earlier: 'When you start learning as hard as you can, I guarantee he'll start treating you differently.'

Henry Chaser knew how much it meant. He just smiled knowingly.

Beside Henry, however, Martha Chaser had become lost in her thoughts again.

At length, Scott Syracuse stood up from the table. 'Thank you all for a lovely dinner, but I fear I have to go.'

'Hey, thanks for coming,' Jason said.

'Don't stay out too late, Mr Chaser. Just because you qualified for the big tournament on Saturday doesn't get you out of classes tomorrow. Lessons will take place as usual.'

'Aw! Don't you ever take a break?' Jason asked.

'See you in the morning, Mr Chaser. Good night, everyone.'

THE INTERNATIONAL RACE SCHOOL
HOBART, TASMANIA
FRIDAY, 31 MAY

The next day was like an episode of that old TV show, *Lifestyles of the Rich and Famous*—albeit an episode that Jason watched in bits and pieces from the window of a classroom overlooking the Derwent River.

Jason knew that the Race School's annual Sponsors' Event was renowned for its carnival atmosphere, but he hadn't been prepared for the sheer *opulence* of that atmosphere.

The whole of the river had been decorated with flags and banners. Hover boats happily tooted their horns, welcoming the flotilla of yachts and hover vessels that descended upon Hobart.

Around lunchtime, *gigantic* hover yachts began to arrive at the Royal Hobart Yacht Club. They variously belonged to famous movie stars, visiting politicians and of course the heads of the major hover car manufacturers and race teams. One wholly-chartered hover-liner pulled into the main dock and unloaded a bevy of glamorously dressed women and powerfully dressed men, the elite of Europe and East-Coast America.

Last and most celebrated of all came the professional racers who had once been students at the Race School.

La Bomba Romba, from Italy.

Fabian, from France.

And Angus Carver, the fighter pilot and member of the elite US Air Force Racing Team.

It was celebrity heaven. The local media just loved it.

Jason, however, didn't really get it.

As far as he was concerned the Sponsors' Event was about winning a knockout tournament. But for all of these people, it seemed to be just as much about attending the School's black-tie Gala Ball that evening and the Victory Dinner on the Saturday evening after the tournament, doing deals and *being seen* at every marquee in between. Apparently, the Sponsors' Event was one of the big events on the global 'society calendar'.

Jason didn't even know what a society calendar was.

And then, around mid-afternoon—to the media's absolute delight—the largest private yacht of all arrived, bearing royal insignia on its bow.

The crest of the Royal Family of Monesi.

Prince Xavier's father, King Francis of Monesi, had come to watch his eldest son compete in the tournament.

And while all this was happening, Jason, the Bug and Sally went to class: Jason and the Bug—watched by Scott Syracuse—did simulator sessions on virtual tracks that featured demag strips.

At the same time, Sally was busy erecting two closed-circuit cameras in their pit bay—pit practice was next and Syracuse, feeling that the *Argonaut*'s pit stops had been somewhat erratic over the course of the season, wanted Sally to see for herself exactly what she did before, during and after each stop.

Curiously, both Horatio Wong and Isaiah Washington were once again too unwell to attend classes.

Jason suspected they were faking it in an effort to get some relaxation time before the big day. Both Wong and Washington had qualified for the tournament, and strangely when they had been ill in the past, they had raced just fine the following day.

For his part, Syracuse barely raised an eyebrow when he got the call from the School nurse about their illnesses. He just went on with his classes.

And in a funny way, Jason felt that Syracuse was treating Team *Argonaut* with more respect than his other two teams simply *because* they came to class, even when they were obviously weary. It was as if just by keeping up with their mentor's tough schedule they were earning respect in Syracuse's eyes.

Jason and the Bug were to meet their parents during lunch, but when they got to the riverside park where they had agreed to meet, only Henry Chaser was there.

'Where's Mum?' Jason asked.

'Said she had some knitting or something to do,' Henry replied. 'Don't know what's got into her head, but when we got home last night, she pulled out her sewing kit and worked halfway into the night on something.'

'Oh, okay . . .'

For the rest of their lunch hour, Jason, the Bug and Henry watched the hover vessels gather on the river, munching on sandwiches.

Then it was back to class, to the afternoon's pit practice.

It was perhaps their most gruelling practice session yet, with Syracuse working them hard—and all of it watched by the two all-seeing closed-circuit cameras.

Syracuse even had them practise an almost archaic form

of pit stop: the manual stop, a stop during which all electric power in the pit bay had gone, meaning that Sally had to attach all six magneto drives to the *Argonaut* manually.

It was the Bug who figured out how to make such a stop happen faster: when he saw Sally struggling, he jumped out of the cockpit and helped her.

When he saw this, Scott Syracuse actually clapped. 'Navigator! Excellent thinking! You don't see manual stops much these days, but they *can* occur. Just because the power's out doesn't mean the race is off. And that's how you handle them: you just get out of your car and you help your Mech Chief. Good thinking, Mr Bug.'

The Bug beamed with pride.

Every few stops, they would crowd around the TV monitors and watch the feed from the cameras. Sally frowned as she watched herself. 'Look at that, I'm all over the shop. Spent mags here, new coolant there, compressed-air cylinders all over the place. My God, I never knew . . .'

Syracuse nodded. 'I can tell you and tell you what you have to do, but sometimes you just need to see for yourself.'

Then, at exactly 4 p.m.—two hours earlier than usual—Syracuse called an end to the session. 'Great work today, people. Grab a drink and take a seat.'

They did so and, utterly exhausted, fell into their chairs.

The thing was, Syracuse still wasn't finished.

He put up a spreadsheet on the vid-screen. 'This just came in. It's the draw for tomorrow. Fourteen starters, rankings based on each racer's current position on the Championship Ladder.'

Jason gazed up at the tournament draw. It looked like the draw for a tennis tournament:

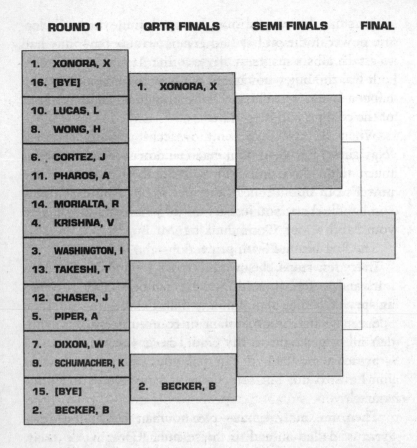

ROUND 1	QRTR FINALS	SEMI FINALS	FINAL
1. XONORA, X			
16. [BYE]	1. XONORA, X		
10. LUCAS, L			
8. WONG, H			
6. CORTEZ, J			
11. PHAROS, A			
14. MORIALTA, R			
4. KRISHNA, V			
3. WASHINGTON, I			
13. TAKESHI, T			
12. CHASER, J			
5. PIPER, A			
7. DIXON, W			
9. SCHUMACHER, K			
15. [BYE]	2. BECKER, B		
2. BECKER, B			

Jason saw himself in the bottom half of the draw. His first race would be against . . .

Oh, no.

Ariel Piper.

His opening race would be against his only friend at the Race School. What was the old saying: 'There are no friends on the track.'

In any case, with Ariel, Barnaby Becker and Isaiah Washington all in his half of the draw, it struck Jason that the lower half was easily the tougher side of the draw.

Since there were only fourteen racers in the draw, the top two ranked racers got the benefit of byes through the first round. It was with great disgust that Jason noticed that both Prince Xavier and Barnaby Becker had scored byes.

The format for the day was known as 'short-course match-racing': two cars raced inside a walled track shaped in a tight figure-8. You won the match-race in one of two ways: first, by lapping your opponent; or second, if neither racer could lap his opponent, by being the first to cross the Start-Finish Line after 100 laps. Since it was a short course—taking about 30 seconds to get around—100 laps would take about 50 minutes.

'So,' Syracuse said. 'Any questions about tomorrow?'

That took Jason by surprise.

It was the first time he could remember Syracuse offering specific advice about an impending race.

'Sure. What's the secret to short-course match-racing?'

'You do get right to the point, don't you, Mr Chaser,' Syracuse mused. 'What's the secret to match-racing? How about this: *Never give up. Never say die.* No matter how hopeless your situation appears to be, don't throw in the towel. Some racers go to pieces when something goes wrong and they find their opponent hammering on their tailfin. They just fold and let the other guy by, thus losing the race. Never *ever* do that. Because you don't know what problems *he's* got under his bonnet. You might throw in the race two seconds before he was going to pit.'

'What about pit stops then?' Sally asked.

'Gotta be fast in match-racing,' Syracuse said. 'When each lap is only 30 seconds long, you can't afford anything longer than a 15-second stop. Any longer and your opponent will be all over you when you come out. Then you're only one mistake away from defeat.'

The Bug whispered something to Jason.

Jason said: 'The Bug wants to know your ideas on *when* to pit. Early? Late? First or always second, like they say in the textbooks?'

'The pits are the X-factor in match-racing,' Syracuse said, 'because whenever you stop your car, you run the risk of it not starting up again. Many a racer has pulled into the pits in a match-race and never come out again, only to watch helplessly as his rival cruises around the track to an easy victory. That's why the books advocate pitting second. I agree. It's also why I wanted you guys to drill pit sessions today.'

He looked over at Sally. 'Pit action becomes even more crucial the longer a match-race goes on—you might have to make decisions about whether to do a full-service stop or just a mag change. The key is to be out on the track. So long as you're out there, even if you're racing on one mag, you can still win. *Never* give up. *Never* say die. But then,' he turned to Jason, 'from what I've observed so far this season, Mr Chaser, I can't see that being a problem for you.'

THE GRAND BALLROOM
THE WALDORF HOTEL, HOBART

It looked like something out of a fairy tale.

The theme for the evening was 'Among the Clouds', so the entire Grand Ballroom of the Waldorf was filled with 80-foot-high blue sails and fluffy machine-generated clouds. The effect was startling—you felt as if you were dining high in the sky, literally among the clouds.

Jason Chaser entered the great ballroom wearing a hand-me-down tuxedo. Beside him, the Bug and Henry Chaser wore regular suits-and-ties—they didn't have tuxedos, so they just wore the best outfits they had. Sally McDuff wore a shiny sky-blue dress that brought out the very best in her busty frame. Martha Chaser continued her peculiar behaviour and did not attend, insisting that she had 'things to do' back in the caravan.

The ballroom before them was filled with wealthy and famous people wearing the best outfits money could buy. Men in designer dinner suits, women in custom-made Valentinos, dripping with jewels.

Famous racers were spread around the room: over in the corner was the reigning world champion, Alessandro Romba; by the bar, the American Air Force pilot, Carver. And at a table near the stage, talking with King Francis and Xavier Xonora, was the much-reviled French racer,

Fabian—the villain of the Pro Circuit: cunning, brilliant and utterly ruthless, and also totally at ease being universally despised by every race fan outside France.

'Hey! Jason!'

Jason turned and saw Ariel Piper—looking absolutely sensational in a figure-hugging silver gown—coming toward him.

'My, don't you clean up well . . .' Ariel said, eyeing Jason's tux. 'Although not as well as your dashing little navigator here,' she winked sexily at the Bug, who flushed bright pink.

'I thought you ran a great race yesterday, Jason,' she said. 'Gutsy stuff skipping your last stop.'

'I had to win,' Jason said simply.

'And so do I in the first round tomorrow, buddy,' Ariel said. 'What is it they say: There are no friends on the track. I'm not going to cut you any slack tomorrow, Jason. I just wanted you to know that.'

Jason nodded. 'Don't worry, I'll be racing as hard as I can, too.'

'So we'll still be friends afterward?' Ariel said, genuinely concerned. And as he saw the look on her face, Jason realised that Ariel Piper had probably lost friends in the past after beating them in hover car races.

He smiled at her. 'Sure.' Then he added mischievously: 'Of course, that's assuming you're not too devastated when I beat you.'

Ariel broke out in a wide grin. 'Oh, you cheeky little man! I'll see you out on the track!'

And with that she danced off to her table.

Jason and his team went to theirs.

★ ★ ★

Scott Syracuse was already seated there when they arrived.

'Hello, Jason, Henry, Bug,' Syracuse said, standing. 'A tad different to our dinner last night?'

'Just a bit,' Henry Chaser said. A simple hard-working man, he was a little intimidated by the wealth and power on show that night. It made him awkward, unsure of how to act in such company. 'Somehow, I don't think they'll be serving takeaway burgers here.'

'If that is what you want, then that is what we shall have!' an Italian voice boomed from behind him.

Henry, Jason and the Bug all whirled around.

Standing behind them was an absolute bear of a man dressed in an expensive dinner suit that struggled to contain his enormous belly. His wobbly jowls were covered by a black beard that was impeccably trimmed.

Jason recognised the man instantly, and his jaw involuntarily dropped.

'Umberto Lombardi,' Syracuse said, 'allow me to introduce to you Jason Chaser, his father Henry, and his brother and navigator, the Bug.'

Syracuse turned to Jason. 'Umberto is an old friend of mine and when we met earlier, I asked him if he would stop by our table later in the evening, but he insisted on joining us for the whole dinner.'

Jason was still gobsmacked.

Umberto Lombardi was the billionaire owner of the Lombardi Racing Team, one of the few privately-owned pro racing teams.

Lombardi was an Italian property developer who'd made his fortune with the outrageously successful 'Venice II' project. When he'd proposed the idea of *rebuilding* Venice fifty miles to the east of the original city—an exact replica, complete with crystal-clear chlorinated canals—

and equipping it with ultra-modern apartments, he had been laughed off as a lunatic.

But as the development proceeded and people saw Lombardi's vision take its wonderful form, the apartments quickly sold out—mainly to playboy race car drivers and the rich and famous of Europe.

Venice II became the hottest address in the world. Venice III quickly followed—where else, but at Venice Beach, California—and then came Venice IV, V and VI.

But Lombardi's passion was hover car racing, and this larger-than-life fellow had become the pleasant oddity of the racing world. Even when his team came dead last in the championship, he still happily threw money at it. He was known as a finder of new talent—talent which was quickly poached by the big-paying manufacturer teams.

'You know,' Lombardi boomed, taking his seat between Jason and Henry Chaser, 'these gala dinners can be so *stuffy* sometimes. Caviar, truffles, foie gras. Bah! Honestly, sometimes all I want is a good hearty cheeseburger!' He nudged Jason with his elbow. 'Don't worry, my young friend. If the food stinks, we'll get some pizza delivered. That'll give these social parasites something to gossip about at their next dinner party.'

Jason smiled. He liked Umberto Lombardi.

It was then that Lombardi—giant loud Umberto Lombardi—saw the Bug sitting on the other side of Jason, eyes wide, almost cowering behind his brother.

'And who do we have here!' Lombardi boomed, delighted. 'My, you are a little fellow to be flying around in an aerial bullet . . .'

From that moment, the Gala Dinner went swimmingly.

★ ★ ★

The night went quickly for Jason.

Umberto Lombardi was the best dinner companion he'd ever encountered. The man talked about racing and building property developments, meeting movie stars and even how he'd been the first person to give Scott Syracuse a start in the pros.

But if nothing else, Jason learned that night that hover car racing wasn't just done on the track. The *business* of racing was done at dinners like this.

Jean-Pierre LeClerq made a speech, flanked by banners covered with the logos of all the School's sponsors. And Jason realised what sponsorship was all about— recognition. As LeClerq was doing now in front of some of the most influential people in the world, you always mentioned your sponsors.

After the speeches were over, the diners spread out around the room.

At one point, as Jason left his table to go to the men's room, he saw Ariel Piper standing at the bar, looking beautiful in her sleek silver dress—but also looking very awkward, seemingly trapped there by a tall guy in his twenties with slicked-back hair and a pointed hawkish nose. The bow tie of his expensive tux was loosened, and he was stroking Ariel's chin slowly with his index finger.

'Hey, Ariel,' Jason came over. 'How's it going? Hi,' he said to the man in the tux. It took Jason a moment to realise that he knew who this fellow was—he was Fabian, the infamous French hover car racer.

'Jason, please—' Ariel said.

'Beat it, kid,' Fabian snarled. 'Can't you see we're busy here.' His French-accented voice was slurred, drunk.

Fabian turned back to Ariel. 'Like I said, there could be opportunities in the racing world for a girl of your ... er,

talents. That is, of course, *if* you play your cards right. Consider my offer, and maybe I'll see you later.'

And with that, he left.

Jason looked at Ariel: she was staring off after Fabian, as if she was making a big decision. Jason watched as a peculiar series of emotions crossed her face—calculation, revulsion, and *ambition*.

'Ariel. Are you okay?' he asked, concerned.

Ariel continued to gaze after Fabian. He had left the dining room now, in the direction of the elevators.

'Jason,' she said, still looking away. 'You're a nice guy and a good kid. But there are some things about the world you don't understand yet.'

She strode off after Fabian.

Jason could only watch her go.

'I understand more than you know,' he said to the empty air behind her.

At 10:30, Jason and the Bug took their leave of Umberto Lombardi and Scott Syracuse.

It was time to get to bed.

They had to race tomorrow.

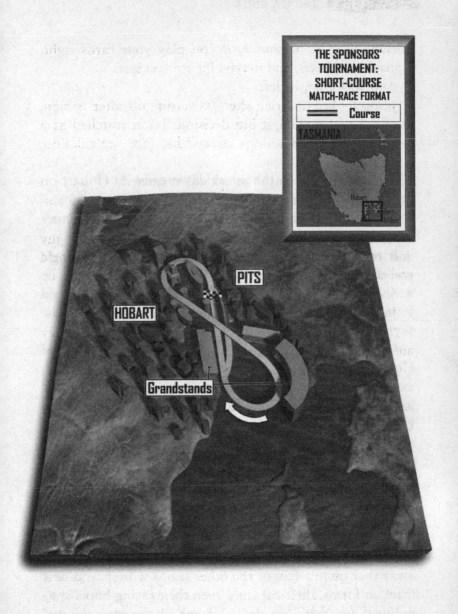

THE SPONSORS'
TOURNAMENT:
SHORT-COURSE
MATCH-RACE FORMAT

━━━ Course

TASMANIA

Hobart

PITS

HOBART

Grandstands

There was tension in the air as dawn came to Hobart on the day of the Sponsors' Tournament.

The rising sun glinted off a *gigantic* temporary structure that dominated the city.

It took the shape of a massive figure-8, with a single walled lane wide enough for two hover cars snaking its way around it. This 'racelane' had walls of clear reinforced Plexiglass bounding it on either side and was open to the sky like a rat-maze.

One section of the figure-8 cut through the canyons of Hobart's skyscrapers, while the main body of the track extended out over Storm Bay, where it was surrounded by immense grandstands, floodlight towers and, today, an ESPN television blimp. In fact, today there were TV cameras everywhere, as the tournament was to be broadcast on racing channels around the world.

The crowds had come out in force: 250,000 people in the stands alone, while experienced locals watched the city-section of the track from rooftops and open office windows.

Jason, the Bug and Sally arrived in Pit Lane at 7:30 a.m. to see the area bustling with activity. Jason noticed right away that quite a few of the other teams wore brand-new team uniforms, their cars and even their racing boots spit-polished for their big day in front of the international sponsors.

And suddenly Jason felt self-conscious in his race

clothes: his old denim overalls, workboots and his battle-scarred motorcycle helmet.

His father was supposed to be with them—he had wanted to experience the tension of Pit Lane with his boys—but at the last moment, Martha had stopped him, saying she needed him to help her with the strange project that had kept her locked away in her caravan the past day-and-a-half.

The tension in the air was palpable.

This was no ordinary day's racing at the Race School. There was more than Championship Points at stake here. Careers could be made or lost today.

Then Jason saw Ariel in her pit bay and he waved. She saw him, but didn't return the gesture. Nor did she look him in the eye.

At 8:45 a.m., a televised ceremony in Pit Lane saw the drawing of the race order. Each first-round race was given a number and Jean-Pierre LeClerq drew the numbers out of a hat.

The first race of the day would be . . .

Chaser, Jason v Piper, Ariel.

Their race was scheduled to start at 9:30 a.m., but before it was to take place, at 9 o'clock, there was scheduled a 'Parade of Racers' in front of the main VIP Grandstand, situated on the Start-Finish Line. And as he looked at the slickly-uniformed teams around him, suddenly Jason didn't feel like being 'presented' to the assembled sponsors in his old denims.

But he had no choice.

And so the Parade of Racers went ahead and he stood there in front of the world, flanked by flags and banners and with the TV blimp soaring in the sky above him, in his threadbare denims . . . and he had never felt more embarrassed in his life. He hated every minute of it.

Then, mercifully, the parade ended, the crowd roared, and the track was cleared for the first race of the day.

Sally prepped the *Argonaut* and the Tarantula.

The Bug worked on pit schedule strategies—in between peering fearfully at the packed grandstands outside.

Jason just sat on his own, centring himself, preparing to race.

The clock ticked over to 9:20 and a loudspeaker boomed with the Race Director's voice: '*Would racers Chaser and Piper please take their positions on the track! Five minutes to racetime . . .*'

Jason got to his feet—

—just as his parents, both of them, ran into the pit area, his mother calling, 'Jason! Doodlebug! Wait!'

She carried a large laundry bag in her hands.

Breathless, she arrived at Team *Argonaut*'s pit bay.

'Mum!' Jason said. 'What is it?'

'I'm sorry I couldn't get them done sooner,' Martha Chaser said, still puffing. She opened the laundry bag—

—to reveal a beautiful set of leather racing uniforms.

Blue.

Silver.

And white.

The colours of the *Argonaut*.

They were full-body uniforms, with the gloves and racing boots seamlessly attached. And the design was *cool*. Mainly white, it looked as if the wearer of the uniform had dipped his arms and legs in blue paint—and, as a nice touch, the blue sections were edged with sparkling silver. Each bore the number '55' on the left-hand shoulder.

There was one uniform for Jason.

A smaller one for the Bug.

And a third one . . . for Sally McDuff.

Martha handed Sally hers: 'I made sure yours has a little extra support in the chest, dear.'

And then Henry Chaser pulled out his surprise: two medium-sized boxes with 'SHOEI' written on the outside.

'No way . . .' Jason said.

He opened his box, and extracted from it a brand-new navy-blue Shoei racing helmet.

The Bug also got one, although his was white. And since she didn't need a helmet, Sally got a blue baseball cap with '*Argonaut 55*' embroidered on it.

Martha said, 'After I watched you all win together on Thursday, the only thing I could think of was: what a great team. But every great team needs to *look* like one. So I got some material, bought some race car magazines to check the current styles, and spent the last day-and-a-half determined to make you look like a team.'

Jason gave her a big hug. So did the Bug. 'Thanks, Mum!'

'Come on, boys,' Henry Chaser said. 'Better get into those suits! You've got a race to win.'

A few minutes later, Team *Argonaut* strode out onto the track, into the sunshine, in front of the roaring crowd, dressed in their spanking new racesuits, Shoei helmets dangling from their hands, eyes fixed, game faces on.

Ariel Piper's team were already on the track, waiting beside the *Pied Piper*.

'What is this? *The Right Stuff*? *Armageddon*?' Ariel's navigator said wryly.

Jason nodded to Ariel as he slid into the cockpit of the *Argonaut*.

'No friends on the track, Jason,' Ariel said.

'Whatever you say, Ariel.'

RACE 1:

 ## CHASER V PIPER

The two hover cars sat side-by-side on the grid, the *Argonaut* on the left, the *Pied Piper* on the right.

From his cockpit, all Jason could see was the wide glass-like corridor of Plexiglass stretching away from him before it banked steeply to the left into the forest of city buildings.

And then—*tone, tone, ping*—the start lights went green and the two cars shot off the mark and the crowds in the stands roared.

Two cars.

One enclosed track.

Hyperfast speeds.

Flashing sunshine.

Blurring walls.

The *Argonaut* and the *Pied Piper* banked and swerved as they rushed like a pair of bullets around the track, ducking and swooping and missing each other by inches as they jockeyed for position.

Out of the corner of his eye on his right side, Jason glimpsed the red-and-white nose of the *Pied Piper* shooting around the track alongside him.

After five quick laps, there was nothing in it.

After ten, they were still side-by-side.

Jason's concentration was hyper-intense, eyeing the speed-blurred track whizzing by him.

Round and round they went, zipping over and under the figure-8 track, at some points side-by-side, at others on each other's heels, swapping the lead but never by more than a couple of car-lengths.

The crowd was captivated.

And then suddenly like a horse throwing a shoe, Jason unexpectedly lost a magneto drive and although more than anything he didn't want to pit first, he peeled off into the pits.

Ariel stayed on the track, shooting off on the next 30-second lap.

The crowd gasped.

Jason had 30 seconds.

He hit the pit bay. The Tarantula descended.

7 seconds . . . 8 . . .

The *Pied Piper* zoomed through the city section.

New mags went on. A splash of coolant.

The *Pied Piper* zoomed over the cross-over of the figure-eight.

13 seconds . . . 14 seconds.

'Sally . . . !'

'Almost done . . . okay! *Go!*'

And Sally cut short the stop and the Tarantula withdrew into the ceiling and Jason hit the gas and blasted out of the pits *just as* Ariel came screaming round the final turn, hard on the *Argonaut*'s heels—now only several car-lengths behind it!

This was classic match-racing, the part of the race known as the 'chase phase'.

The *Pied Piper* (no pit stops) was hammering on the tail

of the *Argonaut* (one stop), chasing it down. If Jason made even the slightest mistake and Ariel got her nose a millimetre ahead of him, it was race over.

And it only had to be a single millimetre—microchips attached to nosewings of both cars would start screaming as soon as they detected one car to be a lap ahead of the other.

Jason had to hold Ariel off until she was forced to pit.

But she didn't pit.

She just kept chasing him.

Charging after him.

Hunting him down, taking each banking turn perfectly, gaining with each lap. Hauling him in metre by brutal metre.

After one lap, she was two car-lengths behind the *Argonaut*.

After two: one car-length.

And after three laps, she had crept *inside* a car-length!

It was relentless. Ariel was throwing everything at him, taking every turn cleanly, searching for a way past him, giving him the race of her life.

On the fourth such lap, Jason's lead became half a car-length.

Hold your nerve . . . he told himself. *Hold your nerve . . .*

Five laps. Most chase phases ended around the fifth lap, with either the pursuer pitting, or the runner crashing out.

Six laps.

And Ariel came alongside him!

She's trying to force you into an error.

Seven laps.

Now it was side-by-side racing!

Jason kept his eyes fixed forward—if he dared to look sideways, he imagined he could see Ariel's eyes inside her racing helmet.

Eight laps, and the crowd rose to their feet.

Eight laps! Jason's mind screamed. *How long is she going to keep this up? When is she going to pit!*

Then on the ninth lap of the chase, he saw the *Pied Piper*'s red-and-white nosewing creep into his peripheral vision.

No! She's gonna take me!

The crowds started cheering.

Never give up. Never say die.

And as they roared down the main straight, commencing Lap 20—the tenth lap of the chase phase—Ariel peeled off and vanished into the pits.

The crowd burst into applause—Jason had just survived a nine-lap chase, almost double the average. An incredible feat of concentration under pressure.

And with Ariel finally off his tail, he gunned it.

Ariel's pit stop was near perfect, and she came back out onto the track slightly ahead of Jason, but now on the same lap.

Lap 40 went by—and there was nothing in it.

Another chase phase took place between Laps 50 and 55, but Jason survived that.

Around Lap 81, Jason had his own chase phase, but Ariel fended him off determinedly.

Then Ariel tried again when Jason pitted on Lap 90, but there was no dice there.

Which meant that after 96 laps and 48 minutes of superb match-racing, it was now a flat-out dash for the line over the last four laps.

The two cars whipped round the track, banking with the corners like a pair of missiles, matching streaks of blue and red.

With three laps to go, Jason was exhausted, his nerves

and reflexes extended to the limit. He didn't know if he could keep this up.

Two laps to go, and his eyes began to blur . . . and Ariel crept ahead of him.

60 seconds of racing left.

Into the city section, and Jason jammed his thrusters all the way forward.

The *Argonaut* roared across the overpass and rocketed into the right-hander at almost 90 degrees to the earth and in doing so gained a metre on the *Pied Piper*.

The two cars screamed out of the final turn, commencing the last lap, the *Pied Piper* less than a metre in front.

Jason clenched his teeth. Gunned it.

His head was beginning to spin.

Through the city buildings, banking hard—the *Pied Piper* just a red shape ahead of him—the roar of the crowd invading his thoughts.

Over the cross-over and towards the final right-hander, all pedals and levers and dials in the red. And then, in a fleeting split-second instant, Jason saw it.

Saw Ariel make a mistake.

She was taking the last turn too wide. The very last turn— the 200th corner of this nerve-shattering, reflex-burning race.

And so, calling on his last reserves of energy and skill, Jason pounced.

He started the turn wide and cut sharply *inside* Ariel—

—and as they took the turn together, the *Argonaut* swooped inside the *Pied Piper* . . .

. . . and came fully alongside it . . .

. . . and the two cars shoomed down the final straight together, and after 100 laps of the most intense match-racing imaginable they crossed the Start-Finish Line almost perfectly side-by-side and the winner was—

—the *Argonaut*.

By the tip of its nosewing.

The official winning margin, taken from the microchips on the nosewings of the two cars, would later be recorded as 0.04 of a second—four hundredths of a second—in favour of 'Chaser, J'.

Physically exhausted and emotionally spent, Jason returned to the pits.

Around him the tournament continued apace; the next pair of racers already lining up on the grid, getting ready to go.

The *Argonaut* slid into its bay—steaming—the acrid smell of overheated magneto drives wafting through the air all around it.

Jason and the Bug stepped out, removed their helmets from their sweaty heads—to be at once embraced in the arms of Sally McDuff and their proud parents.

'You are one gutsy little racer, Jason Chaser!' Sally exclaimed. 'I thought she had you in that first chase phase.'

'Me, too!' Henry said. 'Nine laps! You held her off for nine laps! I've never seen anything like it! How did you do it?'

Jason offered a wry glance to Scott Syracuse, standing nearby: 'Never give up. Never say die.'

With that, Jason's parents let him be, allowing him and the Bug to slump into their chairs in the rear corner of their pit bay.

Syracuse came over. Looked at Jason and the Bug, exhausted, their hair all sweaty and tousled.

And he smiled.

'Nice racing, boys,' he said. 'Very nice. I haven't seen a racer hold his nerve like that for a very long time, Mr Chaser.'

'Thank you, sir,' Jason said.

'Now take a shower and get some rest, both of you. The next round will be here faster than you know and you want to be fresh for it.'

Jason emerged from the showers of his pit bay ten minutes later—just in time to see Ariel over in her pit bay, talking animatedly to Fabian.

Well, in actual fact, only she was talking.

He was walking away, dismissing her tearful pleas with a curt wave of his hand.

Fabian strode off, leaving Ariel standing there in her pit bay, alone, tears streaming down her face.

Jason knew what was going on. Ariel had gone to Fabian's room the night before—he didn't want to think about what happened there—and now she'd lost in the opening round of the tournament, and suddenly Fabian didn't want to know her.

As he gazed at her now, Jason felt for Ariel. She'd given Fabian something last night, something of herself, and for all the wrong reasons, but Fabian had only been using her—

But then Ariel turned suddenly, and caught Jason staring.

And the two of them stood there, on opposite sides of the pits, just looking at each other.

Jason didn't break eye contact. Nor was he going to. It was Ariel who turned away and disappeared into her pit bay.

'I'm sorry, Ariel,' Jason whispered to no-one. 'But there are no friends on the track.'

The tournament continued apace, its carnival-like atmosphere pumping. In between races there were pop music acts, while in the VIP marquees, sponsors and Race School officials did deals over flutes of Moët champagne.

Of the six first-round races, Jason and Ariel's had easily been the longest. The others had been quicker, less-intense affairs, and had variously been won through crashes or mishaps in the pits. None of them had even come close to reaching the 50-lap mark, let alone 100.

And so with the completion of the first round, the tournament draw looked like this:

ROUND 1	QRTR FINALS	SEMI FINALS	FINAL
1. XONORA, X			
16. [BYE]	1. XONORA, X		
10. LUCAS, L	8. WONG, H		
8. WONG, H			
6. CORTEZ, J			
11. PHAROS, A	6. CORTEZ, J		
14. MORIALTA, R	4. KRISHNA, V		
4. KRISHNA, V			
3. WASHINGTON, I			
13. TAKESHI, T	3. WASHINGTON, I		
12. CHASER, J	12. CHASER, J		
5. PIPER, A			
7. DIXON, W			
9. SCHUMACHER, K	9. SCHUMACHER, K		
15. [BYE]	2. BECKER, B		
2. BECKER, B			

The second round—the Quarter Final Round— promised some interesting races and it didn't disappoint.

1ST QUARTER FINAL:

 ### XONORA V WONG

The opening race of the Quarter Final Round saw the first appearance of the top seed, Xavier Xonora, and he showed everyone exactly why he was the favourite to win the tournament.

Up against Jason's stablemate, Horatio Wong, Xonora was quite simply merciless.

His driving around the figure-8 circuit was faultless. He didn't take a corner more than an inch off the optimum racing line and within eight laps, he was a full third of a lap ahead of Wong.

Then Wong pitted—a huge tactical mistake, the Bug commented to Jason; you never *ever* pitted when you were that far behind—and suddenly Xavier was all over him like a rash.

The all-black *Speed Razor* loomed behind Wong's car like a giant hawk—while Wong swerved defensively, panicking, wrestling with his steering vane.

Xavier made a couple of lazy feints to the left, before he just powered easily by Wong on the final turn of Lap 11, overtaking him on the inside, and the race was over almost before it had begun.

It was the shortest race so far. Some likened it to a chess expert dispatching a novice in five quick moves. Others said it was nothing less than the clinical *execution* of a lesser racer by a master.

It even seized the attention of the assembled sponsors.

Xavier Xonora was good, very good. And he had charged into the semis without even breaking a sweat.

2ND QUARTER FINAL:

 ### CORTEZ V KRISHNA

A tight and tense race between the gifted but unpredictable Mexican, Joaquin Cortez, and the No.4 seed, a very gifted 18-year-old racer from India named Varishna Krishna.

It was ultimately won by Krishna on Lap 74, during the race's sixth chase phase.

3RD QUARTER FINAL:

 ### SCHUMACHER V BECKER

This was a race, all agreed, that illustrated the cruelty of match-racing.

The German, Schumacher, had led all the way. He had been pitting superbly—consistently clocking astonishing 8-second stops—and rocketing around the track like a bullet.

By the 50-lap mark, he had built a solid half-lap lead on Becker and all the commentators were certain that after his next pit stop, on fresh mags, he'd pounce.

That pit stop, however, saw Schumacher's pit machine freeze in mid-air.

System crash.

And while Schumacher's Mech Chief swore and rebooted their pit machine's central processing unit, Barnaby Becker just whipped around the circuit—alone, on semi-depleted mags—and lapped Schumacher in the easiest possible way, while he was still in the pits, thus

taking a race that by all accounts he really didn't deserve
to win.

But then, everyone said, that was match-racing.

There was one more Quarter Final race to be run and the
crowd murmured in anticipation.

The public knew that both racers studied under the
same teacher at the Race School—which always made for
interesting racing.

But everyone at the Race School knew that there was more
to it than that: they all knew that Isaiah Washington particularly despised his upstart young stablemate, Jason Chaser.

The stage was set.

The two cars lined up on the grid.

4TH QUARTER FINAL:

 ## WASHINGTON V CHASER

The race between Isaiah Washington and Jason was nothing short of electric.

More than any of the other races in the day so far, there
was *feeling* in this one. The crowd sensed the tension in the
air as the two cars lined up on the grid and Isaiah
Washington glared over at Jason and the Bug.

And then they were off and the race was run at a blistering pace, with multiple lead-changes and daring
overtaking manoeuvres from both racers that had the
crowd gasping.

After 20 laps, there was nothing in it. They were going
stop for stop.

40 laps, and at the Bug's urging, Jason skipped a stop and tried a quick three-lap chase—but Washington held them off determinedly before embarking on a chase phase of his own, but that also failed.

Then, on Lap 57, a mistake.

In this pressure-cooker environment, it was only a matter of time before someone made a mistake and it was the most unexpected person of all who made it.

Sally McDuff.

It was an uncharacteristically rookie mistake, too—co-ordinating her pit gear, Sally mixed up her supply of old and new mag drives and in the lead-up to the next pit stop, she accidentally attached a *used* magneto drive to the Tarantula for affixing to the *Argonaut*.

The stop took place and Jason gunned it out of the pits . . . and immediately knew something was wrong. He didn't have full power.

It was a costly error.

Because it meant that the *Argonaut* had to pit *again* on the very next lap.

'Jason! I'm so sorry!' Sally said as the Tarantula replaced the dud mag. 'It's my fault!'

'Don't worry about it! Just get us back out there!' Jason yelled.

The old mag came off and the new one went on and Jason blasted out of the pits—

—and suddenly found himself only inches in front of the ravenous *Black Bullet*. He was almost a full lap behind now and flying for his life: Washington was on fresh mags, a full tank of coolant and—according to the Bug—his eyes were deadly.

But Jason held on. Drove hard. Concentrated grimly.

That first chase phase melded into a second, then a

third, then a fourth. In each instance, Jason could only pit *after* Washington did: in his position, to pit first was to concede defeat.

Never give up. Never say die . . .

Lap 82 saw Washington pit again—and not a moment too soon for Jason. The *Argonaut* had been almost out of coolant, its mags all but on the point of burning up.

Jason charged into the pits on the next lap for a full coolant refill.

And suddenly his luck changed.

Isaiah Washington was still in the pits when he got there.

Washington's pit machine had frozen halfway through attaching a new set of mags to his car and Washington's Mech Chief was now frantically trying to manually pull the machine clear of the *Black Bullet*.

Jason recalled the words of Scott Syracuse from a few days ago: 'The pits are the X-factor in match-racing, because whenever you stop your car, you run the risk of it not starting up again.'

Which meant that Jason had now reclaimed the lap he had lost earlier—they were now on the same lap.

Jason flung the *Argonaut* into its pit bay—to find that Sally, rattled by her previous error, had misheard the Bug's radio instructions for a full coolant refill.

She had only prepared a top-up.

'Oh, Jason! I'm sorry!'

'Just give me what you've got!' Jason yelled. 'We gotta go!'

The Tarantula's coolant hose pumped a small amount of oily green liquid into the *Argonaut*'s tank and Jason sped off . . .

. . . leaving Washington *still* in his pit bay.

The *Argonaut* shoomed around the track at bullet-speed. Alone.

It had made almost one full circuit when the *Black Bullet* blasted out of the pits—in the nick of time—resuming its place on the track just as Jason rounded the final turn.

And abruptly the tables were turned.

Whereas Washington had spent much of this race hammering on Jason's tail, now—with only 16 laps to go—it was Jason who was almost a lap ahead, and it was his turn to do the hounding.

And despite his own exhaustion, that's exactly what Jason did.

For the next six laps, he rode the tail of the *Black Bullet*, harrying it, hassling it, creeping alongside it until their nosewings were almost side-by-side.

It was all Isaiah Washington could do to stay in front.

But then the Bug issued a warning.

The *Argonaut*'s coolant levels were dangerously low which meant that its magneto drive heat-levels were dangerously high.

Sally's top-up hadn't been enough. It wasn't going to get them to the end of the race. They were going to have to pit one more time, something which would sap the lead they'd just gained and make this race a dash to the finish.

The thing was, Jason was wiped, exhausted from all the previous chases—and he knew it. He didn't think he had the mental energy for another dash to the line.

'Ahhh!' he yelled. 'I just can't do it!'

And then all of a sudden, at the end of Lap 90, something very unexpected happened.

Just as Jason was about to give up on his chase and peel away into the pits and kiss the race good-bye . . .

. . . Isaiah Washington gave up.

Worn out by Jason's brutal six-lap chase—and completely unaware of Jason's own coolant problems—Washington

pulled into the pits, allowing the *Argonaut* to cruise by him, thus winning the match-race.

The crowd cheered.

Jason was stunned.

The overwhelming fatigue that had gripped him moments ago was suddenly transformed into shock.

He had just won this race.

He had just made it to the semi finals.

The *Argonaut* returned to the pits, its mags practically smoking.

Sally McDuff came running over and hugged both Jason and the Bug in their seats. She apologised profusely, but Jason wouldn't hear any of it.

'Sally,' he said. 'Forget it. I've made far more mistakes out on the track than you have in here, and you've always covered for me. Hey. We win as a team and we lose as a team. Don't even think about it again.'

A few minutes later Isaiah Washington came over to their pit bay, with Scott Syracuse by his side. And to Jason's surprise, Washington extended his hand.

'Good race, Chaser,' he said, shaking Jason's hand.

'You too.'

At which point, Washington glanced at the Tarantula and saw the computer readout of the *Argonaut*'s mag and coolant levels. They were all deep into the red, bordering on blowout.

Washington's jaw dropped. 'Wait a minute. You were redlining on coolant *and* mag levels when I dropped out?'

'Er, yeah.'

'But . . .' Washington stammered. 'God, no . . . you were running on empty.' But then his gaze became steely, suspicious. 'How'd you learn to do that?'

Jason shrugged. 'Mr Syracuse taught us. Yesterday, in class.'

'And what exactly did he say?' Washington demanded.

Jason let Syracuse answer that.

'Never give up,' their teacher said.

And so by mid-afternoon on Tournament Day, it was time for the semi finals and the tournament draw looked like this:

ROUND 1	QRTR FINALS	SEMI FINALS	FINAL
1. XONORA, X			
16. [BYE]	1. XONORA, X		
10. LUCAS, L	8. WONG, H		
8. WONG, H		1. XONORA, X	
6. CORTEZ, J			
11. PHAROS, A	6. CORTEZ, J		
14. MORIALTA, R	4. KRISHNA, V	4. KRISHNA, V	
4. KRISHNA, V			
3. WASHINGTON, I			
13. TAKESHI, T	3. WASHINGTON, I		
12. CHASER, J	12. CHASER, J	12. CHASER, J	
5. PIPER, A			
7. DIXON, W			
9. SCHUMACHER, K	9. SCHUMACHER, K	2. BECKER, B	
15. [BYE]	2. BECKER, B		
2. BECKER, B			

It was now the business end of the tournament.

It was time for some serious racing.

It was time for the semi finals.

1ST SEMI FINAL:

 ## XONORA V KRISHNA

If Xavier Xonora's first race in the tournament had been an 11-lap execution, then his semi final against Varishna Krishna was a slightly longer demolition.

It lasted all of 14 laps.

For on Krishna's first pit stop on Lap 10, the young Indian discovered that he'd received two depleted mags. A hurried second pit stop had ensued on the following lap, but by then Krishna's race was over.

Xavier Xonora didn't let mishaps like that go unpunished. Within four laps, he'd shot by Krishna and ended the race, putting the talented Indian racer out of his misery.

And so, having raced only 25 laps in the course of the tournament—all of 12 minutes' racing time—the Black Prince was in the final.

The next race between Jason Chaser and Barnaby Becker would determine who would face him.

'It's over *already*?' Jason said in disbelief.

He had only just stepped out of the shower at the rear of his pit bay, wrapped in a towel, when he was met by

Sally McDuff and the news that Xavier Xonora had already beaten Varishna Krishna and that they were due on the grid in ten minutes.

'What happened to Krishna?' he asked. 'Xavier's good, but he's not that good. Krishna's too talented a racer to go down in fourteen laps.'

'Looks like Krishna got some bad mags,' Sally said. 'The mystery mag-demon strikes again. Hurry up, champ. We're on.'

Jason grabbed his racesuit. 'Geez, I'm still just recovering from the last race.'

The two hover cars sat on the grid, surrounded by their Mech Chiefs, mentors and supporters.

Jason looked over at Barnaby Becker's maroon-coloured Lockheed. Xavier Xonora, fresh from his semi final win over Varishna Krishna, was giving the helmeted Barnaby some tips, while Zoroastro simply glared directly at Jason, trying to psych him out.

'*Racers! This is your five-minute warning! All crew members are to leave the track area immediately,*' Race Director Calder's voice echoed out over the stadium's speakers.

'Stay sharp,' Sally said, slapping Jason's helmet. 'Don't take your eyes off this sneaky bastard.' She turned to the Bug and slapped his helmet, too. 'And you, you look after your brother, okay?'

The Bug gave her a brisk double-thumbs-up.

'Hey, Sally,' Jason said meaningfully.

She turned. 'Yeah?'

'We're gonna beat this guy in the pits.'

'Damn straight,' Sally said.

She made to leave—just as someone else arrived at the *Argonaut* and stopped her.

It was Varishna Krishna.

Dark-eyed and handsome, with smooth chocolate-brown skin, Krishna was a very polite and articulate young man. He was still wearing his sweat-stained racing uniform. He must have come straight from his car after losing to Xavier.

'Jason, Bug, Sally. Hello.'

'Krishna?' Jason frowned. 'What—'

'A word of advice, young Jason. As you may know, I experienced some magneto drive problems in my last race. Let me tell you what happened. Two of my mags were depleted when they went onto my car. However, my Mech Chief, Darius, had checked them all beforehand, and they were okay. Which means that at some point *during the race* my mags were drained of their power. After the race, we found this lying next to our mag storage case.'

Krishna held up a small radio-like device the size of a child's lunchbox.

Jason knew what it was instantly.

It was a portable microwave transmitter. Often used as a back-up radio by race teams, portable microwave transmitters were usually kept as far away from magneto drives as possible—for the simple reason that, if left on, they sapped mag drives of their power.

'I just thought I'd warn you,' Krishna said, eyeing Barnaby, Xavier and Zoroastro disapprovingly. 'I can't prove anything, but Barnaby comes from the same stable as Xavier, and, well . . . let's just say it might be something your Mech Chief will want to keep an eye on.'

Jason nodded. 'Thanks, Krishna. I . . . I didn't know you cared.'

Despite his recent loss, Krishna smiled and placed a

hand on Jason's shoulder. 'Oh, young Master Chaser, do not doubt the impact you make. I know you've had a hard time here at Race School. But know this: some of us enjoy watching you race. You have this delightful habit of hanging on by your fingertips to the bitter end. I suppose I just realised that it was time you knew you had a friend.'

And with that, Krishna turned and walked off.

2ND SEMI FINAL:

 ## CHASER V BECKER

As the *Argonaut* and the all-maroon *Devil's Chariot* had been sitting side-by-side on the grid, waiting for the start of their semi final, Barnaby Becker had called to Jason: 'Hey, Chaser. Time to die.'

Jason replied simply: 'Shut up and race.'

And race they did—in an absolutely brutal contest.

Full-tilt racing.

In a word, Jason raced like a demon. But Barnaby was up to the challenge and for the first 30 laps, it was more a battle of wills than a match-race. The two of them raced almost side-by-side, taking every turn together, every straight, even pitting together.

Indeed, for the first 30 laps, neither of them even attempted a chase phase—which sent a message to the crowd: this was not a chase, it was a 100-lap race to the Finish Line.

In the end, the stalemate was broken in the pits.

At around the 30-lap mark, Sally McDuff lifted her game—and she started sending the *Argonaut* back onto the track, fully replenished, with 8-second stops and even a 7-second one, the first such stop of the day.

The result was a steadily-increasing lead.

The *Argonaut* started to pull away from the *Devil's Chariot*—and by Lap 75, Jason was a full quarter of a lap ahead. And based on the run of the race so far, that would be a lead that Barnaby couldn't surmount.

It was on Lap 75, however—while Sally was busy watching Jason whip down the home straight—that a dark figure slipped into the *Argonaut*'s pit bay behind her and placed something beside her next set of fresh mags.

A microwave radio transmitter.

Sally never saw the intruder. By the time she turned round to prepare for the next stop, he was gone.

A few laps later the *Argonaut* pitted and then shot back out onto the track—where Jason quickly realised that at least two of his new mags were cactus.

'Damn it!' he yelled. 'Not now!'

Furious, he had to pit again.

But Barnaby didn't.

And so as the *Argonaut* pulled into the pits, the *Devil's Chariot* swept past it and all of a sudden, in the space of two laps, the lead was reversed—and with only 19 circuits of the course remaining, Barnaby Becker now held a commanding half-lap lead.

Sadly for Jason, that lead proved to be too big. Desperate and determined, he chased Barnaby all the way to the end, but to no avail.

Barnaby held his lead and after 100 hard-fought laps, he cruised over the Finish Line and claimed his place in the final.

Jason could only punch his steering wheel with frustration and bring the *Argonaut* back to the pits.

His day was over.

He was out of the tournament.

The *Argonaut* returned to the pits—

—to find a large crowd gathered around its pit bay.

And this was no ordinary crowd either. It was a crowd of race officials and teachers, including the School's Race Director, Stanislaus Calder, the man in charge of the tournament, and Jean-Pierre LeClerq, making a rare visit from the VIP marquee.

And in the middle of this crowd stood Sally McDuff, with her arms folded, looking—of all things—pretty pleased with herself.

Jason stepped out of the *Argonaut*, frowning at the sight. He removed his helmet. Truth be told, after three energy-sapping races, he was tired as hell and he was looking forward to having a shower and a rest.

'Sally?' he said. 'What's going on?'

Sally came over. 'Don't put that helmet away, my talented young friend. We're not out of this tournament yet.'

'What do you mean?'

'The judges are checking the video replay,' Sally said enigmatically. 'Come and see.'

The race officials were indeed viewing two video monitors: the monitors that were connected to the two closed-circuit TV cameras hanging from the ceiling of the *Argonaut*'s pit bay; the monitors that Scott Syracuse had employed during pit practice to allow Sally and the boys to see themselves in action.

On one monitor now was a clear black-and-white image of the *Argonaut*'s pit bay: it depicted Sally at work on the Tarantula during the semi final against Barnaby. A computer monitor on the Tarantula showed all the vital stats of the race so far, revealing that this was sometime around Lap 75, racetime 37:30 minutes.

Then Sally moved to the edge of the screen, looking out of the pit bay, and as she did so, a dark figure crept into the *Argonaut*'s pit bay behind her and quickly deposited a portable microwave transmitter next to her stack of magneto drives.

But as the dark figure sneaked away, he inadvertently glanced upwards—looking directly into the camera—and everyone saw his face.

It was Guido Moralez.

Barnaby Becker's Mech Chief.

'Oh my Lord . . .' one of the race officials gasped.

The other School officials swapped shocked glances.

'Gentlemen!' Race Director Calder raised his voice above the murmurs. 'By my order, an emergency hearing will be convened in ten minutes in the Race Briefing Room. Please advise Mr Becker and his Mech Chief, Mr Moralez, that their presence at this hearing is specifically requested. They have some questions to answer.'

Thirty minutes later, the hearing was over.

In the face of Sally's damning video evidence of Moralez planting the microwave transmitter beside the *Argonaut*'s mag drives—thus depleting them of their power and forcing Jason to pit again—Barnaby Becker had been disqualified from the tournament and his semi final victory quashed.

Race Director Calder had been particularly severe in his judgement.

He said that had it been entirely up to him, both

Barnaby and Moralez would have been expelled from the Race School for such disgraceful conduct. But a plea from their teacher, Zoroastro—claiming that this was an act entirely out of character, a stupid act of desperation in the heat of racing—saved their bacon, and they merely had to suffer the indignity of being stripped of their victory.

And with the overturning of that victory came the announcement—an announcement that the 250,000-strong crowd greeted with delighted applause.

Jason and the *Argonaut* were now in the final.

Leaving the Race Briefing Room, Race Director Calder said to Jason: 'Mr Chaser. The final will commence in twenty minutes. See you on the grid.'

'We'll be there, sir,' Jason nodded.

As he strode back to the pits, Sally fell into step alongside him, grinning like a sphinx.

Jason eyed her sideways. 'Why are you smiling like that?'

Sally just raised her eyebrows.

Jason said, 'Now that I think about it, you never switched on those closed-circuit cameras for any of our other races in this tournament, did you?'

'Nope.'

'But you switched them on for the semi?'

'I did. After what Krishna told us, I thought some precautions might be in order,' she said. 'Jason. You race these guys out on the track, but I also race them—in the pits. And I was determined to beat these bastards in the pits. And I did. That was my best race yet, and I sure as hell wasn't gonna let anyone stiff us with some mysteriously depleted magneto drives.'

Jason turned to face her as they walked. In her own way, Sally McDuff was just as proud and determined as he was.

He nodded to her. 'You're a dead-set legend, Sally.'

The next twenty minutes went by in a blur.

With the sun beginning to set, the gigantic track and the bay around it was bathed in a diffused orange glow. The floodlights came on.

The crowds in the hovering grandstands were buzzing with excitement.

The tournament draw itself told the story of a great day's racing:

ROUND 1	QRTR FINALS	SEMI FINALS	FINAL
1. XONORA, X			
16. [BYE]	1. XONORA, X		
10. LUCAS, L	8. WONG, H	1. XONORA, X	
8. WONG, H			
6. CORTEZ, J		4. KRISHNA, V	
11. PHAROS, A	6. CORTEZ, J		
14. MORIALTA, R	4. KRISHNA, V		
4. KRISHNA, V			1. XONORA, X
3. WASHINGTON, I			12. CHASER, J
13. TAKESHI, T	3. WASHINGTON, I		
12. CHASER, J	12. CHASER, J	12. CHASER, J	
5. PIPER, A			
7. DIXON, W		2. BECKER, B	
9. SCHUMACHER, K	9. SCHUMACHER, K		
15. [BYE]	2. BECKER, B		
2. BECKER, B			

But now it all came down to one race and two racers: Xavier Xonora and Jason Chaser.

And they couldn't have been more different.

First there was Xavier who, with his bye in the first round and his two soft victories in the quarters and semis, had raced only 25 laps in the course of the entire day.

Then there was Jason, the very last racer to qualify for the tournament and the driver who had participated in the three most gruelling races of the day. During those three races, two of which had gone the full 100-lap distance, he'd racked up an astonishing 290 laps: 2 hours and 20 minutes worth of racing.

The two cars lined up on the grid.

The *Speed Razor* and the *Argonaut*.

Car No.1 and Car No.55.

The crowd fell silent.

Even the sponsors in the VIP tent lowered their champagne to watch.

This was the big one.

The final.

THE FINAL:

 ### XONORA V CHASER

The final race of the Sponsors' Tournament was nothing short of a match-racing classic.

And for a simple reason: it began with a disaster.

In his superfast Lockheed-Martin, Xavier won the dash from the Start Line and on the first left-hand turn of the race, he cut sharply across Jason's path, clipping the *Argonaut*'s nosewing, snapping it off.

And so, after one lap, Jason pitted and by the time he came out on Lap 2 with a new nosewing, the *Argonaut* was barely a car-length in front of the *Speed Razor*.

The ensuing chase phase was utterly ruthless.

Just as he had done to Horatio Wong earlier in the day, Xavier hounded Jason.

His every turn was perfect. His adherence to the racing line, flawless. It was, quite simply, superb hover car racing, clinical in its precision. He gained a foot on the *Argonaut* with every lap.

But where Wong had failed, Jason didn't falter. He fended Xavier off in the only possible way—by driving equally well, his eyes fixed forward.

And with every lap he survived, the crowd roared ever

louder. After the nosewing mishap on the first corner, no-one had expected Jason to last more than a few laps. But then, this was the kid who'd survived a 9-lap chase phase earlier in the day.

One lap became five.

The chase phase continued.

Five became eight.

Xavier's chase continued.

Nine laps . . . ten . . . *eleven* . . .

Jason raced grimly, his jaw set.

Xavier pursued him like a bloodhound—lap after perfect lap—at one stage bringing his nosecone to within five centimetres of the *Argonaut*'s nosewing . . . but not past it.

In the end, Jason held the *Speed Razor* off for an astonishing twelve laps before Xavier was compelled to pit.

Jason never recovered the lost time from that first unexpected pit stop.

The effect was brutal. It meant that so long as they went stop for stop—with him *always* pitting second—he was always going to be one lap behind Xavier, always being chased.

And so the race became one endless chase phase—with Jason always running and Xavier always pursuing him ruthlessly, relentlessly, only ever one mistake away from victory.

Not even pit stops helped. Sally consistently churned out 8-second stops, but Xavier's Mech Chief, Oliver Koch, was just as good.

20 laps passed—and Jason, exhausted and drained, was driving at the edge of his senses.

40 laps—and Sally wasn't allowed a single mistake in the pits and she didn't make one.

60 laps—and the Bug was starting to get a strained neck from twisting in his seat to check on Xavier behind them.

80 laps—and Xavier just kept on coming.

Kept throwing his perfect laps at Jason, and Jason just kept on going in front of him, equally perfect, like the mechanical rabbit at a greyhound race, forever just out of reach.

And as the race crossed the 90-lap mark, the crowd rose to their feet, many of the students among them saying that if Jason's race against Barnaby had been a grudge match, then this was a death match, a race that was going to go all the way to the 100th lap.

And then on Lap 98 it happened.

Something that no-one could have expected.

Both racers pitted: Xavier first, and then Jason, who had to whip all the way around the track before he could dash into the pits for that one last crucial stop.

He shoomed into the pits, and immediately saw that *Xavier was still there*—indeed Oliver Koch was scrambling around the *Speed Razor* like a crazy man while Xavier yelled at him, waving his fists.

And then Jason saw why.

The pressure nozzle on Koch's coolant hose had broken off, and coolant was spraying everywhere. Koch was now frantically attaching a new nozzle to his hose.

Which meant that suddenly, the *Argonaut* and the *Speed Razor* were back on level terms again.

Sally worked a killer stop—

—just as Koch got his hose working again—

—with the result being that both cars shot out from their pit bays at almost exactly the same time, only now the *Argonaut*, astonishingly, was slightly ahead of the *Speed Razor*!

The two cars blasted back out onto the track, and with only two laps to run, the *Argonaut* was in the lead!

It was now a one-minute scramble for the Finish Line.

Jason flew.

Xavier charged.

Shoom!-shoom!

One lap to go and Jason still held the lead by half a car-length.

The crowd leapt to their feet.

Last lap.

Jason's eyes never left the track.

Left into the sweeper through the city, blurred buildings swooshing by him on either side . . .

Up and over the cross-over . . .

Then into the final right-hander, holding the racing line—and Jason saw the *Speed Razor*'s nosecone enter his left-side peripheral vision, heard the roar of its engines loud in his ears.

The *Speed Razor* was right alongside him! Xavier wasn't giving up.

The two cars took the final turn side-by-side.

Jason gripped his steering wheel tightly, his knuckles white; clenched his teeth. His bloodshot eyes were wide, on the verge of sensory overload.

Still the *Speed Razor* kept coming . . . and slowly, gradually, started edging ahead of him!

Jason couldn't believe it. There was nothing he could do! This was the best he could race and still Xavier was going past him.

And with that, the realisation hit Jason.

Xavier was too good. Too fast.

This race was slipping out of Jason's grasp.

Xavier was going to win.

And then the home straight opened up before them and the *Argonaut* and the *Speed Razor* rushed down it side-by-

side at full throttle, before they shot together through the red laser beam that marked the Finish Line and the winner of the race—of the final—of the day—of the whole entire tournament was—

—Xavier.

By 0.003 of a second. Three *thousandths* of a second.

And as the two cars glided around the track, slowing, Jason sighed with deep relief.

He'd lost. Lost the final—and for that he was bitterly disappointed—but he was also glad that this day, this long day of racing, was finally over.

Almost every member of the 250,000-strong crowd stayed for the winner's ceremony.

They clapped loudly as Xavier stepped triumphantly onto the podium to accept the winner's trophy from Race Director Calder and Jean-Pierre LeClerq.

Jason could only stand behind the podium, behind the 2nd-place-getter's step, and clap too.

He'd come so far, raced so hard, through four of the most difficult races of his life, and he'd missed out by the smallest fraction of a second.

The applause for Xavier and his team died down, and the announcer's voice came again over the loudspeakers:

'*And in second place, Car No.55, Team Argonaut. Driver: Jason Chaser; Navigator: Bug Chaser; Mech Chief: Sally McDuff.*'

Head down with disappointment, Jason stepped up onto the podium.

What happened next made him freeze in shock.

The crowd went nuts.

Absolutely, totally *ballistic*.

The colossal roar that they gave him and Sally and the Bug almost brought down the entire stadium.

Flashbulbs popped, horns blared, people raised their hands above their heads to clap. Even Xavier was taken aback by the strength of their cheering.

But it was true.

The crowd was giving a bigger cheer to the racer who'd come *second* than they had for the racer who'd come first!

Jason was stunned, and at first he didn't understand why this was happening.

Nevertheless, with the Bug and Sally beside him, he took his place on the second tier of the podium and, dressed in his cool new racesuit, waved hesitantly to the crowd.

The crowd went even crazier at the gesture, started chanting: 'Jason! JASON! *JASON!*'

It was then that Jason saw his mother down in the crowd. She was crying with joy. Beside her, his father, Henry, was busily taking audio-included digital photographs for their family album.

And in that instant Jason began to understand.

Xavier had won the tournament, and won it well, and the crowd respected that.

While for his part Jason had lost—but he had lost well.

After a staggering 390 laps of racing, at the edge of total exhaustion, he had lost by less than a second to a guy who had creamed every other opponent he had faced—and the crowd respected that even *more*.

Jason remembered something his father had once told him: *It's not how we win that defines us, Jason, it's how we* lose. *Winners come and go, but the racer who goes down fighting will live forever in people's hearts.*

Jason smiled at that as he gazed out over the roaring crowd—the crowd roaring for him.

As he did so, Race Director Calder handed each member of Xavier's winning team an enormous bottle of champagne, and Xavier shook his bottle hard and popped the cork, sending a geyser of champagne shooting into the air above the winner's podium.

That evening, the Chaser family—plus Sally and Scott Syracuse—returned to Chooka's Charcoal Chicken Restaurant for another celebratory dinner.

'Guess what,' Sally said as she munched on a burger. 'I heard that after the winner's presentation the head of the Lockheed-Martin pro team, Antony Nelson, approached Xavier and asked him if he wanted to apprentice with them at the Italian Run next month.'

'No way!' Jason exclaimed. 'The Lockheed Factory Team. Wow! To the winner, the spoils, I guess . . .'

'Don't you worry,' Henry Chaser said, seeing his disappointment. 'Your time'll come. I don't think your efforts today went unnoticed.'

'Yeah?' Jason laughed. 'Well, I don't see the chiefs of any pro teams walking up to us and offering us a run in a Grand Slam race.'

Just as Jason was saying this, a large figure entered the restaurant.

Heads turned, whispers arose—precisely because you don't often see billionaires in takeaway chicken joints.

It was Umberto Lombardi.

'Ah-ha!' the big Italian boomed. 'Now *this* is my kind of

dinner! Three Super Burgers to go, please, madam, with extra cheese! Oh, would anyone else like anything?'

Lombardi sat down beside Martha Chaser. 'My sincere apologies, Señora Chaser, for intruding upon your celebrations. But I beg your indulgence, I will not stay for long. I do, however, have a serious question for this wonderful young team.'

Everyone at the table fell silent.

Lombardi leaned forward, lowered his voice. 'I thought you all raced well today. Very well. No other team out there came close to surviving almost 400 laps of match-racing. But you did. More than that. You did that *and you almost won!*

'Now. As you are probably aware, the Italian Run is to be held in three weeks' time. Up until now, my team has only ever run one car in pro events, but lately I've been thinking of expanding the team . . . and adding a second car.'

Jason felt a tingle race up his spine. 'Yes . . .'

Lombardi went on. 'What I was wondering was this: would the members of Team *Argonaut* like to race the second Lombardi Racing Team car in this year's Italian Run?'

Jason dropped his fork. The Bug blanched. Sally's mouth fell open. Henry Chaser stopped chewing. Martha Chaser's lip started to quiver. Scott Syracuse just kept eating casually.

'You . . .' Jason stammered. 'You want *us* to race for *you* in the next Grand Slam race?'

'Yes. I do,' Lombardi said simply.

Jason swallowed.

This was too much. The enormity of what Lombardi was suggesting rocked through him with the force of an earthquake.

This wouldn't be like any old School race. Or even like the Sponsors' Tournament, for that matter. This would be bigger—much bigger. This would be a professional race against professional racers, in Italy, beamed live to the entire world.

'Well?' Lombardi asked. 'Do you race?'

Jason looked at the Bug, who nodded once.

He turned to Sally who, still silent with shock, nodded vigorously.

Then he turned back to Lombardi and said, 'You bet we race.'

And so it was settled.

Team *Argonaut* was going to Italy.

PART V

THE ITALIAN RUN

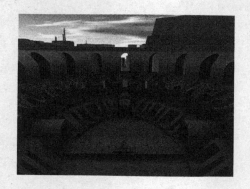

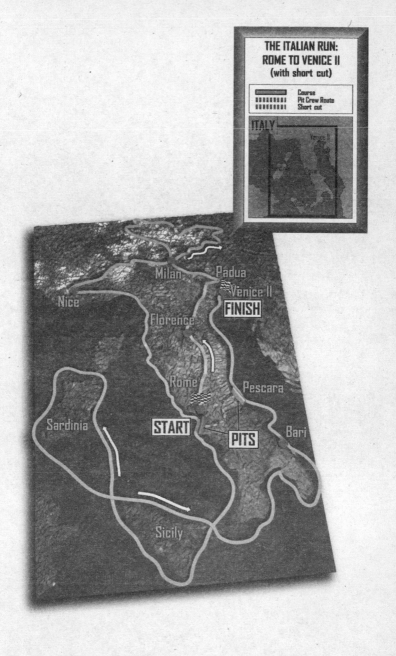

THE ITALIAN RUN:
ROME TO VENICE II
(with short cut)

Course
Pit Crew Route
Short cut

ITALY

Venice II

Milan   Padua
             Venice II
Nice   FINISH
      Florence

         Rome
                    Pescara
Sardinia   START
                    Bari
              PITS

         Sicily

In the hover car racing world, there are four 'Grand Slam' races. In order, they are:

The Sydney Classic, held in February.
The London Underground Run, May.
The Italian Run, August.
And the New York Masters, in October.
Naturally, they are all very different kinds of races.

The Sydney race is a typically Australian event—tough and hard and long, a test of endurance, like five-day-long cricket matches or the old Bathurst 1000 car race. It is a lap race that lasts 20 hours, during which racers do 156 laps of a course that runs past the eight giant ocean-dams that line Australia's eastern coastline, ending underneath the grandest Finish Line in the world: the Sydney Harbour Bridge. Australians call it 'the race that stops a nation'.

The London Underground Run is a gate race—the most fiendish gate race of all. Held in the subterranean dark of the London subway system, it tests every racer's tactical abilities, seeing how many underground stations they can whip through in 6 hours. No racer has ever 'clocked up' every single station.

For its part, the New York Masters is a carnival of racing, four races held over four consecutive days, one race per day—one supersprint, a gate race, one collective pursuit, and finishing it off, an example of the rarest race of all, a long-distance search-and-retrieve 'quest' race that takes racers from New York City to Niagara Falls and back again.

The Italian Run, however, has its own unique format.

Held every year in the baking heat of the northern summer, it is a *unidirectional* race. Racers do not do laps of a circuit. Rather, they start in one city and end in another, on the other side of the country.

The race starts in Rome, inside the Colosseum, after which it shoots north, up the spine of Italy, swinging through Florence, Padua and Milan before it winds up through the Alps and then begins the long trip south down the western coast and between the islands of Sicily and Sardinia. Then it's under the bottom of the boot—where racers can choose to cut the heel if they dare—followed by the final dash up the eastern side of the country to the grand finish in Venice II.

Interestingly, there are *two* pit areas in the Italian Run— one at Leonardo da Vinci International Airport in Fiumicino near Rome and a second directly across the country at Pescara. It is thus the only race in the world where *pit crews* have to travel overland to get to the second stop. It is not unknown for a racer to get to Pescara and find that his Mech Chief has not yet arrived.

Unlike most of the races Jason had run at Race School (which operated under the southern hemisphere rules of racing, such as 'car-over-the-line' finishes), the Italian Run operated under the more traditional rules of the northern pro-racing confederations, including a different finishing rule: 'driver-over-the-line'.

This meant that it was the first racer—driver or navigator, it didn't matter—over the line who won the race, whether *or not* they were in their car. On more than one occasion, a racer, his car broken down or crashed, had *run* (or in Italy, where the Finish Line was over water, swum) over the line to finish the race.

Ultimately, however, the Italian Run was a truly *European* event, and as such it was loved by all of Europe. Every year, millions descended upon Italy for it. Immense crowds line the coastline *of the entire country*, sitting on hills and cliffs and hover grandstands.

For one week in August every year, Italy becomes the centre of Europe, buzzing with tourists and race fans—all of them with money to spend. Economists say that the week of the Italian Run injects $60 billion into the Italian economy.

It was into this surging pulsating world that Jason Chaser was about to plunge.

THE INTERNATIONAL RACE SCHOOL
HOBART, TASMANIA

But before Jason and Xavier were to depart for Italy, there were still almost a dozen school races to be run.

While the Race School was very proud to have two of its racers invited to compete in a Grand Slam event, it was made very clear to both Jason and Xavier that while they were away in Italy, the School season would continue without them.

Which meant they had to put as many competition points as possible in the bank before they left. This was less of a problem for Xavier, who was currently leading the School Competition Ladder by a clear 30 points.

For Jason, it was tougher. As runner-up in the mid-season tournament, he had garnered a solid 18 points (the tournament being worth double points), lifting him to 7th on the overall Competition Ladder. But Italy would take him away from the School Competition for eight days, forcing him to miss three whole races. And Italy aside, he was still mindful that he had to finish the School season in the Top 4 to get an invitation to the New York Challenger Race in October.

He would have to do some catch-up when he returned from his adventure in Italy. But hell, he thought, it was worth it—it wasn't every day a rookie like him got a ride *in a Grand Slam race.*

Boy, he was excited.

Early one morning, a few days after the tournament, Jason went for a walk by himself out across a grassy headland overlooking Storm Bay. It was a place he went to be alone, to think and to breathe, away from the frenetic world of racing.

Someone was waiting for him at his spot.

Ariel.

'Hey.' Jason sat down beside her.

'Hi there,' she said.

Jason hadn't seen her since the day of the tournament, the day he had beaten her, the day after she had—

'You raced well in the tournament, Jason,' she said.

'I almost had him. Almost.'

'Jason, I couldn't believe you kept up with Xavier for as long as you did. No-one could,' Ariel said. 'And after all those races before. You just never give up.'

Jason bowed his head, said nothing.

Ariel said, 'You know, I was cheering for you by the end. Sure, after you beat me, I went back to my room for a while and yes, I cried some. But after a while, I switched on the TV and saw that you were still in it, beating everyone. So for the final, I went back out there and sat up in the back of one of the grandstands and watched.' She turned to him. 'I was proud of you.'

'Thanks.'

'I also felt I let you down by what I did the night before. With that rat Fabian.'

Jason looked at her. 'Ariel—'

'No. Don't say anything. I was stupid. I shoulda known better. He told me everything I wanted to hear. Jason,

you've been the only person who's been good to me this whole time at Race School. I hope you can forgive me and be my friend again.'

Jason was silent for a long time.

Then he said, 'You never let me down, Ariel. So we never stopped being friends. Except, of course, out on the track.'

And with that Ariel gave him a big hug.

The next twelve races went by in a blur.

Knowing he needed to bank some points before he went to Italy, Jason had solid finishes throughout: four 3rds, three 2nds and even two wins—although it had to be said that both of his wins came on days when Xavier Xonora decided to take a rest and sit out the race.

This fact actually bothered Jason.

He realised that he had only ever beaten Xavier on one occasion—in Race 25, and even then, it had been in pretty incredible circumstances, after he'd taken the very non-percentage move of skipping his final pit stop.

In any case, his results catapulted Team *Argonaut* up the Competition Ladder and by the time it came for him to leave for Italy, the Ladder looked like this:

THE INTERNATIONAL RACE SCHOOL CHAMPIONSHIP LADDER			
AFTER 37 RACES			
DRIVER	**NO.**	**CAR**	**POINTS**
1. XONORA, X	1	*Speed Razor*	266
2. KRISHNA, V	31	*Calcutta-IV*	235
3. WASHINGTON, I	42	*Black Bullet*	224
4. CHASER, J	55	*Argonaut*	217
5. BECKER, B	09	*Devil's Chariot*	216
6. WONG, H	888	*Little Tokyo*	215
7. SCHUMACHER, K	25	*Blue Lightning*	213
8. PIPER, A	16	*Pied Piper*	212

Xavier was way out in front. A cool 31 points ahead of his nearest rival, he could sit out three more races and still not lose the Number 1 spot.

Jason was in fourth position—but with a bunch of quality racers nipping at his heels. After missing three races, he'd almost certainly drop out of the Top 4.

But that was a battle to be fought another day.

It was time to go to Italy.

VENICE II, ITALY (MONDAY OF RACE WEEK)

The whole of Italy was positively buzzing with excitement when Jason, the Bug and Sally stepped off Umberto Lombardi's private hover-liner at the main wharf of Venice II.

It was as if hover car fever had gripped the entire nation.

Gargantuan images of Alessandro Romba blared out from building-sized hover-billboards along the coast—pictures of the world champion holding cola cans or driving sports hover cars.

Multi-coloured banners fluttered from every lamp-post—either in the colours of the Italian flag or of some racing team. People danced in the streets dressed in the uniforms of their favourite teams, sang, drank and generally had a great time.

The week of the Italian Run was Party Week in Italy. Magazines and newspapers and TV talk shows spoke of only one thing: *La Corsa*. The Race.

Bookmakers did a thriving trade, offering odds on every available result: the winner, the top three finishers *in order*, any-order multiples, or even just a racer finishing in the top five.

The world champ and local hero, Alessandro Romba, was the talk of the town. His victories in Sydney and London had every race fan wondering if he might be the first racer ever to complete the Golden Grand Slam—

winning all four Grand Slam races in the one year. Indeed, he had not even been cleanly *passed* in a Grand Slam race this year. He appeared on the talk shows and every Italian loved him like a son.

The French racer, Fabian, was also doing the media rounds. On one occasion, Jason saw him being interviewed on a racing show:

The interviewer was asking Fabian about what he had seen at the Race School in Australia.

'There is a lot of talent down there,' Fabian said. 'A lot of talent. And the two students who have come here are two of the best young drivers there.'

'And what about the female driver at the Race School?' the interviewer asked. 'Much fuss was made of her enrolment. What did you make of her?'

Fabian's eyes glinted meanly.

'She was, quite frankly, a non-event. She was defeated in the first round of the tournament, quite comprehensively. Call me a dinosaur, but I personally see no place for women in hover car racing.'

Jason had scowled at the TV.

But then to his surprise the eyes of the media—always hungry, always looking for new fodder—soon fell upon the two young racers who would be making their Grand Slam debuts in the Italian Run: Xavier Xonora and him.

Xavier seemed to take the media attention in his stride. Perhaps it was his experience as a royal figure. Perhaps it was the slick public relations machine of the Lockheed-Martin Factory Team selecting the right talk shows for him to go on. Perhaps, Jason thought, Xavier was just made to be a superstar.

The media (especially the society pages) portrayed him as the dutiful protégé, the sharp-eyed student who would be

watching and learning from the master, his No.1 in the Lockheed-Martin Team, Alessandro Romba. His goals were modest—'I'd just love a top ten finish'—and within a few days he was being hailed as the heir apparent to Romba as the heartthrob of international racing.

Jason had a tougher time of it—just seeing himself portrayed on TV, on magazine covers, in the papers was scary enough.

The media had latched onto his youth. Even though he would be 15 on Wednesday, he was portrayed as a brilliant young upstart, the 14-year-old *wunderkind*—but despite that, still ultimately a boy venturing into a man's world.

He was a curiosity, an oddity—like the bearded lady at the circus—and he didn't like being that.

At the first news story that claimed he was out of his depth, he wanted to write a letter to the editor. After the twentieth one, he just fumed silently.

He wished Scott Syracuse was there, but his teacher had stayed back at the Race School—he did, after all, have other students to watch over in their School races. Syracuse had said he would try to get to Italy for the race on Sunday.

Jason hoped he would make it.

Although the Italian Run actually began in Rome, Team *Argonaut* was based in Venice II, since the entire canal city belonged to Umberto Lombardi.

Jason was staying at the Lombardi Grand Hotel, in a suite that turned out to be the third-best apartment in all of Venice II. The best one, of course, belonged to Lombardi himself. The second-best went to Team Lombardi's No.1 driver, Pablo Riviera.

In any case, Jason's apartment was bigger than most of the houses he knew. Wide and modern, with ultra-expensive hover-furniture, it featured panoramic views of both the Adriatic Sea and Venice II's astonishing recreation of St Mark's Square.

The week stretched out before him:

Today was Monday.

The official Pole Position Shootout session would be held on Friday, on a tight mini-course up the spine of central Italy. That would be followed by a gala dinner on Friday night.

The Italian Run itself would be held on Sunday.

For most racers, this lead-up week would be filled with practice sessions on the course itself, some sponsors' events, and a few invitation-only galas put on by individual teams.

Importantly for Jason, the lead-up week gave him time to meet the members of the Lombardi Racing Team. For while he would be racing with his regular team—the Bug and Sally—they would be supported by a fully equipped engineering and technical team from Lombardi, known as 'E&T'.

Most significantly of all—and a little sadly for Jason—this would be the first time that he would *not* race in the *Argonaut*.

No, in this race he would be flying in a brand-new Ferrari F-3000 emblazoned in the Lombardi Team colours of black-with-yellow-slashes.

Compared to the little *Argonaut*, the Ferrari F-3000 was a beast of a machine: bigger, faster and meaner. A far newer Ferrari, it had roughly the same bullet-like shape as the *Argonaut*, only it was sleeker, more streamlined.

Once Jason had dreamed of driving an F-3000, but now that he was here, he kind of wished he'd be racing in the *Argonaut*.

But he shook the thought away as he gazed at the chunky F-3000.

He and his team had four days to tame this beast.

For the first two days of Race Week—Monday and Tuesday—Jason practised in his new F-3000 under the intense glare of media hovercopters and the paparazzi's telephoto lenses. A crush of journalists was always waiting outside the gates of the Lombardi training course on the outskirts of Venice II.

On the Tuesday, he met Pablo Riviera, the No.1 driver for Lombardi Racing and liked him immediately. Riviera was a 26-year-old Colombian driver. Young and talented but not quite a top-tier racer yet, Riviera was generous in his advice:

'The best tip I can give you,' he said, 'is to go to bed early. Training will weary you, but dealing with the media will wear you out entirely. Trust me. And the only thing that matters is to be ready on race day.'

But then, on the Tuesday afternoon, as Jason and his team were leaving the training track in his hover-limo, he saw that the assembled media crowd at the gates had *tripled* in size.

This media mob was literally bubbling over with excitement when the hover-limo came to the exit gates.

The crowd of journalists and camera crews jostled the car—forcing it to stop—shouting questions at Jason with more force than usual.

And then, beyond them, he saw the reason.

There, grinning like the Cheshire Cat, stood the French driver, Fabian.

★ ★ ★

Jason and the others stepped out of the limo.

'*Jason!*' the reporters yelled. '*Jason!* Over here!'

'Jason! How do you respond to Fabian's invitation!'

Jason frowned. 'Invitation? What invitation?'

Fabian stepped forward theatrically, his French accent oily-smooth. 'Ladies and gentlemen. Ladies and gentlemen. Please! Leave young Jason alone. This is all very new to him.'

The crowd of hacks took a collective step back and fell silent.

'Jason,' Fabian said with more familiarity than Jason liked, 'my personal sponsor, the Circus Maximus Beer Company, has decided to stage an exhibition race tomorrow at sunset, in their newly built Circus Maximus. It is to be a one-on-one match-race between me and an opponent of my choosing. We are calling it Fabian's Challenge . . .'

The media crowd was hanging on Fabian's every word and Fabian knew it.

He went on innocently: 'I just happened to mention on television this afternoon that I would love to race against the determined young driver everyone is talking about. You. What do you say, Jason? Do you want to race?'

Every microphone in the media throng swung to Jason's lips.

And in that instant, the world froze for Jason.

Later, he wouldn't even remember the words coming out of his mouth—but he heard them quite clearly as he saw himself on every news channel on TV later that afternoon.

'You're on,' he'd answered to Fabian's challenge.

The rest of that afternoon and evening was spent talking on the phones with Lombardi and his E&T technicians.

Far from being angry at Jason's acceptance of the challenge,

Lombardi *loved* the idea of one of his drivers participating in an exhibition race against Fabian.

'Jason! I may be rich, but my team—in the broader scheme of the racing world—is a mid-level team. Pablo is good, but he too is mid-range. Certainly not good enough to attract the attention of someone like Fabian. But you! Yes! Lord, think of the publicity such a race will bring!'

But his enthusiasm only went so far.

He didn't want to endanger a new Ferrari F-3000 in an exhibition race. Which was why he allowed his team of engineers to put a brand-new set of Ferrari XP-7 magneto drives and a super-aerodynamic F-3000 tailfin on the *Argonaut*, to bring it up to speed with Fabian's Renault.

The phones didn't stop ringing all evening.

People were running every which way in Jason's apartment.

And in the middle of it all, Jason went into his room and made a single phone call himself.

THE CIRCUS MAXIMUS
ROME, ITALY (WEDNESDAY OF RACE WEEK)

Illuminated by the diffused orange glow of the setting Italian sun the stadium looked exactly like the famous Roman chariot-racing arena—a gigantic oval-shaped racetrack, flanked on the outer circumference by mammoth grandstands; all of it built in a faux-Roman style on a stretch of flat reclaimed land on the western coast of Italy, not far from Rome.

The only difference between this and the Circus Maximus of old was the scale.

Each of its two straights was 12 kilometres long—so that it would take the average hover car roughly two minutes to complete each lap, one minute for each straight.

Red neon signs for the 'Circus Maximus Beer Co.' blazed out from the upper flanks of the stadium.

Before a cheering, heaving, thriving crowd of 2 million spectators—all of them fuelled on free beer—two tiny hover cars lined up on the grid.

Fabian's purple-and-gold Renault Tricolore-VII, known as the *Marseilles Falcon*.

And beside it: the *Argonaut*, looking resplendent in spanking-new coats of white, silver and blue paint. Plus one new feature: its new tailfin was now painted in Lombardi black-and-yellow.

★ ★ ★

Just before the race, Jason and Fabian posed for photos on the track—the modern-day charioteers standing beside their chariots, holding their helmets, flanked by bikini-clad girls and beer company executives, in front of the baying crowd.

By the look on his face, Fabian was clearly pleased by the extra attention the young Chaser boy was bringing to his exhibition event. That today, August 6, also happened to be Jason's 15th birthday was a bonus—the media had painted Fabian as a man giving a boy the most incredible birthday opportunity ever.

For his part, as he stood beside Fabian, smiling for the cameras, Jason eyed the *Marseilles Falcon* and its notorious nosewing.

Fabian's car featured a controversial 'bladed' nosewing. Two vertical fins jutted upward from its outer tips, their forward edges as sharp as knives, hence the term 'bladed'. Renault claimed the sharpness was simply aerodynamic. Other racers claimed Fabian used his bladed fins to damage their cars in the rough-and-tumble of racing. For the moment, the fins were allowed by the governing body of racing, the International Hover Car Racing Association. But every racer knew—stay away from them.

The photo session ended, and Fabian jumped into his car.

Jason, however, dashed to his pit bay, to the toilet there—an act which made everybody in the grandstands laugh. The rookie, it seemed, was nervous.

He emerged moments later, strapping his helmet in place. He stepped into the *Argonaut*, joining the Bug, ready to race.

★ ★ ★

The exhibition race was an absolute beauty.

As the *Marseilles Falcon* and the *Argonaut* shot down the first straight, the delighted crowd did a Mexican Wave alongside them.

The race was twenty laps and at first Fabian took the lead—at times doing playful trick moves to please the crowd.

Jason trailed him doggedly, showing his trademark determination, and during one of Fabian's playful moments, he ducked inside him and overtook him.

Obviously surprised, Fabian gave chase and, after a lap, retook the lead.

But it was to be the first of many lead changes, with Jason entering into the spirit of things—to everyone's surprise, he also performed some daring aerobatics whenever he took the lead: flat lateral skids or the odd corkscrew roll.

The crowd cheered with delight.

But then the race neared its final stages, and the tricks ceased, and when the *Argonaut* slipped inside the *Marseilles Falcon* on the second-last turn, it became a flat-out—and deadly serious—dash for the Finish Line.

Down the back straight.

Twin bullets.

Into the final 180-degree turn—the *Argonaut* taking the standard apex, Fabian starting wide and scything inside with the precision of a surgeon, the *Falcon*'s deadly bladed nosewing coming within inches of the *Argonaut*'s own nose—and the two cars ended up side-by-side as they shot down the main straight, kicking up identical yellow sand-clouds behind them, before hitting the line together . . .

THE CIRCUS MAXIMUS
ROME, ITALY (WEDNESDAY OF RACE WEEK)

The roar of the crowd said it all. They knew who had won. The rookie, Chaser, had got it by half a car-length.

Jason's fist shot into the air as he cruised round the track, waving to the crowd.

Fabian's car came alongside the *Argonaut*, and Fabian offered Jason the 'racer's salute': a short touch of the helmet with his right hand. It was like shaking hands after a tennis match—you always did it after a match-race.

Jason returned the salute.

The two cars completed a full circuit to a standing ovation, before coming to a halt in the main straight, in front of the VIP box.

Fabian stepped out of his car and shook his head in mock disbelief, as if to say: 'Can you believe that? How about this young guy?'

He went over to the *Argonaut* just as Jason and the Bug lifted themselves out of the cockpit. Fabian went to shake Jason's hand, but Jason's gloved hands instead went to his own helmet. He took it off—

—to reveal that the pilot of the *Argonaut*, the racer who had just beaten Fabian in a wonderfully entertaining match-race, wasn't Jason Chaser at all.

Standing there in the middle of the Circus Maximus,

wearing Jason Chaser's racing leathers, holding Jason Chaser's helmet, and standing beside Jason Chaser's pint-sized navigator, stood Ariel Piper.

Live on international television, Fabian's jaw hit the dusty ground.

'But . . .' he stammered. 'We had our photo taken before the—'

'Looks like the Jason Chaser who went to the men's room just before the race wasn't the Jason Chaser who came out,' Ariel said. 'Now, Fabian. What was it you were saying about women and hover car racing?'

The crowd was stunned—at first.

Then they roared their hilarious approval.

Ariel could only smile with immense satisfaction.

And far away to the north, at the empty Lombardi practice track, without a journalist, photographer or hovercopter in sight, Jason Chaser stepped into his Ferrari F-3000 and practised—practised, practised, practised—in glorious peace and quiet.

The best birthday present ever.

THE POLE POSITION SHOOTOUT
ROME, ITALY (FRIDAY OF RACE WEEK)

Jason's black-and-yellow Ferrari F-3000 banked at almost right angles as it blasted in a wide arc around the Colosseum.

Then it executed a quick series of zig-zags through the streets of Rome, before it swung out into the open countryside, onto the final section of the Pole Position Shootout course—a fiendish stretch of track known as the Chute.

This winding S-shaped section of track was actually a long narrow trench dug into the earth, spanned by a multitude of sponsor-bridges.

The key feature of the Chute were the four barriers spaced out along its length. Built into each barrier was an ultra-narrow gateway—so narrow that a hover car could only pass through each opening *on its side*. That the gateways were positioned alternately on the far left and right sides of each barrier made it a brutal driving challenge.

It was hard enough racing through the Chute alone during the Pole Position Shootout—in the Italian Run itself, there were several Chute sections and you had to negotiate them *with other racers buzzing all around you.*

In any case, the Pole Position Shootout was a time trial—with the fastest driver through the Shootout Course starting Sunday's race in pole position—so racers entered the Shootout Course one at a time.

Each was allowed three runs over the Course, and their best time counted.

That Friday morning, one after the other, each racer entered the Shootout Course.

This was Jason's third run and as he hit the Chute he was flying like a rocket. His previous times that day hadn't been spectacular—but this run was *fast*.

The walls of the trench rushed by him at astronomical speed, bending left and right and then—*whoosh!*—he tilted his F-3000 sideways and shot through the first gateway.

Three more banking manoeuvres later, he shot through the final gateway to the roars of the crowd. His eyes flashed to the electronic scoreboard:

THE ITALIAN RUN POLE POSITION SHOOTOUT			
DRIVER	**NO.**	**TEAM**	**TIME**
1. ROMBA, A	1	*Lockheed-Martin*	0:50.005
2. FABIAN	17	*Renault*	0:50.230
3. LEWICKI, D	23	*USAF Racing*	0:51.015
4. CARVER, A	24	*USAF Racing*	0:51.420
5. HASSAN, R	2	*Lockheed-Martin*	0:51.995
6. MARTINEZ, C	44	*Boeing-Ford*	0:52.110
7. IDEKI, K	11	*Yamaha Racing*	0:52.525
8. TROUVEAU, E	40	*Renault*	0:52.740
9. XONORA, X	3	*Lockheed-Martin*	0:53.300
10. RIVIERA, P	12	*Lombardi Racing*	0:53.755
11. PETERS, B	05	*General Motors*	0:54.300
12. CHASER, J	55	*Lombardi Racing*	0:54.841

12th.

12th was good. Jason certainly hadn't expected to win pole. He was just hoping to put in a good performance—and come out of the Chute with his car in one piece. Hell, if he'd managed a place in the top ten, he'd have been over the moon.

But 12th out of a total of 28 starters made him pretty happy.

'Not bad,' Sally said. 'Not bad at all . . . for a first timer.'

She messed up Jason's hair. 'Nice racing, Superstar.'

That evening, even though he really didn't want to go, Jason was obliged to attend the official gala dinner for the Italian Run.

If the gala for the Sponsors' Tournament at the Race School had been opulent, then this dinner was in another league altogether.

It was held in the Piazza de Campidoglio—the famous triple-palace plaza designed by Michelangelo situated on the Capitoline Hill—and in the blazing glare of spotlights pointed up into the sky, the glittering piazza looked like something out of a fairy tale.

Hover limousines unloaded the cream of Europe's rich and famous—billionaires, movie stars, rock singers, and of course, racers. Gushing reporters breathlessly announced each new arrival on the red carpet.

For Jason, though, it was just another dinner.

'How long do we have to stay?' he asked Sally as they walked through the crush of black-tie-wearing guests, searching for their table, the Bug staying close behind them.

'Lombardi says we only have to stay until the speeches,' Sally said. 'Then we're free to leave.'

'Thank God. Any sign of Mr Syracuse? Is he still coming?'

Sally said, 'Last time I spoke with him, he was hoping to get here on Saturday. They had a race on at the School today—you know, the one Ariel had to go back for—and he had to stay for that.'

'Any idea who won—' Jason said as he slid past a tight cluster of people and abruptly bumped into someone he knew.

Xavier Xonora.

An awkward moment.

Jason, Sally and the Bug faced their rival, the Black Prince.

'Hello, Xavier,' Jason said.

'Chaser.'

'Thought you drove well in the Shootout today,' Jason said. 'Tough competition here. Where'd you end up? 9th?'

'That's correct. 9th. But then my goal *was* to finish in the top ten, so all in all, I'm pleased.'

At that moment, Xavier's father, King Francis of Monesi, came up behind Xavier. 'Excuse me, son. I have someone—' at which point the King saw Jason and his team and he cut himself off. 'Oh.'

'Hey there, your Highness,' Jason said good-naturedly. 'Good to see you again.'

The King seemed taken aback, as if he didn't expect Jason to be capable of speech, let alone friendly speech. 'It's, er, nice to see you again, too, Master Chaser. Xavier? I have someone I'd like you to meet. When you're finished talking with Master Chaser.' The King nodded to Jason. 'Have a . . . pleasant evening.'

When his father had gone, Xavier turned to Jason, ice in his glare. 'So. Chaser. Are your parents here? I hear there are some very good caravan parks on the outskirts of Rome.'

'You know, Xavier, you're a great racer. It's a shame you're such a scumbag.'

And with that, Jason went to his table.

Beside his meeting with Xavier, Jason had two other interesting encounters at the gala dinner.

The first came midway through the main course, when he went to the restroom.

As he washed his hands at the basin, a short weedy-looking Indian man came alongside him, also washing his hands. Without even looking at him, the man said, 'Ooh-ooh, my oh my. Look who it is. It's Jason Chaser, hover car racer. How are you feeling, Jason?'

Jason turned. 'Do I know you?'

The Indian fellow extended his hand. 'Ooh. Pardon me, pardon me. How rude of me. Gupta is my name. Ravi Narendra Gupta.'

'Again: do I know you?'

'No, but I know you, Jason.'

Jason said, 'Are you involved in one of the racing teams?'

Ravi Gupta smiled in a way that Jason immediately disliked. 'Ooh, sort of yes. Sort of no. I'm just a very *interested* observer of racing.'

Jason became guarded. 'You're not a reporter, are you?'

'Ooh, no. No-no-no! Certainly not! I promise you, young Jason, I am no reporter. Just an interested observer. For instance, I'm keen to know how you're finding top level racing. You seemed to manage the Shootout very well today.'

'I was pleased to finish mid-field.'

'How do you like the F-3000? Not too much grunt for you?'

'It's a good car.' Jason didn't understand why Gupta was asking him this.

Just then, Umberto Lombardi entered the men's room—and before Jason knew what had happened, Gupta had vanished, gone in an instant.

Lombardi saw the perplexed look on Jason's face. 'Something wrong, my young star?'

Jason looked about himself. The man was indeed nowhere to be seen. 'No . . . no . . . nothing's wrong.'

Jason's second interesting encounter of the evening occurred immediately after the speeches had ended.

Just as the applause for the President of Italy was dying down and Jason was preparing to leave the dinner and go home, an absolutely beautiful young girl suddenly sat down next to him.

'Hi!' she said. 'You're Jason Chaser, aren't you?'

'Er . . . uh . . . yeah,' Jason stammered, awestruck.

She was about his age, 15, with big blue eyes and dazzling blonde hair. She wore an expensive sky-blue cocktail dress that just shone with style. In short, she was the prettiest girl Jason had ever seen in his life.

'I'm Dido,' she said in an Italian–American accent. 'Dido Emanuele, and I'm a *huge* fan. I watched you on TV in that School tournament a few weeks ago and then I saw you in the Shootout today. You're *amazing*, and look at you, you're so young! Okay, that was dumb. Sorry, I don't mean to sound so pathetic, like some starstruck groupie. I just saw you sitting over here and decided I had to say hi. So . . . *hi!*'

Jason was speechless before her. 'Th . . . thanks.'

'Well,' Dido said. 'You look like you're getting ready to

go. I won't bother you any more. Maybe—hopefully—I'll see you round.'

And with that, she stood and flashed her big blue eyes at him and Jason melted.

Dido skipped happily away from the table. Jason just watched her go.

Sally McDuff broke the spell by clapping him on the shoulder. 'Nice work, Romeo. I didn't know you were such a sweet-talker with the ladies. Let's analyse your perform-ance during that conversation: "Er . . . uh . . . yeah," and "Th . . . thanks". Heads up, Champ, I'm sure you'll do better next time. Come on, let's go home and get you to bed. Tomorrow, we rest. Then on Sunday, we race.'

THE LOMBARDI GRAND HOTEL
VENICE II, ITALY (SATURDAY)

Saturday was a 'focus' day for Jason.

A time to sit and contemplate and focus on the big race ahead.

With the press camped outside his hotel, Jason stayed in his suite for most of the day, mainly staring out the window at the sea.

The Bug played headset car-racing computer games, his form of relaxation. Sally paced a lot, and read and re-read her Pro Circuit Pit Bay Rules and Regulations Manual.

In the afternoon, Henry and Martha Chaser arrived in Venice II. They would have come earlier in the week, but Henry had had to work on the farm. Now, they just hung out nearby—Henry marvelling at the suite ('Gosh, it's so big'), Martha knitting as usual.

Midway through the day, Jason's racing leathers arrived: a brand-new black flightsuit with yellow piping down the arms and legs and 'LOMBARDI RACING' splashed across the chest. Yellow gloves, black boots and a sleek yellow helmet completed the package. The Bug and Sally received similar outfits.

And then in the early evening, Jason made a fateful decision. Tired of room service, he went down to the hotel's executive dining room for some dinner.

The executive dining room was an exclusive restaurant reserved for those guests staying in the upper floors of the hotel.

As he sat down on his own, Jason saw Dido sitting at another table with two adults, presumably her parents.

'Dido . . . ?' he said.

'Jason!' Dido came over.

'I didn't know you were staying here.'

'Yeah, I am, well, thanks to my parents,' Dido said. 'They're, well, kinda rich. Listen, you look like you want to be alone, to prepare for the race, so I'll just leave you be—'

'No,' Jason blurted. 'It's okay. You don't have to go. I mean, if you . . . if you wanted and if . . . if it was okay with your folks . . . maybe you'd like to eat with me.'

A wonderful smile sprang across Dido's face. 'I'd like that. Let me go and ask.'

Moments later, Jason was seated by a huge bay window overlooking the Grand Canal, dining with the beautiful Dido Emanuele by the light of a lone candle—two teenagers looking like a pair of adults, dining in one of the most exclusive restaurants in the world.

They talked into the evening, and Jason loved every minute of it. Dido was smart, funny, captivating and *normal*. And better still, she seemed to like him, too! Before he knew it, the restaurant was empty and they were sitting there all alone and it was only when Sally McDuff appeared at his side that he came out of his trance-like state.

'Well, hey there, Superstar,' Sally said. 'We were all wondering where you'd got to. Thought you might have taken an introspective stroll or something. But then it got a bit late for that. It's almost midnight, you know.'

'It's *what*?' Jason looked at his watch. She was right. It was 11:55. 'Dido, I'm sorry. I have to go. I've got to get some sleep. Big day tomorrow.'

'Hey, no problem at all,' Dido said. 'I'm sorry for keeping you this long. I didn't even notice the time. Thank you for dinner.'

Jason nodded. 'No. Thank *you*. I really enjoyed it.'

He left with Sally.

Sally watched him as they walked, bemused. He looked like he was walking on air.

She shook her head. 'You know, that's what I like about you, Jason. You're a quick learner. Yesterday, you were a stammering idiot in front of that girl. Today you're as smooth as Casanova himself. Nice work, kiddo. Nice work. Now get some sleep. Tomorrow's going to be a big day.'

THE ITALIAN RUN:
ROME TO VENICE II
(with short cut)

Course
Pit Crew Route
Short cut

ITALY

Venice II

Sardinia

Rome

Sicily

Milan

Padua

Nice

Venice II

FINISH

Florence

Rome

Pescara

Sardinia

START

PITS

Bari

Sicily

THE ITALIAN RUN
ROME, ITALY (SUNDAY, RACE DAY)

'*Racers. This is your three-minute warning. Would all pit personnel please vacate the start area,*' intoned a stern voice over the public address system.

The starting area for the Italian Run was the Colosseum. Every racer started from the same spot, in the exact centre of the 2000-year-old Roman amphitheatre.

The pole sitter took off first, blasting out of the stadium, followed by the second-placed starter who, sitting on a car-sized conveyor belt, would be cranked out onto the starting grid, ready to go exactly twenty seconds later. Then would come the third car, and the fourth, and so on, all drawn out into the arena on the conveyor belt, a new racer starting every twenty seconds until all 28 had commenced the race.

In the dark stone conveyor-belt tunnel, Jason and the Bug stood a short distance away from their F-3000—now christened the *Argonaut II*—12th in line on the belt.

Jason's eyes scanned the preparation chamber.

'He's not coming,' he said.

Sally had a headset phone strapped to her head. 'He's not answering his phone either.'

There was no sign of Scott Syracuse. He hadn't arrived in Italy yesterday, nor had he left any messages for Jason and the team. No 'Good luck', no anything.

Having his parents here was one thing, but Jason had hoped Syracuse would come—if only to give him some professional words of support.

'*Racers. This is your one-minute warning. Pole sitter to the starting grid, please.*'

'Jason . . .' Sally pressed him towards the *Argonaut II*.

But Jason was still scanning the area for Syracuse.

The simple truth was, he was nervous as hell.

In fact, he'd never felt this nervous before in his life. His stomach was positively churning. He couldn't believe this: *he was about to race in a pro event.* You could watch pro races on TV every weekend, but until you were in one, you never knew what it was really like.

Then, finally, he turned to face his car—and glimpsed a flash of movement near the tailfin of the *Argonaut II*. For an instant, he could have sworn that he'd seen someone lurking there—someone small—a man he had met before.

Ravi Gupta.

Jason went to investigate, but found no-one near the *Argonaut II*'s tail. He scanned the tailfin itself but found nothing out of place or out of order.

And then—lo and behold—he saw Gupta, standing a short distance away, over with another driver.

Gupta caught him looking and waved back happily.

Jason eyed him carefully: 'Sally, do you know that guy? The guy waving at me.'

'Yeah, of course,' Sally's voice became a low growl. 'He's Ravi Gupta, and you don't want to get caught up with him. He's bad news.'

'What's he do?' Jason remembered the weird questions Gupta had asked him on Friday night: how he was coping with top-level racing; how he was finding the F-3000's extra power.

Sally said, 'You don't know who Ravi Gupta is? Sorry, kiddo, but sometimes I forget you're still so young. Ravi Gupta is a gambler. A bookmaker. Hell, one of the biggest bookmakers in the racing world. Now, come on,' Sally handed him his helmet. 'You got other things to worry about.'

'Right,' Jason took the helmet.

Then he and the Bug climbed into the two-man cockpit, strapped themselves in.

Once they were settled, Jason exhaled. 'Hoo-ah.'

The Bug said something in his earpiece.

'Yeah, me too,' Jason replied. 'Mine's churning like a tumble dryer.'

With a dramatic mechanical clanking, the giant conveyor belt rumbled to life and the super-sleek silver-and-black Lockheed-Martin of Alessandro Romba, the pole sitter and current world champion, was drawn out into the main arena of the Colosseum . . .

. . . and the 60,000-strong VIP crowd packed into the ancient amphitheatre roared as one.

Romba's car, *La Bomba*, came to a halt, now pointed like a missile towards the external archway of the Colosseum. The exit to the course proper.

'*Twenty seconds to race-start . . .*' came the voice. '*Would the second place-sitter please stand-by . . .*'

A 20-second digital countdown ticked downwards on a giant scoreboard, beeping with every second . . .

. . . the crowd leaned forward . . .

. . . *beep-beep-beep* . . .

. . . Jason watched Romba's car from the stone tunnel, his heart in his throat.

Sally patted his shoulder. 'Good luck, my boys. I'll be waiting for you at both pit stops.'

'Thanks, Sally. Have a good race.'

Beep-beep-beep . . .

Then the countdown hit zero and a shrill beep screamed and the lights went green and Alessandro Romba screamed off the starting grid, blasting out of the Colosseum and the Italian Run was underway.

As soon as Romba was out of the stadium, the conveyor-belt tunnel erupted with activity.

The great belt immediately rumbled into action once again.

'*Twenty seconds to next racer. Second-placed-racer to the grid . . .*'

The 20-second countdown restarted and the second-placed car—Fabian's purple-and-gold Renault—was drawn out of the prep tunnel and into the sunlight and Jason heard the roar of the crowd.

The conveyor-belt-line of racers shunted forward one place, all of them watching tensely as they awaited their turn to move out onto the starting grid and into the glare of the hysterical crowd.

The countdown hit zero and Fabian shot off the mark.

'*Twenty seconds to next racer. Third-placed racer, to the grid . . .*'

Jason watched each car shunt along the conveyor belt, take its place on the grid, and shoot out of sight—they looked like bullets being loaded into the chamber of a gun and then fired.

His nerves got tighter and tighter with every passing moment. Watching each car go was almost hypnotic—

shunt-shunt, *beep-beep*, blast-off; shunt-shunt, *beep-beep*, blast off . . .

And then, surprising him, the announcer said: '*Twenty seconds to next racer. Twelfth-placed racer, to the grid . . .*'

He'd become so preoccupied with the rhythm of each new car moving out onto the grid and blasting off that it surprised him when his turn came round.

And so Jason sat in the *Argonaut II* as it was drawn out of the tunnel and into the dazzling sunlight—

—where it entered another world.

The crowd packed into the ancient stadium howled and roared, clapped and screamed. They were absolutely *wild*. And these were the VIPs. Jason couldn't imagine what the ordinary race fans out on the course would be like.

The *Argonaut II* jolted to a halt on the starting grid.

Locked and loaded.

The arched exit tunnel leading out of the Colosseum yawned before Jason.

The Bug whispered something.

'You can say that again, little brother,' Jason replied. 'Hang on.'

The digital countdown hit zero, the lights went green and Jason floored it and his Ferrari F-3000 exploded out of the Colosseum and he began his first Grand Slam race.

Speed.

Supercharged, blinding speed.

Rome whistled past Jason's cockpit in a hyperfast blur of horizontal streaks—before abruptly he left the city in his wake and shot up the spine of Italy, knifing up the Autostrada, heading towards Florence.

The entire freeway was lined with spectactors three-hundred deep.

Ahead of him, he could make out the tailfins of the two cars that had started immediately before him. Twenty seconds wasn't much of a head-start and they were already duelling.

And then—*bam!*—Jason swung into the first Chute section of the course and suddenly he was right on the tails of the two racers ahead of him. They'd both had to slow at a gateway when neither would give way and now Jason was on their tails—trying to gauge whether or not he could overtake them before the next narrow aperture.

And that was the thing: multiple cars in a Chute was little more than a high-speed game of 'Chicken'—a who-dares-wins race to each aperture—all played out at a deadly 700 km/h.

Jason waited for his moment, for his chance to make his move when suddenly—*shoom!*—he was himself overtaken by the car that had started *behind* him, in 13th place.

The car—a member of the Boeing-Ford factory team—

had screamed by so close that it actually scratched a chunk of paint off Jason's right wingtip.

'Damn it! Never saw him!' Jason yelled.

'*Make a note, kiddo. We ain't in Kansas anymore,*' Sally's voice said in his earpiece.

And then suddenly, Jason was out of the Chute section and he beheld Florence ahead of him, its famous terracotta Dome rising above a low cityscape in the centre of a wide hazy valley. Every roof on every hill was covered with spectators.

Jason ripped down the Arno River, swooping under its famous bridges. As he swept under the Ponte Vecchio, Jason went left, around a bridge pylon, while the Boeing-Ford that had got him in the Chute went right, and as they came out on the other side, Jason was in front and the crowd on the bridge cheered.

The race shot northward, through Padua—coming tantalisingly close to the ultimate finish of the race, Venice II—and the monumental crowds there.

Giant hover grandstands, floating above the hills, pivoted in mid-air to watch the cars go by, before turning back around, ready to catch them when they would come through in about two hours' time, at the business end of the race.

Then it was into Milan—the cars banking round the great Sforza Castle, before heading into the most treacherous part of the race: the vertiginous cliff-edged roads and tunnels of the Alps.

As always happened in the Italian Run, the field bunched up on the tight twisting roads of the Alps—and here the top racers made their moves.

Showing exceptional skill, Xavier climbed two places, to 7th, whipping past Etienne Trouveau of the Renault team and Kamiko Ideki, the notoriously unpredictable Japanese driver for the Yamaha team, known to fans everywhere as 'Kamikaze' Ideki.

Back in 12th, Jason also moved up the field, first taking the Australian driver, Brock Peters, before sweeping past his own team-mate for the Lombardi team, Pablo Riviera, in a daring round-the-outside manoeuvre.

Up to 10th . . .

And then the first crash of the race occurred and it caused a sensation—because it was the 3rd-placed driver, Dwayne Lewicki of the US Air Force team, who'd bowed out. Lewicki had thundered at 450 km/h into the arched entryway of a tunnel as he'd tried to overtake the 2nd-placed Fabian.

Lewicki had tried to duck inside Fabian, but the Frenchman wasn't going to have any of it, and he'd held his line as he'd entered the tunnel, cutting across the bow of Lewicki's fighter-jet-shaped car—the razor-sharp blades of Fabian's nosewing *shearing the left wing of Lewicki's nosewing clean off*, causing Lewicki to lose control and slam into the archway.

Everyone moved up a place.

Romba was out in front.

Fabian, 2nd.

Xavier, 6th.

Jason: 9th.

In the top ten . . .

Down through the mountains, sweeping through Milan again, then into the third Chute section of the course between Milan and the French border, before making a tight hairpin at the glorious white-walled city of Nice.

And then the racers hit the coastline.

This was the most spectacular section of the course—with every single kilometre of the Italian coast teeming with crowds.

One after the other, the lead cars shot down the coastal straight, shooting through faux-Roman archways that rose up out of the sea a hundred or so metres out from the shore-line. The archways were in a staggered formation—forcing the racers to sweep down the coast in broad S-shaped swoops rather than in a continuous straight line, the whole section—like all the other 'ocean' sections of the course—flanked by red demagnetising lights.

As the ocean swept by under his nosewing, Jason saw on his dials that his mags were way down on magnetic power by now, severely worn by the tight traverse through the mountains and the three Chute sections.

But that was normal—they were coming up on the pit section at Fiumicino Airport outside Rome, and everyone would be pitting there.

The *Argonaut II* screamed down the coast at almost full speed, 810 km/h, ever-closing on the hover car in front of it: Car No.40, the *Vizir*, the second car of the Renault team, driven by Etienne Trouveau.

Jason saw Trouveau's tailfin, saw it wobble slightly after whipping through an archway, losing the 'line' needed to take the next Roman archway properly.

So Jason seized the opportunity, gunned the *Argonaut II* and—to the delight of the crowd—swept past the *Vizir* in a rare straight-line passing move.

He shot through the next archway—now in 8th posi-tion—and flying on adrenalin.

Moments later, he beheld the flashing yellow hover-lights indicating the entrance to the Fiumicino Pits.

He banked left, aiming for the pits, thrilled to be where he was . . .

. . . when disaster struck.

Etienne Trouveau, it seemed, hadn't appreciated Jason's cheeky passing manoeuvre.

As Jason had banked to enter the pits, the Frenchman had accelerated unexpectedly and in a shockingly rude manoeuvre, cut across Jason's nose—swiping it with his bladed Renault nosewing, slicing the right-hand wing of Jason's own nosewing clean off!

Jason watched in apoplectic horror as a piece of his car's nose fell away and tumbled into the sea like a skimming stone: a few bounces and a splash. At the same time, out of the corner of his eye, he saw Trouveau disappear into the pits to the left—

Then reality struck.

Hard.

810 km/h is not a speed at which you want to lose control.

The *Argonaut II* lost control. First it lurched left—then it pitched dramatically to the right—touching the demag ripple strips, causing the car's magnetic power levels to plummet—before Jason engaged his compressed-air thrusters to get them off the debilitating strips.

The *Argonaut II* shot clear off the track, out to the right, *out over* the ripple strips—missing the entry to the pits completely—setting off in a *wide* arc out over the ocean, its mag levels plummeting even further down into the red.

It banked away to the right, out over the sea, out towards

the far western horizon and Jason realised to his horror that after the collision, *he could only steer to the right.*

Then things got worse.

His car slowed. Dramatically.

Thanks to the ripple strip, its magneto drives were now almost dry. The *Argonaut II*—with a broken nosewing and almost zero power—was limping out over the open sea, only capable of turning right.

'*Jason!*' Sally's voice called in his ear. '*You okay?*'

'We're okay . . .' Jason said through clenched teeth. 'Just hacked off. And I can only turn right.'

'*What the hell was that? Is every French driver in this industry a scumbag?*'

'Just stand by, Sally. We're not out of this yet. We're gonna try and make it to the pits . . .'

'How?'

'If we can only turn right, then we'll do it by only turning right . . .'

The *Argonaut II* puttered around in a painfully slow, painfully wide circle, a circuit easily several kilometres in circumference. But a circle that would end at—

—the pit entry.

'*But you're going to have to come back over the demag strip,*' Sally said.

'Then I hope we have enough power to take the hit,' Jason said.

The *Argonaut II* limped around in its arc, at a pathetic 15 km/h—it was almost unnatural to see a hover car moving at such a slow pace.

'Bug,' Jason called, 'do some calculations. How long is this circle going to take us?'

The Bug did the math in his head in about three seconds. He told Jason the answer.

'Three minutes!' Jason exclaimed. '*Minutes!* Damn . . .' As Jason well knew, hover car races were won by seconds, not minutes. Once you went down by more than a minute, your race was run.

But still he flew on.

As he did so, the Bug kept an eye on the pits, on the other cars in the field that were whizzing into them at full speed.

The Bug counted them off: 15th . . . 20th . . . 25th . . . 26th.

He informed Jason.

The 26th car had entered the pits.

They were now officially coming last.

Three minutes later, they came full circle and Jason lined them up with the entrance to the Fiumicino Pits.

By this stage, every other car in the race had sped off into the distance at full speed, leaving Jason alone, foundering off the coast.

But his situation had provided the crowd camped on the rocky coastline with a special spectacle—they were enjoying watching him struggle and as such, were cheering him on, shouting chants, clapping in unison, willing the *Argonaut II* into the pits.

Jason eyed the demag lights directly ahead of him, blocking his way to the pits. The last hurdle.

He checked his mag level display:

MAG 1	2.2%	2.3%	MAG 2
MAG 3	4.1%	2.4%	MAG 4
MAG 5	2.2%	2.3%	MAG 6

Five of his six mags were on 2% power, one a little over 4%.

As he'd learned back at Race School, in Race 25, a standard run over a demag ripple strip robbed you of 3% of magnetic power.

'I only need one per cent to make it,' he said grimly.

But as he also knew, if the *Argonaut II* lingered for too long over the ripple strip, it would lose more magnetic power than that—*all* his power—and that meant dropping out of the sky and into the water . . .

'Hang on, Bug. Here we go.'

The *Argonaut II* banked round towards the pit entrance at 15 km/h, heading right for the line of red demag lights.

The crowd hushed.

Jason held his breath.

The *Argonaut II* crossed the demag strip.

Jason's instrument panel squealed in panic, and his mag levels instantly changed:

MAG 1	0.0%	0.0%	MAG 2
MAG 3	1.1%	0.0%	MAG 4
MAG 5	0.0%	0.0%	MAG 6

The display started flashing and blinking like a Christmas tree. Red warning lights blazed everywhere.

The *Argonaut II* cleared the ripple strip—and by the time it did so, five of its mags were dead.

But one remained.

With a bare 1.1% power left on it, bearing Jason's entire car all on its own.

The *Argonaut II* was still moving—by the skin of its teeth.

The crowd on the coastline roared with delight.

And so, creeping, crawling, hobbling like a wounded soldier leaving the field of battle, the *Argonaut II* entered the pits—

Clank!—Clunk!—Hiss-wapp!

The Lombardi Team Tarantula worked fast.

Old mags came off. New mags went on. Compressed air hoses attached. A brand-new nosewing was attached. Coolant fluid went in.

Every indicator on Jason's dash display sprang upward—refreshed, renewed, recharged.

Jason looked around the pit area.

It was largely empty—all of the other pit crews had left, heading for the second set of pits in Pescara on the other side of the country.

Jason searched the area, half hoping to see Scott Syracuse somewhere nearby, but it was to no avail. Syracuse hadn't come.

Then the Tarantula lifted clear of the *Argonaut II* and Sally smacked the back of Jason's helmet: 'Time to get back in this race! Go! Go! Go!'

Jason gunned everything he had and the *Argonaut II* blasted out of the pits, four whole minutes behind the pack, and headed back into the race.

Behind him, Sally immediately started loading up her stuff—she had to get to Pescara.

The main pack of racers rocketed down the toe of the boot that is Italy before shooting through the Straits of Messina and thus commencing the Figure-8 round the islands of Sicily and Sardinia.

The crowds gathered on the coastlines of both islands cheered loudly as the jet fighter-like cars shot past them at a cool 800 km/h.

But the loudest cheer of all came for the lonely last-placed car: the No.2 car for the Lombardi Team, driven by the kid from the Race School, shooting along at full speed despite the fact that it was a hopeless four minutes behind the others.

The crowds loved it.

This lone Ferrari F-3000 couldn't possibly win the race *and yet it was still trying*.

Thanks to countless headset cell-phones, word travelled along the coastline ahead of the *Argonaut II*, so that when it arrived at a new spot, a super-gigantic Mexican wave followed alongside it, the crowds urging it on.

The Lombardi Team hover-trailer carrying Sally McDuff across Italy shoomed down the freeway in a lane specifically reserved for race crews heading for the pit area in Pescara.

Neither Sally nor her driver saw the two black Ford hover cars cruising down the highway behind them, keeping pace with their trailer . . .

. . . watching them.

When the main pack shot through the Straits of Messina for the second time and rounded the toe of Italy, Alessandro Romba was in the lead, closely followed by Fabian and the second USAF car, with Xavier Xonora now having (impressively) moved up into 4th place.

Jason had closed to within two-and-a-half minutes of the main pack but with the race now three-quarters over, barring a miracle, he was just making up the numbers.

Then the main pack bent right, shooting down the heel of Italy's boot—none of them taking the bait and entering the famously difficult short cut.

Two-and-a-half minutes later, as the rest of them were rounding the base of the heel, Jason sighted Taranto, the town at the mouth of the short cut.

The Bug said something.

'As a matter of fact,' Jason replied, 'I *am* thinking about taking the short cut. Why? Why not? We're screwed as we are. Besides, you never know. We could get lucky.'

The Bug offered some more advice.

'Ouch, man,' Jason said. 'Don't hold back or anything.'

But the Bug wasn't finished.

'I know what Syracuse said,' Jason retorted. 'But he isn't here now, is he?'

'*I wouldn't say that* . . .' a voice said suddenly in Jason's earpiece.

It was the voice of Scott Syracuse.

Scott Syracuse sat in the back of the moving Lombardi Team trailer, alongside Sally McDuff, as it sped across Italy.

He had arrived in Rome only twenty minutes earlier, and had forced his way through the crowds, trying to get to the Fiumicino Pit Lane to meet Sally. But she'd left by the time he'd got there, so he'd chased her trailer down the highway in his black Ford and waved her down from the window of his speeding car.

As soon as he was on board the trailer, Sally had put him in radio contact with Jason.

'*Mr Syracuse!*' Jason's voice came in over the speakers. '*You came!*'

'I'm sorry I couldn't be here earlier, Jason,' Syracuse said, 'but there have been some problems at the Race School in your absence and I couldn't get away. But now that I'm here, I'm going to get you back in this race.'

'*How?*'

Syracuse focused his eyes on the horizon. 'When you hit Taranto, Jason, take the short cut. If I can, I'm going to guide you through it.'

As if the Italian crowds needed anything more to cheer about, they positively exploded when they saw the *Argonaut II* abruptly veer left and shoot towards the yawning Tunnel of Taranto, the wide concrete entry to the short cut.

The *Argonaut II*—last and alone and absolutely delighting the masses—blasted into the tunnel.

A misty concrete-walled labyrinth, illuminated only by the *Argonaut II*'s winglights.

Jason slowed, surveying the tunnel system. The first junction he came to contained *six* forks.

Syracuse's voice said calmly: '*First junction, take the ten o'clock fork.*'

Jason did it, banking left, heading down into the Earth.

The next junction also had six forks. And the next and the next.

But Syracuse's directions were precise. '*Take the two o'clock fork—straight ahead—ninety degree right-hand turn—*'

Down they went, deeper into the tunnel system, before suddenly the tunnel-junctions became even more complex: now they contained *eight* forks—with two extra tunnels shooting vertically upwards and downwards from the centre of each new fork.

'*Vertically down,*' Syracuse said when they came to the first eight-pronged junction.

'Down?' Jason queried. 'We're gonna hit the Earth's core soon.'

'*Yes. Down,*' Syracuse said firmly.

But then he directed them sideways once again and after a few more junctions their tunnels started to take an upwardly-sloping trajectory.

'*Now take the ten o'clock fork at the next junction,*' Syracuse said, '*And get ready . . .*'

'Get ready?' Jason asked. 'For what—'

He took the next fork as directed and—*bam*—his eyes were assaulted by blinding sunlight and the sight of the glittering Adriatic Sea, the blue cloudless sky, the seaside mansions of the city of Bari, and the rugged eastern coast of Italy stretching away from him to the north.

As the *Argonaut II* exploded out from the cliff-side exit tunnel to the short cut, pandemonium broke out among the spectators gathered on the headland all around it. Their collective roar of joy could be heard twenty kilometres away.

The Bug squealed with delight.

Jason swallowed in disbelief.

They'd made it!

They'd come out the other side of the short cut!

But before Jason could revel too much in his achievement—*shoom!-shoom!-shoom!*—he was overshot by three hover cars. The cars of:

Alessandro Romba.

Fabian.

And Angus Carver of the USAF Racing Team.

The fourth car to bank around him was Xavier Xonora's Lockheed, and in a fleeting instant, Jason glimpsed the Black Prince's sideways-turned face and his look of pure shock. Xavier obviously hadn't expected to see Jason again in this race.

Even more satisfying was the car Jason saw in his side mirrors—the purple-and-gold Renault of Etienne Trouveau, the nasty French racer who had almost put Jason out of the race. The *Argonaut II* had come out of the short cut *ahead* of Trouveau!

It took Jason a second to absorb it all.

He and the Bug had just made up three whole minutes on the rest of the field, and in doing so had gone from last to 5th.

'Thanks, Mr Syracuse!' he said into his radio. 'You just got us back in this race!'

As Sally's team trailer entered the outskirts of Pescara, every single giant-screen television in the town was showing replays of the *Argonaut II* blasting out from the short cut.

Every commentator on every TV and radio station was astonished at the *Argonaut*'s recovery. Last to 5th in one fell swoop. *Fifth!* They couldn't believe it. And with the second series of pit stops due in Pescara in about ten minutes, the race was now officially on.

But with that news, as if on cue, the second black Ford that had been following Sally's trailer across the country suddenly accelerated, pulling ahead of the Lombardi trailer.

And as the two vehicles zoomed underneath a freeway overpass the black Ford suddenly jack-knifed sideways, inexplicably cutting across the front of the Team Lombardi trailer, smashing into its front bumper, forcing it off the road and directly into a concrete pylon supporting the overpass.

With a terrible crunching sound, the Lombardi trailer smashed into the pylon, and crumpled like a giant concertina—while the black Ford simply drove off, darting into the distance, disappearing.

Everyone inside the trailer was thrown forward by the impact—the driver, Sally, Syracuse—but luckily they were all wearing seatbelts and the trailer was equipped with compressed-air safety blasters that acted like the airbags of old.

The exterior of the trailer, however, was completely ruined.

And as Sally unbuckled herself from her seat, she realised the situation: she was only two minutes' drive away from the pits. But on foot, that would take . . .

. . . about ten minutes.

Syracuse knew the score as well.

'Grab a handcart and load it up with mags,' he said. 'And start running.'

Ten minutes later, the leaders entered the Pescara pits. The hover cars roared into the pits in single file before branching off into their allotted pit bays.

Their pit crews were waiting.

Alessandro Romba led the way, followed by Fabian. Then the USAF pilot, Carver, Xavier Xonora and . . . Jason Chaser.

The *Argonaut II* swung into its pit bay . . .

. . . to find no-one there.

'Sally!' Jason yelled into his radio. 'Where are you!'

A second later, Jason saw Trouveau slide into his pit bay across the way. Trouveau glared at Jason as his pit machine went to work on his car. But when Trouveau realised that Jason had no pit crew around him, his fierce glare became an evil smile.

At that moment, Pablo Riviera's Ferrari shoomed into the adjoining Lombardi pit bay and his crew went to work. If they could have, they would have helped Jason, but they *were* Riviera's crew, so they had to service his car first.

'Where the hell is Sally!' Jason yelled. Every second he lost here felt like an hour—

'I'm coming!' Sally yelled, appearing from a nearby doorway at a run, pushing a hover handcart stacked with magneto drives and some coolant bottles. Her face and hair were drenched with sweat—she'd been running for some time. Behind her, also pushing a hover handcart, was Scott Syracuse.

Shoom. Romba shot out of the pits.

Sally and Syracuse came alongside the *Argonaut II*. Sally immediately started unloading magneto drives from her handcart, while Syracuse simply hit a button on his cart—causing the entire cart to mechanically unfold *and rise*, transforming itself into: a portable Tarantula pit machine. Sally clipped new mags to the Tarantula's waiting arms, while its other arms started demagging the *Argonaut II*.

Shoom. Fabian shot out of the pits.

To save time, Sally poured coolant fluid into the *Argonaut II*'s tanks by hand. Emptied one bottle. Chucked it. Emptied another. Chucked that one, too.

'Come *on!*' Jason urged.

God, he thought, *after all we've been through in this race, how can this be happening!*

Shoom. Shoom. Shoom.

Carver, Xavier and Trouveau all left the pits.

The Tarantula rose up and spread its arms wide—finished.

'Sally . . . !'

'Just . . . one . . . more . . . second . . .' Sally grimaced as she jammed some fresh compressed air cylinders into the *Argonaut II*'s rear-thruster nozzles.

Shoom. Riviera exited the pits.

Then Sally yanked her hands away.

'Clear!' she yelled. '*Go! Go! Go!*'

Jason punched it and the *Argonaut II* roared out of the pits—in 7th place—and entered the final stages of the Italian Run.

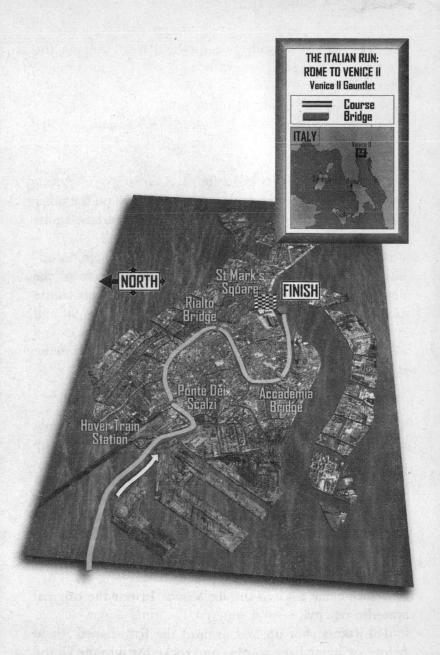

NORTH

St Mark's
Square

FINISH

Rialto
Bridge

Ponte Dei
Scalzi

Accademia
Bridge

Hover Train
Station

The stage was set for a killer finish.

The setting was spectacular: where the seas on the other side of Italy were dark and rough, here the Adriatic shone like a flat turquoise jewel.

And the finishing stages of the Italian Run were notoriously difficult: this would be no full-speed dash to the Finish Line. After they raced up the coast, the racers would face two fiendishly curved sections of track: the tight and twisting—and identical—Grand Canals of Venice and Venice II. The second of these two sections was so intense it had a name: the Venice II Gauntlet.

The field thundered up the coast, bending and banking, swooping left and right to take the archways, kicking up spectacular geyser trails behind them.

Romba was out in front, tussling with Fabian for the lead.

Then there was a gap to the next bunch of racers: Carver, Xavier, Trouveau and Riviera—with Jason hard on their heels.

Behind him, there was another cluster, led by Kamikaze Ideki in his Yamaha.

Venice came into view. Not Venice II, but the original waterborne city.

The racers shot up and around the fish-shaped island before swinging back south—and rocketing into the Grand

Canal from the north. The Grand Canal takes the shape of a wide, swooping reversed 'S' and is flanked on either side by high and historic buildings.

Into the city they went, low and fast, spraying geyser trails as they shot underneath the first of the three bridges that span the Grand Canal, the Ponte dei Scalzi.

Indeed, it was a geyser trail that allowed Jason to get up into 6th place—Etienne Trouveau had seen Pablo Riviera trying to overtake him, so Trouveau had lowered the *Vizir* slightly at the Ponte dei Scalzi and cut across Riviera's path, causing his geyser trail to spray all over Riviera's cockpit.

Blinded by the sudden spray, Riviera had flailed away to the left, out of control, under the bridge, and rocketed like a missile *straight at* an 18th-century church—

—where his Ferrari lurched to a sudden, springing halt, caught in the hover car equivalent of a gravel trap: a magnetic 'Dead Zone'. Naturally, all of Venice's buildings were protected by these negatively-charged dead zones—so that no piece of history could be destroyed by a crashing hover car.

And suddenly Jason—skimming along behind the two racers—was in 6th place and right on the hammer of Etienne Trouveau.

Both cars banked hard, almost at 90 degrees, as they navigated the swinging bends of the Grand Canal. Under the Rialto Bridge with its enclosed shops, then through the wooden Accademia Bridge—Jason flying within inches of Trouveau's tailfin.

And then they were back out over the open sea, flanked by pleasure liners and hover grandstands, shooting round toward the final sector of the race: Venice II and its Grand Canal.

★ ★ ★

The *Argonaut II* shot low over the Adriatic, the Renault of Etienne Trouveau right in front of it.

Venice II loomed on the horizon, its high replica of the great Bell Tower of St Mark's Square standing tall in the afternoon light.

'This is where we make our move,' Jason told the Bug.

Once again, they shot north, preparing for the swinging reverse turn into the Grand Canal.

Jason saw the yawning entrance to the Grand Canal off to his right: flanked by apartment buildings that looked just like those of Old Venice, only these were brand new.

Trouveau hit the Grand Canal on the fly.

Jason charged in after him.

Blurred city buildings rushed by him on either side.

And then Trouveau tried to do to Jason what he had done to Riviera—at the New Ponte dei Scalzi, he cut right, raising a curtain of spraying water across the *Argonaut*'s path.

But Jason's reactions were up to the challenge—he stayed right, and rather than slowing, he gunned his thrusters, rushing perilously close to the dead zone protecting the New Ponte dei Scalzi—and pressed between Trouveau's Renault and the bridge's swooping arch, he banked up on his side, going a full 90 degrees, and with barely an inch on either side . . .

. . . he rocketed out from under the bridge and shot past Trouveau's Renault—now in 5th place!

Trouveau swore. But not before Kamiko Ideki tried to seize the opportunity and swoop past him as well. But Trouveau wasn't going to allow that and he banged against the side of the Kamikaze's Yamaha, fighting him to the finish.

As for Jason, the black V-shaped tailfin of Xavier Xonora's 4th-placed Lockheed-Martin now loomed before him, banking right, taking the sweeping right-hander that led under the Rialto Bridge.

Jason did the math quickly: with only two turns to go, there just wasn't enough racetrack left to catch Xavier before the Finish Line.

Which meant, if he kept his head, he could finish 5th in his first Grand Slam race—not a bad effort at all. Just finishing was an achievement, but 5th was simply awesome. And beating that creep Trouveau would be even more satisfying . . .

Under the Rialto. The crowds roaring. Venice II rushing by him on either side.

Then banking left. The crowds going nuts. Shooting under the Accademia Bridge, after which Jason straightened and suddenly, gloriously . . .

. . . the end of the Grand Canal came into view, the point where it opened out into a wide harbour-like bay, flanked by the red-brick Bell Tower of St Mark's Square on the left and the giant dome of the Basilica di Santa Maria della Salute on the right. Only today, beyond the two colossal structures stood a massive alloy arch, hovering above the water of the bay, covered in chequered flags and a huge digital leaderboard . . .

The Finish Line.

Jason's eyes lit up.

The end was in sight. They'd done it.

It would be the last time he'd smile in a very long time.

For it was at that precise moment that a small explosive device attached to the tailfin of the *Argonaut II* went off.

It was about the size of a pinhead, hardly even noticeable to the naked eye.

An ultra-concentrated military explosive made of SDX-III epoxy. It was used by commando teams to blow open doors. One gram was enough to destroy the average reinforced door—more than enough to completely destroy the light-weight polycarbonate tailfin of a hover car.

It had been surreptitiously placed on the tail of the *Argonaut II* by a lightfingered hand in the last few moments before the Italian Run had begun.

The tailfin of the *Argonaut II* blasted outwards in a shower of tiny pieces.

Jason immediately lost all control—at 740 km/h—his Ferrari lurching downwards with shocking suddenness. He grappled with the steering wheel, but it did absolutely nothing in response.

He looked up and saw the Finish Line approaching and for a brief instant, thought they might make it over the line—

—but then the whole horizon rolled dramatically and abruptly they were travelling on their side, almost upside down—which meant ejecting was not possible—so that now all Jason saw was the surface of the Grand Canal rushing up toward his eyes.

'Bug! Hold on! This is going to be really bad!'

It was bad.

The *Argonaut II* slammed into the surface of the Grand Canal with a terrible splash.

It hit the water nose-first, then tumbled three times, sending debris shooting out in every direction, before—*whack!*—it smacked down on the surface of the Canal and lurched to a halt, floating *upside-down*: its underside pointing skyward, its cockpit underwater.

Every single person in Italy, whether they were at the track or watching at home, stood up and gasped.

The silent underwater world.

Holding his breath, Jason quickly unclasped his seatbelt. He spun, suspended in the water, and saw the Bug grappling with his own seatbelt.

Jason could see that the Bug needed help, but before he could help him, Jason needed more air himself.

He swam four feet upward and broke the surface—to see the high buildings of Venice II flanking the Canal all around him; to hear the crowd cheer briefly, glad to see him alive.

He made to take a deep breath when he saw them.

Saw Etienne Trouveau and Kamiko Ideki round the final turn together, emerging from under the Accademia Bridge, banging into each other, fighting to the end.

And in that instant, it happened.

Trouveau got ahead of Ideki and performed his signature move—he cut across Ideki's nosewing and sheared it off with his own bladed nosewing.

The Japanese racer's nosewing fell clear off, splashing down into the Canal, and Ideki—poorly, in a panic, desperate to finish the race—tried to avoid the safe landing that the nearest dead zone alongside the Grand Canal would have provided him.

Instead, he grappled with his steering wheel and straightened his Yamaha up—but he hadn't counted on how quickly he would lose altitude.

And he realised the truth of his situation too late.

His Yamaha was going to smash directly into the *Argonaut II*, helpless on the surface of the Grand Canal.

Ideki may have realised it too late, but Jason, still treading water, saw exactly what was going to happen.

The Kamikaze's Yamaha was going to slam into the *Argonaut II* . . . and the Bug was still trapped in it under the surface!

Jason gauged the distance and the Kamikaze's screaming speed: impact would come in about five seconds.

And so, with the out-of-control Yamaha zooming like a guided missile toward his upside-down hover car, Jason took a deep breath and went under to try and free the Bug in time.

Underwater again.

Frantically swimming in his flightsuit, Jason came to the Bug, and saw that his brother's seatbelt buckle had jammed. It wasn't coming free.

The Bug was in a fearful panic—tearing at his buckle, screaming underwater, yelling bubbles.

And in that instant, Jason saw the future.

This would take more than five seconds.

Kamiko Ideki's Yamaha shot through the air like a bullet.

A moment before it hit the *Argonaut II*, two blurring objects could be seen rocketing up into the sky above it— the ejection seats of Ideki and his navigator.

Then without slowing or stopping or even veering to the side, the Yamaha slammed into the stationary *Argonaut* at a shocking 700 km/h.

The impact of hover car on hover car shook the world.

And the ensuing flaming explosion filled the Grand Canal, expanding across its breadth in a billowing orange cloud.

Pieces of the *Argonaut II* rained down on the Canal for a full minute, creating a thousand tiny splashes.

A deathly hush descended upon the crowds gathered in the grandstands around the Finish Line. Sitting in his own VIP box, Umberto Lombardi could only stare at the hor-rific scene in disbelief.

The *Argonaut* was gone—blasted to nothing.

And with it: Jason Chaser and the Bug.

'Oh . . . my . . . Lord . . .' Lombardi breathed.

PART VI

THE DEATH OF JASON CHASER

THE FINAL STAGES OF THE ITALIAN RUN
VENICE II, ITALY

The explosion of Kamiko Ideki's Yamaha crashing at 700 km/h into Jason Chaser's stricken *Argonaut II* echoed across Italy—in every grandstand, in every home, on every television, on every digital radio.

For a full twenty seconds, not a single person in all of Italy spoke.

They just stared at the ghastly scene in horror.

Where once there had been two racing cars, now there was just a rising cloud of black smoke.

No-one could believe it.

Jason Chaser and his little brother, the Bug—the two young boys from the International Race School who had won the hearts of race fans with their determined never-say-die attitude; the kids who had turned the tables on Fabian during that wonderful exhibition race—were dead.

Killed in a spectacular blazing inferno.

Watching from a hover stand overlooking the Finish Line, Henry and Martha Chaser were in total shock.

They couldn't move, couldn't breathe, couldn't drag their eyes away from the tall wispy smoke-cloud on the water's surface—the smoke cloud that had once been their sons.

'Oh, no . . .' Martha gasped. 'Dear God, no!'

Henry just whispered: 'Come on, Jason, tell me you got out of there . . . Please tell me you got out of there . . .'

But nothing happened. Rescue vehicles took off from the shore, their siren-lights blazing.

They arrived at the smoke-cloud just as, without warning, two tiny figures burst up from beneath the surface of the harbour twenty metres away from the big black cloud.

Jason and the Bug!

Henry and Martha leapt to their feet.

The crowd—formerly silenced—now positively *roared* with delight.

The rescue vehicles cut a bee-line for the two boys, now bobbing on the surface. Every TV camera in the area zoomed in on them—but on this closer view, the scene took on a disturbing angle.

The Bug was waving frantically, but Jason wasn't moving at all.

Thirty seconds earlier:

The *Argonaut II* lies on the surface of the wide body of water at the end of the Grand Canal, a hundred metres short of the Finish Line. It lies upside-down. Jason surfaces, sees Kamiko Ideki's Yamaha heading straight for him. He holds his breath, goes under to save the Bug. Four seconds later, Ideki's Yamaha *slams* into the *Argonaut II*. Boom.

Seen from under the surface of the water, it is a different scene altogether.

Things are happening.

Jason sees that the Bug's seatbelt is jammed. It cannot be undone in time—certainly not in enough time for them to get away from the blast zone of the impending crash.

So inside four seconds, Jason does the only thing he can think of.

Straddling the Bug's upside-down seat, effectively sitting on his trapped brother's lap, he yanks on the ejection lever.

Shooooooooom!

A supercharged finger of bubbles lances down and away from the overturned *Argonaut II*—it is the Bug's seat ejecting not upward but *downward* into the blue-green world of the harbour, with both brothers sitting on it—a split-second before the *Argonaut II* is hit from above by the Kamikaze and explodes in a burst of roiling bubbles.

The water 'catches' the rocketing ejection seat on its downward flight, slows the boys about thirty metres below the surface.

The Bug is still screaming, blowing bubbles.

Jason has been gripping his seatbelt's clasp for the whole of their downward flight and suddenly—*snap!*—it comes free.

The Bug wriggles out from his seat—and sees that Jason isn't moving. He grabs Jason and kicks for the surface, powered by adrenalin, expelling air as he rises. He cannot know that his brother's lungs are filled with water—water that rushed into his open mouth as they plummeted down through the blue haze.

They hit the surface together and the Bug starts waving frantically, trying to get someone, anyone, to come and help his unconscious brother—the brother who risked his life to save his.

Jason dreamed.

As he did so, his mind raced with fleeting images:

Of himself being loaded onto a hovercopter—of shouting voices—someone pumping on his chest—flying over Venice II with the sun in his eyes, and then abruptly coughing, vomiting water, expelling it from his lungs . . . and then *breathing*, inhaling and exhaling, wonderful deep breaths of glorious air . . . and then falling fast asleep.

Voices in his dreams:

'He's going to be all right, Mr Chaser,' a man's voice said calmly. 'He's just sleeping now. You can go back to the hotel. We'll call you when he regains full consciousness.'

'I'm not going anywhere till my son wakes up,' Henry Chaser's voice replied.

At one point, Jason woke briefly, just long enough to see that he was in a bed and wearing pyjamas. The bed was in a hospital of some sort and it was the dead of night—moonlight streamed in through a nearby window.

And in that brief instant, he saw his father slouched in a chair under the window, sitting upright but asleep, his chin all bristly and unshaven, his clothes rumpled. They were the same clothes he'd been wearing on race day.

His father hadn't left his bedside.

Jason fell asleep again.

Then the nightmares came.

They all involved crashing a speeding hover car.

Hitting the entry pillars of a mountainside tunnel.

Slamming into a cliff-face near the Race School.

And worst of all—in the most often repeated nightmare—Jason would find himself rushing at the surface of the Grand Canal, his car out of control, his steering wheel completely unresponsive.

And as in all the other nightmares, a nanosecond before he hit the water, his eyes would dart open and he would find himself lying in his bed, breathless, drenched in sweat.

Then, one day, sunshine hit Jason's eyes and he awoke fully.

He opened his eyes to immediately see his father staring at him from his chair, smiling. 'Hey there, son.'

'Hi, Dad.' Jason's throat was dry. He blinked, sat up. 'How long have I been asleep?'

'Almost two days now,' Henry Chaser checked his watch.

'Two days . . .'

'All of Italy has been waiting to hear that you're okay. You're a hero, saving your brother like you did—while an out-of-control hover car was screaming right at you. I'm very proud of you, son. Very proud. You could have got away, but you didn't. You didn't leave your brother behind.'

And Henry hugged Jason. Hard. 'Good boy.'

★ ★ ★

Half an hour later, Martha Chaser and the Bug rushed into the hospital room, followed by Sally McDuff and Scott Syracuse.

Martha enveloped Jason in a bear-hug, as did the Bug, who whispered in his ear.

'No problem, buddy,' Jason replied. 'You wouldn't have left me.'

Sally said, 'All right, Hero. I tell you, when you lose, you really do lose in style. You like going out with a bang, don't you? Although, I have to say, reports of your death have been greatly exaggerated.'

She handed him a copy of *Il Corriere Della Sera*, the Italian daily newspaper, headlined 'THE DEATH OF JASON CHASER' and accompanied by a motion-photo of the *Argonaut II* being hit by Kamiko Ideki's Yamaha and exploding into flames.

Sally explained: 'Apparently, the *Corriere Della Sera* prepared two editions for today's paper—one with you alive, the other with you dead—and they accidentally printed 1,000 copies of the wrong edition. I think I'm going to get this framed.'

Jason stifled a laugh.

'How's Mr Lombardi taking it?' he asked.

'At first he was horrified that you might've died driving one of his cars. But then, when he was informed that you were okay—'

'WHERE IS HE!' a loud voice boomed from the corridor outside Jason's room.

Umberto Lombardi strode into the room, his eyes wide. 'Where is the young man *who destroyed my car!*'

Jason shrank into his pillow, not entirely sure if Lombardi was really angry or just faking it.

Lombardi stopped in front of him . . . and his angry face

relaxed into a wide mischievous grin. 'I just have to know, Young Signor Chaser, what does it feel like to *destroy* a 30-million-dollar Ferrari?'

'I'm sorry, Mr Lombardi.'

'Bah! Forget it. It's insured—and I love claiming big payouts from insurance companies! God knows I pay them enough in premiums! But you, you're *a hero*, boy! Which means you've made *me* a guy who *employs* heroes. I just hope you don't mind me basking in the reflected light of your magnificent glow!'

'You can bask all you want, sir. I'm still sorry about the car.'

'Don't even think about it,' Lombardi said kindly. 'Ferraris come and go, but young men like you'—he winked—'come once in a lifetime.'

But Jason couldn't stop thinking about it.

Nor could he rest.

As soon as he was able to, he asked for a video-disc copy of the final moments of the race and he watched his crash over and over again.

He saw his car overtake Trouveau's Renault—moving into 5th place—then saw it swing round the final left-hand turn, banking under the Accademia Bridge . . . before, without warning, its tailfin just exploded to nothing.

Then he watched in horror as the black-and-yellow Ferrari arced down into the water, where it tumbled and splashed and rolled, before it stopped abruptly, upside-down.

And then the Yamaha screamed into it.

Boom.

What the hell had happened to his tailfin? he thought. *What had caused it to explode?*

It was just too weird. And since there was nothing left of the *Argonaut II*, it was impossible to inspect the wreckage.

But Jason knew one thing: tailfins didn't just explode by themselves. Sure, a broken tailfin might get rammed and drop into the airpath of a car's own thrusters, but such instances were rare, and by all appearances, Jason's tailfin hadn't been damaged in any way.

It had just spontaneously exploded.

The truth was clear to Jason: someone had tampered with his car in order to put him out of the Italian Run.

And now, more than anything, he wanted to know who that had been.

At one point, as he was watching the video-disc for the thousandth time, his mother tapped lightly on the door.

'Hello, dear,' Martha Chaser said. 'There's someone here who was hoping to see you.'

Martha stepped aside—

—to reveal Dido, standing shyly in the corridor behind her.

Jason's face broke out in a wide grin. 'H . . . hi,' he said.

'I'll leave you two alone,' Martha said, leaving.

Dido entered Jason's hospital room tentatively. 'How're you feeling?'

Just at the sight of her, Jason felt a lot better.

As Jason regained his strength over the next two days, Scott Syracuse informed him of what had been happening back at the Race School in his absence.

When Jason had come to Italy, he'd been in fourth place on the Race School Championship Ladder. During the week of the Italian Run, he'd missed three races. But now, with his hospitalisation, he would miss at least one more.

The Ladder looked like this:

THE INTERNATIONAL RACE SCHOOL CHAMPIONSHIP LADDER AFTER 40 RACES			
DRIVER	NO.	CAR	POINTS
1. XONORA, X	1	*Speed Razor*	266
2. KRISHNA, V	31	*Calcutta-IV*	259
3. WASHINGTON, I	42	*Black Bullet*	247
4. BECKER, B	09	*Devil's Chariot*	240
5. PIPER, A	16	*Pied Piper*	235
6. SCHUMACHER, K	25	*Blue Lightning*	229
7. WONG, H	888	*Little Tokyo*	225
8. CHASER, J	55	*Argonaut*	217

Jason was stunned.

Just missing three races had seen him drop from 4th to 8th. Xavier, of course, was still coming first, he'd been so far ahead when he'd left.

And Jason was well aware that it was only the top four racers who got to participate in the New York Challenger Race at the end of the season.

Investigations would have to wait.

It was time to return to Race School.

Jason was packing his bags, getting ready to leave his hospital room, when a nurse arrived carrying an envelope.

'This just came for you.' She handed him the envelope.

Jason opened it, and frowned. It read:

SO? HOW ARE THOSE NIGHTMARES GOING?

RUN BACK TO THE PLAYPEN, LITTLE BOY.

REGARDS,

FABIAN.

THE INTERNATIONAL RACE SCHOOL
HOBART, TASMANIA

Jason returned to Race School to find that during his short absence, the world certainly hadn't stopped.

Lessons were still happening in classrooms; the pits rippled with practice sessions; cars darted every which way, shooming up the inland highways or whizzing around Storm Bay.

Since he was still barred from racing for a further two days, Jason was restricted to classroom work only.

At his first lunchtime back, Ariel Piper sat down beside him.

'Hey! Look who's back!' she exclaimed, clapping him on the shoulder. 'The only racer in the world crazy enough to eject *downward*! How're you feeling?'

'Better every day,' Jason said. 'Can't wait to get back out on the track.'

Ariel said, 'Hey, thanks again for letting me take on Fabian in that exhibition race. That was very cool of you.'

'I thought you deserved the chance to take him down.'

Ariel smiled. 'Jase. You can't imagine the impact that race has had on me . . . and on a lot of girls around the world. You should see the fan mail I've been receiving. Lot of chicks wanting to be racers. Lot of girls who were thrilled to see Fabian go down. It made an impact. Thanks for the opportunity.'

'No problem. I was happy just to get some peace and

quiet to practise,' Jason said. 'Looks like you've been racing well back here, too. What are you on the Ladder now? 5th?'

'Yuh-huh.' Ariel grinned. 'One win, one second, and one seventh. 23 points in three races. That race against Fabian gave me my *fire* back. My *desire*. I'm coming 5th now, and the Top 4 beckons. I wanna go to New York.'

Jason nodded, saw the fire in her eyes. The old Ariel was back.

'Good for you,' he said.

As he spoke, he looked around the lunch hall, and noticed that a few new friendships seemed to have formed in his absence: Horatio Wong was sitting at Barnaby Becker and Xavier Xonora's table. So was the young Mexican driver, Joaquin Cortez. At the moment, Xavier's mentor, Zoroastro, was talking to Wong and Cortez and the two lesser drivers were listening to him intently, occasionally nodding.

Ariel saw them, too. 'Yes, hmmm. Zoroastro and Barnaby Becker have been doing a lot of networking while you've been away. *A lot.* They had lunch with Wong and Cortez every day last week. I even saw Zoroastro having dinner with your buddy, Isaiah Washington, one night.'

'What do you think it means?' Jason asked.

Ariel was silent for a moment.

Then she said seriously: 'We're coming to the business end of the season. Everything is up for grabs. The Championship is on the line. Four places in the New York Challenger Race are there to be won. Races are gonna get harder, too—longer, more challenging, more demanding. And don't forget that the last ten races are run under pro rules—demag strips everywhere, dead zones, driver-over-the-line finishes.

'We're entering a whole new world of racing, Jason, and

I think Zoroastro and his boys are creating a few strategic alliances. I get the feeling Race School is about to get very, very serious.'

Ariel couldn't have been more right.

The next day, Jason sat in the stands with Sally and the Bug and watched Race 41. It was so frustrating, just watching, but fortunately this would be the last race they'd have to sit out. The doctors had given Jason the all-clear to race in Race 42.

Sitting with them was one other person: Dido.

It turned out that the last few weeks of the Race School season coincided with her school holidays in Europe, so (at her parents' expense) she had come to Tasmania to support Team *Argonaut*.

True to Ariel's prophecy, Race 41 was a fiercely contested race—Race School had acquired a new level of intensity.

It was also Xavier Xonora's first School race since his impressive fourth placing in the Italian Run.

He didn't disappoint.

He won Race 41 convincingly, prompting many to say that racing at the pro level had steeled him, made him an even better racer than he already was—if that were at all possible.

After the race was over, Sally and the Bug headed off to get some dinner, discreetly leaving Jason and Dido alone in the grandstand.

'So,' Dido said, 'you must be busting to get back out there.'

'Yeah, I guess so,' Jason said.

Dido turned, surprised. 'You're *not* busting to get out there?'

'You wanna know something funny,' Jason said. 'I've never been afraid of getting inside a hover car in my life . . . until now.'

Dido frowned, but didn't speak.

Jason looked away, biting his lip, as if he was deciding whether or not to reveal more.

He took the plunge.

'Everyone assumes that I'm fearless, Dido. That I'm not afraid of the high speeds, and that I just can't wait to get back out on the racetrack. But I'm not fearless. I never was. It's fear that creates adrenalin and it's adrenalin that makes me a good racer. But right now, I'm scared. Dead scared of getting back in the *Argonaut*.'

'What do you mean?'

'Every night I have nightmares, nightmares about my tailfin exploding or some other racer swiping it off during a race, causing me to lose control and crash. Now, I've crashed before, lots of times, but every time I crashed in the past, I knew why. But in Italy, I lost my tailfin for no reason that I can figure out. I lost control and I don't know why.

'I used to love the speed, love racing. But now . . . now I'm not so sure. I'm terrified of getting in that car again, and even more terrified that I'll fail and let my family and my team-mates down.' He turned to her. 'Dido, what happened in Italy changed me. I'm not sure I can be the racer I was before Italy.'

Dido looked at him closely.

Then she gently grabbed his hand. 'You know, my uncle once told me something about heroes: a hero is not a person who doesn't get afraid. No. A hero is a person who takes action *even when they are afraid*. Don't put too much pressure on yourself, Jason. Take it slowly; one step at a time. And know this. *I* think you can do it.'

And with that, she leaned forward quickly and kissed him on the cheek.

Then she dashed off, dancing down the stairs of the grandstand, leaving Jason delightfully stunned by her kiss.

On Lap 29 of Race 42, as they both shot down the southern coastline of Tasmania at full speed, Horatio Wong cut wildly—and inexplicably—across Jason's rear-end and smashed clean through his tailfin, blasting it into a thousand pieces and thus causing Jason to lose all control of the *Argonaut*, just like in the Italian Run.

It was loss-of-control at 795 km/h.

That Wong had been *a full lap behind Jason* at the time and completely out of the race made it worse. He should have just made way for the *Argonaut* to pass. Instead, he hit Jason square on the tailfin.

Wong flailed away to the left, but pulled up safely in a dead zone.

Jason, however, veered right and down, rushing toward the ocean waves, terrified.

He grappled with his steering wheel, but to no avail. He kicked his thrusters, trying to steer that way—and somehow managed to run the *Argonaut* over a full line of demag lights, thus diminishing its magnetic power.

The *Argonaut*'s power drained fast and it slowed and a quick burst from its left thruster caused it to fishtail to a skidding halt a bare foot above the waves.

Other cars boomed past it, shaking the air.

The Bug and Sally were shouting in Jason's earpiece—but all Jason could do was sit there and stare forward and swallow hard.

He looked at his hands.

They were shaking terribly.

When the *Argonaut* returned to the pits, towed by a recovery vehicle, Jason saw Scott Syracuse standing in front of Horatio Wong, letting him have it:

'—what the hell was that! Straight section of track and you suddenly lose control . . . and you take out his tailfin perfectly!'

'I just lost control, sir,' Wong shrugged, looking down. 'Lost my steering and never saw him there. I can't explain it.'

'You just lost control. Lost your steering. Never saw him.' Syracuse shook his head with disgust. 'I'm not so sure about any of that, Mr Wong. Get out of my sight.'

Wong stalked off, glaring darkly at Syracuse.

Sally came over to Jason, who was still badly shaken.

Jason said, 'What's going on?'

'Syracuse just went *ballistic* at Wong for hitting you,' Sally whispered.

'But it was an accident,' Jason said. 'At least, it looked like one.'

Sally said, 'Syracuse didn't think it was an accident at all. When it happened, he was standing next to me, watching on the monitor. He said it was a classic pro tactic: when a young racer is coming back from a bad accident and his self-confidence is shaky, you hit him in a similar way on his return race—and thus crack his fragile confidence. It's a

tactic designed for one purpose: to put a young racer out *for good.*'

'But Wong also put himself out of the race by doing it,' Jason said, perplexed.

'That's what hacked Syracuse off the most. Wong was the patsy, the junior guy who did the deed and took the fall— someone with pro experience told him to take you out. *That's* why Syracuse was chewing out Wong. He reckons Wong was doing someone else's dirty work.'

Jason looked over at the departing Wong, and thought about his new dining companions.

Sally put her arm around his shoulder. 'Confidence hits. Geez. Those sort of tricks aren't gonna be a problem with you now, are they? Jason Chaser, Superstar of the Sponsors' Tournament, Hero of Italy, little guy with nerves of pure steel. Like you'd ever have a confidence problem.'

Jason didn't reply.

He just hid his shaking hands.

Jason had two days till he had to race again.

And he was absolutely dreading it.

Whoever had told Wong to take out his tailfin had been smart. Very smart.

Because it had worked.

Going into Race 42, Jason's confidence *had* been wavering, not that he'd dare tell anybody in his team or family. And losing control in exactly the same way as he'd lost it in Italy had totally freaked him out.

He didn't want to tell the Bug or Sally that he was losing it. Didn't want them to think he was somehow a lesser driver. Nor did he want to confide in his parents: they got such a buzz out of his achievements, he didn't want to disappoint them by revealing his fears.

That was the bonus of having Dido around—she was sort of *external*, not a family member or a team-member. She didn't have any expectations. She just liked him for who he was.

They met each other for lunch the next day, at a coffee shop not far from the Race School.

Jason got there early, and was already sitting at a table when Dido arrived.

And then a strange thing happened.

Barnaby Becker walked into the shop at the exact same moment Dido did, and as he stepped up to the takeaway counter, he checked her out.

Jason was sitting close enough to hear every word of the ensuing conversation:

Barnaby said, 'Hey there, cutie. You're the chickie who's been hanging out with little Chaser, aren't you?'

'Yes, so?' Dido had replied.

'So. You ever want to go out with a real man, Becker's the name, give me a call.'

Dido had snuffed a laugh. 'That's a very nice offer, but I don't like *Neanderthals*. I like cultured and courageous young men. Men like Jason. Good-bye.'

And with that, she'd spun on her heel with the grace of a ballerina—leaving Barnaby speechless—spotted Jason, and waltzed over.

By the time she sat down, Jason was grinning from ear to ear.

RACE 43

Two days later, Jason was back in the driver's seat for Race 43. If he was going to finish the year in the Top 4, he needed to finish in the points today.

He ended up finishing 7th, garnering four points, having spent the greater part of the race staying well clear of all the other cars. It was a timid drive—and both the Bug and Sally noticed it.

That said, there was one hairy moment very early in the race: in the hurly-burly of the start, with all the cars jostling for position, Jason could have sworn that Joaquin Cortez had tried to ram his tailfin.

Jason had swerved wide, clipping some demag lights for his trouble, and the two cars had missed each other by centimetres.

Just racing? Jason thought. *Or was it something more?*

Or was he just getting paranoid?

Either way, he thought, he had to do something about this confidence thing.

The next race was on Tuesday. So he had three whole days to work out a solution.

He started on Sunday morning . . . at 5:30 a.m.

Before first light, he got up and, leaving the Bug fast asleep in his bunk, went down to Pit Lane and in the silence, pushed the *Argonaut* out of its garage.

He clamped some new mags on her, and attached a little hover-trailer to her rear hook. Then he jumped in, and blasted out of the pits, heading inland, up toward the forested northern end of the island.

And there he ran loops around a course of his own design, a tight winding track around the upper forests and islands of Tasmania.

At first he did his laps alone, just timing himself with the *Argonaut*'s digital stopwatch.

Later, he pulled eight mechanical objects from his hover-trailer—hover drones.

Bullet-shaped, superfast and extremely nimble, hover drones were training tools usually used to train very young hover car drivers, giving them a taste of other racers flying all around them, but without risking anyone's safety, since they were equipped with proximity sensors—meaning they couldn't actually collide with a car. For a racer at the Race School to be using them was like an Olympic swimmer using floaties to swim. They were only at the School for Open Days when young kids came to race around the School's tracks and get tips from the teachers.

Jason, however, reprogrammed his drones to race the

course with him in a hyper-aggressive manner, darting and swooping all around the *Argonaut* as it raced—giving him the sensation of closely-moving rival cars, *retraining* himself. That said, he still kept their anti-collision proximity sensors switched on.

At first, the drones whipped across his bow as they raced, cutting dangerously close—then they started zinging across his tailfin, missing it by millimetres.

And Jason drove . . . and drove . . . and drove.

Indeed, he was concentrating so intently that he never noticed the pair of people watching him through digital binoculars from a nearby hilltop.

Monday morning.

And he went up north again, and raced alone in the dewy green forests of Tasmania.

This time he disengaged the drones' anti-collision sensors, and at one point in his racing, one of the drones bounced hard against his tailfin, denting it, creating a loud bang, shocking Jason.

He immediately pulled to a halt.

He was hyperventilating.

'Don't do that!' he yelled aloud to himself. 'Start your car again, and get back up there.'

He keyed his power switch and flew back out onto his track. Immediately, the drones were swarming around him like a pack of killer bees.

Bang! He was hit on the side.

He clenched his teeth, kept driving.

Bang! Again. Other side.

Kept racing.

Bang! This time it was on the tailfin, and the *Argonaut*

lurched violently to the side, losing control . . .

. . . but Jason righted her . . .

. . . and regained control.

In his helmet, he breathed again.

And he smiled.

The two people watching him from the hilltop did not.

He was back at his apartment before eight. The Bug was still snoring.

Tuesday morning. Race Day for Race 44.

Again, Jason headed north before sun-up.

Only this time, when he reached his start point with his trailer full of drones, two people were already there, waiting for him, the same pair of people who had watched him practise by himself the previous two mornings.

Sally and the Bug.

'Hey there, Champ,' Sally said, illuminated by the wing-lights of the *Argonaut*. 'Shouldn't you be in bed?'

Jason froze. 'I . . . I just wanted to practise on my own . . .'

'On your own?' Sally frowned. 'Why?'

Jason winced. 'I just . . . I was . . . I mean—' he sighed. 'I've been a wreck ever since the Italian Run, Sally. That crash freaked me out. And then when Wong hit me in my first race back here, I just cracked. I've been coming up here trying to get my nerve back.'

'We know,' Sally said. 'We've been watching you. The first morning you came, the Bug heard you leave. He followed you, to see where you were going, and then he called me. Why didn't you ask us for help?'

Jason shook his head. 'I didn't want to let you guys down,' he said. 'I wanted to figure it out . . . and fix it . . . and I thought . . . I thought that was my responsibility.'

Tears began to form in his eyes. He bit his lip to hold them back.

Sally saw this, and she stepped forward.

'You know, I screwed up once, and some little punk gave me some good advice. He said, "We win as a team, and we lose as a team." He was right, Jason. We're all in this together. And whether we win or we lose, the members of Team *Argonaut* back each other up. You don't *ever* have to go it alone, Jason. If you've pissed me off in any way by doing this, it's sneaking off and coming up here all by yourself.'

'But I have to be the best . . .' Jason said.

'No, you don't,' a quiet voice said.

Jason started.

So did Sally.

Because it wasn't Sally who had spoken.

It had been the Bug, standing beside her. It was the first time Jason had ever heard him speak to two people at the same time.

'You don't have to be the best. You just have to *do* your best,' the Bug said quietly. 'If you do your best,' he shrugged, 'I'll follow you anywhere, Jason. I love you.'

'Me, too,' Sally affirmed, smiling. 'The follow-you-anywhere part, not the love-you part.'

And Jason laughed.

'Now then,' Sally clapped her hands. 'The whole world's against us, our backs are to the wall, and we need to win some races if we're gonna make the Top 4. But our fearless racer is a little nervy. The question is, what the hell are we gonna do about it?'

In the end, it was the Bug who came up with the answer.

RACE 44

Race 44 saw Jason lead from start to finish, the win earning him ten beautiful points on the Championship Ladder.

That was the Bug's plan.

Win the start—and lead all the way, thereby staying out of range of any would-be assassins—and thus winning the damn race. Simple. Then in the days between races, Team *Argonaut* would work together, helping recharge Jason's broken confidence.

It helped that Race 44 had been a Last-Man Drop-Off, meaning that lapped racers (like Horatio Wong in Race 41) hadn't been a problem.

It also helped that Xavier Xonora had sat out Race 44, choosing to rest, since he was so far out in front of the rest of the field on the Championship Ladder.

Every morning from that day on, Jason and his team could be found practising up in the far northern forests of Tasmania from sun-up to breakfast time. Then they would return to the Race School and commence their daily classes.

Word got around.

The locals and their families—business owners and workers on the School-owned island—many of whom lived up on the northern islands, would come out onto their balconies with their morning cups of coffee and watch the *Argonaut* get harried by its drones in the light of the rising sun.

Soon the local kids would come out and watch, cheering as the *Argonaut* clashed with its drones.

A series of tiny dents now pock-marked the *Argonaut*'s tailfin. It looked shabby, but as far as Jason was concerned, every dent was another brick in his wall of confidence.

He was rebuilding himself.

He was coming back.

He charged through Race 45 like a demon, coming third behind Xavier and Barnaby. Eight points.

More early-morning practice.

Race 46 was a gate race, and guided by a brilliant strategy from the Bug—a course that kept him well away from any assassins—he won, albeit in a tie with Xavier, the two of them ending the race on an equal amount of gate points. Ten Championship points.

More early-morning practice.

Then Race 47: win (over Barnaby and Washington in a race that employed the Port Arthur short cut—the Bug remembered the correct way through; Xavier didn't race).

Race 48: second (to Xavier; in this race, Ariel bowed out with another technical problem, a few of which had started to occur lately).

Race 49: third (behind Krishna and Barnaby; Xavier hadn't even tried to win the race; he'd just cruised over the line in 10th place, needing only the one point to claim an unassailable lead in the School Championship).

And so, with one race left in the Race School season,

Jason had charged up the Championship Ladder:

THE INTERNATIONAL RACE SCHOOL CHAMPIONSHIP LADDER AFTER 49 RACES			
DRIVER	**NO.**	**CAR**	**POINTS**
1. XONORA, X	1	*Speed Razor*	307
2. KRISHNA, V	31	*Calcutta-IV*	296
3. WASHINGTON, I	42	*Black Bullet*	278
4. BECKER, B	09	*Devil's Chariot*	276
5. CHASER, J	55	*Argonaut*	276
6. PIPER, A	16	*Pied Piper*	275
7. WONG, H	888	*Little Tokyo*	274
8. SCHUMACHER, K	25	*Blue Lightning*	273

Xavier was untouchable on 307 points, the Championship his.

Varishna Krishna, on 296 points, was also going to New York no matter what happened in Race 50.

But below them, it was a six-way tussle for the final two invitations to New York. Any one of the next six racers could—depending on the finishing order in Race 50—come in the Top 4.

Jason and Barnaby Becker were level on 276 points, equal 4th on the Ladder (and now one point ahead of Ariel, whose niggling technical problems in recent races had hurt her badly).

But they weren't *truly* equal—if Barnaby and Jason ended the season on equal points (for example, they both crashed in Race 50), Barnaby would beat Jason on a count-back, since he had come 2nd in Race 49 when Jason had come 3rd.

In the end, for Jason, there was only one option in Race 50: *he had to beat Barnaby Becker* and, if he finished low in the placings, he had to hope some other results went his way. But with Barnaby's new allies also out there on the track, just *finishing* Race 50 was going to be a tough prospect indeed.

To cap it all off, the final race of the year was the perfect kind of race to conclude the season.

Designed to test every hover car racing skill imaginable, it was to take place on the rarely-used Course 13—a super-difficult track that began by stretching southward, down over the Southern Ocean along a superlong straight, before it transformed into a twisting turning series of bends that weaved between the outer icebergs of Antarctica.

In that section of the course, racers could—if they were prepared to take the risk—opt to take one of three short cuts between the bergs, but every short cut ran between two bergs that clashed together (thanks to an underwater mechanism), giving them the name: 'the Clashing Bergs'. The standard course did not run through any clashing bergs, but it was longer. High risk, high reward.

After that, the course turned back north, returning to Tasmania, where the racers had to slow dramatically to negotiate the tight highways of the island, before reaching the Start-Finish Line in Hobart.

Each lap took about 14 minutes. And since Race 50 was a 51-lap enduro—that meant a 12-hour race.

But there was one more feature to Race 50 that made it an absolute killer: not only was it a test of endurance and skill, it was also a test of race positioning—Race 50 was a Last Man Drop-Off race.

Technically, it was classified as a '51-3-1 Super-Enduro Last Man Drop-Off' meaning: it would be fifty-one laps, and every three laps, the last-placed racer would be eliminated, until only four racers remained to fight out a six-lap sprint to the finish, a sprint that would involve one last pit stop.

Which made Jason's battle with Barnaby even more perilous: if Jason was eliminated at any time *before* Barnaby, Barnaby would be going to New York.

After all that, perhaps only one thing was clear.

Race 50 would be run on a knife-edge: it would be a dogfight of hardcore racing, under the ever-present threat of last-man elimination.

Race 50 made no allowance for mistakes.

It would be winner take all.

Jason woke with a start, gasping, sweating.

Another crash nightmare.

'What is wrong with me?' he whispered aloud.

He checked the digital clock beside his bed. It was 1:30 a.m. It was the middle of the night—the night before Race 50. Just what he needed.

He sat up, and decided that sleep would be impossible at least for a while.

He went for a walk, wandered down to a small enclosed garden overlooking the river, to gaze at the fountains there.

He sat down on a bench—and suddenly heard footsteps on gravel and voices in the darkness. He ducked behind a statue, listened.

He could make out two voices. One old and deep, the other younger, slimier.

Older voice: 'Good work. You've slowed her rise up the Championship Ladder.'

Younger voice: 'Only doing what I'm told.'

Older voice: 'But she *can* still finish in the Top 4. And this School does not want to see Ms Piper going to New York. It's been embarrassing enough having her study here for the year—and then that Chaser boy gave her a whole heap of publicity in Italy—but it would be beyond the pale if she ended up *representing* the School in New York. I need you to make sure she doesn't.'

Younger voice: 'After the Becker incident at the tournament, we can't deplete her magneto drives with microwaves anymore. Worms and viruses in her pit machine have worked recently, but she put in a new firewall two days ago and it's a good one. That said, I think I can find a newer virus that can bring her system down.'

Older voice: 'Make it happen.'

There was a crunching of gravel and the two speakers were gone.

Jason's eyes were wide with shock.

He recognised both voices.

The older voice had belonged to Jean-Pierre LeClerq.

And the younger one: Wernold Smythe, the nasty grease monkey from the School's Parts and Equipment Department.

Jason returned to bed.

Before the race tomorrow, he'd have to have a word with Ariel.

Dawn came on the day of Race 50.

It found Jason sitting on a clifftop with Dido, the two of them gazing out at the ocean sunrise. Despite his sleepless night, they'd arranged to meet and truth be told, Jason wanted to see Dido alone before the race—her presence gave him strength.

On the horizon, dark clouds framed the rising sun.

'So how are you feeling today?' Dido asked him.

'Better,' he said firmly. 'Stronger.'

His eyes were fixed forward. Game face.

'And your plan for Barnaby?'

'Solid,' he said. 'We've found a chink in his technique. The Bug's been analysing his racing manoeuvres on video-disc. Barnaby's weak on right-hand hairpins—that's where he gets sloppy; he goes too wide, so you can cut inside him. And this track is tight, lots of hairpins.'

Dido grabbed his hand. 'Good luck, Jason.'

'Thanks.'

Jason looked at the dark clouds on the horizon. 'It's going to rain today.'

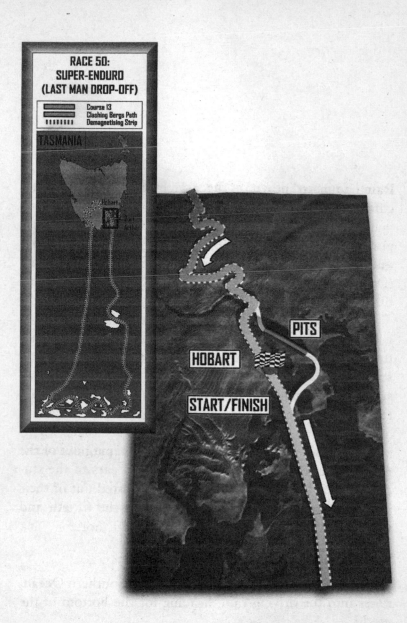

RACE 50:
SUPER-ENDURO
(LAST MAN DROP-OFF)

Course 13
Clashing Bergs Path
Demagnetising Strip

TASMANIA

Hobart

PITS

HOBART

START/FINISH

Rain hammered down on the straight in front of the start-gates.

Sheltered from the driving rain, nineteen hover cars sat poised in their gates, their magneto drives thrumming, pilots and navigators hunched in their cockpits, ready. (Due to mechanical and other issues, six students were sitting out the race.)

The Race School's starting gates were based on those used in old Roman chariot races: a wide arc-shaped structure fitted with thirty archways opened onto the wide straight. Each archway housed one car and at the starter's signal, steel grilles barring them would all spring open together, unleashing the racers.

Clang!

The grilles burst open and, like horses leaping out of the gates in the Melbourne Cup, the nineteen cars of the students of the International Race School blasted out of their archways, into the rain, and commenced the fiftieth and final race of the Race School season.

The field shoomed due south out over the Southern Ocean, noses into the driving rain, heading for the bottom of the world.

Barnaby Becker immediately took the lead—with Xavier slotting in close behind him.

This was unusual.

In previous races, Xavier had shown a clear advantage over Barnaby in straight-line speed, yet now he just settled in tight behind his stablemate . . . as if he were glad to be travelling at three-quarter pace.

Jason saw what was happening at once.

Xavier was riding shotgun for Barnaby.

He was *protecting* his stablemate.

Not needing any points for himself, Xavier was trying to ensure that Barnaby won the race—thus getting Barnaby into the Top 4, and ensuring that Jason didn't go to New York.

But no sooner had he realised this than Jason faced another, more immediate problem.

For it was at that moment—as they swept low over the rain-battered waves of the Southern Ocean—that some of the other racers started targeting the *Argonaut*.

Joaquin Cortez zeroed in on Jason from the right, aiming *straight for* his tailfin!

The blow would have knocked them both out of the race, but Cortez—not in contention for a place in the Top 4—didn't seem to care at all. Jason ducked under him, swooping low, avoiding the blow—

—at which moment Horatio Wong rammed him from the other side, banging into the *Argonaut*'s left wing, before zooming ahead of Jason. Unlike Cortez, Wong still had a chance of making the Top 4 and he wasn't going to jeopardise that just yet.

'*Jason!*' Sally's voice came in. '*What the hell is happening!*'

'Cortez just tried a kamikaze run, tried to knock us out of the race!' Jason called. 'Barnaby must have bought him!'

'*What are you going to do?*'

'There's only one thing we can do, outrun him.'

Jason gunned the accelerator as they hit the pair of icebergs halfway down the Southern Ocean straight—known as the Chicane—and leapt ahead of Cortez, now in 7th place behind Barnaby (1), Xavier (2), Varishna Krishna (3), Isaiah Washington (4), Ariel (5) and Wong (6); but with Joaquin Cortez nipping at his heels, trying to find an opportunity to take him out.

Then it was into the iceberg section.

If he could have, Jason would have gaped at the spectacle of the field of mammoth bergs, but there was no time for gawking now. He banked the *Argonaut* between the white monoliths, following the path of the demag lights.

At this early stage in the race, everyone took the standard route between the icebergs.

But as Jason well knew, as the race went on and things got desperate, that would change.

After three laps, the eliminations began.

At first, they were relatively unobtrusive. Minor racers crashed in the tight land-bound sections of the course, or racers succumbed to technical mishaps—thus eliminating themselves.

Barnaby continued to lead, with Xavier shadowing him in second place.

Then came Krishna, Washington, Ariel and Wong.

Followed by Jason and Cortez.

But then, as the number of racers diminished, things started to get desperate.

By Lap 35, Jason was still in 7th place—second last.

He was starting to worry.

The main thing he had to do in this race was beat Barnaby and at the moment, Barnaby was way out in 1st place, protected by Xavier, while Jason was still way back in 7th—with a total of eight racers still on the track and five of them between him and Barnaby.

Jason still had Horatio Wong directly in front of him in 6th and Joaquin Cortez behind him in 8th.

Cortez continued to harry Jason, especially in the iceberg section of the track—trying to axe through the *Argonaut*'s tailfin by taking the turns straighter than Jason—recklessly straighter.

In the end, it was Cortez's determination to nail Jason that was his undoing. At one point amid the icebergs, Jason took one turn a little too wide, offering Cortez a clear straight-line charge at his exposed tailfin. Cortez took the opportunity, not realising that it wasn't an opportunity—it was bait.

Because suddenly Jason banked the other way, leaving Cortez to smash hard into the side of an iceberg.

Ejection. Explosion.

Cortez's car was history and the Mexican racer and his navigator soon found themselves floating down to earth on hoverchutes, and as Jason completed Lap 36 several minutes later, Cortez was eliminated.

But now Jason was in last place—with Horatio Wong banking and bending in front of him.

Jason had three laps to overtake Wong.

Lap 37—no dice. Wong fended him off grimly, at times using dubious defensive tactics.

Lap 38—Jason flew the entire lap within a metre of Wong's tail, but no matter what he tried, he *still* couldn't take Wong.

Jason began to panic. He was running out of time and track.

He zoomed through Hobart again, and commenced Lap 39, knowing it could well be his last.

And as he rocketed down the long Southern Ocean straight, eyeing Wong's weaving tail-lights, he made the call.

'Bug,' he said. 'Either we get past this bastard on this lap or we're out! Out of the race, out of contention to go to New York, out of everything. I say we take him via the Clashing Bergs. Opinions?'

The Bug replied instantly . . . and firmly.

'I'll take that as a yes,' Jason said.

The leaders rushed into the iceberg section of the course, all taking the standard route, Wong among them.

But as Wong swept right, taking the regulation route, Jason abruptly cut left, slicing between some smaller icebergs before he beheld two clashing bergs.

They were absolutely gigantic.

The rough seas of the ocean and the underwater mechanism caused the two big icebergs to alternately slide apart and then clang back together like a pair of god-sized cymbals. The enormous bulk of the two bergs—each was easily 100 metres long—meant that a racer had to really floor it in order to get through.

Jason floored it.

The *Argonaut* screamed into the shadowy canyon between the two bergs, just as they reached their widest point.

Then the two bergs converged.

The *Argonaut* sped—

The canyon narrowed, its towering white walls closing—

The Bug screamed—

And Jason flipped the *Argonaut* onto its side as the canyon's walls became unbearably close and— *CRASH!*— the two icebergs came together with a deafening boom *just as* the tiny *Argonaut* blasted out from between them, house-sized chunks of ice raining down into the water behind it.

'*Hoo-ah!*' Jason yelled, blood pulsing through his veins as he swooped back onto the track proper . . . three car-lengths ahead of Wong!

In 6th place.

Wong's eyes went wide. He couldn't believe it—Jason was now in front of him!

'Okay . . .' Jason said, his eyes now laser-focused. 'Time to put you *out*, Horatio.'

And put him out, he did.

No matter what Wong threw at him, Jason fended him off, and as Lap 39 ended, it was Wong who found himself in 7th place, last place.

And out of the race.

So by Lap 40, the race order was this:

1st: Barnaby.

2nd: Xavier.

3rd: Krishna.

4th: Ariel.

5th: Isaiah Washington.

6th: Jason.

As one would expect of such an important race, it was super close—while he was in last place, Jason was still flying within sight of the leaders.

Then, at the end of Lap 41, everyone pitted.

Jason swung into the pits, to see all the other pit bays teeming with activity. In a race as long as this one, pit stops were longer, taking anywhere between 30 and 50 seconds.

As he arrived, he saw Barnaby shoom back out onto the track—closely followed by Krishna and Ariel, but not, surprisingly, Xavier Xonora. For some reason, Xavier was still in his pit bay.

Jason came to his own bay.

Sally immediately went to work, and outdid herself.

She performed a superb stop, so superb that Jason came out of his pit bay before Isaiah Washington did, leapfrogging him into 5th place.

He gunned the *Argonaut* out of its pit bay—

—only to slam on the brakes a moment later.

A car was blocking the exit tunnel that led back out to the track.

Xavier Xonora's *Speed Razor*.

It was just splayed across the tunnel, completely blocking the exit—as if it had stalled in the process of leaving its own pit bay. Xavier offered Jason a disingenuous shrug: 'Sorry. But it's not my fault.'

Seconds ticked by.

Jason fumed. 'The son-of-a-bitch is blocking us!' He couldn't believe it. Every second he was held up here by Xavier, Barnaby was racing away to victory.

And then Isaiah Washington appeared in Jason's rear-view mirrors, looming up behind the *Argonaut*, only Washington didn't appear to be slowing: at this rate, *he was going to ram Jason's tailfin—*

To evade him, Jason started edging around Xavier's car. But then, just as he was about to get round Xavier, surprise-surprise, Xavier got the *Speed Razor* started and darted off ahead of Jason.

Jason could only swear and chase after him, still in 5th place ahead of Washington, but now a *long* way behind Barnaby Becker.

Jason raced hard through the rain.

He was now second-last and so safe from immediate elimination, but directly in front of him was the tailfin of the all-black *Speed Razor*. And Jason had a feeling that

Xavier wasn't going to let him past lightly.

At the end of the next lap, Lap 42, Isaiah Washington bowed out.

Five racers left.

Nine laps remaining.

One elimination to go, before the six-lap dash to the Finish Line.

The race order was:

1st: Barnaby Becker.

2nd: Varishna Krishna.

3rd: Ariel Piper.

4th: Xavier.

5th: Jason.

And suddenly Jason was again in last place—only now his situation was especially dire: Barnaby was way out in front and the racer directly in front of him was Xavier, Barnaby's team-mate.

Thus they began Lap 43 and, with a gulp, Jason saw what he had to do: he had exactly three laps to get past the best racer at Race School—perhaps the best racer to have *ever* come to Race School—or else he'd be eliminated.

The *Speed Razor* and the *Argonaut*.

Going at it hammer and tong.

Jason threw everything he had at the Black Prince, but try as he might, he just couldn't get past the *Speed Razor*.

Xavier was simply too good.

He just wouldn't let Jason by.

On Lap 43, Jason even tried another daring dash through the first pair of Clashing Bergs—just as he had done with Wong—but to his total horror, Xavier outran him by going *around* on the standard route!

That's impossible! Jason thought. *If he can outrun me going around the Clashing Bergs, there's no way I can take him . . .*

For the rest of that lap, Xavier held him off easily, anticipating every one of Jason's overtaking manoeuvres through the tight land-bound section of the course.

Lap 44: still no luck. Xavier seemed to be enjoying this, blocking Jason, ruining his chances of beating Barnaby.

And then they hit Lap 45.

Jason's last chance.

The *Speed Razor* and the *Argonaut* shot down the Southern Ocean Straight, zig-zagged through the Chicane— and suddenly the Bug made a suggestion.

'*You've got to be kidding . . .*' Sally said over the radio.

The Bug said he wasn't kidding.

'*That's totally crazy, Bug! Even by your standards!*' Sally said. '*You'll be killed for sure!*'

But Jason liked the plan. 'Nice thinking, Bug. You always were a daredevil at heart. Hang on to your hat, little brother, because this is gonna get hairy . . .'

They came to the iceberg section—

And true to form, Xavier kept to the standard track—

While Jason took the Clashing Bergs track—

And, as before, Xavier beat them to the other side, even though he'd stayed on the regulation track. But Jason had gained a whole car-length on him.

Then they came to the second fork in the track—leading to the second set of Clashing Bergs—and again Xavier took the safe option, but not Jason.

To everyone's surprise, including Xavier's, he took the Clashing Bergs track *again*—

And this time, he came out the other end *alongside Xavier*—

They hit the third and last fork together . . . and *again* Jason took the Clashing Bergs option!

Xavier went the long way—

Jason shot through a quickly-narrowing chasm of two gargantuan icebergs—

—and blasted out the other end just as they clashed, only this time when he emerged, he came out exactly one car-length *ahead* of Xavier!

It had taken not one, not two, but three short cuts to do the impossible: they had overtaken Xavier!

Xavier charged, threw all he had at Jason, trying to retake him. But now that he was in front, Jason wasn't going to let go of his lead.

He and Xavier fought all the way around the track, but when they hit the Start-Finish Line seven minutes later, it was Jason in the lead.

The 15th and last elimination of the race would be Xavier Xonora.

Now there were only four racers left, and with six laps to go, they alone would fight it out to the finish.

But not before one last pit stop at the end of Lap 48.

Jason knew this pit stop would be his last chance to catch up to Barnaby—who by this time was almost 40 seconds ahead of him.

'Sally!' he called over the radio. 'This is your moment!'

'*I'll be waiting*,' came the reply.

Jason wound through the land-bound section of the course, until finally he beheld Hobart.

He swept into the city and dived into the pits—

—saw the usual buzz of activity, Mech Chiefs running every which way, pit machines rising and falling, electric lights everywhere blazing.

He saw the other three racers still in their pit bays, their Mech Chiefs working away already, halfway through their stops:

Barnaby.

Krishna.

Ariel.

And then, just as Jason swung the *Argonaut* into its pit bay, there came a loud dying whine from somewhere above him and all of a sudden . . .

. . . *every single electric light* in Pit Lane went out!

Pit machines froze in mid-air.

Computer monitors crashed to black.

Everyone looked about themselves in confusion.

Sally, now standing beside the *Argonaut*, swapped a look with Jason.

They didn't even need to say it out loud.

Power failure.

Manual pit stop.

Jason and the Bug were out of their seats in seconds, and by hand they attached six fresh magneto drives to the *Argonaut* while Sally added coolant and compressed-air cylinders, also by hand.

The other teams obviously hadn't practised manual stops much—if at all—and they just stood in their pit bays, confused.

Barnaby yelled at his Mech Chief, swearing, pointing, telling him to hurry up.

Krishna deduced that he had to help his Mech Chief, and so he leapt out of his car.

Ariel did the same—and while she may not have practised manual stops as well as Jason's team, of the other three racers, she did the best at it.

As he screwed on his mag drives with a cordless drill, Jason heard Ariel's Mech Chief yell to Ariel: '—can't explain it! Some kind of virus just hit us like a goddamn anvil! Ripped down our firewall! But it was so powerful, it spread into the wider system and brought down the entire Pit Lane power grid!'

In the end, the big winners from the unexpected power shutdown were Ariel and Jason.

Having entered the pits in 3rd place, Ariel shot back out onto the track in 1st place!

Krishna shot out next, in 2nd.

Barnaby was the biggest loser—perhaps because he hadn't got out of his car for the whole of the manual stop, choosing instead to simply abuse his Mech Chief. As such, he came out of the pits in 3rd place . . .

. . . a single car-length ahead of Jason Chaser.

Game on.

With two laps to go, Jason hammered on the heels of Barnaby Becker.

In a funny way, Jason felt confident now.

Xavier was out of the race, as were those racers like Cortez and Wong who had tried to take him out. And now he had Barnaby in his sights.

And he knew Barnaby's weakness—right-hand hairpins—and there were plenty of those coming up.

Through the Chicane . . . into the icebergs.

Jason lined up Barnaby.

Got himself into position behind him.

The best option was at the very end of the iceberg section, at a hairpin turn inside a tunnel carved into the last iceberg.

They weaved through the icebergs, Jason coming closer and closer to Barnaby—looming ominously.

Then they hit the last iceberg, and Jason made his move, ducked inside Barnaby, expecting him to take it wide, as usual . . .

. . . only Barnaby didn't do that at all.

Instead, he took the hairpin perfectly, and cut Jason off . . .

. . . and held his position!

Jason was shocked.

That wasn't supposed to happen! his mind screamed.

Barnaby never took hairpins like that—not even in the most recent race, Race 49.

He must've got lucky, Jason thought, and he prepared to take Barnaby at a right-hand hairpin up in the land-bound section of the track.

But again Barnaby confounded him—taking that hairpin perfectly as well, and thus fending Jason off again.

'How are you doing this, Barnaby!' Jason asked aloud. 'How do you know . . . ?'

He cut himself off.

At that moment, like a sledgehammer-blow, it hit him . . .

. . . and it broke his heart.

Dido.

Flashback:

Jason and Dido that morning, sitting on the clifftop watching the sun rise. And Jason telling Dido how he planned to beat Barnaby that day:

'We've found a chink in his technique. The Bug's been analysing his racing manoeuvres on video-disc. Barnaby's weak on right-hand hairpins—that's where he gets sloppy; he goes too wide, so you can cut inside him . . .'

Then another recollection struck Jason.

The time he had told Dido about his nightmares and his greatest fear: having his tailfin taken out. Then, the very next day, Horatio Wong had ruthlessly taken out his tailfin, almost killing him and the Bug.

His greatest fear at the time had come true.

And the event had all-but taken Jason over the edge, shattering his race confidence.

Oh, Dido . . . he thought. *You didn't . . .*

But the evidence was clear. Whenever he told Dido something, his enemies seemed to know it the following day.

Dido was in league with Barnaby and Xavier.

Jason's brain returned to Race 50.

The *Argonaut* screamed across the Start-Finish Line and started the last lap, Lap 51.

Ariel was leading.

Krishna was in 2nd place.

Then a gap.

Then Barnaby in 3rd.

And Jason in 4th.

Race 50 had essentially become two races: one between Ariel and Krishna for the win; and another between Barnaby and Jason for 3rd place.

But as far as Jason was concerned, Krishna and Ariel didn't matter—however they finished, it didn't affect him on the overall Ladder. All he had to do was beat Barnaby to get to New York: as things were, 3rd was as good as 1st in this race.

Down the Southern Ocean Straight, through the Chicane for the last time.

He was still all over Barnaby, probing for a way past.

Into the iceberg section.

Jason thought about taking the three Clashing Bergs routes again, but figured his luck there couldn't last. Better to hang onto Barnaby's tail—he could still take him.

But he couldn't pass him in the icebergs.

Barnaby held him out, sometimes just by flagrantly taking up all the track, blocking Jason's path.

Northward, back towards Tasmania.

Then into the land-bound section.

More hairpins, and belying his previous efforts, Barnaby took them all beautifully—but now Jason was charging, pushing Barnaby on every turn, the two cars almost side-by-side.

As Jason and Barnaby fought in the central region of Tasmania, ahead of them, Ariel Piper—having flown a near-perfect race—crossed the Finish Line five seconds ahead of Varishna Krishna, taking 1st place.

But Barnaby and Jason were still racing.

And with Ariel and Krishna coming 1st and 2nd, everything was still on the line for the two of them—whoever won this tussle would go to New York.

Screaming with speed, they came roaring over the magnificent Tasman Bridge, approaching the last corner of the race—a sharp *left*-hand hairpin underneath a freeway flyover—and Jason made a sudden inside move on the turn . . .

. . . and he got him!

As the Finish Line swept into view, the *Argonaut*'s nose inched in front of the nose of the *Devil's Chariot*.

'Noooo!' Barnaby yelled.

And then he did something totally unexpected.

Panicked and desperate, Barnaby rammed Jason hard—driving *both* of their cars across the nearest set of demag lights.

Jason fought with his steering wheel, but to no avail—he saw his mag levels deplete with shocking speed.

Luckily for him, the same thing was happening to Barnaby's car. It, too, was losing all its magnetic power.

At which point Jason saw where he was heading—straight for a big concrete pylon that supported the freeway bridge above them.

With a terrible shriek, the *Argonaut* glanced off the pylon and flipped up onto its side, ending three-quarters sideways, lying up against the next concrete pylon.

The *Devil's Chariot* performed a similar crash, but it finished right-side-up, resting on the roadway, pointing backwards.

Both cars just sat there, under the concrete overpass, smoking and still.

'You okay?' Jason yelled to the Bug, both of them hanging sideways in their seatbelts.

The Bug said he was.

Jason was all right, too, but the forward half of the *Argonaut* was now resting on its side up against the pylon, so Jason couldn't get out of the cockpit even if he tried.

'Bug! Pro rules! Driver over the Line. You've got to get to the Finish Line! Here!'

Jason removed the *Argonaut*'s steering wheel—fitted as it was with a transponder. Pro rules dictated that if a car couldn't cross the Line, a racer could still finish the race by having either himself or his navigator *carry* his transponder-equipped steering wheel over the Line.

Jason offered the steering wheel to the Bug. 'Run! *Run!*'

The Bug's eyes boggled for a moment, then he unbuckled his seatbelt and literally fell out of the cockpit, dropping clumsily to the ground. Then he stood up, took the steering wheel from Jason, and ran.

Down the highway.

As fast as his little legs could carry him, down the last 500 metres of the track.

The crowd gathered to watch the final race of the season had never seen anything like it.

There was the Bug, *running* down the finishing straight, his little legs pumping, his round bespectacled face pink with exertion, clutching a steering wheel in his right fist.

Trapped in the cockpit of the *Argonaut*, Jason could only watch him run.

'Go, Bug! Go!'

Vmmmmmm.

Just then, an ominous thrumming sound came to life beside Jason.

Jason turned—to see the battered and dented *Devil's Chariot* lift up off the asphalt and resume a hovering position. It seemed wounded, broken. But it was working.

Slowly, it pivoted in mid-air and Jason saw Barnaby at the controls, his face set in an evil grimace.

Jason snapped round—and saw the Bug still running down the road.

Barnaby hit the gas.

The Bug ran. Hard.

He was hardly built for speed: short legs, little pot belly, big glasses, helmet. Sweat had fogged up his glasses by now, but he kept on pounding the pavement anyway.

The crowd was now on its feet—but silent. Stunned into silence.

And then everyone saw it.

Saw Barnaby Becker's battered *Devil's Chariot* come lurching down the highway behind the Bug . . .

Chasing him to the end.

It wasn't trying to run him down. Far from it. It was trying to beat him to the Line. After all the racing, all the pit stops and overtaking manoeuvres, it had come down to this. One racer on foot, the other in the air, in his dented, broken car.

And as all could see, even at their wildly differing speeds, they would hit the Line almost together . . .

Then, a man's voice in the crowd yelled, 'Go Bug! *Go*!'

The voice of Henry Chaser.

And as they watched this bizarre contest, the rest of the crowd joined in.

'GO BUG! GO!

'*GO BUG! GO!*'

The Bug's little legs pumped up and down.

The *Devil's Chariot* gained speed.

Jason could only watch, helpless in his seat.

The Bug ran over the giant white letters painted on the road just before the Finish Line—'START-FINISH'—just as the *Devil's Chariot* roared up behind him, accelerating . . .

. . . coming closer and closer and closer . . .

. . . and the Bug saw the Line—the actual Finish Line, a thick white band stretching across the road in front of him—and as the roar of the *Devil's Chariot* filled his ears and rushed alongside him, he dived . . .

It would go down in Race School history as one of the most bizarre photo-finish photos ever.

It depicted the Bug, frozen in mid-air, *diving* over the Start-Finish Line, the *Argonaut*'s steering wheel held in front of him in his outstretched hands—while the *Devil's Chariot* hovered, also frozen, in the background of the photo, its body blurred with speed . . . and its nose a bare ten centimetres *short of* the Line.

Thanks to the Bug's little legs, Team *Argonaut* had beaten Barnaby Becker by less than a foot.

Afterwards, Henry Chaser would ask if he could have a copy of the photo and the School gave him one.

It now hangs in the Chaser family living room.

Pandemonium reigned in the pits after the consequences of Race 50 became apparent.

Jason leapt out of the recently towed-in *Argonaut* and threw his fists into the air. Sally caught him, also jumping for joy.

They knew the score.

The results of Race 50 had changed the Race School Championship Ladder dramatically.

It now looked like this:

THE INTERNATIONAL RACE SCHOOL CHAMPIONSHIP LADDER AFTER 50 RACES			
DRIVER	NO.	CAR	POINTS
1. XONORA, X	1	*Speed Razor*	313
2. KRISHNA, V	31	*Calcutta-IV*	305
3. PIPER, A	16	*Pied Piper*	285
4. CHASER, J	55	*Argonaut*	284
5. BECKER, B	09	*Devil's Chariot*	283
6. WASHINGTON, I	42	*Black Bullet*	283
7. WONG, H	888	*Little Tokyo*	278
8. SCHUMACHER, K	25	*Blue Lightning*	275

Suddenly the Top 4 looked very different.

Barnaby and Isaiah Washington had both dropped out of it completely, replaced by Ariel—who with her 10-point win had leapt up from 6th to 3rd—and Jason, who had gone from 5th to 4th with his 8 points for coming third.

Along with Xavier and Krishna, Jason and Ariel were going to New York.

Almost as pleasing to Jason was the result that Barnaby Becker and Isaiah Washington wouldn't be going anywhere.

But then something else happened—ripping Jason from his thoughts.

Dido ran into the pits.

She spotted Jason, smiled with joy, and hurried over to the *Argonaut*.

Dido threw her arms around Jason . . .

. . . but Jason didn't hug her back.

She noticed his lack of response immediately, and drew away. 'What's wrong, Jason? You did it. You made the Top 4. You won your ticket to the New York Challenger Race.'

At first, Jason didn't speak. Truth be told, he actually didn't know what to say. He'd never had someone so brazenly betray his trust before.

For a long moment, he just looked at Dido—scanned her eyes, her face, searching for something . . . anything. Something he could trust, something he could believe in.

But he found nothing there.

Both the Bug and Sally saw at once that something was very wrong—but they kept their distance.

'Jason? Are you okay?' Dido asked.

'I have something to tell you,' Jason said, 'something very personal . . .'

'Yes,' Dido said gently.

'. . . so I hope when you relay it to Xavier and Barnaby, you tell it to them word-for-word.'

The blood drained from Dido's face.

The Bug spun in disbelief. Sally McDuff turned, too.

Dido stammered, 'Jason . . . I . . . what are you say—'

'I know what you did, Dido,' Jason said. 'You were feeding them everything I told you. About my fears. About my strategies, like overtaking Barnaby on hairpins. Stuff I never told anyone else. You were probably also updating them about my health. I'm also now wondering about some of those late nights we had before important races—like in Italy. I'm wondering if you were *keeping* me out late.'

Dido fell silent.

By now Sally was staring daggers at her. The Bug's mouth was just open in shock.

Jason went on: 'Even that time in the coffee shop, when Barnaby hit on you and you blew him off, I bet that was a set-up, too.'

As if in reply, Dido bowed her head.

'So when you see them next time,' Jason said, 'tell them this from me . . . *Jason Chaser is back. Back to full strength.* Which means the next time we're all on the same track, they're going *down*. As for you, Dido, please leave.'

Dido clutched her face, then turned and ran away.

Steely-eyed, Jason could only watch her go.

In the immediate aftermath of Race 50, questions were asked about the catastrophic power failure that had occurred during the final pit stop on Lap 48.

Race Director Calder led the investigations . . .

. . . and quickly made some sensational findings.

Ariel's Mech Chief had been right: on Lap 48, Ariel's pit machine had indeed been hit by a super-powerful computer virus.

But only that morning, Ariel—tipped off by Jason before the race—had installed a new firewall on her system and it had repelled the sinister virus. Unfortunately, the virus then searched for a new host and it found it in the School's power grid.

And so, like a constricting python, the virus wrapped itself around the School's power system . . . and brought down the entire grid!

The source computer for the virus was soon found: Wernold Smythe's computer in the Parts and Equipment Department.

Smythe was confronted and he broke down in seconds, implicating no less than the Principal of the School, Jean-Pierre LeClerq, in a plot to damage Ariel Piper's chances at the Race School, a plot that went all the way back to her depleted mags in Race 1. And why?

Because she was a girl.

LeClerq protested his innocence, but the look on his face said it all. He'd done it, all right.

The School's Board held an emergency meeting that night and suspended LeClerq pending further investigation. In the meantime, Race Director Calder—a man of impeccable integrity—would be Acting Principal in his place.

Ariel and Jason just watched the drama unfold from afar.

'Thanks for the tip-off this morning,' Ariel said as they watched LeClerq skulk away from the Race School, get into his car and drive off in a huff.

'Anytime,' Jason said. 'Anytime.'

The following evening, the School held its annual end-of-year Presentation Dinner.

It was a formal affair, with parents, friends and some sponsors in attendance, and hosted by Acting Principal Calder.

Jason sat at a table with Team *Argonaut*, plus his parents and—for the first time that year—Sally's entire family, including her parents and all eight of her very proud rev-head brothers, newly arrived from Scotland.

As he sat down, Jason noticed Dido over at Xavier Xonora's table, sitting alongside Xavier.

'I asked around,' Sally whispered to Jason, seeing him looking at Dido. 'She's Xavier's cousin. But she's not royalty. Her mum is the Queen of Monesi's sister; lives in Italy.'

'We met in Italy,' Jason said. 'Just before the Italian Run. I thought it was luck, coincidence, fate. But it wasn't. It was a set-up, a big set-up, and I fell for it.'

Sally tousled his hair. 'Jason, if it makes you feel any better, if Xavier had sent a gorgeous young Italian hunk to flirt with me for our race secrets, I woulda told him everything, too.'

'Really?'

'Oh, sure,' she said, 'but not before I *snogged the living daylights* out of him!'

She roared with laughter, clapped Jason on the back. 'Now, shut up, eat, and enjoy yourself, you big superstar.'

★ ★ ★

After the main course had been served, the usual prizes were handed out.

It was virtually a clean sweep for the *Speed Razor*.

First-placed driver on the Championship Ladder: Xavier. For that he took home a huge trophy.

The Race School Medal for the year's best driver also went to Xavier.

The teachers' choice of Best Mech Chief was Xavier's crew chief, Oliver Koch—although his victory was narrow: he only beat Sally McDuff by two votes.

Jason didn't win a single prize.

But then he didn't actually mind that.

He'd had an incredible year at Race School, but for him, Race School wasn't about winning prizes, it was about scoring a contract with a pro team—and he'd already had one run with a pro team in Italy this year.

And if he—just maybe—won the New York Challenger Race, he might race again in a pro event: for the winner of the Challenger got an automatic 'exemption invitation' to participate in the Masters.

That said, there was one prize handed out that evening which Jason felt he had played some part in.

For one prize eluded Xavier's table—the prize for Teacher of the Year. It was a peculiar omission, as many would have credited Xavier's winning efforts to Zoroastro's superior instruction.

But then, not a few officials at the Race School still recalled Barnaby Becker's disgraceful acts during the Sponsors' Tournament—and they secretly thought Zoroastro had played a part in that.

Which was why the prize for Teacher of the Year went to Scott Syracuse.

Last of all, and rather fittingly, the night ended with the

four racers who would represent the Race School at the New York Challenger Race—Xavier, Krishna, Ariel and Jason—called to the stage to receive a standing ovation from their family and friends.

A week later, Jason found himself sitting once again on a grassy headland, watching the sun rising over the ocean. With him were Sally and the Bug, also gazing at the dawn.

Suddenly—*vroom!*—a police hovercopter roared by overhead, invading the view.

It flew away to the left, out toward the spectacular skyline of New York City.

Jason eyed the dense collection of towering skyscrapers, swooping suspension bridges and countless lights of Manhattan Island.

And his eyes narrowed.

PART VII

CHALLENGER

NEW YORK CITY, USA

New York City, glorious in the Fall.

Rust-coloured leaves littered Central Park. The Chrysler Building glittered like a diamond. The Brooklyn Bridge floated high on its new hover-pylons. And the Twin Pillars of Light—the pair of light-shafts that rose from the spot where the Twin Towers had once stood—soared into the sky.

And with the Fall, came the race teams.

Because in the Fall, for one week, the largest city in America was transformed into a series of the most incredible street circuits in racing.

Fifth Avenue became Race HQ, with the Start-Finish Line set up outside the main entrance to the Empire State Building. Super-steep multi-levelled hover stands lined the broad boulevard.

The pits were situated in Sixth Avenue, parallel to Fifth—racers reached them by branching off Fifth Avenue at the New York Public Library and running southward behind the Empire State Building.

Filling the air above the avenues and streets of New York City was a phenomenon peculiar to Masters Week: *confetti snow*.

It filled the concrete canyons of the city—a beautiful slow-falling rain of white paper. In celebration of their racing carnival, New Yorkers hurled tiny pieces of shredded paper out of their windows, creating a constant—and stunning—mist of white confetti that floated down into their streets. The roads themselves had to be cleaned each evening, since by the end of a given day they would be three inches deep in the stuff.

Today was Monday—a general preparation day.

Tuesday would see the running of the Challenger Race—widely regarded as a showpiece for the world's up-and-coming drivers.

Wednesday was Parade Day—when all of the 16 racers who had qualified for the Masters would travel down Fifth Avenue before the adoring crowds.

Then on Thursday, it would all start, one race per day over four sensational days, with the number of racers reduced by four every day. It was kind of like a Last Man Drop-Off, *but over the whole series of races*—after each race, the last four-placed racers on the leaderboard were eliminated—until only four racers took part in the fourth and final race.

On Thursday, **Race 1: The Liberty Supersprint**—a tight lap-race through the streets of New York, with a short section of track that whipped out and around the Statue of Liberty. It was here that the racers had to negotiate the sharpest turn in the racing world, a 9-G hairpin corner known as Liberty's Elbow. It was not unknown for racers to knock themselves out on this notorious bend.

Friday, **Race 2: The Manhattan Gate Race**—250 gates set amid the labyrinthine grid of New York streets.

Saturday, **Race 3: The Pursuit**—a collective pursuit race in which the drivers raced in circuits around Manhattan Island. Its main feature: bridge-mounted ion waterfalls—glorious but deadly curtains of ionised particles that fell from each of Manhattan's many bridges; the waterfalls nullified *all* magnetic power in any hover car that strayed through them. The final turn of every lap of this race was Liberty's Elbow; the Finish Line: the Brooklyn Bridge.

And then, on Sunday, came the final race of the series, **Race 4: The Quest.** The longest race of the Masters, it took racers away from Manhattan Island, up the rural highways of New York State and through the great underground water-caverns to Niagara Falls on the Canadian border. There, each racer had to grab their 'trophy'—an item they had sent there earlier in the morning—and then bring it back to New York City. The first racer across the line with their trophy won.

Jason loved it. Every year, he would sit at home and with his dad beside him, watch every minute of the Masters Series on TV over the course of the whole week.

He'd always dreamed of coming to New York to watch the Masters in person, but it was a long way and tickets were terribly expensive and his family had never been able to afford it. The closest he'd come to seeing it was staying with his cousins in New Jersey and watching some of the races from a distance.

But now, now he was here, in New York (albeit staying with those same cousins in New Jersey), racing in the Challenger Race—with an outside chance of participating in the Masters.

Hell, he thought, even if he bombed out of the Challenger, he'd hang around for the Masters festival just for the chance to watch it up close.

This, for Jason, was *fantastic*.

This was a dream come true.

THE CHALLENGER RACE (TUESDAY)
15 MINS TO RACE START

The start-gates stretched across Fifth Avenue. Like School races, the Challenger Race didn't have a pole position shootout. It gave everyone an equal start.

Cars entered their gates from behind, getting ready to race.

Jason eyed the other racers—the best from their respective leagues, regions and schools.

Markos Christos—from Greece, in his car, the *Arion*, numbered 12 in honour of the twelve labours of Hercules. Christos was the first-placed driver in the European Satellite League, a sub-division of the International Pro Circuit.

Edwardo—from the Central & South American Race School in Brazil. Like Xavier, he had won his School Championship, and from that, a pro contract with the low-level Castoldi Team. Since the CSA Race School wasn't as highly regarded as the International Race School, it had only been given two invitations to the Challenger Race.

Praveen Chandra, from the intense Indian Race School.

Zhang Lao, the third-placed driver from the Russo-Chinese League—a gun pilot from the Chinese Air Force. His fighter-shaped car, the *Chun-T'I*, was numbered 8, since the Chinese believe eight to be the luckiest number of all.

And, most fearsome of all, the two top-placed drivers from the Russo-Chinese League: the Russian twins, Igor and Vladimir Krotsky. In their sleek, identical Mig-90s, the *Red Devil I* and *Red Devil II*, Igor and Vlad had been responsible for no less than sixteen crashes in their League races, none of which had injured them, and one of which had been fatal. But then the Russo-Chinese League was known for its rough racing.

But the name on everyone's lips was Xavier Xonora.

He was the hot favourite to win with the bookmakers—his exceptional fourth placing in the Italian Run had made a huge impact. And word had spread of his dominance at the International Race School.

In total, there were 30 racers in the Challenger Race—talented young drivers from all over the globe, every single one of them knowing that victory here could change their lives.

Standing behind the line of start-gates, Jason was just stepping into the *Argonaut* when someone arrived at his car.

Xavier. Dressed in his black racesuit and holding his helmet.

And standing with him—just for psychological effect, Jason figured—was Dido.

'Just thought I would swing by and share with you an interesting statistic I've only just discovered, Mr Chaser,' Xavier said.

'And what's that?'

Xavier smiled meanly. 'Only on one occasion, when we've both raced, have you actually *won the race*. And that was way back in Race 25. And today, there's no prize for second place. Only the winner gets the exemption invitation

to the Masters Series. And based on the statistics, when we race, *I don't often come second.*' Xavier turned to go. 'Just thought you should know.'

'Thanks,' Jason said. 'I'll keep that in mind.'

In truth, Jason had been thinking a lot about Xavier.

He knew full well his head-to-head record against the Black Prince: with the exception of Races 25 and 50 (and Xavier's lazy effort in Race 49, which didn't count), whenever they'd raced, Xavier had beaten him.

The simple fact of the matter was that Jason just couldn't overtake Xavier.

It had only been an outrageous move in Race 50— whipping through all three sets of Clashing Bergs—that had got him past Xavier then.

And so, this past week, Jason and his team had been working on strategies to get by the *Speed Razor*.

They'd watched the video-discs of all the televised races Xavier had been in, both at Race School and outside it. They'd analysed his pit stops, and how his pit crew behaved during races.

And their conclusion: Xavier was the perfect racer. His defensive techniques were impenetrable; and his crew-work all-but flawless. Indeed, his Mech Chief, Oliver Koch, was so good, not only did he provide lightning-fast stops, he also kept Xavier appraised—on every lap—as to how far he was ahead of his rivals, and whether he was extending his lead, or whether they were gaining on him.

It was the total package.

'He's too good,' Sally had said as they'd sat in front of the television the night before, watching Xavier's finish in the Italian Run: the *Speed Razor* whipped across the Finish

Line, Xavier punching a fist into the air. 'I can't find a single chink in his armour.'

The Bug said something as well.

'*Nobody's* perfect, Bug,' Jason said, staring closely at the TV. 'Hey. Sally. Can you bring me the video-disc of the Sponsors' Tournament?'

Sally brought the disc, and they watched it. Watched Xavier cross the Finish Line ahead of his opponents, including Jason in the Final. Every time he crossed the line, Xavier did the same thing: he punched his fist into the air.

Sally shrugged. 'I think the pattern's pretty clear, Jason. Xavier races. Xavier wins.'

'Yes, it is,' Jason said quietly. Then abruptly his eyes lit up. 'Sally. Race 25. The race where I beat him. Is there any tape of that one?'

'No,' Sally said. 'It wasn't recorded.'

'But it *was* a photo finish. Do we have a copy of the photo?'

Sally shrugged. 'Sure. I have it here somewhere.' She grabbed her race file and pulled a photo from it, handed it to Jason.

Jason examined the photo closely.

And he smiled.

Both Sally and the Bug saw his lips curl upward.

'What have you found?' Sally asked.

Jason stared at the photo intently. 'Xavier's weakness.'

'And what exactly is that?'

Jason turned to face her. 'Xavier *thinks* he's a great racer.'

NEW YORK
CHALLENGER RACE:
SUPERSPRINT
Greater New York, USA
=== Course

NEW YORK

Yankee
Stadium

Queens

JFK
Int. Airport

Brooklyn

Yankee Stadium

Central Park →

PITS

START/FINISH
(Empire State Bldg)

Hudson River →

THE CHALLENGER RACE
LAP: 13 OF 30

The Challenger Race was run at a blistering pace—if you took a turn an inch too wide, you were overtaken by the car behind you. If you missed a turn by a few metres, *three* drivers would shoot past you.

You also had to take into account the constantly-falling rain of confetti in the city sections of the course—it made the air misty, cloudy, affecting visibility. The bullet-paced cars left spiralling snow-trails of the shredded paper in their wakes.

The Challenger course was a super-tight track that twisted and turned through Greater New York—from the home straight on Fifth Avenue, out to JFK International Airport via Brooklyn, and then back to Manhattan via Queens, the Bronx and Yankee Stadium. The intricacy of the course made it especially tough on magneto drives—each racer would require no less than five pit stops over thirty relatively short laps.

Right out of the gates, two drivers had zoomed out to the front.

Xavier and Jason.

Xavier had gone straight into the lead.

Jason had tucked in close behind him.

A larger chase pack of ten racers loomed behind them—with Ariel and Varishna Krishna embedded in it.

Then, on the third lap of the race, as the chase pack came roaring down the home straight, the nasty Russian twins, Igor and Vlad Krotsky, claimed their first victim: the Indian racer, Chandra.

The result was catastrophic.

In fact, it would go down as one of the most spectacular chain-reaction crashes in recent hover car racing history.

Chandra had been leading the chase pack, and the Krotskys, in an attempt to push past him, had squeezed Chandra from either side, one hitting him on the front left side, the other pushing on Chandra's rear right flank, forcing him into a sideways lateral skid.

The problem was, Chandra—intent on winning this vital race—didn't give in.

And he made his biggest mistake. He powered up . . . and flipped . . . turning his car fully sideways into the wind and as such, he lost speed instantly—

Bam!

Bam!

Bam!

The next three racers slammed into him at full speed.

Carnage.

Hover cars flew every which way across Fifth Avenue.

Chandra's car hit the ground hard, crumpled against the asphalt—then Zhang Lao careered straight into it.

Ejection. Explosion.

Varishna Krishna came next. Boxed in by two other racers, there was no way he could avoid the ugly pile of metal that was Chandra's and Lao's cars. He and his navigator ejected a nanosecond before the *Calcutta-IV* hit the pile and also became shrapnel.

The fourth and last car to hit the pile was Markos Christos's *Arion*. It banked to avoid the pile, but clipped it with its left wing, snapping the wing clean off—which caused the Greek racer to lose all control and shoom at right angles across Fifth Avenue and take out three more racers!

It was only the magnetic dead zone protecting the nearest building that stopped them all from smashing right through its windows.

The four cars hit the dead zone, stopped, then fell, dropping like shot birds down to the roadway.

The end result of this great conflagration was twofold.

First: the crash left two high piles of battered and crumpled hover cars on either side of Fifth Avenue, creating a kind of gateway between them, a gateway big enough for only one car to fit through at a time.

And second: it left Xavier Xonora and Jason Chaser well clear of the rest of the field.

The New York Challenger Race, winner take all, was now a two-horse race.

Xavier and Jason.

Out in front.

On their own.

Engaged in the race of their lives.

Left and right, they weaved through the city section of the track. Then blasting out through the streets of Brooklyn, before shooting up and down the runways at JFK, slowing dramatically at the ultra-sharp hairpins there.

And all the while, Xavier drove perfectly, never once giving Jason a chance to get past him.

Jason hung in there, only a few car lengths behind the *Speed Razor*.

On each lap, he actually *gained* on Xavier in the super-tight city section of the course just before the home straight—banking left and right in the confetti-filled canyons of New York City—but in the straight-line sections of the track, Xavier would power away from him, cancelling out the gains Jason had made.

The situation was all too familiar.

No matter what he tried, Jason just couldn't get past the Black Prince. He was half a second behind Xavier, but it might as well have been half an hour.

Lap 20 went by, and still Xavier remained in front.

Lap 25—and Jason was still on his tail.

He's just too good! Jason's mind screamed. *Too good! But that's also his weakness: he thinks he's too damned good.*

'Sally!' Jason called into his radio. 'Time to start the plan! You ready?'

'*You're absolutely crazy, Superstar,*' came the reply, '*which is why I love you so much. Let's dance.*'

Jason flew around the next lap—Lap 26—like a bullet, hanging onto Xavier's tail, but if anything, compared to his previous laps, it looked like Jason had actually lost ground to Xavier.

He had.

'*Okay!*' Sally called. '*You just lost a second to Xavier on that lap!*'

'One second is okay,' Jason said grimly. 'I hope Oliver Koch noticed.'

Lap 27—and Jason lost more ground to Xavier.

'*Another half second . . .*' Sally called. '*He's pulling away from you!*'

It was true. Xavier was pulling away from him—even the crowd could see it now.

But that was part of the plan. It could only work if Xavier *thought* he was pulling away from Jason.

And with only three laps remaining, the race looked over.

It was Xavier out in front.

Then Jason.

Then daylight, thanks to the big crash, followed by the Russians and Ariel Piper.

Lap 28—and Xavier was ahead of Jason by two full seconds.

★ ★ ★

In the pits, Sally looked over at Oliver Koch—the *Speed Razor*'s Mech Chief was looking at his race computer and speaking into his radio-mike.

'Oliver's taking the bait, Jason,' she reported.

'He *should be taking the bait,*' Jason said. '*It was this kind of attention to detail that won him Mech Chief of the Year. Now it's gonna lose him this race.*'

Lap 29—and the lead extended another 0.2 of a second.

Sally took a deep breath. 'I hope you're right about this, Jason,' she whispered.

And with that the last lap began.

At the start of the final lap, Xavier's lead over Jason was a full 2.2 seconds. Even if Jason hauled him in amid the city S-bends near the home straight, he'd only gain a second.

Xavier was out of reach.

But then a strange thing happened.

As soon as the last lap began, Jason started gaining on Xavier—just slowly, in a measured way, over the course of the entire lap.

They hit JFK and the lead was 2.0 seconds.

Up through Queens and it was 1.7 seconds.

Then over the East River and down through the Bronx and the lead was down to 1.5 seconds.

The Bug said something.

'I know! I know!' Jason said. 'If I'm right, this one's gonna go right down to the wire. That's what I'm banking on! The home straight *on the last lap* is the only place I can get him!'

Then the two cars swept around Yankee Stadium and headed south, into the confetti-filled canyons of the city for the last time.

★ ★ ★

And here Jason made his move.

As he'd done the entire race, he gained on Xavier amid the right-angled turns of the city.

The gap between them narrowed quickly now:

1.2 seconds . . .

1.1 seconds . . .

1.0 second . . .

As he banked and swerved through the buildings of the Upper West Side, Jason saw the *Speed Razor* through the veil of falling confetti—saw it getting nearer and nearer.

Hopefully Xavier was expecting this, having seen it the whole race.

And that was the key, Jason thought. This was all about what Xavier expected.

Then the two leaders shot across Central Park at the 79th St Transverse—and when they blasted out of Central Park on the Fifth Avenue side, the lead was half a second.

Now there were only about twenty seconds of racing left. They came down through the Upper East Side, through the confetti snow, Xavier taking turns perfectly— impossible to pass—Jason edging closer.

And then the final turn onto Fifth Avenue came into view.

'Here we go . . .' Jason said.

The *Speed Razor* and the *Argonaut* hit the left-hander almost together.

As they did so, Jason swung in low, lower than usual, diving through the confetti, looking like he was going to go under the *Speed Razor*.

But he wasn't going under it—he was just aiming for its blind spot, and with all the confetti floating around, Xavier's navigator was more blind than usual.

The two cars hit the straight.

And then Xavier did it.

Just as Jason had hoped.

Three hundred metres short of the Finish Line, he punched his fist into the air in triumph.

Just as he had done in each of his victories at the Sponsors' Tournament.

And at the Italian Run.

And whenever he'd won a race at Race School.

Xavier, as Jason had noticed during their study sessions, had a habit of celebrating prematurely.

As so, at that moment, Jason jammed every thruster forward.

It made for an astonishing sight.

Xavier in the *Speed Razor*, roaring down Fifth Avenue to the cheers of the crowds, blasting through the confetti rain, with his fist thrown into the air in triumph . . .

. . . before suddenly, there was the *Argonaut*, zipping alongside him from out of nowhere!

And as the two cars came to the crumpled piles of broken cars on either side of the home straight, Jason darted ahead of Xavier and whip-weaved quickly in front of him!

The crowd gasped at the audacity of it.

Xavier's eyes boggled.

And the *Argonaut* roared through the narrow gap between the two piles of smashed-up hover cars and shot like a rocket across the Finish Line.

In.

First.

Place.

It was the photo that had done it.

The photo from Jason's only victory over Xavier Xonora—his photo-finish win in Race 25.

Gazing closely at the photo the evening before the Challenger Race, Jason had seen something very peculiar in it.

Whereas before he had only ever seen the nose of the *Argonaut* sneaking across the Finish Line inches ahead of the *Speed Razor*, on this occasion, he had seen something else entirely.

There in the photo, frozen forever in that moment in time, Jason had seen Xavier's fist punching the air.

Xavier, thinking he had won when in fact he had not, had prematurely pumped his fist into the sky.

And so Jason had formulated his plan—he would use Xavier's perfect pit crew against him, allow them to feed Xavier information about his increasing lead, *and then on the last lap Jason would pounce*. He would gain on Xavier over the course of the final lap and then overtake him *on the home straight*, the one place Xavier dropped his guard, the one place on a race course where he was vulnerable.

The New York crowds roared with both delight and disbelief at such a daring strategy.

Jason had caught everyone by surprise.

By the time he swung into the pits, every television crew in the city was camped outside his pit bay.

After a well-earned team hug with Sally and the Bug behind the closed doors of their garage, he came out to face the media.

'Jason! Jason! Did you plan it from the start?'

'Jason! How did you know Xavier would make such a rookie mistake?'

'Jason! How does it feel to know that you just qualified for the New York Masters?'

It was the last question that caught Jason short.

'It feels . . . great,' he said. 'Only I . . . I don't have a licensed team to sponsor me. And without a team, I can't race.'

'You can race under my name anytime, my young friend!' a familiar voice boomed from somewhere nearby.

Umberto Lombardi stood behind the assembled media throng, grinning from ear to ear.

He spread his arms wide. 'I used to have a second car, but some young driver destroyed it in Italy earlier this year! If you're prepared to race in your own car, young Jason, you can race under my licence in the Masters Series!'

The media swung their microphones to Jason.

But just as Jason was about to answer, another voice rose above the throng.

'I have another suggestion,' the voice said.

Everyone turned—

—to see a very well-dressed man in a suit standing beside Lombardi. He was younger than Lombardi, mid-40s, American, with perfectly groomed hair, and he wore a suit that screamed money.

He was one of the most well-known figures in racing.

He was Antony Nelson, head of the Lockheed-Martin Factory Team.

'For I *do* have a spare car,' Nelson said imperiously. 'My team was ready to run a third car in the Masters, but sadly, our first-choice racer'—he glanced across at Xavier's pit bay—'didn't make the grade in the Challenger. You did, Mr Chaser. As such, the Lockheed-Martin Racing Team would be honoured if you would race for us in the New York Masters Series.'

The offer hung in the air.

The media people froze, their eyes locked on Jason.

Alone on the stage, Jason gazed out over the crowd of reporters and photographers—saw their eager hungry faces, hungry for the story.

Then he looked at Nelson and Lombardi—and found a study in contrasts. One small and slick, the other broad and loud. One had a top-tier car waiting for him, the other had nothing but an International Racing Federation Licence.

And one had eaten greasy chicken burgers with Jason . . . and the other, quite obviously, hadn't eaten a chicken burger in years.

Jason took a deep breath.

'I think I'll race with Team Lombardi.'

The media scrum erupted—with shouted questions and flash photos, but Jason was done.

He just stepped back into his pit bay, ignoring them, ending the press conference. He looked at his team: the diminutive Bug, the smiling Sally McDuff, and the serious Scott Syracuse.

'Well, people,' he said. 'I don't think I believe it yet myself. But in two days' time, we're gonna be racing in the New York Masters.'

★ ★ ★

Thirty minutes later, the media throng had departed, having got their story, and Jason found himself standing in his pit bay, alone, tidying up after the race.

Across the way from him, he saw Xavier, also alone, also packing up his gear.

For some reason that he didn't understand, Jason went over to him.

'Good race today, Xavier,' he said.

Xavier didn't even acknowledge Jason's presence, just kept packing.

'Okay, then . . .' Jason turned to go.

'By any reckoning, I'm a better racer than you are,' Xavier's voice said from behind him.

Jason turned back.

Xavier was glaring at him now, his eyes icy. 'All year it's been apparent. My speed tolerances are better. My cornering. My passing. My crew. In every facet of racing, *I am better than you are*. Which is why I cannot understand how on earth you beat me today. I should be racing in the Masters.'

Jason just stared back at him, held his ground.

'You know why I beat you today, Xavier?'

'Why?'

'Because of everything you just said. You *are* better than me. You have heaps more natural talent than I do. *But I work harder than you do.* That's why I won. And that's why you've been scared of me all year—that's why you sent Dido to distract me, that's why you sent her to get information on me. And that's why, Prince Xavier, if we ever meet again on a racetrack, *I'll beat you there too.* Have a nice life.'

And with that, Jason turned his back on Xavier and walked away.

NEW YORK CITY, USA (WEDNESDAY)
PARADE DAY

The floats worked their way down Fifth Avenue, bearing on their backs the sixteen racers who would compete in the Masters.

All of New York had come out to see them. The streets of the city were lined with over 10 million people, waving and throwing streamers. Ticker-tape fell from the upper heights of the skyscrapers, mingling with the ever-present confetti snow.

Jason, Sally and the Bug stood atop a gigantic papier-mâché float—built in the shape and colours of the *Argonaut*—waving to the cheering crowds.

On the other floats, Jason saw some familiar faces.

Alessandro Romba.

La Bomba Romba. The current world champion and, this year, the winner in Sydney, London and Italy: if he won the Masters this week, he'd become the first racer ever to win the Golden Grand Slam, all four Grand Slam races in a single calendar year.

And on another float: Fabian.

The nasty Frenchman whom Jason had humiliated in the exhibition race in Italy.

Etienne Trouveau—Fabian's equally villainous team-mate—the man who had taken out Jason's tailfin so ruthlessly in Italy.

And the two US Air Force pilot-racers, Angus Carver and Dwayne Lewicki—the crowd gave them a huge cheer.

At one point during the parade, Jason made eye-contact with Fabian.

The Frenchman smiled at him, and then formed his fingers into a gun and—his smile vanishing—pulled the trigger.

While Jason and the others were out on Fifth Avenue, the *Argonaut*—the tough little *Argonaut*—sat in a Team Lombardi pit bay on Sixth Avenue being overhauled.

Umberto Lombardi may not have been able to give Jason a brand-new race-ready car to compete in the Masters, but, as he had done in Italy, he could give the *Argonaut* a bit of an upgrade: some brand-new compressed-air thrusters, another new tailfin and a crate-load of the best magneto drives money could buy—Ferrari XP-7s.

No longer was the *Argonaut* a hodge-podge of wildly different parts—now, internally at least, it was the complete package.

Externally, however, Lombardi didn't change a thing.

The only thing he got his workmen to do on the outside of the car was give the *Argonaut* a complete repainting and polishing—not in the colours of Team Lombardi, but in its own original colours: blue, white and silver.

When it came out of the garage later that afternoon—when Jason and the others had returned from the parade—the *Argonaut* positively sparkled.

It was ready to race.

★ ★ ★

Throughout the rest of the day, Jason and his team stayed away from all the formal race functions—dinners, sponsors' events, drinks parties.

Having seen how vacuous those things were both in Italy and at Race School, Jason, Sally and the Bug didn't care for them.

They just stayed at the official practice track out on Long Island Sound—putting the new-and-improved *Argonaut* through its paces—before returning to Jason's cousins' house in New Jersey late in the afternoon.

That evening, the entire extended Chaser family, the McDuff clan, Ariel Piper and Scott Syracuse sat around the dinner table, discussing tactics.

'The important thing is the elimination system,' Syracuse said. 'Over the course of the four races, a leaderboard is used. Like at Race School, you get 10 points for winning, down to 1 point for coming 10th—and a flat zero points if you DNF. At the end of each race, the last four racers on the leaderboard get eliminated. So: in Race 1, 16 racers compete; in Race 2, 12; in Race 3, 8, and in the final race, only 4.

'As such, the first race is simple,' he said. 'If you come in the last four, you're out. If you survive the first race, then elimination depends on everyone's scores in the subsequent races.'

'And don't forget the Bradbury Principle,' Henry Chaser, ever the armchair expert, said. His eyes twinkled as he said it.

'Yes, Dad,' Jason sighed, shaking his head.

'Hey, look!' one of his cousins yelled from in front of the TV. 'You can bet on Jason!'

Everyone turned to see that the TV news was reporting on the gambling odds being offered for the Masters. A representative from the main internet gambling company, InterBet, was summarising the available odds.

Jason was a rank outsider to win the Masters—his odds were the highest of any racer: 1500-to-1.

But what surprised Jason was the amount of different betting options that were available to the keen gambler:

You could bet on Jason making it through Race 1 (100-to-1).

You could bet on him making it to Race 4 (575-to-1).

But then there were the more complex bets.

Jason coming in the Top 3 overall.

Jason coming in the Top 5 overall.

Jason placing in the Top 3 in any race (naturally the odds for Race 1 were shorter than those for, say, Race 3, since he'd have to avoid eliminations to get to Race 3).

Jason placing in the Top 5 in any race.

Jason was a little overwhelmed by it all. He'd always loved racing, but he'd never taken an interest in the gambling side of it.

'Hmmm. I'm not much of a gambler,' Martha Chaser said tentatively, 'but I might just put a dollar on you to win the whole thing. I could buy myself one of those fancy new sewing machines. Mmmm.'

After a time, dinner broke up, and Jason and the Bug went to their bedroom. They wanted a good night's sleep before tomorrow's racing.

Before he climbed into bed, though, Jason had a thought—and he went online, checking something . . . something about the gambling odds on him in Italy.

Hmmm, he thought, gazing at the screen, before flicking it off.

Then his parents came in, wished him and the Bug good night, switched the lights off, and left.

Jason lay in the dark for a long time—long after the Bug had fallen silent—staring at the ceiling. Then he rolled over to go to sleep.

As he did so, someone came into the bedroom behind him and sat down on the floor between his bed and the Bug's.

It was their father, Henry Chaser.

'Boys,' he whispered, assuming they were asleep. 'I just wanted you both to know something. I am so very proud of you—not for reaching the Masters, but just for being who you are and conducting yourselves as you have. Tomorrow, win or lose, it doesn't matter, I still love you both. You just do your best and enjoy the experience. I hope you have the time of your lives.'

Henry sniffed back some tears.

Then he stood up quickly and left the room.

Jason smiled in his bed.

He didn't know it, but across from him, in the other bed, the Bug was also wide awake and listening.

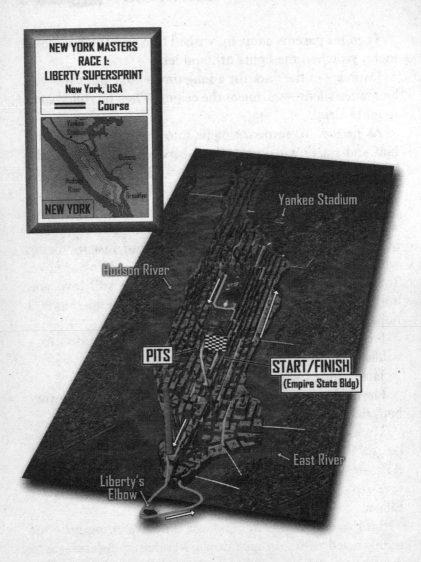

NEW YORK MASTERS
RACE 1:
LIBERTY SUPERSPRINT
New York, USA
▬▬▬ Course

Yankee Stadium

Queens

Hudson River

Brooklyn

NEW YORK

Yankee Stadium

Hudson River

PITS

START/FINISH
(Empire State Bldg)

East River

Liberty's Elbow

Lightning speed.

Blurring skyscraper canyons.

Slow-falling confetti.

Roaring crowds.

And absolutely *brutal* racing.

Race 1 of the New York Masters introduced Jason to a whole new level of hover car racing.

This wasn't just *fast*.

It was desperate. You did everything you could to stay out of the bottom four . . . and stay alive.

The course for the Liberty Supersprint wasn't dissimilar to the course Jason had raced in the Challenger Race—except that this track never left Manhattan Island, save for the downward run to the treacherous Liberty's Elbow.

But this course was *tight*, sharp, a never-ending series of right-angled turns up and down Manhattan Island—as a driver, you never got a chance to rest your mind. If you lost your concentration for a second, you'd find yourself missing a turn and skidding out over the demag lights or into a dead zone.

In short, Race 1 was murder on mag drives—which was

very deliberate. It made taking Liberty's Elbow even harder.

On the first corner of the race, Etienne Trouveau made a barely concealed swipe at Jason's tailfin.

But Jason—wiser from his similar experience at Race School and loving the extra speed of his new-and-improved *Argonaut*—had expected it and he evaded the move with skill.

Welcome back to the big leagues, was the message.

Twisting, turning, banking, racing.

Sixteen racers, but only twelve could progress to Race 2.

Fabian shot to the lead—

Closely pursued by La Bomba Romba—

Jason slotted into 14th place, racing hard, yet within range of elimination.

But he liked this course. It suited the light-and-nimble *Argonaut*. The never-ending sequence of short straights and 90-degree turns suited the smaller cars—in the city, there wasn't a single street-section long enough for the heavier big-thruster cars to gather any straight-line speed.

Where they gained a slight advantage was on the short straight leading down to Liberty's Elbow.

And that was where things got hairy.

LAP: 17 OF 40

On Lap 17, Liberty's Elbow claimed her first victim.

Kamiko Ideki, running on worn mags at the back of the field and hoping to pit at the end of that lap, lost control taking the notorious left-hand hairpin.

He lost it wide, understeering badly, and pushing his struggling mags to the max, he blew them and flipped—

—and rolled wildly—

—tumbling out of the turn, heading at phenomenal speed toward one of the giant horseshoe-shaped hover grandstands that lined the corner, before he was caught—abruptly, instantly—like a fly in a spider's web in the protective dead zone enveloping the Elbow.

Out of the race, Kamiko would now automatically be eliminated.

LAP: 32 OF 40

Into the pits. Frantic activity everywhere.

And Sally did well, very well, sending Jason out ahead of two racers who'd actually entered the pits *before* him—Raul Hassan, the No.2 driver for the Lockheed-Martin Team, and Jason's Lombardi team-mate, Pablo Riviera—the in-pit overtaking manoeuvre elevating Jason to 12th.

He felt a little relieved—with Ideki already out, so long as he didn't come 13th, 14th or 15th, he'd be returning for Race 2.

But as the race entered its final stages, things were about to get nasty.

LAP: 35 OF 40

Raul Hassan in his Lockheed tried to overtake Jason at the Elbow.

After Jason's in-pit overtaking on Lap 32, Hassan had hounded him for the next three laps, snapping at Jason's heels—so that when they hit the Elbow on Lap 35, they hit it almost together.

The two cars banked sharply, side-by-side, Jason on the inside, Hassan on the outside.

Jason felt the immense G-forces of the turn assaulting his body. He gripped his steering wheel for dear life, as if it were the only thing holding him inside the *Argonaut*.

The G-force meter on his dashboard ticked upwards:

6.2 . . .

7.1 . . .

8.0 . . .

And then—just as Hassan had planned—it happened.

For the briefest of instants, as his car hit 8-Gs, Jason blacked out.

A squeal from the Bug roused him—

—and he decelerated, wrestling with his steering wheel, and caught the *Argonaut* just before it hit the dead zone—

—but not before Hassan, Riviera and a third driver, Carlo Martinez in a Boeing-Ford, all snuck past Jason.

It was a costly mistake.

Suddenly the *Argonaut* was in 15th place.

Suddenly Jason was coming last.

The last four laps of the race went by in a blur.

Jason raced as though his life depended on it, zigging and zagging through the tight New York streets.

Yet his error at the Elbow had hurt him—on every lap, he took it ever more gingerly . . . and he gradually fell further behind the others.

But he kept on driving anyway, keeping them in sight, staying close.

Something could happen.

Anything could happen.

So long as you were there at the end, you had a chance.

This was Henry Chaser's 'Bradbury Principle', in reference to that time at the Winter Olympics when the Australian short-track speed-skater, Steven Bradbury, had dropped back behind the leaders, only to see them *all* fall—taking each other out in a spectacular crash—on the final turn of the race.

As all the lead skaters lay splayed everywhere on the ice, Bradbury had simply skated past them and won the gold, incidentally the first gold medal Australia had ever won at a Winter Olympic Games.

The Bradbury Principle: stay alive and you never knew.

And in Masters racing, it had particular relevance: year after year, the final laps of each race saw some of the most

downright dangerous driving ever, as racers sought to avoid elimination at any cost.

This reckless driving was so common, it had a name: Masters Madness.

LAP: 40 OF 40

Into the last lap, and Jason was lagging behind the next five racers by about six car-lengths.

Raul Hassan had moved up through the field, as had Pablo Riviera, both now well clear of the bottom three.

Immediately in front of Jason were:

In 12th (and thus safe from elimination): Helmut Reitze, the German driver from the Porsche Team.

In 13th: Carlo Martinez, in his Boeing-Ford.

In 14th: Brock Peters, from the General Motors Team.

And then Jason.

Whipping through the financial district, and he couldn't haul them in.

Down to the Elbow, still no decent gain.

And then it was back up through the city, bending and banking furiously, before he crossed Central Park for the last time and came to the final few corners of the course.

Jason kicked himself for his earlier mistake, but strangely, he was happy.

He'd made it to the Masters.

And that in itself was an extraordinary achievement. He'd be back in future years, he was sure, but he'd be older then, wiser, a better racer. He was, after all, only fifteen.

And then, as the racers in front of him hit the final left-hand turn of the race he saw—spectacularly, gloriously—the Bradbury Principle in action.

It was largely the fault of the 13th-placed racer, Carlo

Martinez, as he tried to avoid elimination by overtaking the 12th-placed driver, Helmut Reitze, in his Porsche.

By any reckoning, there was no room to move, but Martinez tried anyway—Masters Madness—thrusting his Boeing inside Reitze's silver Porsche on the final turn.

The result was as tragic as it was spectacular.

Martinez collected Reitze—and the two cars rolled together, but not before the car immediately behind them, the GM of Brock Peters, slammed fully into the back of them. Peters and his navigator ejected an instant before their car disappeared in a billowing explosion of flames.

All three cars crashed to the roadway, their charred remains littering the final turn on both the left and right.

At which point, the *Argonaut*—left for dead in last place—just cruised by them, banking round into Fifth Avenue, slicing past the dark columns of smoke rising from the wreckage, before it zoomed across the Finish Line, the last car to cross the Line in Race 1, but safely in 12th place.

By sheer good fortune, by just hanging in there when all seemed lost, Jason was through to Race 2!

NEW YORK CITY, USA (THURSDAY)
AFTER LIBERTY SUPERSPRINT

As soon as the Liberty Supersprint was over, gigantic score-boards sprang to life across New York City: above the Start-Finish Line on Fifth Avenue, in Times Square, on the Brooklyn Bridge and in hundreds of other locations.

The leaderboard looked like this:

DRIVER	LIBERTY SUPERSPRINT	MANHATTAN GATE RACE	THE PURSUIT	THE QUEST	TOTAL
1. ROMBA, A (1) Lockheed-Martin Racing	10				10
2. FABIAN (17) Team Renault	9				9
3. TROUVEAU, E (40) Team Renault	8				8
4. CARVER, A (24) USAF Racing	7				7
5. LEWICKI, D (23) USAF Racing	6				6

DRIVER	LIBERTY SUPERSPRINT	MANHATTAN GATE RACE	THE PURSUIT	THE QUEST	TOTAL
6. SKAIFE, M (102) General Motors Factory Team	5				5
7. HASSAN, R (2) Lockheed-Martin Racing	4				4
8. REIN, D (45) Boeing-Ford Team	3				3
9. CHOW, A (38) China State Racing	2				2
10. REITZE, R (51) Porsche Racing	1				1
11. RIVIERA, P (12) Lombardi Racing Team	0				0
12. CHASER, J (55) Lombardi Racing Team	0				0
13. REITZE, H (50) Porsche Racing	DNF				
14. MARTINEZ, C (44) Boeing-Ford Team	DNF				
15. PETERS, B (05) General Motors Factory Team	DNF				
16. IDEKI, K (11) Yamaha Racing Team	DNF				

While Jason had been struggling at the back of the field, a fierce battle had been going on up front—between Alessandro Romba and the two Renault Team drivers: Fabian and Etienne Trouveau. In the end, Romba had held out against the two Frenchmen and won, claiming 10 points

and inching one step closer to the Golden Grand Slam.

The last four drivers—all of them having crashed out during the race—were blocked out in red, eliminated.

After the next race, four more would go.

That night, Jason went to bed both exhausted and exhilarated. Sure, he was last on the scoreboard, but he had high hopes for the next day's race—for it was a gate race, his and the Bug's specialty.

As he slept an army of workers went to work reconfiguring New York City—erecting arched gates and towering barricades—preparing it for the Manhattan Gate Race.

NEW YORK CITY, USA (FRIDAY)

Dawn on Friday found the streets of New York City eerily deserted. Not a single car, cab or truck could be seen on any of its wide boulevards—vehicular traffic was banned today.

If you moved through those streets, however, you would find that many of them were now fitted with high metal archways—race gates—250 of them.

You would also find that dozens of the city's streets had been blocked off—by massive temporary barricades—transforming them into dead-ends.

The island of Manhattan had been turned into a labyrinth.

Every year the configuration of New York's streets was altered—racers and navigators would receive a map of all the gate locations and dead-ends three minutes before racetime.

As with all gate races, the farthest gates were worth 100 points; the nearest, 10. And since no racer could possibly race through every single gate within the time limit, this was a battle of strategy—choosing the optimal course.

The time limit for the race was 3 hours.

The punishment for a late return to the Start-Finish Area was severe: 2 points *per second*.

So if you were a minute late, you lost a massive 120 points.

The Manhattan Gate Race was also the only race in the New York Masters to operate under the 'Car Over the Line' finishing rule. Driver Over the Line wasn't good enough in this race—your whole car had to make it back.

The message was clear: go out, get through as many gates as you could, and get back on time.

Jason arrived in the pit area on Sixth Avenue very early on Friday morning.

Nervous, he'd slept fitfully and woken terribly early, around 4:30 a.m., so he'd decided to go down to the pits and tinker with the *Argonaut*.

He was looking inside its rear thrusters when a voice behind him made him jump:

'Ooh, hello there! Why if it isn't young Jason.'

It was Ravi Gupta. The creepy guy Jason had met in Italy—whom Jason had subsequently discovered was a leading bookmaker.

Gupta stood a few yards away from Jason, with his hands clasped peacefully in front of him—but he had arrived all-but silently, as if he had appeared out of thin air.

'What are you doing in here?' Jason asked. 'This area is restricted.'

'Ooh, I have been involved in racing for a long time, Jason,' Gupta said slyly. 'I know people.'

'What do you want?'

Gupta held up his hands quickly. 'Me? Ooh, nothing, Jason. Nothing at all. I thought you were lucky yesterday—ooh, yes, very very lucky—with that crash on the last turn.'

'A race is never over until everyone crosses the line,' Jason said warily.

'Yes, ooh yes. So true, so true,' Gupta said. 'But now the simple fact of the matter is that you are in Race 2, the gate race, and everyone knows how much you like gate races. Feeling confident then?'

Jason didn't like talking to Gupta—it was as if Gupta was plying him for information, looking for the inside scoop on how he would perform that day, so he could adjust his betting odds accordingly.

Too late Jason had realised that this had been exactly what Gupta had done in Italy.

Smiling, Gupta said, 'Enjoying your new and improved *Argonaut*. I must say it looks a million dollars.'

'It's great,' Jason said.

A door slammed somewhere. Jason turned. Saw a security guard walking down the length of the pits.

Jason swung back to address Gupta—

—only to find that the Indian had disappeared.

Gone.

As suddenly and silently as he had arrived.

Jason scowled. 'Hmmm . . .'

By 8 a.m., New York City was once again snowing with confetti.

The city was absolutely overflowing with spectators.

They lined every street, hung from office windows, lay on deckchairs on rooftops. Sizeable crowds gathered around the two 100-point gates in the Cloisters (at the extreme north of the island) and at the Brooklyn end of the long Brooklyn-Battery Tunnel (the southernmost point of the course), ever hopeful that this would be the year that a racer claimed both 100-pointers.

But by far the largest crowd of all lined Fifth Avenue: an

unbroken multitude that stretched from the New York Public Library on 42nd St all the way down Fifth Avenue to the 4-way Start-Finish Line that stood beneath the Empire State Building at the junction of Fifth and 34th St.

The stage was set.

The crowd was ready.

The race would begin at 9 a.m.

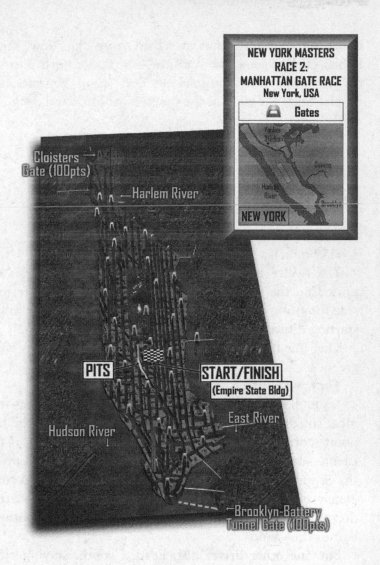

NEW YORK MASTERS
RACE 2:
MANHATTAN GATE RACE
New York, USA

Gates

NEW YORK

Cloisters
Gate (100pts)

Harlem River

PITS

START/FINISH
(Empire State Bldg)

East River

Hudson River

Brooklyn-Battery
Tunnel Gate (100pts)

NEW YORK CITY, USA (FRIDAY)
RACE 2: THE MANHATTAN GATE RACE

12 racers. 250 gates. 3 hours.

8:59 a.m.

The twelve remaining racers in the Masters Series sat poised on the square-shaped Start-Finish Line, three to a side, pointing in the four cardinal directions—their initial starting direction determined by lot.

Then the clock struck 9:00 and—*bam*—the lights went green.

They were off.

Jason had drawn an east-pointing grid position—the most sought-after were the northward ones, since the key point-scoring area was in the mid-to-north section of the island—and while all the racers around him blasted off to the east and then turned north, he just swung around completely *on the spot* and—at the Bug's instruction—darted due south down Fifth Avenue, heading for the southern half of the island.

But one other driver also headed south, staying close behind Jason.

Fabian.

And as Jason weaved his way southward, whizzing through the picture-postcard gates at Washington Square Park, the World Trade Center Memorial and Wall Street, it quickly became apparent that Fabian hadn't just followed Jason southward.

Fabian was following Jason everywhere.

Every single time Jason turned for a new gate, Fabian turned after him.

'Damnit, Bug!' Jason yelled. 'He's tailing us! He doesn't trust his own navigator, so he's using our race-plan!'

'Tailing' in a gate race (in the southern hemisphere it was called 'sequencing') wasn't unheard of: it was technically within the rules, but it was also regarded as a cheap and cowardly way to race.

All the way down Manhattan, the crowds cheered the *Argonaut* on . . .

. . . cheers that became boos as the purple-and-gold *Marseilles Falcon* shot by a split-second later.

Through more gates at the south-western corner of the island. Every time the *Argonaut* passed through an archway, that gate emitted a shrill electronic ping:

Bing! Bing! Bing!

The Bug's race-plan was near perfect—plotted to pass through the maximum number of worthwhile gates while by-passing those that offered only minimal points for inordinate effort.

And all the while, he kept Jason close enough to the pits for necessary mag replacements and coolant refuellings.

By the time they took their second pit stop at the 1-hour mark, the *Argonaut* was sitting on an incredible 750 points—and in the lead!

Unfortunately, Fabian—because he was following exactly the same course—was on the same number of points and thus sharing the lead.

But then Jason did something unexpected.

He went south again, this time taking the superfast route down the FDR.

He was going for the Brooklyn-Battery Tunnel. And the prized 100-point gate at its end.

Fabian visibly doubted whether or not to follow, but in the end, he did.

In hindsight, it was a very canny plan—take on the tunnel with six full-strength mags, a full tank of coolant and no distractions.

The Brooklyn-Battery Tunnel came into view, and without missing a beat, the *Argonaut* shoomed into it, closely followed by the *Marseilles Falcon*.

A minute later, Jason emerged at the turnaround at the other end of the long tunnel—the Brooklyn end—to be met by the roars of the crowd gathered there, and he banked hard, swooping through the 100-point gate . . .

Bing!

. . . before he roared back into the tunnel to start the return journey.

But while Jason was plundering the southern areas, others were progressing well in the northern half of the island.

Chief among them were the two USAF racers: Carver and Lewicki.

They were gate race specialists, the US Air Force priding itself on its pilots' abilities to most efficiently navigate any course.

Word was, Carver and Lewicki's Air Force navigators trained on state-of-the-art computer navigation simulators for ten hours a day, so that optimal race-plotting became almost second nature to them.

But when it was revealed at the 1-hour mark that at 740

points each, they were both ten points behind the leaders, Jason and Fabian, the crowds and the commentators went wild.

The television commentators—with the help of their own course-plotting computers—immediately analysed Jason's possible race-plans based on his course-plotting so far.

'Check this out,' one of them said. 'From the start, Chaser went south, while everyone else went north. Now, he's coming back north, where the streets aren't as congested with other racers anymore, and he's stealing solid 20-point gates on his way. And now look here—he's just jumped onto the Henry Hudson Parkway, still heading north. Now where could he be heading? Okay, here comes the computer's assessment of his plan: what the hell—?'

The same thing happened on every other sports channel.

Shocked commentators saw the Bug's plan.

'No way!'

'He can't be serious!'

'The computer must be wrong . . .'

'No, it's working all right . . . and, holy Toledo, it'd bring him back to the Start-Finish Line way ahead on points, easily in 1st place! Folks, according to our race-plan computer, Jason Chaser, the popular young racer in Car No.55, is going for the Cloisters. He's going for the 100-point double! And, by God, if he makes it, according to our calculations, he's gonna win this race, too!'

RACETIME: 1 HOUR 30 MINS

At the halfway mark, the top five racers on the scoreboard were:

	DRIVER	NO.	CAR	POINTS
1.	CHASER, J	55	*Argonaut*	1,250
2.	FABIAN	17	*Marseilles Falcon*	1,250
3.	CARVER, A	24	*Mustang-I*	1,220
4.	LEWICKI, D	23	*Mustang-II*	1,210
5.	ROMBA, A	1	*La Bomba*	1,160

Jason was racing well—fast and hard—but it was the Bug who was having the race of his life. Word of his daring plan had spread, and every race fan in New York was on the edge of their seat, wondering if the *Argonaut* could possibly complete the double *and* win the race.

But Fabian stayed with him. And in the southern part of the course, the two US Air Force racers were now accumulating points very well. It was also widely known that Alessandro Romba, the world champion, intensely disliked gate races—he would be thrilled if he retained his 5th placing in this race.

Elsewhere, other things were happening.

As the race entered its last hour, racers again began to

get desperate, and they started taking more risks, started taking corners more recklessly—and when two speeding hover cars hit the same intersection from different directions, catastrophe could occur.

It was one such collision that took the Chinese racer, Au Chow, out of the race. He'd been in 7th place when he'd come blasting out of Central Park—just as one of the other tail-enders, the American Dan Rein in his Boeing-Ford, had been zooming down Fifth Avenue to pit.

The two cars clashed at right-angles—with Rein careering spectacularly through Chow's nosewing, shearing the Chinese racer's entire nosecone clean off, in the process almost taking Chow's legs off.

Rein came out of it with a crumpled nose, but he managed to limp back to the pits. Chow's race was over—and since he'd only garnered 2 miserable points in Race 1, so was his time in the Masters.

RACETIME: 2 HOURS 45 MINS

'I like your style, Bug!' Jason yelled as the *Argonaut* roared up Riverside Drive, occasionally ducking inland to plunder some 40-point gates on the high Upper West Side—all the while with Fabian hammering on their tail.

'Everyone thinks you're this sweet little mousy guy, but I always knew you were a glory-seeker!' Jason said. 'Only you could come up with a race-plan that's points-heavy and history-making!'

The Bug replied with three words.

Jason nodded. 'Death or glory. You bet your life, little brother.'

Up and up they went, zooming northward toward the Cloisters, their race now an equation of distance and time.

The 100-point Cloisters Gate was the single farthest point on the course from the Start-Finish Line, and they had 15 minutes left in this race.

But the Bug had planned well—basing his decision on the distance to the Cloisters, their speed, the big points available and the ever-diminishing state of their mags. He'd planned it down to the second.

But there was still the Fabian issue.

Try as he might, Jason just couldn't shake Fabian.

The wily Frenchman was clinging to his tail, riding on the Bug's brilliant strategy—no doubt informed by his pit crew that it was a winning one.

A couple of times, Jason tried to lose Fabian in the maze of the Upper West Side, but to no avail.

And then, as the race-clock hit 2:45 and Jason set his course for the Cloisters, Fabian did it for him.

Either he lost his nerve or he took a call on his radio to try a new plan—most observers thought he lost his nerve.

Whatever the reason, Fabian pulled off Riverside, swinging right, and headed back down toward Midtown—not prepared to take the risk of going all the way up to the Cloisters; preferring to take the points from lesser gates and get back within the 3-hour time limit.

Now the *Argonaut* shoomed northward, alone.

Heading for the Cloisters.

Jason gripped his wheel tightly as the minutes ticked by.

At 2:50 exactly, the *Argonaut* roared into the Cloisters, the crowd there rising in a delighted Mexican wave as it zoomed past them and—*bing!*—whipped through the archway there, collecting 100 points for its trouble.

'Yee-ha!' Jason yelled.

The Bug whooped it up too.

'Right,' Jason said. 'Now it's time to get back.'

RACETIME: 2 HOURS 52 MINS

Overcautious racers rushed back over the Start-Finish Line, finishing a full eight minutes early, determined to bank their hard-earned points and avoid penalties for returning late. It was conservative racing, but in gate races, one never knew . . .

According to the Bug's plan, the return journey was to be swift and simple.

Zoom due south all the way down Central Park West, along the border of the Park, and then swing onto Broadway as it angled in toward Midtown—collecting a couple of easy 10-pointers there—before turning onto 42nd St and heading for Fifth Avenue.

It was all going to plan until, at the very bottom of Central Park, the two Renaults of Fabian and Etienne Trouveau appeared from out of nowhere, slotting into identical positions on either side of the *Argonaut*.

Ostensibly, they were just other racers legitimately trying to get back home as fast as they could—but the way they buffeted the *Argonaut*, slashing at it with their razor-sharp bladed nosewings, Jason knew that this was something more.

They were trying to put him out of the race.

For good.

He held them off grimly, banging from one to the other,

hemmed in on either flank, at one point roaring down Broadway on his side—but then as he turned left onto 42nd St, only one right-hander away from home, the French racers got him.

The three cars took the left-hander onto 42nd St together—with Fabian on the inside, Jason in the middle, and Trouveau on the outside.

And at that point, with cool calculation and in a manner that just looked like vigorous racing, Fabian pushed Jason into Trouveau.

With nowhere else to manoeuvre, the *Argonaut* slid right, its nosewing coming closer and closer and closer to Trouveau's glistening bladed nosewing . . .

. . . and they hit.

CRACK!

The *Argonaut*'s nosewing splintered and broke and Jason lost all control.

The *Argonaut* veered downward, rushing toward the hard surface of 42nd St—while the two Renaults flittered away like a pair of nasty ravens, their job done.

Jason somehow managed to pull his nose up and the *Argonaut* slammed into the roadway, landing awkwardly on its belly, right on top of its magneto drives.

Mags flew left and right, out from under the bouncing car: one, two, three, four of them . . .

. . . and the *Argonaut*—once beautiful, now battered and smoking—slid to a screeching halt in the middle of 42nd St, one turn and 500 metres away from the Finish Line.

RACETIME: 2 HOURS 56 MINUTES

The crowd in the grandstand closest to the crashed *Argonaut* sighed with dismay at the unexpected crash.

The commentators on TV went bananas:

'Oh, no! Chaser is down! Chaser is down—!'

'Ladies and gentlemen, the race leader has crashed—!'

'And with only four minutes to go! In what could have been one of the best gate-race runs ever! Oh, the shame!'

Fabian and Trouveau both swung right, onto Fifth Avenue, and a few seconds later, roared over the Finish Line on 34th St, eight blocks away.

The *Argonaut* sat nose-down—crumpled and broken—on 42nd St, alongside the majestic New York Public Library.

Inside the stationary car, Jason raised his head weakly. The first thing he did was check behind him.

'You okay?'

The Bug groaned but nodded.

Jason keyed his power switch.

The *Argonaut*'s internal organs ticked over but did not catch. The car remained still.

Jason tried to start her up again. No luck.

'Come on, car!' Jason yelled. 'Don't let me down! You've still got two mags! There's still time for us to get over the Line!'

He keyed the power switch one last time.

Vmmm.

The *Argonaut* rose exactly two feet off the ground—

—and stayed there.

Jason pushed forward on his thrusters, but the car remained in a stationary hover—its compressed-air thrusters coughing pathetically—the car held up only by its two remaining magneto drives.

It had lost forward thrust.

The *Argonaut* wouldn't—couldn't—go forward.

Jason's face fell. If this had been a regular Masters race, he could have run for the Finish Line with his steering wheel, as the Bug had done back in Race 50 at Race School. But this was the only race in the Masters that was Car Over the Line: the *Argonaut* had to cross the Line.

Jason looked up. 'Oh *damn*.'

RACETIME: 2 HOURS 57 MINS

With three minutes to go, 8 of the 12 starters had crossed the Finish Line. Four remained out on the course: the crashed Au Chow, Raul Hassan, the second Lockheed-Martin driver, Dan Rein in his mended Boeing-Ford (both trying to get more points), and Jason.

At the time he crashed, Jason was in the lead on points.

But now, unmoving on 42nd St, all agreed that his race was over.

The TV commentators overlooking the Finish Line bemoaned his crash.

'This is such a shame . . .'

'Could have been a history-making drive . . .'

'But he's young, he'll learn . . .'

'That's right, Bob, a gate race is never over until you're over that line.'

But then, one of the commentators kicked back his chair and stood, pointing up Fifth Avenue, and raised his voice above them all:

'Wait a second! *What is that!*'

Every spectator on Fifth Avenue turned northward at the same time, and they all saw it together.

And for the first time in history, Fifth Avenue fell completely and utterly silent.

For what they saw totally took their breath away.

Through the glorious slow-motion confetti snow, they saw an object emerge from 42nd St and come out onto Fifth Avenue.

It was the *Argonaut*.

Hovering low above the street.

And behind it, bent low with exertion, were two small figures.

Jason and the Bug were pushing it.

Slowly, gradually, with all their strength, Jason and the Bug pushed the *Argonaut* out onto Fifth Avenue.

The wide avenue stretched away before them—to the Finish Line, 500 metres away.

They kept pushing, and at first, their slow journey went in silence—the crowds massed in the stands on either side of them just watched them in sheer speechless shock.

And then someone yelled in a classic Noo York accent: 'Come on, kids! Push that sucker home!'

And with those words the spell was broken and the crowd exploded with applause and started urging Jason and the Bug on with roars that shook the heavens.

RACETIME: 2 HOURS 58 MINS

Two minutes to go. 200 metres to go.

Step by agonising step, Jason and the Bug pushed the *Argonaut*—their *Argonaut*, their tough little car—down the home straight.

The crowds on either side of them were now in a frenzy, urging them on with rhythmic chants of:

'*HEAVE! HEAVE!*'

Sweat dripped off Jason's brow, splashed to the ground.

The Bug leaned with all his might against the tailfin of the hovering *Argonaut*, pushing with his back.

The race-clock ticked over to 2:59.

One minute to go.

But still 120 metres to travel and the boys were exhausted.

The commentators were abuzz with excitement:

'. . . In all my years calling sport, I have *never* seen anything like this . . .'

'. . . We'll have to look at the points tally. Chaser was 60 points ahead of his nearest rival before he crashed. At this slow speed, he can't possibly get to the Line before the 3-hour mark. The question is: How many points will he lose for being late?'

The tiny figures of Jason and the Bug pushed their car down Fifth Avenue, in front of the seething cheering roaring crowds in the multi-tiered grandstands.

'*HEAVE! HEAVE!*' came the chant.

Jason lowered his head, pushed.

Step, heave.

Step, heave.

But then, the Bug slipped . . . and fell.

Jason stopped, picked him up, put the Bug back where he had been standing.

'Keep pushing . . . !' he gasped. 'We . . . have to . . . make it!'

And then the race-clock hit 3:00.

Every second now would cost them 2 points . . . and they still had 80 metres to go.

'*HEAVE . . . !*'

20 seconds gone.

'*HEAVE . . . !*'

40 seconds gone.

'*HEAVE . . . !*'

A minute.

And then, 70 seconds after the 3-hour time-limit for the race had expired, to a million camera flashes exploding all around them, Jason Chaser and his brother, the Bug, pushed the *Argonaut* over the Finish Line and collapsed together in a heap.

Had he not wiped out on 42nd St, Jason would have won the Manhattan Gate Race by 60 points—his dash to the Cloisters Gate would have been the difference.

As it turned out, however, with his 70-second-late finish—incurring a whopping 140-point penalty—Jason ended up coming 3rd, behind the two US Air Force gate race specialists, Carver and Lewicki.

Fabian had come 4th—aided by his early tailing of the *Argonaut*—and Romba was very satisfied to finish 5th.

But other results had gone Jason's way. The lesser-placed racers coming into the Gate Race—Hassan, Rein, Chow and Reitze—had either crashed (Chow), come in late (Hassan and Rein) or simply not fared well (Reitze), all of them coming in the bottom four.

Consequently, after the Gate Race the Masters Scoreboard looked like this:

DRIVER	LIBERTY SUPERSPRINT	MANHATTAN GATE RACE	THE PURSUIT	THE QUEST	TOTAL
1. ROMBA, A (1) Lockheed-Martin Racing	10	6			16
2. FABIAN (17) Team Renault	9	7			16
3. TROUVEAU, E (40) Team Renault	8	3			11
4. CARVER, A (24) USAF Racing	7	10			17
5. LEWICKI, D (23) USAF Racing	6	9			15
6. SKAIFE, M (102) General Motors Factory Team	5	4			9
7. HASSAN, R (2) Lockheed-Martin Racing	4	0			4
8. REIN, D (45) Boeing-Ford Team	3	1			4
9. CHOW, A (38) China State Racing	2	DNF			2
10. REITZE, R (51) Porsche Racing	1	2			3
11. RIVIERA, P (12) Lombardi Racing Team	0	5			5
12. CHASER, J (55) Lombardi Racing Team	0	8			8
13. REITZE, H (50) Porsche Racing	DNF				
14. MARTINEZ, C (44) Boeing-Ford Team	DNF				

DRIVER	LIBERTY SUPERSPRINT	MANHATTAN GATE RACE	THE PURSUIT	THE QUEST	TOTAL
15. PETERS, B (05) General Motors Factory Team	DNF				
16. IDEKI, K (11) Yamaha Racing Team	DNF				

In one fell swoop, with his 8 points for coming 3rd, Jason had leap-frogged Hassan, Rein, Chow and Reitze, not to mention his Lombardi team-mate, Pablo Riviera.

He was now 7th on the overall points ladder.

Which meant, incredibly, after two races, he was in the final eight racers.

Jason Chaser was still in the Masters.

And only two races away from glory . . .

PART VIII

JASON AND THE GOLDEN FLEECE

The *Argonaut* screamed down the Hudson River at top speed, with Etienne Trouveau's *Vizir* right alongside it, banging against it, ramming it—on the very last lap of Race 3—and with only one turn to go, the fearsome Liberty's Elbow, Jason and Trouveau were out in front of the other racers, battling it out for the win.

The world blurred around Jason. The buildings of New York City. The bridges. The vast hoverstands flanking the river.

This race had been bitter. Bitter and tough.

But now it had come to this—one turn, two racers.

The *Argonaut* dived into the Elbow. So did the *Vizir*.

Jason battled the G-forces, gritted his teeth.

6-Gs . . .

The *Vizir* was still beside him.

7-Gs . . .

The *Argonaut* began to shake.

Jason gripped his steering wheel with all his might.

8-Gs and Jason's vision started to darken, the initial stages of blacking out.

Gotta stay conscious! he told himself. *Gotta stay conscious!*

But the *Vizir* was still beside him.

Worse, it was creeping *past* him, round the outside on the terrible turn!

How was Trouveau doing it! Jason's mind screamed.

8.5-Gs . . .

Jason started to feel nauseous. He'd never survived this many G-forces before—but all he could think of was the *Vizir* edging away from him, slipping out of his grasp, *beating him* in this race that he had to win to stay in the Masters.

Had to win.

Win.

Then the end of the giant hairpin came into view and—

—Jason blacked out.

The *Argonaut* was instantly flung clear of the Elbow.

Jason flopped back in his seat like a rag doll. Dimly, he heard the Bug scream in terror as their car rocketed out of control over the demag lights flanking the turn, screaming like a wounded fighter jet, before it flipped and bounced horribly on the surface of the harbour—pieces of it being stripped away in the process. Then the *Argonaut* slammed at tremendous speed into the carcass of another car that had crashed in the same manner earlier in the race and which was blocking the nearest dead zone.

There was no chance to eject.

No chance of survival.

The *Argonaut* hit the wreck and exploded.

Jason awoke with a shout—dripping with sweat and breathless to the point of suffocation.

He caught his breath, and recognised his surroundings: he was in his cousin's bedroom in New Jersey. The Bug lay in the single bed beside his, snoring happily.

The digital clock next to Jason ticked over to 4:44 a.m.

It wasn't yet Saturday.

Race 3 had not been run.

It had just been a bad dream. A really bad dream.

But the emotions of it lingered: Jason's overwhelming desire to win, his pain at watching Trouveau pull away, the nausea of the G-forces, the descent into black-out, and worst of all, Jason's fear of that turn, Liberty's Elbow.

He just didn't like Liberty's Elbow—it was perhaps the toughest turn in racing and today, like it or not, Jason was going to be taking it once every minute for two hours.

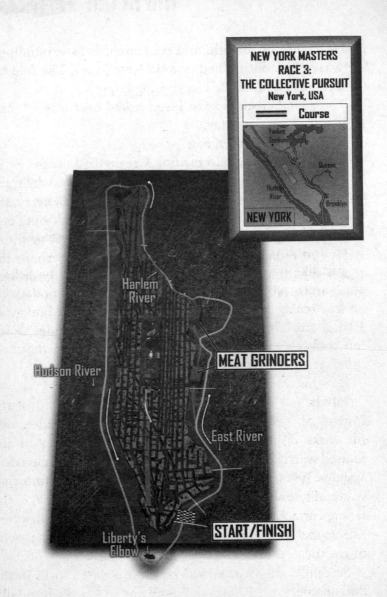

NEW YORK MASTERS
RACE 3:
THE COLLECTIVE PURSUIT
New York, USA

Course

Yankee
Stadium

Queens

Hudson
River

Brooklyn

NEW YORK

Harlem
River

Hudson River

MEAT GRINDERS

East River

START/FINISH

Liberty's
Elbow

NEW YORK CITY, USA (SATURDAY)
RACE 3: THE PURSUIT

Race 3 of the New York Masters is a variety of race known as a 'Collective Pursuit Race'.

Just like the pursuit races Jason had run in the School tournament, it involved racers blasting around a relatively short circular track—in Race 3, it was a lap of Manhattan Island, starting and ending at the Brooklyn Bridge. Each lap took approximately one minute: redefining the term 'quicker than a New York Minute'.

But this track featured obstacles:

Firstly, *ion waterfalls* that rained down from all of the bridges of New York City. They looked like upside-down fireworks displays: the luminescent gold particles of the ionised waterfalls wreaked havoc on magnetic and electrical systems. If you missed the one-car-wide gaps in the (moving) waterfalls, and accidentally drove your car *through* the falling curtain of golden ions, your car emerged on the other side as merely the shell of a hover car—no power, magnetic or electrical. A horrible crash usually ensued.

Secondly, *the Meat Grinders*: there are two forks in the Pursuit course, at Roosevelt Island and at Ward's-Randall's Island (they are in fact one island, but were once two, hence the double name). At both forks, racers can take a longer, less dangerous route to the right-hand side.

The *left*-hand fork, however, is much shorter—but in both cases it contains an enormous iron wall, forty metres thick, blocking the way completely. In the centre of each iron wall is a narrow cylindrical tunnel. The thing is, the walls of this tunnel—the *entire* tunnel—open and close in an iris-like fashion. If a racer chooses to take the short route, and gets caught in the closing tunnel, that racer can be crushed, hence the name 'meat grinder'. More often, desperate racers opt to take the short route, miss the opening of the tunnel, and lose even more time waiting for it to re-open.

And, of course, at the very end of each lap, at the end of the superlong and superfast Hudson River Straight, *Liberty's Elbow* loomed. It was the final challenge for every racer—pitting one's body against one's desire to win. As had happened to Jason in his dream, it was not uncommon for drivers to knock themselves out taking the Elbow, allowing their desire to win to overcome their good sense.

There was also one extra feature, unique to this race, known as *The 15-Second Rule*.

In short, every racer had to stay within 15 seconds of the lead car. As the leader passed underneath each bridge, a timer was initiated. After 15 seconds, the ion waterfall on that bridge flicked from gold to red—and the gap in the waterfall closed, turning it into an impassable wall of ions. Meaning if you failed to stay within 15 seconds of the leader, you could physically go no further. You were out of the race.

At this point in the Masters, since there were only eight contenders left, the scoring system also changed.

For the final two races, the winner still got 10 points.

The 2nd placed racer, however, now only got 8 points; 3rd got 6 points; 4th: 4 points; 5th: 2 points; and the last three drivers, nothing. Those racers who DNF'd—Did Not Finish—still got a flat zero points.

For Jason, the situation was clear.

Sitting on only 8 points, a full 8 points behind the leaders in the series, he needed a good finish in this race—top two at least—and he needed some of the other racers to finish poorly or not at all.

But if he'd learned anything this year, it was that in hover car racing, *anything could happen.*

As daylight broke on Saturday, Manhattan Island had essentially become one gigantic stadium.

Enormous crowds swarmed all over the outer banks of the East River, the Harlem River and the Hudson River, all facing inwards. While on Manhattan itself, New Yorkers had commandeered every piece of available viewing space—from parks and buildings to the major freeways that ringed the edges of the island: the Henry Hudson Parkway, West St and the FDR—all looking outward.

And the subject of their collective gaze:

The eight humming rocket cars hovering above the waves of the East River, in the shadow of the mighty Brooklyn Bridge.

Jason and the Bug sat hunched in the *Argonaut,* eyeing the river stretching away before them.

Fabian's *Marseilles Falcon* sat on their left and Trouveau's *Vizir*—Jason had discovered that it was named after Napoleon's horse—on their right.

'Anything can happen . . .' Jason said aloud.

It was about to.

The lights went green and the race began.

Eight cars.

120 laps.

On one very short track.

To Jason, the three rivers of New York resembled one continuous watery trench, flanked by hills of roaring spectators and spanned intermittently by sweeping bridges, from which cascaded the spectacular golden ion waterfalls.

The first bridge after the Brooklyn was the Manhattan Bridge, but since it was so close to the Brooklyn, its waterfall wasn't initiated till Lap 2. But the next bridge, the colossal Williamsburg Bridge, like the first turn of any race, was a crunch point.

Its golden waterfall was most certainly active—and by the time the eight racers reached it, they had to be in single file in order to pass through the narrow opening in its curtain of golden ions.

The surface of the East River rushed under the nose of the *Argonaut* as Jason threw every lever forward, banking with the leftward bend in the river toward the tiny gap under the Williamsburg Bridge.

He saw the bridge, saw the gap, saw all the speeding

cars around him and wondered: *How the hell are we all going to fit through?*

But in the moment before the bridge was upon them, all eight cars converged like the teeth of a zipper and roared— *shoom-shoom-shoom-shoom*—through the narrow gap.

But then as he shot through the gap in the waterfall in the middle of the field, Jason saw that one car hadn't quite made it through, and had instead shot right through the ion cascade.

It was the second US Air Force driver, Dwayne Lewicki, in his modified F-55 fighter, Car No.23.

Trailing two cars behind Jason, Lewicki's car emerged on the other side of the waterfall, seemingly all right—but it wasn't.

It was completely without power.

Slowly, painfully, inexorably, the car peeled away to the right in a soaring downward arc, before it came to an abrupt jarring halt in a dead zone in front of the spectators on the eastern shore—out of the race.

'Game on,' Jason said.

Jason roared around the track—all but overwhelmed by the intensity of the racing.

This was unlike anything he'd experienced at Race School. Cars whizzed across his nose at reckless speeds. Racers bumped and pushed each other. And the crowd, it was always there, always around him, roaring, cheering, almost . . . well . . . *baying* for blood. It kind of felt like an old Roman chariot race.

The two Renault drivers, Fabian and Trouveau, had obviously decided to make Jason's life hell. All round the first lap—and then the second and the third—the two Frenchmen badgered Jason, the pair of them taking calculated swipes at

both his tailfin and his nose, zeroing in on the *Argonaut* with their bladed nosewings.

Every time they cut in, the New York crowds booed.

And every time Jason evaded their thrusts, the crowds cheered. He held them off doggedly.

But it was only a matter of time till their attacks did some damage and on Lap 6 they did.

At Liberty's Elbow, the two French cars cut across the bow of the *Argonaut* in such a way that Jason either pulled out of the turn or lost his nosewing.

He pulled out of the turn—

—and decelerated—

—and watched as the field raced away from him.

'Damn it!' he yelled.

He gunned the *Argonaut* once more, and shot off in pursuit—now chasing the 15-second rule.

At each bridge now, he saw a giant digital countdown, telling him how far ahead the leader was (of course, it was Alessandro Romba).

Jason hit the Start-Finish Line at the Brooklyn Bridge eleven seconds behind Romba. Close. But okay.

But in a race like this—by its very nature, tight and close—that kind of lead could only be regathered in the pits or with the help of a crash.

In the end, Jason would benefit from both.

Pit stops in a collective pursuit race were pre-set—so as not to allow cheap knock-outs when someone pitted. In this race, they were pre-set to take place every 20 laps.

At those stops, Sally performed like a genius. And it was she who hauled in Alessandro Romba's lead—in stops on Laps 20, 40, 60 and 80, in one of those stops, hauling in three whole seconds.

And then things started to get interesting.

LAP: 105 OF 120

Romba was still in the lead, in his silver-and-black Lockheed-Martin.

The USAF pilot, Carver, was in 2nd in his military-blue F-55.

Then there was a pack of four—among them, Jason.

Last of all, in 7th place, came Jason's quasi-team-mate in the Lombardi Racing Team, Pablo Riviera.

Riviera was languishing in last place, having woefully botched a pit stop on Lap 100, and was now travelling along only just inside the 15-second mark.

And so, in a moment of desperate insanity, he took on the second meat grinder—since it afforded the single greatest gain on the course. It could turn a 13-second deficit into a 3-second one.

He didn't know—or perhaps he didn't have the skill or the nerve to know—that in order to overcome the meat grinders of New York, you had to take them at absolutely full speed: 810 km/h.

And entering a tight iron tunnel no bigger than a garage door at close to the speed of sound is even harder than it sounds.

Riviera shot into the meat grinder at a cool 750 km/h.

The long dark cylindrical tunnel enveloped him.

And then the tunnel around him began to iris shut, its gigantic iron cleaves squeezing inward with a loud mechanical clanking, like a giant industrial python swallowing its prey.

And in a moment of clarity, Riviera realised he wasn't going to make it.

He screamed.

The meat grinder squealed with rust as it closed around him.

Its shrieking walls sheared off the tips of his wings first . . . then they crushed his side air intakes . . . and his tailfin . . . and . . .

The crumpled remains of Riviera's F-3000 were spat out the other end of the meat grinder, battered and unrecognisable; it tumbled into the river, the only thing that had survived: the driver's reinforced safety cockpit. Riviera was alive—just—and only because of the super-solid construction of his car (and the fact that the meat grinder didn't squeeze all the way inward). Not in any way because of his own skill.

Now only six drivers remained in the race.

Two separate battles were now taking place on every lap.

Romba and Carver for the lead.

Jason and the two Renault drivers for 3rd. And trailing behind them, only just managing to keep inside the 15-second rule, the General Motors factory team driver, an older Australian driver named Mark Skaife in car 102.

In fact, the 15-second rule performed an admirable service: it kept all of them bunched close together—within striking distance—so that when the chance came, every driver was in a position to strike.

Then the chance came.

When two things happened at once:

First, Angus Carver tried to overtake Alessandro Romba as they roared up the side of Ward's-Randall's Island on Lap 110. Carver tried to sneak inside Romba, but Romba held his line stubbornly and as they hit the left-hander at the top of the island, they collided—badly—and separated, lurching wildly in either direction, *both of them* hitting the nearby demag lights.

The other thing that happened (at the exact same time) was this: as they shot up the East River behind the two leaders, Fabian and Trouveau, working together, boxed

Jason in on the left-hand side of the track, so that when they hit Ward's-Randall's Island, Jason had only two options: crash into Ward's Island, or go left—toward the second meat grinder.

Jason went left.

And he accelerated.

Gave it everything he had. He'd seen the meat grinders enough on TV over the years and every year the commentators said the same thing: you couldn't beat them at anything less than top speed.

So he hit the gas and rushed round the base of Ward's-Randall's Island and beheld the entry to the second meat grinder.

It looked tiny.

Really tiny.

This would be like firing a bullet into a keyhole.

The *Argonaut* rushed toward the tiny opening. Its speedometer topped 800 km/h . . .

805 km/h . . . then 810 km/h before—

VOOOOOOM!

The *Argonaut* blasted into the tight cylindrical tunnel—and immediately the tunnel began to iris inwards.

Jason leaned forward in his seat.

The Bug looked up at the rapidly 'collapsing' tunnel all around them.

Then the irising walls were so close, they started sparking against the *Argonaut*'s wingtips and Jason thought his car was almost certainly going to die when—*whoosh*—they blasted out into dazzling sunshine again and found themselves . . .

. . . in the lead.

With only ten laps to go.

The Bug exclaimed something.

Jason smiled. 'I'm telling Mum you swore.'

But the jackals weren't far behind.

Because of their collision, Romba and Carver were cactus, and they were quickly swamped by Trouveau and then Fabian and then Skaife. (Romba and Carver would ultimately duke it out for the still-important 2 points available for the 5th placed racer, fighting right up until they were both eliminated by the 15-second rule—in the end, Romba outlasted Carver.)

Meanwhile, up front, it was Jason against the rest—and with ten laps to run, he now had a golden opportunity *to win the race!*

And from that moment, with adrenalin coursing through his entire body, Jason flew nine of the best laps of his life.

The two Frenchmen couldn't believe that he'd come out the other side of the meat grinder. They charged with a vengeance.

It was Trouveau—needing the points more than Fabian—who charged harder, and when he stormed through the first meat grinder on Lap 115, he was suddenly hammering on Jason's tail.

The last four laps of the race would be four of the toughest Jason had ever experienced.

Trouveau hounded him.

But Jason took every turn perfectly.

Well, almost every turn. On each lap, Trouveau gained on him at Liberty's Elbow. The French driver seemed to know it was Jason's weak point—it was as if he could *smell*

Jason's fear. He knew that Jason took it gingerly, frightened of the G-forces, frightened of knocking himself out.

And as they commenced the last lap of the race—Lap 120 of 120—Trouveau was travelling almost alongside the *Argonaut*.

And deep in his heart of hearts, Jason knew what Trouveau was going to do.

Trouveau was going to take him at the Elbow.

Up the East River, following the safe route now. Into the narrower Harlem River, under all the bridges spanning it—before blasting out into the Hudson, down its long wide straight, hitting top speed, before suddenly, *she* came into view.

Lady Liberty.

Jason saw her and grimaced.

He knew the score—the Bug had done the math after Romba and Carver had been eliminated: an 8-point 2nd-placed finish wouldn't be enough to beat Carver on the overall ladder. To go through to the next race, Jason needed the full 10 points. He needed to win.

Death or glory, he thought.

And as he hit the Elbow, he knew which one he'd choose.

Into the Elbow, banking left, their cars almost vertical, flying hard.

And then Trouveau—as expected—made his move.

But this time, Jason held his line.

And Trouveau was a little shocked.

Halfway round the Elbow—

—and Jason's vision began to blur at the edges.

7-Gs . . .

Further round the enormous hairpin . . . and his vision began to *darken*.

I can make this . . . he told himself.

I can make this . . .

8-Gs . . .

Blinking. Trying . . . so hard . . .

8.5 . . .

. . . to . . . stay . . . conscious . . .

Trouveau was almost beside him now, but the Frenchman couldn't get past.

9-Gs . . .

And Jason's face was pressed against his skull, his cheeks sucking backwards, his teeth clenched hard and he realised with a thrill that this time—yes!—he was going to make it . . .

Then he blacked out.

Jason awoke—

—to the sound of ecstatically cheering crowds . . . and to someone banging on his helmet.

It was the Bug hammering on his helmet, trying to rouse him.

As for the crowd, they seemed to be cheering: 'We love the Buuuuug! We love the Buuuuug!'

Jason was sitting in the *Argonaut*, but it was stationary now—caught in a dead zone—hovering above the low waves of the East River, but *past the Finish Line*.

Jason looked about himself in astonishment—he had no recollection of how he had got from Liberty's Elbow to the Finish Line.

Then he saw an action replay on a giant-screen TV on the riverbank: saw the *Argonaut* blast out of the Elbow, levelling out of its high-banking turn ahead of the *Vizir*, and roar past the camera.

And there, depicted in glorious slow-motion on the television image, leaning over Jason from behind, clutching at the *Argonaut*'s steering wheel, guiding the car over the last few hundred metres, was the one student at the International Race School who had survived a 9-G banking turn.

The Bug.

More than that, the *Argonaut* had retained its speed from the turn (evidently, despite losing consciousness, Jason had kept leaning on his thrusters), and with the Bug at the controls, it had outrun Trouveau to the Brooklyn Bridge!

The *Argonaut*, with its pilot unconscious and its navigator leaning over him to steer, had won the damn race!

Now the Bug was smiling broadly. He explained to Jason what had happened.

'I what?' Jason asked. 'I kept all our thrusters on, even after I knocked myself out?'

The Bug nodded, added something.

'You could say that,' Jason replied. 'You could say I wanted to win this race *really* badly.'

The points immediately went up on the leaderboard.

10 points for Jason.

8 for Trouveau.

6 for Fabian, who took 3rd place easily.

4 for the Australian Skaife—a fine effort, but not enough to take him to the final round.

And a most unusual 2 points for Alessandro Romba, for his 5th placing; while the USAF pilot, Carver, got zero for coming 6th.

And suddenly, with the two USAF pilots both scoring no points at all and the overall leader scoring poorly, the scoreboard told a new tale:

DRIVER	LIBERTY SUPERSPRINT	MANHATTAN GATE RACE	THE PURSUIT	THE QUEST	TOTAL
1. ROMBA, A (1) Lockheed-Martin Racing	10	6	2		18
2. FABIAN (17) Team Renault	9	7	6		22
3. TROUVEAU, E (40) Team Renault	8	3	8		19
4. CARVER, A (24) USAF Racing	7	10	0		17
5. LEWICKI, D (23) USAF Racing	6	9	DNF		15
6. SKAIFE, M (102) General Motors Factory Team	5	4	4		13
7. HASSAN, R (2) Lockheed-Martin Racing	4	0			4
8. REIN, D (45) Boeing-Ford Team	3	1			4
9. CHOW, A (38) China State Racing	2	DNF			2
10. REITZE, R (51) Porsche Racing	1	2			3
11. RIVIERA, P (12) Lombardi Racing Team	0	5	DNF		5
12. CHASER, J (55) Lombardi Racing Team	0	8	10		18
13. REITZE, H (50) Porsche Racing	DNF				
14. MARTINEZ, C (44) Boeing-Ford Team	DNF				

DRIVER	LIBERTY SUPERSPRINT	MANHATTAN GATE RACE	THE PURSUIT	THE QUEST	TOTAL
15. PETERS, B (05) General Motors Factory Team	DNF				
16. IDEKI, K (11) Yamaha Racing Team	DNF				

All of a sudden, Angus Carver had gone from leading on 17 points, to being eliminated on 17 points, while Fabian—wily Fabian—had shot up the scoreboard with his solid 6-point finish, surging into first place on 22 points, three points clear of his nearest rival, his team-mate, Etienne Trouveau.

But most astonishing of all was Jason, who with his massive 10-point bonanza, found himself on 18 points, and in the top four, leapfrogging three racers with one big jump. The Bug had been right: that final turn had made all the difference; 8 points would not have been enough.

Jason couldn't believe it.

His parents couldn't believe it.

The crowds couldn't believe it.

The commentators couldn't believe it.

Thanks to the Bug, the one and only Bug, the *Argonaut* was in the fourth and final race of the New York Masters.

That evening, a silence fell on the New Jersey home of Jason's cousins.

After Team *Argonaut*'s efforts in the Pursuit earlier that day, one would have expected an uproarious celebration, with champagne corks popping and soft drink spraying.

But no, that wasn't happening tonight.

The weight of it all had finally hit home: the magnitude of what Team *Argonaut* had achieved this week. After three ultra-tough pro-level races, tomorrow Jason, the Bug and Sally would be participating in one of the most prestigious events in world racing—and also one of the most dangerous.

Everyone sat around the dinner table in contemplative silence: Jason, the Bug, Henry and Martha Chaser, the Chaser cousins, Sally McDuff and her family, and Ariel Piper.

Indeed, the silence—a grim hush of fear and awe—was deafening.

The only one who wasn't fazed by it all was Scott Syracuse, but then, he'd been here before in a professional capacity and so was used to the pressure.

'You know . . .' Syracuse said, breaking the uncomfortable silence, 'the other racers, they're only men.'

Others in the room kept their heads bowed. Jason alone looked up at his teacher.

Syracuse shrugged. 'People see racers like Fabian and Romba, and they think they're superhuman. Men of steel. Bold champions who fly at astronomical speeds without fear or nerves. But they're not superheroes. Oh no, they're not. They are ordinary men, with fears and loves and weaknesses like you and me.

'This is why we love sportspeople—from Tiger Woods to Donald Bradman to Muhammad Ali—they handle a kind of pressure that most people cannot even imagine. They stand on a golf course or in a stadium or in a ring, with hundreds of thousands of viewers watching them and somehow their legs don't fall from under them. And then— *then*—they *keep* standing and, under all that scrutiny, *they do what they have practised for so long and they do it well.* That's why we love them. We think *we* would fail, and yet they don't. But that doesn't mean they aren't afraid.

'Jason, Bug, Sally. As your teacher, I've watched you develop this past year; watched you grow from young wide-eyed hopefuls with some talent . . . into *racers*. When you started with me, you were good. Now you are great. Great at your individual duties, and a great team—from going to lessons when you were too tired to think; to pitching in together to perform manual pit stops; to pushing your car over the Line; to the Bug taking over the steering when it was necessary.

'You're *racers* now. And believe me, you're ready for this. You may not think so, but as someone who knows racing, trust my judgement: you are ready to stand up in front of the world, and your legs will not fall out from under you. You've done the work, you have the skill and you most certainly have the desire. It's time for you to do what you came here to do: win the Masters.'

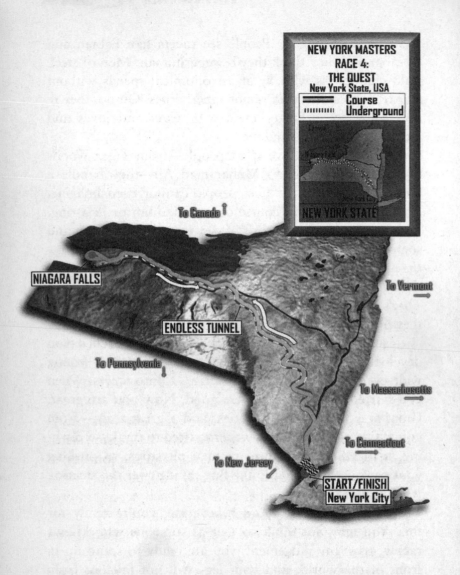

NEW YORK MASTERS
RACE 4:
THE QUEST
New York State, USA

━━━━━ Course
┅┅┅┅┅ Underground

Canada

Money Fall

New York City

NEW YORK STATE

To Canada

NIAGARA FALLS

To Vermont

ENDLESS TUNNEL

To Pennsylvania

To Massachusetts

To Connecticut

To New Jersey

START/FINISH
New York City

NEW YORK CITY, USA (SUNDAY)
RACE 4: THE QUEST

'Do you have it, Mum?' Jason asked as they arrived in the Sixth Avenue pits for the fourth and final race of the Masters series.

Martha Chaser opened her purse for him to see inside, and sure enough, there it was, his 'trophy' for the Quest.

The format of a quest race is simple: all racers head out from the Start-Finish Line to a faraway point, where they pick up their chosen trophy—it can be anything really, but usually racers choose something of significance to them: a medal they won once, perhaps, or their national flag.

Either way, the first racer to come back across the Start-Finish Line *with his or her trophy in their possession* wins. The twist comes in the journey itself—and the journey in the Masters' Quest was a particularly difficult one.

Typically, Jason's mother had fashioned a very appropriate trophy for Team *Argonaut* to use in Race 4.

'I think we have to give it to one of the officials,' Jason said, taking it from her.

As they reached their pit bay, he handed it to the race official who would transport all four racers' trophies to the farthest point of the Quest course.

★ ★ ★

The *Argonaut* sat in its pit bay, glistening, shining, *waiting*. It was as if the little blue-white-and-silver car was alive, energised, ready to go, stamping its hoofs in anticipation of the challenge ahead of it today.

Jason eyed his car with pride, thinking of all they had been through together—from the Regional Championships in the swamps of Carpentaria, to his epic efforts at Race School: the gruelling tournament, taking on the Clashing Bergs in the final race; and now, his feats here in New York.

He patted the *Argonaut*'s left wing.

'Well, car,' he said, 'here we are again. One more race, that's all I ask of you. One more race. Let's do it.'

And with a final pat, he strode away from the car to go and get suited up for the race.

He never saw the tiny explosive device—it was the size of a pinhead—attached to the tailfin of his beloved *Argonaut*.

It had been placed there during the night by a light-fingered hand . . . a hand that had paid off one of the security guards to gain access to the pit area . . . a hand that had laid a similar device on another *Argonaut* once before.

NEW YORK CITY, USA (SUNDAY)
RACE 4: THE QUEST
SECTION: OUTBOUND JOURNEY

The four cars sat on Fifth Avenue, all aimed northward.

Alessandro Romba—in his silver-and-black Lockheed-Martin.

Fabian and Etienne Trouveau in their purple-and-gold Renaults.

And Jason—in the *Argonaut*.

This is what it came down to.

Four contenders.

All within four points of each other.

Romba, Trouveau and Jason had to win Race 4—and have some other placings go their way—in order to take the Masters.

Fabian, however—three points clear of his nearest rival—could come 2nd, garnering 8 points, and still take the overall title.

The course for the Quest was a long and arduous one—taking the racers all the way across New York State, right to Niagara Falls on the US-Canadian border. There the racers would collect their trophies from a platform suspended high above the falls and begin the journey back to Manhattan.

Now, while the journey both ways was extraordinarily difficult, it was also astonishingly beautiful, but in an unusual way.

For the main feature of the course was a superlong underground highway known as the Endless Tunnel. Before the invention of hover cars, the US Government had started construction of an underground superhighway designed to go from the Canadian border all the way down to Florida, to be known as Superhighway Two.

But then along came hover cars and the project was abandoned: and only the section through New York State was completed—and even then, only roughly.

What remained was a rough-hewn network of long octagonal tunnels cutting through all sorts of underground environments—old mines, subterranean chasms, rivers and waterfalls. Indeed, the construction of the highway had led to the discovery of the now-famous Twin Caves, the largest underground caverns in the world.

Naturally, the Endless Tunnel was now equipped with many small ion waterfalls that cut the tunnel's width in half. Plus lots of single-file-only bridges over the underground gorges and rivers, and not a few dead-end forks: navigators were provided with a map of the Tunnel and their role in the race was crucial.

Jason sat in his cockpit, eyeing the skyscraper- and grandstand-lined canyon of Fifth Avenue stretching away before him.

'Your legs will not fall from under you,' he said aloud.

The Bug didn't hear him properly, asked what he'd said.

'Nothing, little brother. Nothing.'

The crowd murmured—would Alessandro Romba win

this race and take the Grand Slam? Or the two Frenchmen? Or perhaps even the young outsider, Jason?

Jason's parents watched from the grandstand nearest to the Start-Finish Line. Sitting with them were Umberto Lombardi, Scott Syracuse, the McDuff clan and Ariel Piper. Henry Chaser was literally on the edge of his seat with excitement.

Then suddenly a loud electronic tone warned everyone that the start lights would ignite in three seconds.

Red light—

Yellow light—

Green light—

Go!

The world blurred.

Super speed. And Jason found himself pushing the *Argonaut* to new limits.

Skyscrapers became bridges then houses then open highway as the racers shot up Interstate 87, charging northward, with every piece of available land covered with spectators.

Then the landscape quickly became tree-covered hills, bridges and rivers and—all too soon—the Catskill Mountains came into view. And waiting for him at their base, Jason knew, was the entrance to the famed and feared Endless Tunnel.

Romba was in the lead, where he liked to be, while Jason and the two Renaults swapped and jockeyed for 2nd place, overtaking each other regularly—and all the while, the two French drivers flashed their razor-sharp nosewings dangerously close to Jason's flanks.

And then Jason beheld the entrance to the Tunnel.

It was a massive grey concrete arch, solid as hell, with a dark passageway behind it that yawned black. The opening was flanked by a sea of cheering spectators.

Shoom!

Jason rushed into the blackness.

Arched concrete pillars whistled by overhead in a dizzying display of hyper-repetition. Actually, they weren't so much pillars as 'ribs'—the ribs of the octagonal tunnel.

The four cars roared like rockets through the winding passageway, banking with the bends, flattening out with the straights.

Romba—Jason—Fabian—Trouveau.

At certain points, ion waterfalls halved the width of the Tunnel, and they had to form up into single file to get past the glittering golden curtains—and sometimes weave left and right when a second or a third ion waterfall appeared directly after the previous one, but on the other side of the underground passage.

And then, gloriously, Jason burst out onto a superlong natural bridge that spanned a subterranean gorge. Bottomless black raced by on either side of the fenceless bridge. But before he could gaze in wonder at the spectacular scenery, Jason was plunged into claustrophobic tunnel-territory once again.

Forks began to appear in the tunnel system.

And for a time everyone just followed Alessandro Romba—trusting his navigator's map-reading skills—but then Romba got ahead of the others and suddenly the Bug had to make the *Argonaut*'s navigation calls.

But not for long.

Fabian—keen to stay in 2nd place and thus ensure that

he won the Masters—started harrying Jason with the help of Trouveau.

The *Argonaut* sped round a bend, avoiding an ion waterfall, before—*whoosh*—it blasted out into an absolutely enormous cavern, the first of the Twin Caves, known as the Small Cave.

Stunning waterfalls blasted out from fissures in the side of the immense cavern, falling 700 feet down a multi-tiered rock wall before disappearing into darkness. Temporary underground hoverstands filled with spectators lined the cavern, their chants echoing in the massive space.

A wide bending S-shaped bridge snaked its way across the face of the multi-streamed falls—at some points dipping behind the curtains of rushing water. The hover cars on the bridge were dwarfed by the sheer size of the underground water system.

It was here that the two Renaults tried to finish Jason off for good.

The bending bridge was wide enough for the three of them, but it narrowed to a two-car-wide tunnel at its end.

Ominously, the two Renaults swept up on either side of the *Argonaut*.

Jason snapped left, then right. Saw Fabian at his left, Trouveau on his right—both of them so close that he could almost touch them.

A Renault sandwich.

'Uh-oh . . .' Jason said.

The Renaults had him exactly where they wanted him—in a technique they'd used so many times before to nail their rivals. All Fabian had to do now was push Jason onto Trouveau's bladed nosewing.

Fabian started ramming Jason, forcing him right, forcing him towards . . .

. . . Trouveau's flashing nosewing.

Jason rammed Fabian back, fighting the push—nervously eyeing the rapidly-approaching tunnel entrance ahead.

Then Trouveau also pulled in close, bringing his fearsome silver nosewing to within centimetres of the *Argonaut*'s.

Jason swung his head left and right. There was nowhere to go. He was being run onto Trouveau's blades and there was nothing he could do about it.

Any second now, they would have him . . .

Any second . . .

Fabian gave him a final push.

Got him.

But as Fabian made the killing blow, Jason did something totally unexpected.

He slammed on his brakes.

The *Argonaut* slid backwards in the air and the result of this sudden action was as spectacular as it was surprising.

Fabian—previously pushing hard against the *Argonaut*—suddenly found himself pushing against nothing at all, so his car lunged forward in the air and before he could do anything about it, Fabian saw his own bladed nosewing shear right through Trouveau's!

Trouveau's eyes bulged as he saw his nosewing drop away—at which point he lost all control of his vehicle and the *Vizir* veered to the right, speeding perilously close to the edge of the winding bridge and the deep drop below it, before it smashed with terrible force into the vertical concrete frame of the tunnel entrance at the end of the gigantic cave.

Car hit stone.

At 700 km/h.

In a single instant, the *Vizir* transformed from hover car to fireball.

The explosion rang out in the cavern—and the crowds in the stands rose in horror. Trouveau and his navigator

would ultimately walk away from the crash, dazed and dizzy, saved only by their reinforced cockpit and anti-crash features. The *Vizir*, on the other hand, would never race again.

It was left splayed across the right-hand side of the tunnel entrance, blocking half of the way.

As for Jason, he was still rocketing along at speed—his braking manoeuvre had only been brief, so he hadn't lost that much ground on Fabian—and the two of them shot past the wreckage of the *Vizir* in single file, and disappeared into the two-car-wide tunnel at the end of the Small Cave.

The tunnel that led out from the Small Cave bent in a wide, wide curve to the right—testing each driver's G-force-resistance like Liberty's Elbow did—before it opened onto the second of the Twin Caves.

This was the Big Cave.

And it made the Small Cave look puny.

It was the largest natural underground space in the world, discovered only a few years previously, and it was utterly breathtaking. Towering waterfalls and rocky pinnacles as high as skyscrapers lined the superlong cavern. Magnificent naturally formed aqueducts connected some of the pinnacles, and the water running down them spilled off their ends, spraying into the air before dropping away into darkness.

A gently-sloping bridge of rock ran all the way down the length of the mighty cave, stabbed here and there by thin vertical waterfalls that over many years had cut clean through its edges, and it was along this that the racers sped, winding between the thin but powerful jet-streams of water.

Romba, then Fabian, then Jason.

To the roars of the crowds in the hoverstands, the three remaining racers blasted down the rockway and disappeared into the final section of the Endless Tunnel—a section that ended at Niagara.

Niagara Falls.

The sight, glorious. The sound, deafening. The crowds flanking the world's most famous outdoor falls: massing and roiling and bursting with anticipation.

All eyes were glued to the tiny pipe-like tunnel that poked out from the base of the main falls, waiting to see which racer would emerge first.

Alessandro Romba did.

And the crowds went nuts.

Fabian blasted out next, followed last of all by Jason.

The three cars banked quickly, sweeping up the hill on the US side of the Falls, before they all stopped at the landward end of a long thin rail-less footbridge that extended out over the flowing river, at the very precipice of the Falls.

Jason leapt out of the *Argonaut* and, chasing Romba and Fabian *on foot*, he dashed out across the long narrow bridge.

Sitting on a platform at the end of the footbridge were four podiums and on each podium sat each racer's trophy.

Romba's trophy was the Italian flag. He snatched it and turned and began the run back to his car . . . and the return journey home.

Fabian's trophy was typically Fabian: it was a framed picture of himself standing with the *Marseilles Falcon*. He grabbed it and dashed back to his car, pushing roughly past Jason as they ran past each other on the narrow bridge.

Last of all, Jason came to his podium.

And he beheld his trophy, crafted by his mother.

It shone in the sunlight like a treasure, haloed by the rainbow created by the spray of the Falls.

A small piece of soft wool.

Painted all in gold.

A golden fleece.

Like his classical namesake, Jason grabbed the fleece, turned, and then ran as fast as he could back to his chariot, and thus began the most thrilling hour of racing he had ever experienced in his short life.

RACE 4: THE QUEST
SECTION: THE ENDLESS TUNNEL (INBOUND)

Jason jumped into the driver's seat of the *Argonaut* and hit the gas.

The little Ferrari roared off the mark, swinging in a wide circle in the turnaround at the top of Niagara Falls, before descending down the roadway to the base of the Falls, where it swung out over the river and shot like a bullet back into the Endless Tunnel.

Into the dark again.

Heading for home.

Roaring, charging, chasing, racing.

Jason hammered the *Argonaut* through the branch-like passageways of the Endless Tunnel, ducking left, veering right, now engaged with Romba and Fabian in a headlong race for home.

He saw Fabian's tail-lights glowing red not far ahead of him—and suddenly, there came a voice in Jason's helmet earpiece, a French-accented voice that shouldn't have been there.

'*You cannot win, boy.*'

It was Fabian.

He must have discovered Jason's radio frequency and now, in the crunch-zone of the race, decided to put in a taunting call. This was very improper, but not technically illegal.

'*Why keep trying?*' Fabian said. '*You've done so well for a child. Why not leave the rest of this race to the men?*'

Jason eyed the Frenchman's tail-lights.

'I'm coming after you, Fabian . . .' he said firmly.

And he was.

He was gaining steadily on Fabian as they shot through the dark rocky tunnels, so much so that when they hit the Big Cave, the *Argonaut* sprang alongside the *Marseilles Falcon* on its right-hand side.

Fabian saw Jason and frowned—

'Peek-a-boo,' Jason said.

In reply Fabian rammed him.

But Jason swung wide, softening the blow.

This only seemed to enrage Fabian even more and as they shot up the long ramp of the Big Cave, Fabian slammed the *Marseilles Falcon* into the *Argonaut* again.

Jason, however, was up to the challenge, and he held his line as the two cars swooped up the bridge side-by-side and shot into the long sweeping (now) leftward curving tunnel that connected the Big Cave to the Small Cave.

Banking with the turn.

Flying hard.

Flying fast.

Fabian on the inside, Jason on the outside, their cars positively galloping, tearing the very fabric of the air with their speed.

And then, in a fleeting moment, Jason saw Fabian's eyes in his helmet—saw them glaring over at Jason with pure derision and hatred.

'*I'm gonna get you, you little punk!*'

'Not today,' Jason said.

'*And why exactly not?*'

'Because I've remembered something you haven't,' Jason said.

And as he said it, they rounded the final segment of the curve together, perfectly side-by-side—Fabian on the left, Jason on the right—and the thing that Jason had remembered suddenly came upon them.

The wreckage of Etienne Trouveau's car.

It was still crumpled up against the entrance to this tunnel—now the exit—blocking the entire left-hand side of the track.

Fabian's side of the track.

Fabian saw it too late—and his eyes boggled at the sight—and at the realisation that Jason had got the better of him; had deliberately got him to travel on this side of the track, heading straight for his team-mate's wreck.

Fabian screamed.

Then he covered his head as the *Marseilles Falcon* exploded *clean through* the remains of the *Vizir*, sending pieces of the two Renaults showering out in a huge star-shaped spray—while at the same time, the *Argonaut* shot past the double wreck in total safety.

The central core of Fabian's car actually survived the trip through the *Vizir*—although unfortunately for Fabian, its wings, nosewing and tailfin didn't.

The battered remains of his car shot off the nearest edge of the S-shaped bridge in the Small Cave and sailed down into blackness . . .

. . . where, perhaps undeservedly, it would be caught in a safety dead zone, its race run.

Needless to say, the crash's effect on the race, on the entire Masters Series, was electrifying.

Fabian had just DNF'd—meaning he would get *no* points at all for this race. His Masters Series was over.

Now the Masters would be fought out by the last two racers on the track: Alessandro Romba and Jason Chaser.

With the two Renaults out of his hair for good and flying on outrageous amounts of adrenalin, Jason now eyed the tail-lights of Alessandro Romba.

La Bomba Romba.

The No.1-ranked driver in the world, the man seeking to become the first racer ever to claim the Grand Slam, the man who this whole year had never been cleanly passed.

Until today, Jason thought.

A two-horse race.

Romba fleeing.

Jason chasing.

Chasing him as hard as he could.

Down the length of the Small Cave, then into the labyrinthine passages of the Tunnel.

Romba drove hard.

Jason drove perfectly.

And over the course of twenty minutes, he *gained* on the World No.1, moving within a car-length of him before—

—sunlight assaulted them both as they blasted together out of the Tunnel.

Onto the Interstate now, sweeping left and right between the trees and hills—with Jason hammering on Romba's tail, giving the World No.1 absolute hell.

Then Jason made his move, tried to get past Romba on the inside left.

Romba blocked the move—legally, fluidly.

Jason tried again, this time on the right.

And Romba blocked him again.

Jason persisted, left, then right, searching doggedly for a gap, showing the World No.1 no respect.

Then again Jason went left—and Romba went that way too—but this time it was a perfectly disguised fake and Jason suddenly cut right . . .

. . . and zipped past Alessandro Romba as Romba over-balanced to the left!

The crowds lining the highway gasped.

Then they *roared* with joy, delighted at Jason's skill.

It wasn't a crash or luck or some foul move that had got Jason past Romba.

It had just been damn good driving.

And suddenly, with only ten minutes left in the New York Masters, *Jason found himself in the lead.*

New York City rose in the distance.

Whizzing down the Interstate, Jason saw its high sky-scrapers stabbing the sky.

He gunned the *Argonaut*, trying to shut out all thought of being *in the lead*, being *out in front*, being on the cusp of achieving everything he had ever dreamed of.

Don't think about winning! he told himself. *Don't jump the gun!*

Win the race first.

So he concentrated with all his might.

And in the final run-up to Manhattan, he actually extended his lead on Romba, moving at first a car-length, then a few lengths ahead of the Italian.

Then it was over the Broadway Bridge at the top of Manhattan Island and suddenly he was back in the city and its maze of hard right-angled corners.

The assembled crowds roared at his every turn.

Romba was now seventy metres behind him.

And as he swung out onto Fifth Avenue and realised that he had no more turns to take—that this was the end—that he'd done it—Jason allowed himself a half-grin.

He'd done it . . .

And then a figure in the crowd watching Jason shoot down Fifth Avenue toward the Finish Line pressed a button on a remote control, triggering the pinhead-sized explosive device attached to the tailfin of the *Argonaut*.

For the second time that year—and for the second time in a Grand Slam Race—the *Argonaut*'s tailfin spontaneously exploded.

No! Jason thought. *Not on the home straight!*

'Hang on, Bug!' was all he had time to yell.

Its tailfin gone, the speeding *Argonaut* dropped its nose instantly and ploughed at a sizzling 790 km/h into the pavement of Fifth Avenue.

Sparks flew everywhere.

The *Argonaut*'s nosewing dislodged immediately and flew away, loose pieces of the car were stripped off by the wind, while its wings bounced against the pavement and were torn clean off.

And the battered little *Argonaut* skidded to a sideways halt in the middle of Fifth Avenue, a tantalising two hundred metres short of the Finish Line, before it tipped clumsily onto its side, its cockpit pointed towards the Line.

Jason snapped his neck upwards and saw—tilted sideways—the Finish Line, so close but so far away.

'Bug! You okay?'

The Bug said he was.

In a flash, Jason assessed his options.

He knew Romba was close behind him—and by the sound of it, almost on him—too close to beat to the Line on foot as the Bug had done to Barnaby back at Race School.

'Damn it!' he yelled. 'I am *not* gonna lose this race!'

And as he felt Romba's car come up beside his stationary position, inspiration struck and Jason jammed his golden fleece in his lap, unclipped his transponder-equipped steering wheel, and did the only thing he could think to do to win the race.

He yanked on his ejection lever.

RACE 4: THE QUEST
SECTION: FIFTH AVENUE (INBOUND)

It was an image no race-goer would ever forget.

The black Lockheed of Alessandro Romba sweeping past the crumpled wreck of the *Argonaut* just as—*shoooooom!*—Jason, on his ejection seat, came shooting out of the wreck, rocketing horizontally and head-first, like a human cannonball, a bare two feet above the surface of Fifth Avenue where he . . .

. . . *overtook* Romba's car in flight . . .

. . . and shot over the Finish Line one single foot ahead of the shocked Italian!

No sooner was the ejection seat over the Finish Line than it lost all its horizontal momentum and arced downward, and hit the ground and skidded—on its side—kicking up a million sparks all around Jason, but protecting him with its reinforced construction.

And then it stopped.

A sizzling, steaming crumpled wreck.

Race officials came running from all sides, concerned.

The crowds were stunned into silence.

Henry and Martha Chaser just stared, searching for a sign of life in the smoking ejection seat and the crowd of officials gathering around it.

No-one had ever seen anything like it—the kid had *ejected* over the Line to win!

And then an official lifted Jason from the crumpled mess of his ejection seat and Jason stood, wobbling, and held his steering wheel and golden fleece aloft—

—and the roar that went up from the crowd gathered around the Finish Line was like no other that had ever been heard in the history of hover car racing.

It was so loud, it almost brought the city down.

And Henry and Martha Chaser both breathed a sigh of relief—before Henry leapt into the air, pumping his fists.

'*YOU . . . LITTLE . . . BEAUTY!*' he yelled.

Delirious scenes followed.

Like a dam breaking, the ecstatic crowd burst through the barricades and stampeded onto Fifth Avenue, massing around Jason's crumpled ejection seat.

Jason—now flanked by officials and security guards—sought out Alessandro Romba nearby and shook his hand.

'I'm sorry about the Grand Slam, Mr Romba,' Jason said.

Romba just smiled ruefully. 'I have a feeling that today might have been my last chance to get it—from now on, I'll be facing a tough new opponent in every race.'

Jason nodded. 'Good race today.'

'You too. Now go, young Chaser. Celebrate.'

'I will,' Jason smiled broadly.

And he ran off down Fifth Avenue, to the wreck of the *Argonaut*, still lying on its side in the middle of the wide boulevard, where he found the Bug, now standing beside the wreckage.

The two brothers embraced—as camera flashes blazed all around them.

'Jason! Doodlebug!' Martha Chaser came running from the VIP stand, with Henry behind her.

Martha grabbed Jason in a great big hug and squeezed him tight.

Henry Chaser stopped a few steps behind her, knowing that the Bug—currently unhugged—didn't like to be held by him.

He was, then, quite stunned when the Bug leapt up into his arms and cuddled him warmly, resting his head on Henry's shoulder.

'Well *done*, son,' Henry said, his voice breaking slightly. 'Well *done*.'

'Thanks . . . Dad,' the Bug whispered softly—the first words he'd ever spoken directly to Henry Chaser.

Martha released Jason. 'I almost had a heart attack when your back fin exploded in the final straight. What was that all about? Why did that happen?'

'I have an idea,' Jason said, turning to see Ariel arrive on the scene, escorted by two New York cops who held between them: Ravi Gupta, the Indian bookmaker, with his hands cuffed.

'Is this him?' one of the cops said to Jason.

'Yeah. That's him,' Jason said. 'That's the guy who put the explosives on my car in Italy and here.'

Both Martha and Henry whirled around. So did all the race officials nearby, levelling their eyes at Gupta.

Jason explained. 'I realised it the other night when we saw the gambling odds on TV. In racing, you can bet on all sorts of results: me winning, me coming in the Top 3 overall. But what really caught my attention were the odds for me coming in the Top 5 in any race. And suddenly I thought about the Italian Run.

'Twice in the Italian Run, our team encountered unusual difficulties: that explosion in the home straight, but also before that, just before the second pit stop, when Sally was blocked from getting to the Pescara Pits.

'And I realised: in both instances those difficulties arose only when I moved *into* 5th place. On the way to the

Pescara Pits, I leapfrogged into 5th by cutting the heel. Then my tailfin exploded just after I got past Trouveau and looked like finishing in 5th.

'And suddenly, I realised: someone didn't want me to come in the Top 5 in Italy. So I thought about who that could be . . . and came to one conclusion: gamblers. And there's been only one bookmaker who's shown any interest in me. Gupta.

'So the other night, before I went to bed, I checked his odds on me both here and back in Italy, in particular, Gupta's odds on me coming in the Top 5 in Italy. They were huge. Gupta stood to lose a fortune if I'd come 5th there, so he'd ensured that I wouldn't: first by blocking Sally at the Pescara Pits, and second by planting an explosive on my tailfin.'

'But how could you prove it?' Henry asked.

'I couldn't. I just had to wait—and see if something similar happened today. So I got Ariel to get some cops to watch Gupta for the whole race and . . .'

He turned to the cop beside Ariel.

The cop said: 'We have digital surveillance footage of Mr Gupta pointing a remote control at the *Argonaut* and pressing a button on that remote a moment before the car's tailfin explodes. Radio-signal surveillance also recorded seek-and-respond signals passing between Gupta's remote and the *Argonaut* an instant before the explosion. Which is why Mr Gupta is coming with us now.'

With that, the cops took Gupta away.

'Gambling . . .' Sally growled. 'It's bad news.'

'Oh, it's not that bad,' Martha Chaser said daintily.

'And why do you say that, Mum?' Jason asked, surprised.

'Well,' she seemed a little embarrassed to say it, 'as I said I would, I put a dollar on you to win the Masters, way back before the first race of the series, when you were at 1500-to-1. So I just made $1500. I think I might get myself that new sewing machine now.'

Jason just shook his head and grinned.

And so he was left with his family and his friends and his fleece and the massing cheering waving crowd in the middle of Fifth Avenue, New York, on the Sunday of the Masters . . . as the winner.

That same grin was still fixed on his face as he stood on Liberty Island, at the feet of the Statue of Liberty, behind the winner's podium, watching Romba (26 points) and Fabian (22 points, having received no points in Race 4 for crashing) receive their wreaths for coming 2nd and 3rd in the Masters.

Then came the moment.

'And, now, ladies and gentlemen,' the announcer proclaimed, 'in 1st place, with a series total of 28 points, two wins, and one 3rd placing, the Masters Champion for this year . . . Jason Chaser! Team: *Argonaut*/Lombardi. Navigator: Bug Chaser. Mech Chief: Sally McDuff.'

The three of them leapt up onto the podium.

Jason, the Bug and Sally.

And they accepted their wreaths, and the gigantic Masters Trophy.

Then Jason hefted the enormous trophy aloft, above his head, and the crowd just went ballistic.

And as he looked out over them, Jason thought about everything he'd been through the previous year.

It had, without a doubt, been the most incredible year of his life—a year that had begun in the swamps of Carpentaria, proceeded through the many trials of Race

School and featured an appearance at the Italian Run, before he had finished off the year winning—yes, *winning*—the most prestigious and demanding race series of all: the New York Masters.

And now, to cap it all off, in his pocket sat a contract from Umberto Lombardi offering him and his team the privilege of racing full-time for the Lombardi Racing Team on the Pro Circuit next year.

Jason held the trophy high and smiled.

He was Jason Chaser.

Hover car racer.

AN INTERVIEW WITH MATTHEW REILLY

THE WRITING OF *HOVER CAR RACER*

Where did the idea for Hover Car Racer *come from?*

A bit like *Contest* before it, *Hover Car Racer* arose from my love of sports. I have always loved watching professional sports, from gruelling 5-day Test cricket matches, to soccer, tennis, golf and Formula One.

I just wondered what it would be like to have a sport that was *totally* wild. Super fast, super dangerous, and utterly electrifying. And so I came up with the idea of rocket cars that hovered above the ground and raced at 800 km/h, kind of like racing fighter jets.

I then made this futuristic sport of hover car racing into a *world*—a world that was essentially an amalgam of existing sports:

Hover car racing has four 'Grand Slam' races (like tennis and golf).

It has a qualifying school (like professional golf's Q School).

It has gate races (which are similar to the bushwalking sport of rogaining).

It has match-races and pursuits (like cycling).

It has race teams (like Formula One, NASCAR and Indy car).

It has a rich and glamorous global tour (like Formula One).

By giving hover car racing all these familiar features, I felt readers would understand it quickly . . . and then just settle back to enjoy the story.

Hover Car Racer *sees you return to science fiction for the first time since* **Contest.** *Is there any particular reason for this?*

It's funny, but I don't divide novels into categories like 'literary fiction' or 'action thrillers' or 'science fiction'. To me, they're all just stories, to be read and enjoyed.

Hover Car Racer, then, is a story that happens to take place in the near future. And to me, its themes are universal: a young outsider dealing with a hostile entrenched world; never give up, never say die; how determination against all odds will win out in the end. And, perhaps most of all, how a determined young hero (Jason) will ultimately beat a super-talented but snobby older person (Xavier): having guts is better than having sheer talent alone.

The thing about science fiction is that it can give you *options*—options that a story set in the present-day doesn't have.

Contest was sci-fi because I wanted the biggest, cruellest and meanest creature-villains ever seen, and I couldn't get them with regular animals. So I used aliens.

Hover Car Racer required an advanced society that had embraced a new technology and a wild new sport.

So for me, I use a particular genre to support the story I want to tell, not the other way around.

What are some of the classical references in **Hover Car Racer?**

There are lots of in-jokes in *Hover Car Racer*, and not just classical ones!

- First and foremost is **Jason and his car, the *Argonaut*—** their names are derived from the Greek tale of Jason and the Argonauts going in search of the fabled Golden Fleece. The Argonauts were the crew members of his boat, the *Argo*. (By the way, that story is called *The Voyage of Argo*, or the *Argonautica*, by Apollonius of Rhodes, and it is one of the best action-adventure stories you'll ever read! It was written in the third century B.C. and it still rocks along at a cracking pace!)

- **The Clashing Bergs** in Race 50 (in Part 6), are based on the Clashing Rocks in the *Argonautica*.
- **Dido** gets her name from the doomed princess in Virgil's *Aeneid*. The *Aeneid* details the adventures of Aeneas, a survivor of the sack of Troy, who goes on to found Rome. A cool part of the story is this: Juno, the wife of Jupiter, is the patron goddess of Carthage; and being a goddess, she knows that Rome will one day annihilate Carthage; so she tries to stop Aeneas from founding Rome long before this can happen (sounds like *The Terminator*, doesn't it!). In any case, to this end, Juno makes Aeneas fall in love with Dido, a princess of Carthage. Aeneas ultimately tears himself away from Dido to fulfil his destiny, while she burns herself on a pyre as he sails away. I wanted my Dido to be like the classical one: a love interest who is actually there to hinder Jason in his quest.

Other references include:

- **Trouveau's car, the *Vizir*,** is named after Napoleon's horse.
- **La Bomba Romba** is named after an Italian Olympic skier nicknamed La Bomba Tomba.
- **Stanislaus Calder** is named after an Australian car racing track named Calder Park.
- **The Greek driver's car, the *Arion*,** is named after Hercules' horse.

- **The Chinese driver's car, the *Chun-T'I*,** is named after the Chinese god of war.
- Two drivers in the Masters are **'Brock Peters' and 'Mark Skaife'**: Peter Brock was one of Australia's greatest touring car drivers (and my hero as a kid) and Mark Skaife is a current top driver whom I admire. Both raced or race in Holden Commodores.
- **The bookmaker Ravi Gupta** and his questions are loosely based on the minor cricket scandal involving Shane Warne and Mark Waugh a few years ago: these two (excellent) cricketers were asked by an Indian bookmaker about seemingly innocuous subjects: pitch and weather information. Ravi Gupta's questions to Jason seem to be of little importance, but to a bookmaker they are crucial. I wanted to show how any sport, even hover car racing, can have a darker side.
- The Sydney Classic is described as **'the race that stops a nation.'** This is actually the phrase used in Australia to describe the Melbourne Cup, Australia's biggest horse race. It is the one day of the year when nearly everyone in the entire country stops work and watches the race on TV; it really is the race that stops a nation.
- Oh, and **Fabian's 'sequencing' of Jason** in the Masters Gate Race is a cheeky reference to my own book, *Contest*. In that novel, if you followed another contestant around, you were deemed to be *sequencing* them.

As the author, what do you like most about Hover Car Racer?

That's a good question. I guess, more than any of my other novels, *Hover Car Racer* has heart. And that's what I like about it most.

I particularly love two scenes involving Jason's father, Henry Chaser: where he sits beside Jason's bed after he has survived the crash in the Italian Run and says how proud he is of Jason; and where, before the New York Masters, he speaks to the two boys when he believes they are sleeping, again saying how proud he is of them.

When all is said and done, this book is about pride and never giving up.

Henry shows great pride in his sons. Jason always races for pride—even if he can't win, he will finish the race anyway, if only for pride's sake.

Look at what happens in the Sponsors' Tournament: Jason loses, he comes second, and yet the crowd cheers for him even more than they do for the winner, Xavier. Winning and coming first are not the same thing. You don't have to come *first* to win. As the Bug says, You don't have to be the best, you just have to *do* your best. (I love the Bug—in the same way I love Mother in *Ice Station*. He's just one of those characters you can do anything with!)

And that's what *Hover Car Racer* is about: you don't have to be the most talented person in the world to succeed. You just have to do your best. If you do that, you win every time.

Whether in sport or in life generally, you *are* always in the race.

Any other things you'd like to mention?

Nope. That's about it. As always, I just hope you enjoyed the book!

Matthew Reilly
Sydney, Australia
August 2004

DOUGLAS ADAMS

THE HITCHHIKER'S GUIDE TO THE GALAXY

Losing your planet isn't the end of the world.

Earth is about to get unexpectedly demolished to make
way for a hyperspace bypass. It's the final straw for Arthur
Dent – he's already had his house bulldozed this morning.
But for Arthur, that is only the beginning . . .

In the seconds before global obliteration, Arthur is
plucked from the planet by his friend Ford Prefect – and
together the pair ventures out across the galaxy on the
craziest, strangest road trip of all time.

The Hitchhiker's Guide to the Galaxy is a best-selling cult
classic – and the funniest adventure-in-space you will ever
read.

ALEX SHEARER

BOOTLEG

All chocolate will be illegal from 5 p.m. today!

The Good For You Party is running the country, and forcing everyone to lead healthier lives. Chocolate addicts Smudger and Huntly watch in horror as their favourite food is swept from the shops and Chocolate Trooper police arrest anyone caught with sweets.

When the boys discover the recipe for making chocolate and a hidden store of the right ingredients, they fight back. Their secret bootleg operation is soon a brilliant success – but how long can they keep selling illegal chocolate before the Good For You thugs catch them?

A selected list of titles available from Macmillan Children's Books

The prices shown below are correct at the time of going to press. However, Macmillan Publishers reserves the right to show new retail prices on covers which may differ from those previously advertised.

Douglas Adams

The Hitchhiker's Guide to the Galaxy	0 330 43895 6	£6.99

Terence Blacker

The Transfer	0 330 39786 9	£4.99
The Angel Factory	0 330 48024 3	£4.99
Boy2Girl	0 330 41503 4	£4.99
ParentSwap	0 330 43464 0	£9.99

Alex Shearer

The Stolen	0 330 39892 X	£4.99
The Speed of the Dark	0 330 41538 7	£4.99
Bootleg	0 330 41562 X	£4.99
The Hunted	0 330 43190 0	£4.99
The Lost	0 330 43188 9	£4.99
The Great Blue Yonder	0 330 39700 1	£4.99

All Pan Macmillan titles can be ordered from our website, www.panmacmillan.com, or from your local bookshop and are also available by post from:

Bookpost, PO Box 29, Douglas, Isle of Man IM99 1BQ
Credit cards accepted. For details:
Telephone: +44(0)1624 677237
Fax: +44(0)1624 670923
Email: bookshop@enterprise.net
www.bookpost.co.uk

Free postage and packing in the United Kingdom